THE
EMERALD SPY

NICOLA CASSIDY

POOLBEG

Published 2022
by Poolbeg Press Ltd
123 Grange Hill, Baldoyle
Dublin 13, Ireland
E-mail: poolbeg@poolbeg.com
www.poolbeg.com

ISBN 978-1-78199-706-2

Printed and bound by CPI Group (UK) Ltd, Croydon, CR0 4YY

www.poolbeg.com

ABOUT THE AUTHOR

Nicola Cassidy grew up in the quiet countryside outside Drogheda in County Louth and started writing stories at a young age. Encouraged by her English teacher, she chose to study journalism at Dublin City University and worked for a short time in local and national newspapers before turning to a career in political PR and marketing management. She studied creative writing at the Irish Writers' Centre and wrote her first novel while on maternity leave for her daughter. She now works as a full-time ghostwriter and screenwriter. She lives in Termonfeckin, County Louth, by the sea with her husband and two daughters.

ALSO BY NICOLA CASSIDY

December Girl

The Nanny at Number 43

Adele

For the Displaced

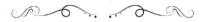

"Hitler brought into the world misery such as no man had previously conceived possible. It had to be combated. The British were slow to observe this. The Irish never did."

Hubert Butler, *The Children of Drancy*

Gisela

CHAPTER ONE

June 1939

"Don't cry, Mama."

"I'm not."

It was a lie. A kind lie, but a lie all the same.

Gisela's mother took a white handkerchief from her sleeve and wiped her nose.

Her father was silent.

He held onto her arms, his hands like glue.

All around, people jostled by.

The train would be full.

The fumes from the engine choked the platform.

They had to talk loudly over the noise, standing beside a telephone box.

It at least offered a shade of privacy.

"You will write?" her mama said.

"Yes, as soon as I can. I will send a card."

"And you'll eat?"

"Of course."

Gisela's father's face was the colour of summer tomatoes.

The only other time she had seen it such a colour was the day he argued with the shopkeeper Herr Krehl over bread and milk.

JUDEN VERBOTEN.

"I have been coming to this shop for years!" her father had said.

Herr Krehl said, "Things are different now."

"But you know me," her father had answered.

"I know you are a Jew."

She had stood silent beside her father, wretched with embarrassment.

Tugged at his arm as he tugged at hers now.

Let's go. Somewhere else. Somewhere that still serves Jews.

As they left the shop, her papa kicked at a sack of oats near the door.

A shower of dust rose, white, like a puff of smoke.

Herr Krehl yelled.

On the street she'd noticed her father's face and neck had gone red, the same red as the tomatoes they grew on the windowsills and balcony of the apartment.

Shiny red.

And now, here was the colour of tomatoes again.

He could not speak, his voice caught up in the lump in his throat.

He held her arms, squeezed.

And then, it was time to go.

A last embrace from Mama.

And for Papa.

His hands, stuck, peeled off, then gripping again, and pulling away, because it was time to go.

Gisela climbed the steps of the train and waited by the door, so that when it closed she could put her hand out the open window.

We will see you soon.

Take care.

We love you.

The train shunted with a jolt.

Goodbye.

Goodbye!

Her mother's handkerchief fluttered in the wind.

Tears openly flowing now.

No hiding the crying anymore.

Gisela touched her cheek and found there were tears there too.

She hadn't even realised she was crying.

Her parents faded from view, the platform with them, until the station was gone and there were only flashes of shrub along the train track.

Goodbye.

Gisela made her way down the train, looking for space, compartment by compartment, feeling as though she might stumble with nausea and shock.

It was the first time she had ever been separated from her parents.

She was twenty-two.

And yet, she felt like a child.

A seat in the middle of a compartment, free. She opened the door and dragged her case in.

A man helped her lift it overhead.

He had kind eyes.

Gisela sat and felt a pain in her chest, like when Rudy used to sit on her in a game, pretending to be an elephant, trapping her on the bed.

Let me up! Let me up!

Say the magic word!

She felt as though something had broken and leaked all inside her.

And then she realised it had.

Of course it had.

It was her heart.

It had broken and spilled out, and now it drained, painfully, endlessly, right in the centre of herself.

* * *

The train swayed as it picked up speed.

Clack, clack, clack.

Salzburg, Munich, Stuttgart.

All of these places she would see.

She was used to trains.

She had taken so many journeys with her father over the years, right from when she was very small.

He called her 'his little companion' and his 'good luck charm'.

His job was to bring tourists into Austria, and he travelled often, for meetings and day trips, showing off the beautiful alpine mountains and lakes, the quaint villages and towns, the peace and serenity sought by Germans, Bulgarians and Yugoslavians.

But now she would be seeing these cities knowing that she would not be back.

It was not a day trip.

And she would not have her father at her side.

As the train rattled on, the rhythm calmed her somewhat.

The other passengers were reading, smoking, looking out the window.

Gisela opened the hatbox that sat on her knee and sifted through the papers inside, feeling the smooth, flat surfaces.

The hatbox was her mother's, passed on to her by her mother.

The hat had been long lost.

But the box remained.

"This will do for my papers," Gisela had said as she'd packed.

It was large and round and awkward but it was a piece of her mother and her grandmother that she would carry with her on her journey.

Gisela checked her documents, over and over.

Passport.

Letter from the Society of Friends.

The bundle of letters from her Irish sponsor.

Visa from the Legation. *Permission to visit Great Britain, June 1939.*

Train ticket.

Her purse was full of notes and coins, her money to buy her onward ticket from Amsterdam.

She looked at the steamer timetable. Touched her ticket for the S.S *Amsterdam*.

For over a year her father had worked to secure this passage.

Visiting every agency in Vienna.

She is only a quarter Jew.

Can you do anything for her?

She has good English.

She is nearly finished her education.

She is a good worker.

Help us.

Within a few weeks the Quakers had presented a job offer, to the south of England, at Dover.

She would be a hotel chambermaid, changing bedsheets and scrubbing toilets for travellers.

"No," said Gisela, when her father brought home the job offer. "No, Father, I cannot. I cannot!"

"Gisela," her father said sternly.

"How could I, Papa?"

"You will be safe."

"But for how long? The channel is so close to France."

France was so close to Germany.

If the job had been offered in the north of England, perhaps.

London even. But not the very south.

Not within view of France.

What was the point of leaving Vienna to sit at the Channel, a target waiting?

And a chambermaid?

She was willing to work, yes, she did not really mind what she did.

But a chambermaid offered no opportunity to climb upwards.

She had hoped she would be put in an office.

Put somewhere where she might use at least part of her university education.

"What about my qualifications?" she'd said to her father.

"You did not graduate."

"But I have four years of college done."

"It does not matter."

"I am not taking it."

"What will I tell the agency?"

"Tell them to find me something better, please. I can't do it."

"Gisela, no one else has said no, you can't say no."

But she did.

She knew it was not her future. She knew it was wrong.

And so, her father wrote back to the agency, explaining the situation.

"Gisela is a very bright, intelligent girl and seeks a position where she can in some way contribute to society at large. We very much appreciate the good work you have done so far. If you could look to see if there are other possibilities – in administration perhaps? She is willing to assist any professional and has, as you know, four years attendance at Vienna University in the study of mathematics."

They waited.

Nothing came through for months.

Her mother said she should have taken the chambermaid job.

The borders were packed.

And you refused a job, a ticket out?

She had been out walking the streets, doing the morning shop to see what rations she could get, the day the letter arrived.

She went out early every morning and walked as far as she could.

The rations were becoming less and less.

There was no meat, no butter, no milk.

There were only certain shops they could visit now, now that they had been classed as Jews.

"*Gisela!*" her mother called, when she came in the door. "A letter! A letter for you!"

There were two letters inside the envelope.

One, handwritten, from a lady who had a farm in Ireland called Mrs. de Freyne.

Another, from the Society of Friends, typed.

She had been offered a position as a companion to Mrs. de Freyne's daughter.

The whole way across England and the Irish Sea.

Far enough away from the Channel.

Far enough away from France.

And from Germany.

She took it, without question, without protest.

They sent the acceptance letter back the very next day.

Now the time was right, she knew.

Now, she would leave Vienna and make her journey to that Atlantic island.

She would leave her parents behind, for her safety, her new start away from the oppression and the disaster back home.

What would Ireland be like?

Did it matter?

The decision was made.

She was getting out.

She was lucky to get a visa, she knew.

There was no such visa for her parents.

She and Rudy would be safe.

And that, her parents said, was all they could ask for.

* * *

The afternoon became dusk. The dusk became a dark black night broken only by the station lamps they passed.

Gisela ate in the dining carriage, a plate of grey mashed potatoes and fried onions.

There were pork chops, but she decided to save her money.

Who knew what she might need it for on this unwanted adventure?

She walked up and down the aisle a few times outside her compartment, trying to stretch her legs ahead of the long night, before settling back in her seat.

The man who had lifted her case smiled at her, but she did not want to engage in conversation with him, so she made sure to look away.

She read her book until she felt tired and then tried to get into a comfortable position to sleep.

It was impossible.

She could not relax among these strangers.

She was terrified that the hatbox would slip off her lap, that her papers would scatter, that she'd lose something important – a ticket, a visa.

The man with the kind eyes saw how unsettled she was and whispered about how uncomfortable the seats were.

Gisela took her scarf, wrapped it around her face and pretended it was a pillow.

The smell of its perfume was a comfort.

The same one her mama wore.

She wished there were no passengers in the compartment, that she could stretch out across the seats, her feet up like in a bed.

Later she was woken by the smell of cigarette smoke and she opened her eyes to see a glowing red dot, waving back and forth.

The cigarette was stubbed out in an ashtray but the smell lingered, pungent.

Back to a groggy sleep, in and out, limping on towards dawn.

She was glad to see the sun creep over the horizon, brightening as it rose, the dark fading into a grey.

The black bushes became brown.

Street lights glowed against the light in the sky.

The clatter and movement outside the compartment caused everyone to wake.

When the woman in the corner opened the compartment door to

leave for the toilet, they smelt coffee from afar.

Gisela's stomach gurgled with hunger.

"If you wait until Frankfurt, I know a lovely café for breakfast," said the man with the kind eyes. "Better than the dining car."

He spoke German with an accent.

The train had an hour wait at the station.

"That sounds nice," she said in response.

She needed to get off to post a card anyway.

She scratched her note: *Reached Frankfurt. I will write from Amsterdam. Love, Gisela.*

On the platform she carried her hatbox and felt weary as she made her way through the throng.

It was as though she hadn't slept at all.

"I saw you with your family," said the man from the carriage.

His name was Dirk.

He was Dutch and was on his way from Vienna to Amsterdam, where he lived.

"You must be going far away?" he said.

"Yes. I'm going to Ireland."

"Ah," he said. "You are escaping."

Gisela needed to be careful in what she said. She did not know where this man's loyalties lay.

"I'm going to work. Well, I am going to be a companion."

"Sounds very nice," said Dirk and he smiled again.

Gisela looked up at him. He towered over her diminutive height.

Could she trust him?

There was a queue at the café. It seemed its reputation for good food and coffee was true.

Gisela posted her card in a post-box near to the café door.

They got sausages and bread and ate them from the paper they were wrapped in.

"It's not easy saying goodbye," said Dirk.

"No."

"I felt quite sorry for you all. It's not nice to see people so upset."

Gisela realised he was being kind. He had seen her parents on the platform.

He was sorry for her was all.

She took the gold chain from around her neck and fingered the well-worn cross. She had worn it since she was twelve, a present from her godmother for her Confirmation.

It was a comfort.

Dirk's eyes lingered on it.

She felt he was going to ask the question.

I thought you were a Jewess?

But the truth was, she was not. Her parents had converted, years ago.

She thought of her passport in her hatbox, the large J stamped across the page.

Jewish by birth. Catholic by choice.

Still it was not enough.

"There are lot of people leaving Vienna," he said.

There were a lot of Jews leaving Vienna, he meant.

He was handsome, Gisela realised. Blond and tall.

In another time perhaps they would have exchanged addresses.

Started a long-distance friendship.

"It is crazy what is happening," he said. "In Holland too."

Nowhere was safe.

But she did not want to talk about it.

Not with Dirk.

Not with anyone on these trains.

They took a walk down the platform and, well before their time for departure, they boarded the stuffy train again and settled into their seats.

A few more hours to the border crossing into the Netherlands.

She was braced for it.

She checked her paperwork over and over again.

Eventually Dirk laughed and said she must relax.

"You will be fine," he said. "Stop worrying."

But he did not know that she would be fine.

He did not have a J on his passport.

And he was a Dutch citizen!

She put the paperwork away, but when Dirk went to the toilet, she allowed herself another little sift, stacking the papers and pressing them into place.

Getting out of Germany was not an easy task.

Especially for a Catholic girl who was still, on paper, a Jew.

G2 INTELLIGENCE REPORT

STATUS: INFORMATION
LOCATION: NEWTOWN HOUSE,
TERMONFECKIN, CO. LOUTH

Hans Schmitt is a quiet, reserved member of the Austrian Kagran group. His file notes that he has military training and served as part of the Austrian Armed Forces in the 1920s, dates unknown. His demeanour is secretive and aloof. Marked for attention.

MARRIAGE STATUS: Unknown

RESIDES: Cottage at back of Newtown House

ACTION: Close Observation

Hans

CHAPTER TWO

Anja Schafer's otherwise perfect smile was made all the more interesting by her two lateral incisors, which Hans noticed turned outwards.

It wasn't a defect.

To him, it made her more beautiful.

Sharpened.

It was the first thing he noticed about her the day she climbed onto his tram and made her way towards him with her gloved hand outstretched.

He held out his for hers.

She dropped the coins, waited for her ticket and swung around the hand-pole, falling elegantly into a seat.

He wasn't supposed to stare.

And in truth, he never did.

It wasn't his style to look longingly at the many young women that took the tram each day.

But he could not take his eyes off Anja.

Or her teeth.

Because she smiled for the whole length of her journey.

It was as though someone had delivered the most wonderful news to her before she boarded for Westbahnhof.

She was a beacon of brightness among the dour, lifeless souls who sat glaring out the fogged-up windows till it was time to dismount.

It would be another week before Hans saw Anja again.

This time, she was not smiling, but had a faraway look.

As if she were distracted.

He spoke to her this time, a *thank you* and *good evening* and she looked back at him surprised.

"Good evening to you, too."

And then she disappeared again.

For the following two Thursday evenings, at exactly ten minutes past five, he hoped she would climb onto his tram, with her gloved hand outstretched and her ready smile.

Where, he wondered, had the beauty with the slightly crooked teeth gone?

Was she but a visitor to Vienna?

Would she be back?

He was thinking of his ailing mother the next time she boarded.

His mother had caught a respiratory illness and had not slept the past two nights. When she coughed she sounded like she was drowning. As she was already of a weak disposition, having never recovered properly from a bout of whooping cough as a child, Hans worried that this time she might not pull through.

His father, who himself was elderly and infirm, insisted that his wife certainly would.

"It's only a cough," he said. "She's had worse before."

But Hans couldn't remember his mother ever sounding like that.

As he stood, thinking about his mother and what he might be able to purchase in the pharmacy on the way home that could perhaps soothe her poor, racking chest, Anja Schafer appeared.

He barely even noticed her, so engulfed was he in his thoughts.

Should he call the doctor, he wondered.

Would his father remember what the doctor said if he called when he was at work? His memory was so poor now and agitated.

Should he try to take an hour off work to be there for the visit?

But the doctor could never give an exact time when he could call.

And it was not easy to get off work.

Not if you wanted to keep your job.

"You are lost in your thoughts," Anja Schafer said.

"Excuse me?" said Hans.

He looked and saw that it was her.

Up close.

Such beauty.

"Yes," he said. "I am. Forgive me. Where to?"

She told him that she was travelling to Westbahnhof.

Her usual stop.

"Shopping?" he asked, desperate to speak to her for a moment more.

"No," she said, shaking her head. "Music lessons. I play the oboe."

She held up a small, long black case.

Ah.

The case.

Of course, he had noticed it before, but not known what was inside.

"The oboe," he said.

Not his favourite instrument.

Though it was powerful in its solos, he supposed.

It was the nasal quality that he disliked.

"The saddest instrument in the orchestra," he said.

She laughed.

"Do you think so?"

"I do. Are you any good?"

It was quite a forward question for Hans.

Not something he might usually ask of a young woman that he did not know.

"I'm terrific," she said.

He laughed.

How forward she was too.

And, he suspected, she was right.

"Do you play in an orchestra?" he asked.

"Next year I want to audition for the Vienna Philharmonic."

Surely not, he thought.

A woman auditioning for such a prestigious position?

He liked her gumption.

He was very attracted to Anja Schafer and her outward disposition.

* * *

Now, on this rattling, bone-shaking bus, Hans thought back to the smooth tram where he had met Anja.

How long ago that had seemed.

How far he had come.

How everything had utterly, immensely, changed.

He had not seen any trams in Ireland.

In Waterford City where they had visited once there were only buses. In fact, the spacious streets laid out by the wide river port had been filled with many horses and carts, and pony traps.

Ireland was nothing like Austria.

In Cork, where their steamer ship had landed, there were only buses too.

He supposed, where they were going now, out to the countryside, north, beyond Dublin, to their next, new village there would be no trams either.

Their third accommodation in just six months.

Nowhere kept them too long.

He'd had a vague idea before he came to Ireland that perhaps he could take up a job as a tram conductor.

When he'd first arrived, he reasoned that his poor grasp of English might hold him back.

After a week he realised it wasn't just his language skills that would be a barrier to that particular job; outside of Dublin, Ireland simply didn't have any trams.

It was something they had taken for granted back home in Vienna.

He knew there would be nothing for it but to remain working as a farm labourer.

Hans had felt quite lucky when he'd joined the Kagran Gruppe, an agricultural collective which had formed in Vienna to train and organise emigration visas and tickets out for hundreds of Jews.

The scheme was overseen by the Government but supported by charities and Christian churches anxious to get Christian Jews to safety.

Hans had not found the labouring too intensive.

He was used to standing on trams all day.

It was the businessmen who struggled to cut trees, lay roads and plough fields.

It was their upper-class wives who found it impossible to carry heavy stones and watch their manicured nails turn black with soil.

They had weakened and faded.

Hans had not.

It was at Kagran, the wide expansive area of flat fields where they trained, that he had met the Hettingers.

They had been glad to be sent to Ireland together.

Most evacuees were being sent to Bolivia. Or Peru.

He would have gone to America, had he any choice in the matter.

But, by the spring of 1939, the embassies were crowded and countries had shut their doors.

He was grateful to have been sent anywhere at all.

They were the lucky few.

Now, on the ground in Ireland, he could see why visas had become so scarce.

Ireland, as a country, as an economy, was rural and poor.

A woman in Ardmore in Waterford had explained it quite simply to him.

"People wonder how we could take *you* in when our own sons and daughters must leave because there's no work for *them*."

He understood then that they were on shaky ground.

No matter where they went, they would be unpopular.

They were not wanted and it hung over them all, heavy on their backs.

They were a burden.

Displaced.

And unwanted.

Looking out the window, Hans saw that the fields had gone from flat and green to hilly and blue as the bus climbed an incline.

They were coming up to the Dublin Mountains.

The bus strained, loudly, diesel fumes pouring out from behind, completely clouding the rear of the bus in black smoke.

Eva Hettinger held her stomach.

She was not a good traveller.

She had been sick on the crossing from Holland to England and from England to Ireland.

She said she never wanted to see another boat again.

Hans worried that she might never return to Vienna again, so awful had the sea journeys been for her.

Then he wondered would any of them ever return again.

He had no intention of returning home.

But he knew that Eva would wish to.

She still had family there.

He would never need to return to Vienna.

Not now.

"Please," said Eva to her husband Fritz. "Please, tell him to pull over."

Fritz got up and weaved his way up to the bus driver.

The bus driver flashed a look of annoyance but soon they slowed and when the bus came to a stop Eva lurched forward, out the front door and tried to vomit discreetly by the side of the bus.

They all, politely, looked away.

Poor Eva.

She had dreaded the journey.

It was going to take over five hours, a long time to be in a bus.

But they were not at sea.

At least they could stop for moments of relief.

After Eva composed herself, she climbed back on and collapsed onto Fritz's shoulder.

They were on their way again.

After a short while, the driver stopped at a large inn, which was busy with other travellers.

They were glad to take soup and bread and rest for an hour.

The Hettinger boys, Otto and Max, sat with their long legs stretched out across the patterned carpet.

The inn's tables were low and small.

Otto took after his mother Eva and had dark features; his hair and thick eyebrows were black, but his eyes were bright blue.

He was quite striking.

Max, more like his father, had sandy hair and fairer skin.

Hans envied them their youth and their language skills.

Otto was finished with high school. Max had only one year left.

Their English tumbled from their mouths and they had no problem listening to and understanding everything that was said to them.

They would likely, if they wished, go on to college.

They would be educated, meet and mingle with young Irish people their age, set up their new lives in Ireland and adapt better than he ever could.

At 43, there was no such hope of assimilation for Hans.

He knew he would always speak with a heavy accent and that he would have to listen carefully to everything that was said to him.

Perhaps he could take language lessons.

Apart from that though, he really had no idea what was to become of him.

After the inn, the bus resumed its journey down a busy main road, accompanied by flashes of an azure blue sea to their right.

He liked that they were near the coast.

It was different than what they were used to.

He enjoyed the sea air and the fresh, skin-cutting winds that blew there.

They were told that the place where they were going, the village of Termonfeckin, was home to a long sandy beach.

The soup had settled Eva's stomach and she chatted in a low voice with Fritz and the boys.

Both Eva and Fritz had aged since Hans met them at Kagran.

Eva had long grey streaks that spread across her hair. Her cheeks were high and hollow.

He hoped that in Termonfeckin she might have an easier time of it.

He had grown very fond of Eva and the kindnesses she showed him.

So far, during their stays at Ardmore in Waterford and the lonely, cold house in Enniskerry in Wicklow, they'd stayed off site and had to travel to work on the farm each day.

In Termonfeckin they would be living onsite at the farm, which they were told was a chicken farm with some dairy.

Now Hans' stomach began to feel a bit queasy.

He too, was getting travel sick.

Or, he wondered, could it be nerves?

After passing along the coast for a long distance, the bus drove down a steep hill into a small busy town and the bus driver told them that they were near.

They looked out the windows at the shoppers and delivery boys making their way up and down the paved streets.

There was a port, overlooked by a giant viaduct bridge with ships lined up at the quay.

Large cargo ships waited beyond the bridge to dock.

A herd of liver-and-white cows stood patiently on the quay, lowing loudly.

Past the bustling town, they took a scenic road along the river.

A few minutes later, the bus slowed down and turned right, into a long avenue.

The driver drove slowly past neat green lawns, featuring thin, youthful trees tied to narrow posts.

When they got to the top of the avenue, Eva, Fritz and the boys all audibly gasped.

This was much grander than the other two houses they'd stayed in.

This place was a large manor house.

Eva looked at Hans and raised her eyebrows.

"My Queen, you are home," said Hans to lighten the mood and Eva laughed.

"My goodness," she said.

My goodness was right.

What a place Newtown House was.

It was not what they expected.

Things were looking up.

Gisela

CHAPTER THREE

"What about your family?" Dirk asked. "Will they leave Vienna too?"

Gisela shook her head.

"My father does not want to leave."

She thought of her father's stubborn face.

The city had been his home for fifty-seven years.

"My brother has already left."

She did not tell Dirk where.

She did not like to say these details out loud.

It was a habit they had learned.

To stay quiet.

To keep everything close.

"Good for him," said Dirk.

Was it though?

Rudy was a concert pianist.

Now, he worked as a grocer's assistant in a tiny village in Czechoslovakia.

He was safe, but it was not his life.

Not the life he was born to.

In his letters he told Gisela that his fingers were being worn by sacking and twine and the hard graft of lifting, pulling and dragging.

His wounds took a long time to heal.

He missed home, his friends.

His language.

His piano.

He was lonely, she knew.

She wished she could go visit him.

Now, she was going even further away, right to the tip of Europe!

She had no idea when she would see him again.

As the morning became day, Gisela and Dirk looked out the windows and saw that the landscape was changing.

It was so flat.

The horizon visible for miles.

Gisela couldn't help but notice guns appearing, lined up at stations, ready for transport, some the size of small motorcars, pushed and pulled by young-looking men in uniform.

The gun barrels were black, shiny, monstrous.

Trucks drove along parallel roads and sometimes it felt as though both train and car were on the same track, moving together.

Army trucks carried soldiers, sailing along the narrow, flat roads.

"So much artillery," said Dirk, as they passed another train station with its shiny guns on show.

It reminded Gisela of last year when Adolf Hitler drove into Vienna in his motorcar, saluting.

The clack-tap of the soldiers who marched behind him.

Sieg Heil, Sieg Heil.

She remembered the blood red of the giant red party flags.

The crowds who waved and wore swastika armbands.

Children laughing, gleeful.

That was the day everything changed.

That was the day they knew there was no hope left and the only way she could have a future was to leave.

"Where is all the artillery going, do you think?" Gisela asked Dirk.

"Who knows?" he said. "But it's going somewhere. And it's hard to believe that all those guns are needed just for defence."

Of course.

They were being transported for attack.

Not defence.

The sight of the ammunition made Gisela's stomach sick.

The closer they got to the border, the more weapons they saw.

"I'm worried about crossing the border," she whispered behind her hand to Dirk, as the train slowed.

"Don't be," he said.

"I have my papers but ..."

"It will be all right."

She admired his positive manner, but it was different for Dirk.

The train came to its final stop.

They had reached the border.

They were crossing from the Rhine Province into the Netherlands.

From one country to the next.

The sick feeling in Gisela's stomach worsened.

She had a bad feeling about this.

* * *

They stood in a long winding queue on the platform, waiting to visit the customs office where they had to have their paperwork checked.

Dirk chatted to Gisela in low, hushed tones.

He helped to calm her nerves.

She worried that if she looked nervous they would definitely stop her and possibly even detain her.

She tried to look confident.

Breezy.

She was doing nothing wrong; she had her paperwork.

But if she did not get through here, she would have to turn back.

And she did not want that.

Three stern German officers sat behind desks in the customs office, paper piled high, cigarette-butts tumbling from pyramids of ash in their ashtrays.

They smoked while they checked everyone's papers and mumbled only to each other, ignoring whoever was in front of them.

Gisela showed her passport when it was her turn and watched the officer's eyes fall to the 'J'.

His eyes came back to her face, then back to the 'J'.

Her gold cross was neatly tucked inside the neck of her blouse.

She had to be who the papers said she was.

The officer sighed and flicked through the passport.

He examined the stamp from when she visited Budapest in Hungary with her father.

He had taken her for her sixteenth birthday treat.

1933.

Before everything had gone wrong.

The officer cleared his throat.

He coughed and reached for his own stamp.

He lifted his hand.

Gisela held her breath and watched as the official stamped her passport with force.

She was through!

She had passed border control.

She took her passport and carefully put it back into her hatbox before turning and leaving the office as quickly as she could.

She marched back to the train, not daring to wait for Dirk.

Back in the compartment the atmosphere had lifted.

There were smiles.

Relief.

Dirk arrived back and nodded at her.

It turned out he was right after all.

Gisela reached into the neck of her blouse and took out the gold cross, pulled it up to her chin and felt the tiny chinks of chain press against her flesh.

Thank God.

And then some noise.

There were soldiers on the train.

Walking the corridors.

Murmuring.

Then, the voices got louder.

A face appeared at window of their compartment.

"She's here!"

Who was there?

Her?

Did they mean her?

The door opened. The soldier pointed.

At her.

"Passport!" he barked.

Gisela opened her hatbox quickly, searching for her passport.

When she gave it to the solider, he shook his head.

"No. *Out!*"

"What is the problem?" asked Dirk, his voice firm. "This girl is for Amsterdam. She is with me."

The soldier shook his head again.

"She does not have the correct visa. Please, take your baggage and dismount the train."

Dirk protested. "There must be some mistake!"

"I was told I did not need a visa for this border!" said Gisela, the horror of being taken off the train making her stomach curdle.

"You need a Dutch visa."

"I have a British visa. Letters of permission to travel."

"*Out.*"

She gasped as she walked down the passenger aisle, clutching her hatbox to her chest.

On the platform, she watched the train shunt forward.

Dirk handed her case out the window. She was forced to run to catch hold of it.

"You will be all right!" he shouted.

Out of breath, she carried her luggage, following behind the guards, as the train pulled out of the station.

It was leaving.

Without her on it.

Dirk waved, his hand jittering like a landed fish out the window.

Within a minute the train had gone, a flood of fumes in its wake.

Tears sprang to the corners of Gisela's eyes and she swiped at them, shocked at the situation she had just found herself in.

She wished Dirk had been able to get off with her, to stand beside her and protect her.

Dirk had seen her with her parents.

He was the last link she had to them.

The last person to understand the love they had for each other.

Now she was on her own.

Was she for a prison camp?

Is that why they had taken her off the train?

She wondered if Dirk thought so.

She'd seen the flicker of fear in his eyes.

* * *

She was told to sit in a chair.

The official made a telephone call on the large black phone, curling his fingers around the wire, leaning back on his chair, lighting up another cigarette while he talked.

He was loud, boisterous.

He made small talk, about his wife and children, a joke – he laughed showing a set of yellow stained teeth.

"Yes. Yes. A Jew," he said.

A pause.

"Yes."

Another pause.

He slammed the telephone into its receiver and looked at her.

And then he turned and started talking to the other official in the office as if she was not even there.

In the distance, another train screeched and slowed.

Soon, there would be another passport queue into the office.

Men, women, children, holding out their papers.

Gisela stewed.

What had been said about her at the end of the telephone line?

Was someone coming to get her?

Within a few minutes, bodies had pushed and shoved from the other train into the office and she sat and watched the officials in their nonchalance.

It took forty-five minutes for the passengers to be dealt with and another ten minutes after that before the official looked back in her direction and remembered her.

He rooted in his desk.

"*You*," he pointed at her.

She stood up and felt her heart beat in a *drum-drum-drum*.

"You need a visa to enter Holland. You need to go back to Duisburg, get off the train at the station, go to the customs office there and they'll direct you," he said.

Was it a ruse?

Who would really meet her at customs office? A solider to collect her for camp?

All along she'd been told she did not need a Dutch visa.

They had spent months organising the British and Irish visas, weeks organising her exact travel.

She took her hatbox and case and went outside, crossing the bridge to the other platform.

Her tears had dried.

Now she needed to wait for a train to take her back the way she had just come.

She thought of Dirk, hurtling into the distance, towards Amsterdam, further and further from her.

She was stuck in limbo, her parents on one side, her destination and her new friend on the other.

She thought about writing another card to her parents.

They are sending me to Duisburg. I hope this is not the end.

But how could she?

It would terrify them.

It was just ... what if that was her last chance to write?

She wondered where the closest camp to Duisburg was ?

They would never get her out if she was sent to a camp in the Rhine Province.

Father's friends from work, the Koppels, their sons had been taken to a camp.

Herr Koppel went to the camp, with bribes, with letters and documentation.

If you had a letter to show that you would be leaving Germany and draining the fatherland of another Jewish family – *we are leaving, we have family in Gdansk, we must take our sons with us* – then it was possible.

But that had been last year.

Now things were different.

She watched more trains pull in.

Passenger coats, brown and grey.

Hats and stoles, even in the summer heat.

Women wore pearls and thick gold necklaces; they were laden down with jewellery.

She pulled her beret over her head to straighten it.

She felt thirsty, desperate for some cool water for her tight throat.

But there was no hunger.

Only fear.

Only a great big knot of anguish in her stomach, right where her lunch should have been.

* * *

The frustration of being sent back the way she came, of not having made it over the border, made Gisela's head want to burst.

She had been only moments away. Her passport carried the stamp.

And yet here she was, still in Germany, waiting.

And waiting for what?

In Duisburg she was relieved to see that no solider was waiting at the customs office for her, only another grumpy official sitting behind a desk.

This one smoked cigars. The smell, overpowering, permeated her clothes, making her eyes water.

There were no other travellers there.

As she had done at the border, she handed her paperwork over again.

The official told her to sit and so again she did, watching the ticking hands of the clock, minute after minute.

She had noticed that the clocks were all the same in every station.

Standard issue.

The same clock here, as throughout the stations in Linz, Salzburg, Vienna.

She sat for two, then three hours.

Her stomach gurgled and she rubbed it and held it, to try and cover the noise.

Finally, the official called her over.

"Come back tomorrow. We cannot process this today," he said matter-of-factly.

He dismissed her with a wave of his hand.

"But where will I go?" said Gisela. "I am supposed to be in Amsterdam – where will I go?"

He looked up and sighed.

He reached for a notebook and scratched an address onto it with his fountain pen.

He tore the page with a force that said *I do not care where you go.*

Gisela read the address and left the station, walking past industrial buildings and large ugly warehouses.

She had no idea where she was.

Would she get to the address and find out it was a holding centre full of Jews like her?

Waiting.

For departure.

After walking in circles and going back the way she came twice, she found the building.

Pale-pink paint.

Nothing too sinister.

She rang the bell.

It was answered by a nun.

"I was given this address at the train station. I have to wait for my visa until tomorrow." Gisela reached into her blouse and pulled out her cross. An indication she was a Catholic. And also, a comfort.

The nun said nothing, but stepped back from the door to let Gisela in.

Her expression did not change.

Gisela felt she could say she was Mary Magdalene and still the nun would not smile or move her statue face.

In the kitchen, the nun gave her soup and bread.

The knot in her stomach had turned to acid. The soup soothed it. She wiped the bowl with the bread.

The nun offered tea and crackers, soft from being left out uncovered.

Finally, the old woman spoke and asked Gisela if she would like to pray with her.

She answered yes.

She felt she could do with all the prayers she could get.

They went to a tiny chapel in the basement of the house and there she found three more kneeling nuns, old and wrinkled.

They prayed in silence and Gisela welcomed the familiar prayers and the serenity of the small chapel.

The thoughts rushing round her head began to calm.

Surely no solider would appear now to take her away?

Surely this was not an elaborate ruse, involving four devout nuns?

After prayer, she was shown to a simple dormitory room with bunk beds.

There were no other boarders tonight.

She picked a bed near the window and lay on top of the blankets, holding her hatbox.

She closed her eyes and wished that she could open them and find herself back on the train with Dirk, the other side of the Dutch border.

When she opened them, she saw that someone had scrawled something on the bunk above her head, the laths dark with pen-marks, unseen to the nun's bed-making eyes.

Satan will get you.

She stared at the graffiti.

Then she sat up, opened up her hatbox, and took out her own pen.

Not if God gets you first.

She lay back and examined her handiwork.

Never before had she defaced anything.

Although never before had she been sent to a convent while trying to cross a border to save her life.

Memorandum

From: Under Secretary of State (SS-Brigadeführer) Ernst Woermann
To: The Foreign Ministry, Germany

The Irish Republican Army (IRA) is a secret military society which fights for the union of Northern Ireland with the Irish Republic and the complete separation of Northern Ireland from the British Empire. This is also the ultimate objective of the present Irish Government. The difference between the government and the IRA lies mainly in the method. The government hopes to attain its objective by legal political means while the IRA tries to achieve success by violent means. Most of the members of the present Irish Government formerly belonged also to the IRA. By reasons of its militant attitude towards England, the IRA is a natural ally of Germany.

Hans

CHAPTER FOUR

In the dining room an evening tea of sandwiches and salads had been laid out.

Eva was so sick that she was barely able to eat anything, but Otto and Max tucked in hungrily.

Hans took some crusty bread and spread thick white butter on it.

It tasted delicious.

Mrs. de Freyne was most welcoming.

She was soft in her stature, padded about the stomach and bust.

Her grey hair was cut short.

They had been met at the steps of Newtown House by Mrs. de Freyne and her daughter Nola, who was young and striking, her red lips pursed in suspicion as they climbed down off the bus.

When she saw Otto and Max her face brightened.

Hans could see the attraction.

Here were two young men close to her age.

There was something about her, Hans thought.

A glint to her eye.

She looked the complete opposite of her kind, matronly mother.

Maeve, the housekeeper, had shaken their hands heartily.

She had a deep Irish accent, and spoke so fast Hans had trouble keeping up with her.

Fintan Walshe, who managed the farm, held tightly onto Hans' arm as he shook his hand.

He was small, with narrow shoulders and a red-brown moustache that almost covered his mouth completely.

He said he was glad they had arrived and that plenty of work awaited them.

After their refreshments, they were shown to their accommodation.

They were to be housed at the back of the grand manor house where small, self-contained stone cottages sat behind a wide farmyard.

They would have their own privacy and comforts, but they could use the house too if they wished, Mrs. de Freyne said. Her dining room and drawing room were always open to them.

Hans couldn't believe he had his own place to himself.

In their other accommodation he'd shared a dorm with the Hettinger boys.

His cottage had a kitchen and fireplace and a small upstairs bedroom with a large bed.

It was ideal.

The Hettingers had been given a much larger cottage and Hans knew by Eva's face that she felt relieved that they could live as a family again.

Properly, with some privacy.

Fintan Walshe helped them with their belongings.

Hans towered over him and he had to bend his head to get into his cottage.

"You're a tall fellow anyway," said Fintan, staring at Hans' legs, which he seemed quite fascinated by.

"My mother is Dutch," said Hans and he shrugged as if in apology.

He had always been conscious of his height and as a youth had felt gangly, as though he'd been made all wrong.

Now, he was more concerned about understanding what Fintan was saying and responding using the right words and grammar.

Was Dutch, he corrected himself in his mind.

His mother *was* Dutch.

It was hard to get used to.

The death of a parent.

Fintan seemed to take to Hans and while the Hettingers settled into their cottage, he asked if he'd like a tour of the farm.

Hans was glad to take a look around and get his bearings.

He felt that he and Fintan were going to get along.

The evening light was settling and the sun sent yellow rays over their heads.

Crows cawed in their rookeries and small birds flitted and sang loudly from green, bushy branches.

Invisible.

Hans couldn't help but notice how beautiful it all was.

How calm.

Fintan asked about Hans' farm experience and Hans had to explain that he had been a tram conductor but had been retrained as a farm labourer under a programme to help Austrians who wished to leave the country and resettle.

"We learned many things," he said. "But I have still a lot to learn."

He wanted Fintan to understand that he was willing to work.

That he was not there to be idle.

Fintan nodded and said he would help him with any questions he had.

"I've been on this farm since the beginning," he said. "Mrs. de Freyne wasn't here a wet week when I got the job. So, there's nothing I don't know about how she likes to run things."

He showed Hans the various stone sheds, the large hay barn and Bessie the red tractor.

"The most important woman on the farm," he said, laughing.

Hans smiled too.

He had driven a tractor at the training camp and told Fintan he would be happy to do so here too.

"Good, good, that's great you can do that."

Mrs. de Freyne's large walled garden would likely be attended to by Eva Hettinger, said Fintan.

He saw it as women's work.

Herbs grew, potted and in a small raised beds.

Against the walls were splayed pear trees.

There were orchards behind the walled garden and Mrs. de Freyne was very keen on tree planting, Fintan said.

"We've put in a thousand since last year but she wants more, so you may be helping with that."

Hans nodded.

It was good work.

The land here was green and flat, so different to the tall, triangular mountains that rose all around Vienna.

Here the odd pine tree poked out from in between oaks, beeches and sycamores.

There was no lake.

But there was the sea.

He could hear it in the distance.

"You'll do well here if you work hard," said Fintan after their tour as he stood at the door of the cottage while Hans attended to starting a fire in the grate, over which he would boil a kettle.

Hans nodded.

"Are you a political man?" asked Fintan.

"Politics?" said Hans.

Politics.

How to explain German and Austrian politics.

"Not really," said Hans thinking how politics had led him to where he was now.

How politics had utterly and irreversibly changed his and the Hettingers' life.

"And is it a Jew you are?" said Fintan.

The words rang out.

Jew.

Is it a Jew you are?

The sentence structure was strange to Hans' ears, but he understood well enough what Fintan meant.

Even here they wanted to know.

"No," said Hans. "I am not."

He did not indulge Fintan further. Did not go into his complicated story.

It wasn't, he felt, any of the man's business.

"Ah sure, that's grand," said Fintan.

He smiled at Hans.

Hans didn't feel like smiling back but did, all the same, weakly.

"Welcome to Newtown," said Fintan before he left. "I'm sure you'll be very happy here."

Hans hoped that he was right.

He was ready for some calm.

He was ready for some peace.

* * *

Each week when Anja boarded the tram for her oboe lesson, she sought out Hans and they chatted for the whole journey towards Westbahnhof. Their conversation was punctured only by the brief pauses as Hans took coins from other passengers and handed out tram tickets.

Their conversations developed beyond the musical peculiarities of playing a woodwind instrument.

Hans told Anja about his family.

About his ailing mother.

About his fears for his father who, he thought, was showing signs of dementia.

"He is making mistakes," he told her. "He is confusing things."

She in turn told him about her large family, who were younger and healthier.

They lived in a large town house in Alsergrund, a family of musicians, though their business was tailoring and her father owned two large, thriving shops.

His specialty was tuxedos.

When Anja disappeared on a two-week midterm break from her lessons, thus depriving Hans of a chance to see her for a whole fortnight, he plucked up the courage when she finally returned to ask her to see him outside of their tram journey.

He couldn't bear the uncertainty of their relationship.

He lived in anxiety and hope of seeing her for seventeen minutes each Thursday.

If she was late or missed her stop, he spent the rest of the week angry and disgruntled.

"Anja, would you like to have a cup of coffee?" he asked. "I am free on Saturday afternoon."

She did not pause before she answered. "Yes, I like Café Rose – will we meet there at half past two?"

When they met, he wondered if she thought he looked strange out of uniform.

Did she feel differently about him deprived of his leather bag and ticket-punch?

If she did think anything of it, she did not say.

They sat over three cups of coffee.

By the end of their meeting, he knew that he would marry her.

He did not have the courage to ask her, but he wondered, desperately, if she felt the same.

She had held his hand.

Smiled.

Laughed.

A week after their wonderful meeting in Café Rose, Hans' mother's cough worsened to the point where she could not breathe.

Hans carried her in his arms the whole way to the Sisters of Mercy hospital. She was taken into a room where she slipped into unconsciousness.

She died only a few hours later.

Hans sat for a long time holding her hand, finding it hard to believe that the warmth would soon disappear forever.

How could this woman he'd known for nearly four decades, this constant in his life, never come home again?

He dreaded breaking the news to his father.

He knew that he would get upset and then later forget and have to be told all over again.

Now that he had Anja's address, he sent word that his mother had died.

He was surprised and overcome when he spotted her at the funeral, in a pew in the middle of the church.

She had curled her lips sympathetically, given him a look that said, *I am sorry*.

Afterwards she had embraced him, the first time they had shared such intimacy.

She smelt musky, of expensive perfume.

When she stepped back, he didn't want to let her go.

He was given a week off work and when he returned he worried constantly for his father, left at home now, alone.

"Please come to meet my family," Anja said, after they had met two more times.

Hans could feel it now, that her own emotions were growing towards him.

He knew that she understood that he wished to marry her.

Still, he would not ask till he had met her family.

That would not be fair.

In their large townhouse in Alsergrund, Hans stood nervously, wringing his hat in his hands.

Gerhard Schafer was a small immaculately dressed man.

He had a tightly cut beard and he surveyed Hans with complete suspicion.

Again, Hans hated his height and his awkward limbs and the way that he had to look down upon this man who he wished would become his father-in-law.

Other men did not like to be looked down upon.

This, he had come to know.

Miriam Schafer was also cool but she at least smiled and made small talk over dinner.

Anja looked anxiously from Hans to her parents to her brothers who laughed and sniggered, caught up the tension overhanging the dining table.

They could not help it.

They were not cruel, but young.

After the dinner Hans confessed to Anja that he thought he would never be accepted by her family.

"No, that is not true," she said. "They just need to get to know you."

Dogged, Anja continued to invite Hans for dinner.

Eventually the tension thawed.

Hans came to realise that the main issue they had with him was not that he wasn't a Jew, but that they had expected Anja to marry a businessman.

Gerhard had two tailoring shops.

Her brothers would inherit one each.

Anja needed to be supported by her husband, as was right.

A tram conductor was not a businessman.

They wanted more for their only daughter.

Still, Anja persisted.

She told Hans that she loved him.

And she told him she could convince her family to accept him too.

"My father wants to see you," Anja told him breathlessly as she climbed aboard his tram one Thursday evening, her oboe case in hand.

"He does?" he said. "What for?"

Horrible thoughts crossed his mind.

Was he going to tell him that he longer wanted his daughter to be seen walking out with him? That he was to leave Anja alone, that he was finished?

"I told him last night," said Anja, a shine to her eyes. "I said, this man will make me happy, Father. You must see that. It is what I want. And it will be done."

"You said that?" said Hans, shocked.

"Yes, I did and he wants to see you!"

"Do you think –"

"Yes. I think you must talk to him and then it will be arranged."

Hans could barely speak to Anja the whole way to Westbahnhof.

Could it be true? That she had convinced Gerhard?

When she alighted the tram, after he'd kissed her on the cheek and smelled her musky scent, he realised his stomach was all full up.

It was as if he'd eaten a heavy dinner or pastries by the bucketload.

It was a heavy, strange feeling.

He realised, as he arrived back home to see what damage might have been caused that day in their apartment by his wandering father, that the feeling was hope.

For the first time, he was filled with pure, sickening hope.

Could it really be done?

Could Anja Schafer really be his wife?

Gisela

CHAPTER FIVE

All night Gisela dreamed of her cousin Wolfgang who was due to meet her at the station in Amsterdam.

She had thought about sending a card last night but she knew it would not have reached him in time.

She wondered how long he waited for her?

How many trains had he watched arrive at the station and leave without her ever stepping off?

Did he think she had been taken somewhere?

That she was gone?

Would he write to her parents?

No sign of Gisela. Did she change her mind?

She tossed and turned in the dark and longed for morning to come.

But what would morning bring?

What it brought was a knock on the door and the elderly nun beckoning her for breakfast.

The other sisters were at the table, their faces pale, watery beneath alabaster under-veils.

They asked where she was travelling to.

They asked about her family.

Gisela was warmed by their kindness.

They asked if she wished to pray with them again before she left.

She said yes, again.

After breakfast she packed up her barely unpacked things and went to the small chapel.

When she bowed her head, she imagined her mother and father in front of her.

She directed all her prayers to them.

Outside, after she said her goodbye, the big wooden door of the convent slammed behind her.

She was back to being alone.

A scattering of starlings fluttered through the sky.

The air was warm.

She felt hopeful.

At the train station she found to her relief that it was not busy.

She explained her situation to an official, a man she had not seen before.

She kept her voice bright. *Thank you, sir, kindly.*

The official nodded, reached for the phone.

While he was speaking, he reached for his stamper.

He stamped her passport quickly and closed it.

Hung up the phone.

Handed the passport over to her.

She was free to go.

She tried not to run from the office.

She tried not to bound down the platform, smiling.

Could it really be all right? In just a few moments, it had all been resolved?

She glanced at the timetable.

The next train was due in only ten minutes.

She walked all the way down to the other end of the platform, the furthest from the customs office she could get.

She began a prayer in her head, then mumbled it out loud, pulling on her gold chain out of habit.

Thy Kingdom come, Thy will be done ...

In the distance she heard the train approach. The travellers on the platform gathered their bags and stood to attention.

She kept her eye on the door of the customs office, almost afraid to breathe.

Give us this day our daily bread ...

A glorious screech of metal on metal, the wonderful fumes filled her nose.

She opened the door, put her foot on the steps, and launched herself inside.

Forgive us our trespasses as we forgive those who trespass against us ...

The train started with a jolt, moved, further, further along the track.

She had her visa, she had her paperwork, soon she would be across the border and on to Amsterdam.

But deliver us from evil.

She'd done it.

Amen.

* * *

Wolfgang waved madly as he ran towards her.

"Gisela! Gisela!"

She couldn't help but throw her arms around him.

"You waited."

"I came to meet every train! What happened?"

"They wouldn't let me through. I had to go back to Duisburg. I had to wait for a visa. They sent me to a convent. I thought I was done for!"

"Oh my goodness!"

"Thank you for waiting for me."

"Of course I waited!"

He carried her case while Gisela held onto her hatbox.

She had not seen Wolfgang in years. Now he looked quite mature, filled out in the face, his shoulders wide.

"I had planned on taking you to Scheveningen. But that was with you arriving yesterday. Do you still want to go today? Are you tired?"

Gisela looked up at the blue sky, the clouds puffing along, pure white against cornflower blue.

Yes, she wanted to go somewhere nice for a treat.

First Wolfgang led her through narrow paved streets, past gambrel-roofed houses, to his flat, tucked up in the eaves. His place was small, but it had a canal view.

His rooms were neat and tidy, sparse.

He made her a coffee while she changed into a lighter blouse.

She told him all about her fears, about how frightened she was when the guard took her off the train.

He seemed to think it was a funny story, rather than a terrifying one.

She wasn't sure he quite understood what had been going on in Vienna.

Before they left, Gisela wrote another card to her parents.

Thank goodness she had not sent that card from Duisburg yesterday.

They would have been distraught had it arrived.

They walked towards the tram and Gisela felt herself relax, now that she had a few hours to pass amiably with her cousin.

Wolfgang was an accountant in a small and old family firm.

He pointed towards his office as they passed.

The building was three storeys high with semicircle windows in its attic.

"I could have saved my day off yesterday," he joked.

"I am so sorry about that," said Gisela.

"No, no," said Wolfgang. "It is quite all right. I always wanted to spend seven hours at a train station just for fun."

"Wolfgang!" said Gisela, doffing him on the arm for his teasing.

The warm sun shone down while they waited for the tram to pull up.

Gisela felt a weight lift from her and evaporate into the canal-odoured air around her.

Was she really so worried just a few hours ago?

On the tram they stood, watching tall buildings flash by.

She was looking forward to seeing the sea.

It was so long since she'd been to the coast.

She once visited Trieste and saw the wide water with her father.

It was so different to the lakes outside Vienna.

As the coast finally appeared so too did rows and rows of squat sandbags. They sat, scattered in places like pebbles.

"The sandbags," Gisela said, pointing. "What are they for?"

Wolfgang shrugged. "Perhaps they are expecting flooding?"

"In the summer?" asked Gisela.

Wolfgang shrugged again.

Gisela thought of the giant guns she had seen all along the train line.

Were these sandbags the intended protection against those great big guns on wheels?

One rocket would blast all those sandbags into the air.

She shook her head.

In the distance, a Ferris wheel appeared.

They watched its buckets turning over and over in the sky.

"Will you have a go?" Wolfgang asked.

"I think I'm having enough of an adventure," said Gisela.

The air was fresh and salty – it flowed in through the open window of the tram and Gisela breathed it in, feeling her chest expand and rise.

The refreshing smell of the sea.

How wonderful it was!

They dismounted from the tram and made their way down the long pier.

Seagulls screeched overhead and descended on an old man who had brought a canvas bag of crusts.

Beneath their feet, the wooden boards showed cracks of the water. Dark-blue.

Down, down, down.

"Imagine you'll be out there soon," said Wolfgang when they sat on a bench and looked out to the horizon. "It's exciting."

"Is it?"

If only it were a holiday.

Wolfgang put his hand on hers.

"You will be fine. Try not to think of it as long-term. When all this is soon over, we will see each other." He paused. "Is it very bad? In Vienna?"

They weren't looking into each other's eyes and so it was easier to talk.

To say what she was really thinking.

"It's been bad for a long time. I think it's hardest on Papa. He was so sure that he would keep his job. That we would not get caught up in all the … I mean we're Catholics, not Jews. What more do they want from us?"

"I'm glad I'm living here," said Wolfgang

"They could come here too."

"Never."

Gisela realised that Wolfgang really did not understand at all.

He was naive.

They had thought it impossible too, all that happened, all that they'd seen since Adolf Hitler and his Nazi Party rose to power.

The freedoms lost over the past six years.

The jobs being stripped away, the right to education, the access to any entertainment, even to food.

Never had they imagined it could happen.

"I'm glad I am going across the water," she said. "And I'm glad I'm going to Ireland, which is safer than England even."

They sat in silence again, thinking.

"Are your friends leaving?" Gisela asked eventually. "Your Jewish friends?"

"Some."

"What will you do?"

Wolfgang shrugged.

His family had never converted. Not like hers had.

If the Nazis did come to Holland, they would not be safe.

"Let me see how Ireland is," she said. "You could come there?"

He laughed. "Ireland!" He shook his head.

Gisela hoped he was right. She hoped that the soldiers carrying their red swastika-ed flags would never come to Holland.

"Now," said Wolfgang. "Would the lady care for some luncheon?"

They walked back up the pier while Wolfgang decided which hotel they would visit.

He settled on the Kurhaus Grand.

Before they reached the wide hotel steps, a man in a Tyrolean hat stopped, put his foot on the kerb and tied his shoelace.

Gisela stared at him.

The sight of him brought her back to an afternoon in Vienna last year, when she had been out shopping, trying to see if she could get some meat for their dinner.

She'd walked by a group of soldiers who were laughing, making noise.

In the centre of the group was an older man in a Tyrolean hat, the hat perched at a funny angle on his head, as if it had nearly been knocked off. He hunkered, brushing at the kerb with a toothbrush.

They were making him clean the street!

One soldier kicked him hard as Gisela passed, right in the back.

The man wobbled and shot out his arms to steady himself.

The toothbrush fell out of his hands, the bristles black with dirt.

Haha.

Haha, laughed the soldiers.

The man began to cry.

Hahahaha.

"Are you alright?" asked Wolfgang.

Gisela broke herself from the memory.

"Yes. Yes, I'm fine."

There was no point discussing the man in the Tyrolean hat with Wolfgang.

She wasn't even sure that he would believe her.

They walked by a grand fountain in front of the hotel.

The water cascaded in a noisy torrent.

The doorman in a top hat bowed slightly as he opened the door.

Music tinkled, low, from an unseen pianist.

Potted plants sat, green against red-and-gold wallpaper, under low gaslights on the wall.

A beautiful smell of perfume permeated the air.

"Do you have a luncheon booking?" asked the maître d' with smile.

"We do not," said Wolfgang but he opened his wallet and discreetly shuffled two guilder notes.

The maître d' nodded and led them to a window table overlooking the beach.

It was okay to forget for an hour, Gisela told herself.

It was okay to forget about the tiny sandbags and the black metal guns.

It was okay to forget about the man with the toothbrush, forced to scrub the streets.

And it was okay to forget about the steamer boat that would sail her away from everything and everyone that she knew this evening.

"Think about it," she said to Wolfgang as they looked at their menus. "If I settle and get a good job perhaps you could come over to me. I'm sure they need accountants in Ireland."

"To count all the sheep?"

"Stop it!" she said, laughing.

Gisela thought of Mrs. de Freyne and her words in her introductory letter; *I am a chicken farmer with a large holding.*

"To count all the chickens," she said, to Wolfgang's bemused face.

G2 INTELLIGENCE REPORT

STATUS: INFORMATION
LOCATION: NEWTOWN HOUSE, TERMONFECKIN,
CO. LOUTH

Fritz Hettinger has a degree in chemistry and is known to have a knowledge of explosives.

He and his family arrived in Ireland through the farming scheme, despite his university education.

All speak excellent English and could provide very useful services to any covert German operations.

To pay close attention.

MARRIAGE STATUS: Married to Eva Hettinger, two sons, Otto and Max

RESIDES: Private Cottage at back of Newtown House

ACTION: Observation, particularly in relation to any purchases of farm chemicals/fertilisers

Hans

CHAPTER SIX

The chicken farm turned out to be two very large coops, which could, by way of a contraption, be moved onto new grass every few days.

Hans, Otto and Max helped manoeuvre it around when needed on account of Fritz Hettinger having a bad back.

Otto and Max were tasked with feeding the hens and cleaning out their coops, rather an unpleasant task, as the eye-watering ammonia emanating from the urine-soaked hay forced them to wear scarves around their noses and mouths.

They collected the eggs, graded them and packed them for the suppliers for market.

Hans quite liked watching the hens waddle round their coop, stretch out their claws and scratch in the grass for corn. They needed to be moved so often because in a day or two they could tear a lawn dry.

Fritz was helping with general odd jobs around Newtown House. With his easy manner and excellent English, Mrs. de Freyne took to him straight away. She seemed to relish both Fritz and Eva's company in the house.

Hans preferred to be out on the farm and he found himself tasked with helping Fintan Walshe milk the cows. The milk was plentiful now that it was coming into high summer.

They poured the milk into huge churns that were collected for the creameries in Dublin.

As well as looking after the animals there was a huge amount of upkeep on the land and buildings that Fintan assigned to Max.

Fritz had to be given the low-impact jobs when it was realised that he simply wasn't able to do any heavy lifting.

Hans knew that Fintan favoured him over Fritz on account of his strength and willingness to tackle any job asked of him.

Fritz's response of, "I'm sorry, Mr. Walshe, is there something else I could do?" visibly irked the farm foreman.

Hans realised that Fritz had been lucky to escape with the Kagran Gruppe and get his family to safety, being as it was that he was not quite fit to work on a farm.

But Hans would have done the same thing.

Fritz was a good man.

Fintan liked to chat to Hans as they worked out in the fields or in the yard. He let him drive Bessie to bring feed and tools around the farm.

In two weeks, the Garden Fête, an event organised by Mrs. de Freyne whereby she invited the whole parish to see the house and gardens, would take place.

Fintan had a long list of jobs that needed to be done.

"Good man," he said, whenever Hans completed a job.

He was particular about the work, taking time to inspect any task Hans carried out.

Sometimes Mrs. de Freyne came to talk to them while they were at work.

She was very interested in Hans' background and when he told her that he had no experience of farming prior to his training, she smiled.

"I knew nothing about farming before I came to Ireland either," she said. "But, by God, I've learned."

Fintan told Hans that Mrs. de Freyne had grown up right in the heart of London, in a place called Belgravia. Her father had been an MP and an industrialist and it was this inheritance that she had bought Newtown with. He often referred to her as 'Lady de Freyne', but as far as Hans knew, she was not a titled lady.

Hans had noticed that Mrs. de Freyne's accent sounded a bit different to everyone else, but because his English was poor, he wasn't sure if it was just his ear.

Never one to pry, he did not ask any more questions about Mrs. de Freyne, but he was curious. Where was her husband? Was she a widow?

She was a charitable kind woman and yet, apart from Nola, she seemed to live totally alone.

The walled garden was filled with flowers that Fintan had either imported or seeded and sometimes crossbred in the glasshouses.

He was an efficient foreman, thought Hans.

In a small, growing way, Hans felt that he could carve out a place for himself here.

There would be plenty of work all year round. The gardens were so large and the house in need of constant maintenance that his hands would never be idle.

He was comfortable to be left to his work and to take his meals in the house with the other Austrians.

He enjoyed his privacy in the cottage with his little warm fire to himself.

Newtown was so calm in its surroundings, scenic and peaceful, the sound of cows lowing in the field and swallows dipping overhead until the sun finally set on the horizon.

Yes, he thought, of the three places they'd stayed since they'd come to Ireland, this was the best.

In the six months since they'd left Vienna, he now felt most content.

He could see that perhaps he could be happy here.

It was something he had not expected.

There was a point, not so long ago, when he thought he would never be happy again.

Never, ever again.

He had contemplated the worst at his lowest points, when the days were so dark that he could not find the energy to rouse himself from his bed.

How could he go on?

Why would he want to?

Coming to Newtown had changed that.

And he was thankful.

He felt he had arrived somewhere special.

Somewhere where he could be at peace.

* * *

When Hans proposed to Anja she smiled, nodded and embraced him round his neck.

She did not say the word "yes".

It was simply to be done.

Instead, she curled her fingers around his and they stayed, huddled close at the bottom of the Wedding Fountain in Hoher Markt Square, whispering and making their plans.

Hans thought the fountain appropriate enough.

Ideally, he would have taken Anja to the mountains and made a day of it, hiking and picnicking and finding a cool, shady spot in which to explore each other.

It was one of the reasons he knew Anja wanted to get married.

They were both curious. They both wanted to know what it would be like.

But with his father's health deteriorated now to the point where he could not be left on his own for any length of time, Hans knew a mountain trip was impossible.

The problem was that his father liked to wander.

If he found the door unlocked, he would bolt and because he was now completely unaware of his own personal safety he could run down the street, straight under a tram or the wheels of a motorcar.

At first Hans had asked some of the neighbours to watch him while he was at work.

But they soon grew tired of looking after an adult man who acted like an unruly child.

When his father left a pot on to boil, burning the pot and its contents to black and causing a near fire in their apartment, his neighbour Frau Leitner told Hans that he'd have to do something.

Frau Leitner, who had seven children of her own to watch, said Hans' father needed someone with him at all times.

"He is like a child now himself," she said, in her no-nonsense loud voice. "Since your mother died, he has got very bad."

It was true.

Hans' mother's death had set his father back in so many ways.

It had set them both back.

Hans hated coming home now to her aching absence.

Everywhere he looked he was reminded of her empty presence.

He could not bring himself to sort out her things.

Her cooking pots and implements lay around the kitchen unused.

Her toiletries still sat in the bedroom.

Sometimes he opened the wardrobe just to smell the perfume on her clothes.

Anja, being Anja, offered to mind Hans' father and, although Hans knew it would likely be another strike against him as far as her family were concerned, having their daughter as some sort of nursemaid, she said none of that mattered.

Each morning before Hans went to work, she arrived at the apartment bright and full of energy.

Hans' father took to her like the daughter he never had.

He told her constantly how beautiful she was and wanted to know if she was married.

It became a running joke as each day Anja answered, "Soon, soon."

Through dogged persistence, Hans had eventually made Gerhard see that his intentions were honourable.

Gerhard admitted that they could see Anja was happy.

"She tells me it is what she wants," he said to Hans the evening when Hans had gone to Alsergrund to formally ask Gerhard for Anja's hand, before his proposal to her.

"I know you worry about my job," said Hans. "But I am a hard worker and I will always provide for your daughter."

"All right," Gerhard had sighed. "I know that you love her. Although I always thought that my daughter would marry a –"

Gerhard stopped.

"Jew?" said Hans.

"Businessman," said Gerhard.

They both laughed.

"You have my blessing," said Gerhard.

The next day, Hans asked Frau Leitner to look after his father for just an hour and took Anja to the Wedding Fountain.

"Mary and Joseph," said Hans, pointing up at the monument. "Their wedding."

"Yes," said Anja. She was familiar with the statue.

Hans had asked her to take a moment and sit down under it.

"Well, I thought it appropriate. For us. If you can imagine the same thing for us. I would very much like that. I would like to ask you to marry me. I have already asked your father."

Anja looked into Hans' eyes intently before throwing her arms around his neck.

They remained there for many minutes, unable to break away.

They wanted to get married as soon as possible and so the date was set for just three months' time.

Hans counted down the days, marking an X each day into the calendar that hung on the kitchen wall.

He felt ecstatic as the day drew nearer and nearer.

When the day did dawn, it was a cold, frost-tipped morning and Hans awoke to a ball of nerves in his stomach.

What if Gerhard had changed his mind and talked Anja out of it?

What if his father threw a tantrum, or escaped from the church?

They had chosen St. Rupert's church, the oldest church in the city.

Anja was not religious and had decided that she would be happy to marry in a church.

It had resulted in much discussion among the Schafers, and Hans feared they would think it was at his insistence that Anja had agreed to marry in a Catholic church.

But it was Anja who pushed it. What did it all matter, she said, when her family, although Jewish by birth, had never really practised? Whether she married in a synagogue or a Gothic church, made no difference to her.

Hans was coming to see how forthright his young bride was, how she had her own opinions and ideas and was not afraid to push for them.

It was possibly what he loved about her most.

Hans was sad that his mother did not live to see Anja walk down the aisle, radiant.

He was sad that she did not live to even meet her, or hold her hand or know her embrace.

She would have loved her, he knew. She would have welcomed her into her home and there would have been no animosity between the two, which he knew could so often be the case when a young woman swept into a home to marry the only son.

After the church they went to a hotel where they had hired its dance hall for their wedding breakfast.

Anja's family, in their finery, were warm and friendly and sang songs and clapped their hands, wishing the couple well on their lifetime ahead.

A cousin played the accordion and soon the dance floor was filled with stomping feet.

Hans and Anja were pushed into the middle as the Schafer extended family encircled them.

He had never felt such love.

Later he and Anja danced together, quite a deal for Hans who had never liked dancing in public.

Hans' father stayed for most of the celebrations and seemed to enjoy dancing with all these people he didn't know.

Afterwards, tired from all the excitement, they left the hotel and returned to their apartment where earlier, Frau Leitner had put Hans' father to bed.

"I'm sorry we couldn't stay in the hotel," Hans said.

"I don't mind," said Anja. "This is home now anyway."

Hans left the curtains apart to allow the lamplight from outside to shine in.

Under the yellow glow he followed the lines of Anja's body, not quite believing that after that all that time waiting and wondering, here she was now in front of him.

If it hurt, she did not say.

But she clung to him all night, like a mussel on a rock and he knew that he made her feel safe, his arms wrapped around her tight, in her new home, in the life she had chosen to spend with him.

Gisela

CHAPTER SEVEN

The breeze was warm on the pier at Scheveningen but at sea it turned cool.

Gisela stood on the deck of the S.S. *Amsterdam* as it cut through the water, feeling the sharp sting of the wind on her face.

The sea air whipped her hair, against her brows, it tugged at her skirt and sleeves.

Last night she had stayed on the deck as long as she could, but when she couldn't take the wind and biting cold anymore, she made her way into the warm fug of the ship's interior to go and find supper.

There were many families travelling together.

Plenty of single men.

And the odd young woman.

She wondered who was escaping like her. Who else had a single ticket with no idea when they would be back?

She shared her cabin with two women.

One was older, with deep lines on her face, dressed all in black as if in mourning.

The other was younger and kept her mouth shut in a tight line.

Neither wished to converse with her.

She watched as they got ready for bed and then climbed under the sheets and pulled them up to their chins.

She was reading her book on her bunk and sensed they wished to extinguish the light so she left the cabin and went for a walk about the ship, finding herself back on the freezing deck as the dark night settled in.

An overwhelming sense of loneliness swelled.

Never before had she been so far from home.

Never before had she been so alone.

When she went back to her cabin, she got undressed in the dark and climbed into the unfamiliar bed.

She listened to the soft sounds of the two strangers sleeping.

Tears threatened but she pushed them away, gritting her teeth and squeezing the blankets in protest.

It was useless to get upset.

She had to be strong.

In the morning she was awoken by the women getting dressed and ready for breakfast.

She waited till they left before getting up to pack up her own case and put on her clothes and face the day.

When she made her way to the dining room, she saw that England had come into view.

There it was, dark, green-brown, flat then rising, closer and closer. Harwich.

The churning of the ship was slow on approach.

Gisela stood and watched as the ship was directed into port, while men in caps scurried, pulling, shouting, making big wide circles with their arms.

The ropes were the size of her torso.

The ship docked with a thud.

Inside, the passengers shuffled and lifted their bags.

Gisela's legs shook a little when she reached terra firma.

She listened to the voices as she walked into the terminal.

It felt so different already – the signs, the furniture, the babble and flow of English.

In the crowd at arrivals a man from the Jewish Society held her name on a piece of cardboard.

He turned as soon as she greeted him and she had to follow him through the crowds, to descend steps into a train station.

The man was brusque.

"The train will take you to Euston. When you get there, you will need to take the underground to get to your hostel. I've written down the stops and the address."

He spoke so fast.

She strained to understand the words.

He handed her a slip of paper.

"Have you everything you need?"

"Yes."

He did not offer to carry her bags. Not like Wolfgang did.

Gisela got the impression he was tired of ferrying Jewish refugees about the place.

He pointed her towards her train.

The train was up so high, it looked like ...

"I ..."

"What's wrong?"

"The ..."

The carriage looked like the ones they used to take Jews out Vienna. To the camps.

The Society man watched her, waiting impatiently.

"What is wrong?"

She could not tell him her thoughts.

They were irrational.

She had to get on.

She was safe here, surely?

"Hurry now. Go and find a seat," said the man.

When Gisela pulled herself up the train steps, she found that inside the seats were covered in leather.

People were not pressed up against the sides, peering to get out.

It was not a cattle train.

She took a seat and held her hatbox and case close to her.

Soon the train moved off.

Soon, she would be in London.

* * *

The smell of cooked food wafted each time the door opened into the dormitory.

It smelled like sausage in bolognese.

It made Gisela's stomach curl.

The hostel was busy.

She was glad she only had to stay there for a night before taking a train right across England to Wales and the port of Holyhead.

For her free day, she was keen to see London.

She did not know if she would ever be back.

Despite the tiredness tugging at her eyes and the tightness in her calves, she took her hatbox and pushed her case under her bed.

While checking her hair in a small mirror nailed to the wall beside her bunk bed, a young sandy-haired man appeared from behind her.

"Hello," he said.

Gisela turned around.

"Hello," she said back.

He sat on her bed while she hunted for her jacket.

"My name is Magnus," he said, speaking German. "Where are you from?"

"Vienna," said Gisela. "My name is Gisela."

"No!" said the boy, his voice lighting up. "I knew it! I knew you were Austrian. I am from Linz!"

Gisela did not share the young man's joy. She did not appreciate his forwardness in sitting on her bed but, as the dormitory was quite open, she felt that she could not stop him.

"Where are you going?" he asked. "Are you in London for long?"

Gisela shook her head. "I leave for Ireland tomorrow."

"Oh," he said, looking disappointed. "Where are you going now?"

"I am going sightseeing. I want to see the Tower of London."

Gisela realised her mistake as soon as she said the words.

"Oh! I would love to see it. Can I come with you? It would be nice to speak to someone in German for a while."

His face was childish, his freckles dark on his skin.

He was too young to be handsome, thought Gisela.

She couldn't help but feel sorry for him.

She sighed. "All right," she said.

Apart from Dirk, she hadn't really spoken to anyone friendly since she'd left Vienna.

Magnus was overjoyed.

They took an underground train, which was stuffy and choking, to Big Ben first, before making the long journey over to London Bridge and the famed Tower.

All the while Magnus talked, telling Gisela of his home in Linz and his family who had sent him to London with the only money they had ever saved.

His babbling irritated Gisela.

She wanted to take in the calm serenity of the ancient buildings, to consider the history of the city and the people who had gone before them.

She had a book on Henry the Eighth and was fascinated by his six wives.

As she studied the huge, carved sandstone bricks, and looked at the Tudor garb of a Yeoman Warder who stood at the entrance gate, she felt a warm hand slip into hers.

She pulled her hand away in shock.

"Magnus!" she said.

He laughed.

After the tower, Magnus suggested they get something to eat and, thinking of the sausage bolognese back at the hostel, Gisela reluctantly agreed.

They found a café and Gisela watched Magnus' eyes light up when his mashed potatoes, pork chop and apple sauce landed in front of him.

"What would you say if I asked you to stay in London?" Magnus said while licking his knife.

"What do you mean?" said Gisela.

"What would you say if I said: don't go to Ireland?"

"Why would I not go to Ireland?" Gisela said with a chuckle.

"I'm serious," he said.

Gisela noticed his two front teeth, which overlapped slightly.

She shook her head in confusion. What was he talking about?

"You are from Vienna, I am from Linz," he said. "We should marry. You would find work easily – your English is very good."

Gisela let out a great big burst of laughter.

She tried to stifle it when she saw the incredulity on Magnus' face.

"I'm sorry," she said and she shook her head firmly. "I cannot."

"Two are stronger than one," he said.

"It's all set up. I am going to Ireland and I'm not going to back out now."

But what she really wanted to say was *Magnus, you idiot! You silly boy!*

He was crestfallen.

As a waitress served them tea after their dinner plates were cleared, his upset turned to anger.

"You should not laugh," he said. "It is not nice. Who do you think you are anyway? Some stuck-up cow from Vienna – think you're better than me?"

Gisela stared at her cup, refusing to meet his eyes.

He should not have asked such a question of her.

Now, everything had gone sour and she desperately wished that she were back at the hostel and away from him.

They took the underground back to the hostel in frosty silence.

There were no stabbing grabs for her hand.

That night, as Gisela fell asleep to the rustles and panting of amorous couples all around, she understood why such a thought must have got into Magnus's head.

In the morning as she packed her case to leave, he turned his head to the wall and she could not help but feel sorry for him.

He was all alone in the world.

And they both knew that neither of them would ever see each other again.

* * *

Gisela met the man from the Jewish Society at Euston Station again.

He had a list of Jews that he was in charge of meeting, seeing that they made it to their trains and buses, as they tumbled in from all parts of the former Austria and Germany.

He walked her to her train bound for Holyhead. As they waited for the train to pull into the platform, Gisela absentmindedly played with her gold cross, running her fingers up and down the links in its chain.

She saw the man's eyes grow wide.

"May I see your passport?" he asked.

Gisela took it from her hatbox, and watched him stare at the letter 'J'.

She tucked her cross away and smiled at him.

He said nothing further but Gisela could see he was not happy.

The society was only interested in helping proper Jews.

She had slipped through the net.

On the train, she slept in bursts, her head rolling on the rest.

In her rattled dreams she saw Dirk, then Wolfgang, then Magnus, then the Society man.

All the men she had met on this journey.

By the time she got to Holyhead, her body felt coiled as a snake.

In the terminal she spied the steamer in port.

Her ship.

Her final vessel.

Thick, angry raindrops lashed at the windows as the boat moved up and down in the grey foamy sea, pushing forward towards Ireland.

Gisela felt as though her energy was draining the nearer she got to her destination.

Everything she'd saved up inside to get her through this journey had now been spent.

She didn't expect to meet and lose a good friend that she suspected she might have had in Dirk.

She didn't expect a near trip to a local concentration camp.

She certainly had not expected a marriage proposal from a young, het-up Austrian man.

No wonder she felt weary.

At Dublin Port the clouds had rained themselves out but the late June day was overcast and shadowy.

Finally, her feet touched Irish soil.

She passed through the terminal and met another man with a sign saying "*Gisela Moller*".

He had spelled her name wrong, with an 'o' were the 'ü' should have been.

As they exited the port in the man's motorcar and drove into the city, Gisela noticed how flat Dublin was.

There were no tall structures like Big Ben or rope bridges like in London.

Up ahead along the quays, she saw a dome, copper-green on top.

The buildings they drove by were sooty and black.

Broken windows stuffed with rags were dotted in nearly every building she saw.

Down one street, she spied a row of houses with no doors at all.

Children darted everywhere. They thronged the side streets, barefoot with blackened faces.

When a boy ran out in front of the car, her driver had to press hard on the brakes.

He rolled down the window and shouted, "*Get out of the way, you little blaguard!*"

Gisela wondered what a "blaguard" was.

They reached a wide bridge where horse and carts moved among the motorcars and flat-bed carts carried people, furniture, goods.

Green buses drove by advertising Cadbury's and Horlick's.

Around a corner a bushy-looking park appeared.

"Stephen's Green," said the driver.

Past a hotel called the Shelbourne, the car pulled to a stop.

"Here you are," said the driver.

He had informed her he was the harbour master but liked to help out the Society of Friends when he could. He referred to them by their popular name of "Quakers".

"Safe and sound. Just up them steps," he said as he opened the boot to retrieve her case.

Gisela read the Society of Friends plaque on the wall.

"Thank you," she said.

"You're very welcome, love – you look after yourself now, won't you?"

She nodded.

"Good luck, Fraulein."

He mispronounced the word but she appreciated his effort.

He had been kind to her.

He meant well.

She took a deep breath and climbed the steps.

She rang the doorbell and waited.

The door was opened by a slight-looking man wearing a purple tie.

It was quite dazzling against his pale-grey suit.

"Miss Müller?" he said.

She nodded.

He smiled.

"You are most welcome. Your host is upstairs, all ready to meet you."

Gisela walked past the man with the purple tie and took a deep breath.

G2 INTELLIGENCE REPORT

STATUS: INFORMATION

LOCATION: KELLY'S NEWSAGENTS, DROGHEDA, CO. LOUTH

We have information that Victor Kelly has been receiving and supplying indecent magazines from London against the Censorship of Publications Act, 1929. The magazines are stored under the counter and have been supplied to a number of gentlemen from the town. It's understood the password is 'Jellybeans and Jam'.

MARITAL STATUS: Married, to Jacqueline Kelly, three children

ACTION: Please organise an officer to purchase the evidence and pursue appropriately

Hans

CHAPTER EIGHT

A smelly man with long grey hair protruding from a greasy hat sat beside Hans on a bench in Drogheda Garda Station.

Hans tried to shift away from the man, due to the odour that permeated the air all around him, but the waiting room was full.

His stomach lurched.

At least there were high ceilings in the old Georgian building.

At least there was that.

He had taken the bus that morning on his own; the Hettinger boys signed their paperwork on Mondays, while their parents signed on Tuesdays.

His turn was Wednesday.

He presumed it would be easier for them to travel as a group, but perhaps the staggered approach was intentional.

He had come to understand that they caused great suspicion when they travelled as a group, having already felt the eyes of the parish on them when they'd arrived for Sunday Mass.

On the bus, he had looked out at the estuary marsh that ran all the way along the river towards the town.

He spotted birds he'd never seen before. Birds with long necks and wide wings, birds with semicircle beaks, for sticking right down into the sand.

He thought how free those birds were.

How they could spread their wings and up and leave and fly to another marsh all the way across the country if they wanted.

If he disappeared down the country there would be a warrant out.

A missing alien.

Still, he was aware of the freedom that he had here.

He could wander around the town if he so wished.

He could visit any shop, museum or picture house.

There be no questions asked of him or paperwork to be shown.

The man beside him grumbled and spoke out loud. He was annoyed at the waiting time. He was annoyed at the heat. He was annoyed at everything it seemed.

Hans very much wanted to escape the muttering man but now that a seat had become free, right up next to the hatch where a policeman was seeing to the long line of enquiries and complaints, he felt it would be rude to move.

He realised, now that he knew about these things, that the man smelled of manure.

Cow manure to be precise.

He really stank.

Hans looked at the man's shoes and saw that along the sole, near to where a crusty sock and toe peeped out, was fresh, wet, green manure.

There was the source of the smell.

A man at the hatch needed to renew three dog licences.

The woman who came next wanted to report her neighbour for stealing coal from her coal shed.

She didn't have any evidence, she told the policeman, but she was fully sure it was him.

Hans watched the policeman sigh and fill in a report.

Finally, the stinking man beside him was called to the hatch and Hans was relieved.

Curious to see what the man's business was, Hans strained to hear as the man spoke in a low mumbling voice to the policeman behind the hatch.

The policeman leaned forward to hear.

After repeating himself a number of times the man eventually roared at the top of his voice: "*Jews! Fucking Jews! There's a load of them hiding in a shed in Sheepgrange, didn't I tell ya, didn't I warn ya? They're everywhere. Coming in off the ships like rats. Now are you going to go and do something about it or what?*"

The policeman stood up from his chair and raised his arms in a calming gesture.

"Mr. McCormack, there's no need to be shouting. We'll take the details and look into it, all right?"

Hans felt the hairs rise on the back of his neck.

Did the man know who he was?

That he was of the Austrian contingent?

The manured man looked around, rather pleased that he had now garnered everyone's attention.

"They're everywhere!" he said to his new audience, grinning, before turning back to the policeman.

The policeman wrote down the details of the shed (*Reilly's shed, no, not the new one, the old one, the one with the thatch roof, the one with the hole in it*) and its exact location. (*The field behind the field with the horse in it, there's no gate to the road, you have to go in from another field, that's why it's such a good hiding place*).

With his report made, the man was now satisfied and thanked the policeman. As he left the barracks in a waft of dung, he tipped his hat to Hans in goodbye.

Hans gave him a small polite wave.

Hans was called next.

He handed over his passport while the policeman went to fetch the file.

He wrote in his notes and held out the passport for Hans to retrieve it.

As Hans reached for it, the policeman said with a nod towards the door, "Don't mind that McCormack fella. He's in here every day reporting something or other. All up here!" and he tapped his temple knowingly.

Hans smiled.

He appreciated the policeman's words.

Leaving the station he felt the summer sun fall on his head and shoulders.

He had an hour to kill before it was time to take the bus back to Termonfeckin.

A bit of freedom for himself.

As free as a bird.

Almost.

He ambled along the street, enjoying the sunshine on his face, watching the shoppers and people who walked by.

They looked different, he realised, the Irish.

More pale around the face, even some adults with freckles.

The women wore their headscarves tucked tight under their chins and there was little colour to their clothes.

The streets were a little shabby, he felt.

There was no paving like in Vienna, no handsome statues with gold, no ornate carved stonework on the shops.

At the picture house he stopped to see what was showing.

He wondered whether he would go, with the others perhaps.

It would be an excursion.

They had all gone to see a film when they stayed in Ardmore and once in Enniskerry too.

The Hettingers had been thrilled as they'd not been able to go to the cinema since the regime clamped down on entertainment for Jews at home.

Hans stared at the fine-looking picture house beside a ballroom called The Abbey.

He wondered if Maeve, Newtown's housekeeper, liked dancing.

He could picture her waltzing around a ballroom with her sturdy legs and long graceful neck.

He had taken quite a shine to her and found her presence, in a way that was different to Eva Hettinger's, comforting.

The funny thing was he felt that she, in some way, felt it back.

That they liked each other.

They exchanged pleasantries in the kitchen and in the hall, whenever they passed, and he did every errand she asked of him and more.

In the evenings when they settled in the drawing room for tea before bed, they found themselves falling into conversation.

He thought her a very interesting woman as she talked about her love of her country and the struggles of the past years as Ireland sought its freedom from the rule of England.

She had a great respect for Mrs. de Freyne, who she told him was a deeply kind woman who had improved the parish immensely by opening up Newtown House and employing locals.

"You know, when she came here first, nobody thought much of her because she was another British landlord as such and we didn't expect much at all. The house has always been closed up. Nobody ever got in really – they didn't have many local staff. But Mrs. de Freyne seemed to make jobs for people. And then when she realised what things were like here, she made a special effort to help. Building homes for people – oh, there's not a soul I don't think in this parish who doesn't know her generosity."

Hans had listened with interest.

It confirmed what he had felt on meeting Mrs. de Freyne, that she was at heart a very good and conscientious woman.

Maeve told him that the Garden Fête was the highlight of the year for the parishioners.

It was a day out for the whole family, with competitions and music and dancing and novelty things to see.

"You'll enjoy it," she told Hans.

"After all the hard work is done," he had joked.

"Yes, well, we will all be run ragged, but it will be worth it," she said.

As he left the Abbey ballroom and picture house behind him, Hans thought how strange it was that he felt such warm feelings towards Maeve.

He had never expected to feel anything for another woman other than Anja.

He should not let them take hold.

He would not let them take hold.

How would that make her feel, he wondered?

How devastated would she be?

Further down the street, on his left loomed a cathedral church, behind black iron railings.

He considered going up the steps to light a candle but decided against it and walked on.

He was not feeling very religious today.

In fact, the issue of religion had been bothering him greatly lately.

The fuss it caused, the animosity and hate.

Perhaps they would be better off if no one had any religion at all?

Under a large limestone clock tower, Hans turned right down a busy street called Shop Street.

He looked in a hardware store and noted some implements that might work well at Newtown. Like him, Fintan Walshe had a great interest in carpentry.

He wondered if perhaps they could work on a project together, when the farm work was at a lull. When the Garden Fête was over and things had quietened down.

For Christmas perhaps? Wasn't that funny, he thought, as he spied a newsagent's called Kelly's near the bottom of the street. He was already thinking of Christmas, six months away!

It seemed he was settling in.

He was thinking about the future.

Dusty-looking jars of sweets sat in the window of Kelly's.

Hans stopped and stared at the jars of bullseyes and apple drops and thought how he could take a small bag home for Maeve.

She would like that, he thought.

It would make her smile.

Hans pushed open the door of the shop and a little bell jingled.

A balding man in a brown coat looked up from behind the counter and smiled.

"Good morning," he said.

Hans nodded in hello and asked for a quarter of the sweets.

While the shopkeeper busied himself, Hans went to look at the newspapers and magazines.

Danzig Youth and Labour Conscripted shouted a headline in the *Irish Press*.

The article underneath it told how thousands of men and women in Northern Poland had been called up by the Nazi authorities to carry out police service.

Hans bought the paper.

Since coming to Ireland he had kept abreast of the news as best he could.

They liked to talk about it over dinner – what was happening back home.

Sometimes it was too much and Eva especially got upset, worrying about their relatives left behind.

She had a sister in Vienna with a small family and Fritz had cousins he was very close to.

"Not looking good on the Continent, is it?" said the shopkeeper, pointing to the *Irish Press* newspaper. "There'll be a war for Christmas, mark my words."

Hans nodded.

Was he right?

Probably.

"Desperate for Poland he is. Won't stop till he has Poland," said the shopkeeper as he pushed buttons on his cash register. "I can see him aligning with the Soviets. And we don't want that, by Jesus, we don't want that."

He handed the brown-paper bag of sweets and newspaper to Hans and took the coins.

"It is very worrying," said Hans.

"Is that an accent I hear?" said the shopkeeper, his eyes lighting up.

"Yes," said Hans. "I'm from Vienna. I'm staying in Termonfeckin, at Newtown House."

"Ah!" said the shopkeeper.

This news seems to terribly excite him.

"The refugees! I've heard about you. Well, of course, you'd be glued to the news!"

He pointed again at the newspaper in Hans' hand.

"And how are you getting on, out in Termonfeckin?"

"Good," said Hans.

"Right," said the shopkeeper.

He stared at Hans, his eyes taking him all in.

It made Hans feel uncomfortable.

It felt as if he'd be reported on, that his very presence would be talked about with every customer who came in that day.

"You know ..." said the shopkeeper and he leaned forward, lowering his voice, "I might have something for you."

From under the counter the shopkeeper lifted a flat brown-paper bag.

He eased a magazine out of it and turned it round ever so slightly to Hans.

Pictured was the top half of a woman, nude.

Hans' eyes fell to the dark, round nipples.

"Oh," said Hans, taken quite aback. "Eh ... no. No, thank you."

"Are you sure?" said the shopkeeper, shuffling the magazine out a little further to reveal the woman's belly and a small triangle of thick black pubic hair.

The image, so unexpected, made Hans blush.

He shook his head.

"All right," said the shopkeeper and he pushed the magazine back into its paper bag. "But if you do change your mind, or you want to let your fellow countrymen know, you know where I am. Could do with a bit of distraction, I expect."

Hans nodded.

Turning, Hans walked towards the door, feeling desperately embarrassed.

"Tell them to ask for Jellybeans and Jam," said the shopkeeper to Hans' back.

Hans nodded again and escaped out onto the street and its fresh air.

"Take care," said the shopkeeper, as Hans pulled the door shut behind him.

Gisela

CHAPTER NINE

In an upstairs room at the Society of Friends building on Stephen's Green, five women sat round a table, waiting to greet Gisela.

They all stood when she entered with the man with the purple tie.

The two older women put out their hands in greeting.

The first woman was large in her presence, soft. She wore a hat with a veil.

She smiled widely at Gisela.

The other woman was thinner.

Her smile was thin too.

The other three women were younger – they looked to be in their late teens.

"Mrs. Laila de Freyne," said the larger woman, introducing herself and pumping Gisela's hand up and down.

Her host and sponsor.

Thank goodness she looked friendly.

"Mrs. Mulvany," said the other woman. "Pleased to meet you."

"My sister-in-law," explained Mrs. de Freyne.

Mrs. Mulvany's grip was limp and bony.

Gisela turned to a blonde girl who had pushed herself forward.

She was tall and quite a beauty.

Gisela's fingers were crushed in her long, white grip.

She held her stare, not a hint of a smile on her lips.

"Nola de Freyne," said the girl.

Nola.

Mrs. de Freyne's daughter.

Her companion-to-be.

She was surprised by her height, by her long blonde hair, by her beauty.

She had expected someone darker, someone more demure.

Someone ... more like her.

"How do you do?" said Gisela.

Nola continued to stare, rudely.

Gisela's instinct was to drop her hand, for here was a girl ungracious in her hello.

Gisela was older by more than four years. Surely she deserved at least a modicum of courtesy?

Suddenly, a smile burst forth from Nola with a flash of her large white teeth. She whipped Gisela's hand from her grip and pulled her into a bone-crunching embrace.

The shock of her body against hers, pinning her arms, made Gisela gasp.

It had been a joke.

Nola was playing a trick.

She whispered into Gisela's ear.

"I'm so glad you've come."

Gisela couldn't help but laugh.

The other two girls, tall and wiry, did not come forward to shake her hand.

"Girls!" admonished the older thin woman, who Gisela realised now must be their mother.

The girls reluctantly offered two limp handshakes.

"Kate."

"Margaret."

They snapped their hands back and Gisela saw them wipe them on the hips of their dresses.

She was too unclean for them.

They saw her as a dirty Jew.

So it was the same in Ireland.

"You must be exhausted?" said Mrs. de Freyne.

She had a lovely smile, though she was not beautiful.

"I am alright," Gisela said.

The reaction of the young girls had annoyed her.

She wasn't expecting it.

The truth was that she was absolutely exhausted, but felt it would be rude to state so to her host.

"Well, I can imagine what an arduous journey it was. We are so happy to finally see you. Are you hungry?"

"A little."

"Let's go and get some refreshments," said Mrs. de Freyne, looking disapprovingly at the tea and plate of custard creams that had been set up in the middle of the table.

Downstairs, they said goodbye to the charity workers who sat behind desks piled high with paper and folders. A woman was bent over a typewriter, clacking with force.

"All in order?" said the man with the purple tie.

"All in order," said Mrs. de Freyne. "We are going for high tea!"

"Wonderful," said the man.

He nodded to Gisela as she made her way to the front door.

"If you need anything at all, you have our address," he said.

"Thank you," said Gisela.

And she meant it.

She was more grateful than he could possibly ever understand.

* * *

Nola carried Gisela's case up a wide street called Grafton Street where they followed the footpath past slow-moving motor vehicles.

She talked non-stop.

"What was the boat like? I've only ever taken a steamer to England. I'd imagine it's much more exciting coming from the Continent. Is it? Did it take long? Were you down near where the animals are kept? Marguerite, she's a friend from Powerscourt, she told me when you go on a long crossing like that all you can hear is the cows mooing, poor things – they've no idea they're on their way to be slaughtered, do they?"

"No," said Gisela. "No, I could not hear the cows."

"Was it very rough?"

"Not really."

"You don't get sea sick, do you? That's an awful rotten experience. We might get out on a boat at home, I have a friend who has a rowing boat, we can go out around the head at Clogherhead. Would you like that?"

"I suppose so."

Gisela knew she should have said yes. With enthusiasm. Nola was being kind.

But she was so tired.

Kate and Margaret followed their mother up the street, ignoring her. Nola made a face behind their backs.

"Don't mind them, they're a bit snooty!" she said.

Gisela gave her a weak smile.

Dublin, so far, was a bit of a shock. She felt as though she'd got off the boat into another era.

Endless children ran past barefoot, faces smudged black as if they'd been eating coal.

The buildings were cracked, grey and shabby.

They looked like the children, dirty and unkempt.

The streets were pockmarked and broken.

Poor.

She found herself longing for the smooth streetscape of her home city, for the swept flagstones and ornate windows, pretty in their plaster, crafted by the hands of Renaissance masters.

She wasn't sure if she liked it here at all.

How would she get by in such a place?

Ahead, Mrs. de Freyne stood outside a café with mosaic tiles on its front.

A large sign over the door read *Bewley Oriental Cafes Ltd.*

She waited for Gisela to approach and smiled, while the others went in. She didn't look very much like a chicken farmer, thought Gisela. She held the door open for her, which was a kindly gesture.

Gisela was quite taken aback when she got inside.

She could have been walking in to have coffee with Mama and Papa in a café on Stefansplatz!

Waiters hurried by and, all around, diners clinked their coffee cups, read their newspapers or chatted.

Tall stained-glass windows looked down on low sofas and shiny brass lights.

The mahogany chairs at the tables were upholstered in red velvet with yellow swirls.

When they sat, Mrs. Mulvany asked a few polite questions of her – *what was school like, college my goodness, what did your family actually do* – but soon she fell back into conversation with her daughters. They were going shopping it seemed – there was quite a lot to get.

Tea was served in white porcelain pots. Red and blue flowers entangled on the china cups. Small cut sandwiches and cakes, sliced for dainty hands, nestled in their afternoon-tea stands.

"Eat up," said Mrs. de Freyne.

Gisela's cream bun oozed with jam, the sugar coated her fingers and she had to wipe her hands on her napkin.

Too sweet. Her stomach swirled.

"Do you like to dance?" asked Nola.

"Yes."

Nola smiled. "Oh goody. We have a lot of parties to attend. Did mother tell you my coming out ball is in October?"

Gisela had not yet been furnished with that information.

"You will need some dresses, Gisela," said Mrs. de Freyne.

"I brought dresses with me," Gisela responded.

"We'll go to Switzer's after this," said Mrs. de Freyne.

A shopping trip.

Ach nein.

* * *

Switzer's smelled of musky perfume.

No matter which floor they trooped to, it choked.

Gisela wondered if it was somebody's job to go round spritzing all day?

"Yellow is divine," said Nola as she held a taffeta material across her rather flat bosom.

Gisela spied a chair and went and sat in it, putting her case on the ground and using it as a footstool.

She held her hatbox tight to her chest out of habit.

She thought how she didn't need to be so security conscious anymore.

She had made it to her destination.

Well, nearly.

"Are you all right, my dear?" asked Mrs. de Freyne, when she noticed how Gisela had opted out of sifting through dress-racks.

"I am a little tired," she said.

"Of course you are. Goodness, you must be exhausted. I will try to hurry them up. We'll go to our car after this and start for home. But you will need some dresses, my dear, and this will save you another trip back to the city."

Reluctantly Gisela stood and searched through a near rail of dresses. She took three and tried them on in a dressing room.

Nola popped her had round the door.

"*Woo!*" she said, waving her hand under her nose. "Perfume pong. It's to hide the smell of feet!" She stood on one leg and put another into a pair of women's slacks. "I'm going to get these. Mother will hate them!"

Gisela was surprised at Nola's willingness to undress in front of her, still quite a stranger.

She smiled at her reflection while Gisela stared back at hers.

Gisela examined her long plaited hair and her white face.

They looked so different.

Nola had golden-blonde hair – she looked like a German film star.

Gisela had dark eyes, her features sharp.

Nola looked like she belonged in a movie.

Gisela? Well, she wasn't quite sure where she belonged.

* * *

The Isotta Fraschini car was narrow and long, and George, Mrs. de Freyne's chauffeur, tied Gisela's case to the back of the car with twine as the boot was full of their shopping purchases.

Mrs. de Freyne asked gentle questions as they made their way out of Dublin city.

How are your parents doing?

Do you miss your studies terribly?

Did you manage to rest at all on your journey?

"Do you have a boyfriend?" asked Nola.

"Nola! Don't ask personal questions," said Mrs. de Freyne.

"That's not personal, Mummy," said Nola.

"It is."

Nola whispered to Gisela: "I just want to know the facts."

Gisela shook her head. She whispered back, when Mrs. de Freyne was talking to the chauffeur, that a boy asked her to marry him in London.

Nola gasped.

"Oh my goodness! What did you say?"

"No, of course."

"Oh, I would have said yes," said Nola.

On and on the car drove, out of the city, where the road narrowed and green and yellow fields appeared.

Gisela began to feel carsick and after some time had to ask the driver to stop.

Nola put a hand on her arm.

How, Gisela wondered, after all the miles she'd travelled, was it only now that she felt travel sickness?

Outside the car, on a green grass verge, she bent low with her head in her hands.

Would she ever get there?

Would she ever get to her wretched destination?

Back in the car and after many, many meandering miles alongside hedges, fields and coastline, they came to Drogheda.

"This is our nearest town," said Nola. "The shopping's not great – that's why we go to Dublin."

"You'll have to sign on at the police station weekly," said Mrs. de Freyne. "We can drive you there if you need."

A river cut through the town and a startling viaduct bridge overlooked it, high in the sky.

"Nearly there!" said Nola, a few miles past the bridge.

Gisela had begun to feel calmer now. Now that she knew her journey was finally coming to an end.

Soon she would unpack her case and her hatbox and then she could rest, rest, just rest, without having to move anywhere again for a while.

White-and-brown cows stood in fields, munching.

Nola squeezed Gisela's leg as the car turned up an avenue.

Gisela strained to look out the window.

No muddy driveway to a farm.

Instead, neat lawns, with new trees, some older, bushier.

It took an age to get to the top of the avenue where the car turned a corner and there was Newtown House.

My God!

It was gigantic. A stately home!

This was not the chicken farm she had expected.

"Here we are," said Mrs. de Freyne, as the Fraschini pulled to a stop.

Low limestone steps led up to a columned porch. Bay windows sat to the front and side.

A woman came to the front door.

Gisela got out and stared for a moment, her mouth open, before going up the steps where the woman shook her hand and introduced herself as the housekeeper.

"I'm Maeve," she said. "You're very welcome."

Inside, the hall was large, square and filled with the smell of fresh flowers.

Would she like some tea before being shown to her room, asked Maeve, who was graceful and ladylike in her manner.

"No, thanks," said Gisela.

She was so weary.

She just wanted to fall into bed.

The stairs were wide and sweeping, like the stairs in a concert hall, reaching to the balconies.

An ornate window box in the centre of the roof allowed light to cascade down.

Maeve explained to Gisela that her room was next door to Nola's as she opened the door into a large, cosy room with pale-pink wallpaper.

The pillows were fluffed on top of a pink bedspread, which matched the wallpaper.

This was more like a hotel, Gisela realised, than a house.

"I'll leave you to get settled," said Maeve.

She winked.

Gisela smiled at her.

There was something about the woman. Something knowing and kind.

Out the window Gisela saw a neat lawn, dotted with small fruit trees.

To her left was a redbrick walled garden, colourful flowers in bloom and pear trees flailed against the brickwork.

A knock came to the door.

Gisela opened it to find a man in a chequered shirt with her case.

"Fintan Walshe," he introduced himself.

Gisela stood back and he entered the room and put the case on the bed.

He stood back and smiled.

"Can I get you anything?" he said kindly.

Gisela shook her head.

She just wanted to be left alone.

"Thank you," she said, wishing the man would disappear.

He seemed to want to stay, to chat.

"Just let me know," he said, "if you ever need anything. You'll find my cottage and workshop there in the yard, just behind the house. Vienna is it, you're from?"

"Yes. Vienna. Thank you," said Gisela again, this time more firmly, hoping he would read her tone.

"A long journey, I expect. Where was it you sailed from?"

"I am very tired," said Gisela. "Please. Can I talk to you later?"

"Of course," said Fintan and he nodded his head and left the room.

She hoped she hadn't come across as rude.

Had she?

Perhaps she had?

But she was beyond caring.

She had nothing left to give.

She touched her case on the bed, before shifting it onto the floor.

Something about the warmth of the leather and the room and the strange, unfamiliar smell overwhelmed her.

Tears filled her eyes.

She got into bed fully clothed, buried her head in the odd-smelling pillow and let herself cry, with exhaustion, with homesickness, with relief.

Another knock came to the door.

Not somebody else!

It was Nola.

"Are you alright? Is everything okay?" she said, coming over to the bed to look at her new companion.

Yes, everything was okay.

She was here now.

She was safe.

"Everything's fine – I'd just like to be left alone," said Gisela from under the covers.

"Oh," said Nola and she turned to leave the room. "Okay. Well, we'll be eating in half an hour."

Gisela shook her head.

"If it's all right, I am just going to sleep. Please give my apologies to your mother."

Nola stood, stared.

Another meal with strangers, thought Gisela.

There were so many people around, so many who wanted to welcome her and speak to her and wish her well and yet she felt completely, utterly and overwhelmingly, alone.

She wished she were a thousand miles away.

She wished she were home.

"All right," said Nola and she smiled kindly as she closed the door.

G2 INTELLIGENCE REPORT

STATUS: INFORMATION
LOCATION: COTTAGES, STRAND ROAD,
NEAR HANRATTY'S FIELD

Mrs. Maeve McGorry (widower, housekeeper at Newtown
House) is a known IRA sympathiser. Her husband
Malachy McGorry was active in the IRA until his death
in 1931 and took part in the anti-treaty guerrilla
campaigns.

Her cottage, located beside Mrs. Walshe's cottage on
the Strand Road, is a known safe house.

G2 will continue to monitor her movements and report
any suspicious activity.

Hans

CHAPTER TEN

Hans had come to love the breakfasts at Newtown House.

Each morning they sat down to fresh breads, butter, jams and preserves, and bright-yellow eggs laid by the chickens.

On Saturdays Maeve cooked up sausages and bacon which was a real treat.

Maeve bustled about with tea and coffee and fresh toast and Hans sometimes felt as though they were on holiday, rather than there to work.

The Hettingers were enjoying their time at Newtown too.

They looked fresher about the face, less haggard.

Otto and Max had ventured as far as the town and Fintan Walshe had told them about the parish dance that was taking place the next week and said they should go, for something to do.

He told Hans he should accompany him to Patton's pub for a drink sometime and Hans said he'd like that.

It would be nice to spend time with the farm foreman in a social setting, he thought.

Away from the other Austrians and the pull of the farm.

Hans wasn't comfortable in social situations, though he felt a quiet drink with the man he was becoming closest to here would be alright.

"More toast?" asked Maeve.

She had bent her head right down to Hans and he could smell a floral scent.

He liked it very much.

He waved his hand to say no and smiled at her.

It was too much food.

His stomach couldn't handle it in the morning.

The dining-room door opened and in came a petite young woman, her hair plaited, a look of surprise on her face.

So here she was.

Nola's new companion, another visitor from Vienna.

Nola had talked of nothing else over the last few days and Maeve had made a great deal of airing the new woman's room out.

They had all been expecting to meet her last night, but Mrs. de Freyne said she was completely exhausted and had gone to bed.

Hans was glad they'd have another woman to join their troop.

He knew Eva would love to have a confidante from home to speak with.

The young woman stared at the diners and then at Mrs. de Freyne.

"Ah, Gisela!" said Mrs. de Freyne. "Come, come, join us! What do you think? We brought a few German speakers for you!"

The young woman sat down silently.

"I wanted to surprise you," said Mrs. de Freyne, who was seated at the head of the table, her hands beneath her chin, smiling. "I thought you might be feeling homesick and the sound of the mother tongue would be welcome."

Gisela smiled.

She looked pale.

Tired.

"You are not the only Austrian here, my dear. Meet Fritz and Eva Hettinger," said Mrs. de Freyne. "Their sons Otto and Max. And that man there is Hans Schmitt."

Hans waved.

Gisela smiled widely and gave a wave to the whole group.

"Hello," she said.

Her eyes flicked to Otto and Max, the nearest to her age.

Hans guessed Gisela was in her early twenties, but with her plaits she could have been younger.

She reminded him a bit of Anja.

It was the curve of her face, the roundness to her cheeks.

"This group have been travelling for quite a while," said Mrs. de Freyne. "They came through a farm scheme, part of the Kagran Gruppe. When I was contacted by the Society of Friends to see if we could help you out, I thought, why not, we've plenty of room. So, you will not be alone, Gisela. You'll have many friends here."

The group nodded and smiled.

Hans thought Gisela might break down into tears.

The Society of Friends along with Christian and Jewish charities, had been helping Jews to escape. It was easier for converted Jews, though, to get a visa, especially to Ireland.

The Hettingers had converted to Christianity in 1934.

Hans wondered where Gisela stood.

When she took her out gold cross and held it to her mouth and played with it, he knew.

"So, Gisela," said Eva, conscious of how the young woman might be feeling, "was your journey all right? You got here okay?"

Gisela nodded. "I was stopped at the German border and detained for a night. They said I did not have the right visa. But I got through the next day."

"That must have been frightening," said Eva.

"I thought I was done for," said Gisela.

The Austrians nodded in agreement, understanding the perils she had just been through.

In English, scattered with words in German, Eva explained how this was the third home they'd had in Ireland since they arrived.

The first house they'd stayed in was put on the market and they'd had to move out.

The second house had structural problems and they were also told they had to leave.

"We expect Mrs. de Freyne will sell up soon and throw us out any day now!" joked Fritz Hettinger.

The others laughed and Eva playfully cuffed her husband on the arm.

"I can assure you I am not going anywhere!" said Mrs. de Freyne.

As the conversation reverted to Gisela's journey, a red blush crept up her cheeks and spread to her neck and chest.

Hans could understand her embarrassment. He too loathed being the centre of attention and hated when the focus was on him.

"Tell me," said Eva, "are things very bad now? It is six months since we left."

Gisela looked down at her plate.

Hans knew she was thinking of her family.

She shrugged slightly. "Things have got bad," she said, quietly.

"I cannot even imagine it being worse," said Eva.

A silence descended on the table.

Sensing the mood change, Mrs. de Freyne asked in a loud voice, "Where is that daughter of mine? Did you see her upstairs, Gisela?"

Gisela shook her head.

"She hates getting out of bed," said Mrs. de Freyne. "She'd quite happily live in bed forever."

Hans watched Gisela smile in response.

He felt quite sorry for her.

She reminded him of a bird.

Tiny, in need of protection.

Like Anja.

"I'll knock again," said Maeve.

"Knock?" said Mrs. de Freyne. "Have you a pneumatic drill? That would do the job."

Everyone laughed.

As though on cue, the dining-room door opened and Nola appeared, yawning, her hair tousled.

Mrs. de Freyne clapped, followed by Otto and Max, then they all found themselves applauding Nola's arrival.

"Oh, do shut up," said Nola, smiling.

"Coffee?" asked Maeve.

"You're a mind-reader, darling," said Nola.

"Your family," said Eva to Gisela, "are they still in Vienna?"

"My parents, yes," said Gisela.

"Will they try to get out?" asked Eva kindly.

"I hope so," said Gisela.

"The Quakers might be able to help them too?"

Gisela smiled awkwardly. "Perhaps."

Another silence descended before Mrs. de Freyne, changed the subject again onto something brighter. "What do you plan to do with yourselves today? I thought you could get to know the place. Walk the village. See the beach. You have so much to explore."

"It's all rather boring really, but I can show you around," said Nola.

Nola made Hans smile.

She was young and couldn't see the simple beauty in the quiet, peaceful surroundings where she lived.

She craved adventure.

And, he feared, the way she was going, she was going to get it.

* * *

After they married, Hans suggested to Anja that he would like to find a new job.

He wanted to earn more money – in truth, he wanted to provide the things that Anja was accustomed to.

She had come from a large three-storey house to his apartment.

She had swapped her full wardrobe for a share of his.

There hung plain, practical day dresses, seeing as they had no socials planned.

He wanted to give her more.

He wanted to give her what her father gave her.

"We have everything we need," Anja said whenever Hans discussed a career change to earn more.

And there was an element of truth to that.

The apartment was cosy and warmly furnished.

Hans had made a few adjustments when Anja came to live, adding some extra shelving to store her things.

She had him hang new wallpaper in their bedroom and she had hand-sewn some cushions for the old sofa, which brightened things up.

Hans enjoyed making the shelves and sanding down the banisters outside the apartment for repainting.

He redid the doors and then the kitchen cupboards.

After that he moved on to the kitchen table.

To mark their three-month wedding anniversary, he presented Anja with a picture frame he'd made from some of the leftover wood from the shelves.

He had sanded and smoothed it carefully and painted it blue with small yellow stars.

In the frame he'd put a picture of them on their wedding day.

The photographer had come to St Rupert's church and snapped them standing outside.

In it, Hans did not smile, but he held the crook of Anja's arm tight.

She beamed.

He'd realised, as he'd worked on refurbishing the apartment in the early days of their marriage, that he'd always been drawn to woodwork and confessed to Anja as they lay in bed on cold winter mornings, their breath moistening the air around them, that if he could do any job in the world, it would be what Jesus' father, Joseph, did.

He would be a carpenter.

Anja suggested, if he was really interested in pursuing his passion, that he take up some night classes, particularly when she succeeded against the odds in securing a place in the Vienna Philharmonic Orchestra.

"We must do what we are good at," she told him.

Hans found a class that met on a different night to Anja's rehearsals, meaning they could continue to look after Hans' father, whose health was as variable as the weather.

Hans felt as though he had already lost his father. It was only his body that was left – his mind had disintegrated and it seemed, floated away, little by little, over time.

Anja found it very sad and said she wished she had met Hans years earlier, so that she could have had time with his father, before he got sick.

It bothered her greatly that she had never known his mother.

Because of his father's health, the couple could rarely attend Anja's parents' home for a visit together, but after work sometimes Hans would drop by or he would visit the family shops to chat with Anja's brothers and father.

He wanted to be part of their family.

He wanted to get to know them better.

More, he wanted to let them see how much he cared for their sister and daughter, how happy they were together and how, even though it had been against their initial wishes, the marriage was a successful one.

Hans and Anja had yet to have an argument.

It simply had not happened.

If anything, Hans felt he loved Anja more and more each day. Even when he didn't think that was possible.

Hans' woodwork lessons at the technical school became a life force within him.

He looked forward to the three-hour class all week and, when he came home, he didn't feel tired, but elated.

They were given two projects to complete over term and with their savings he bought new tools so that he could practise at home.

Hans had left school early to work and help support his parents. He had never been academic.

His father was a tram driver with the Vienna Transport Company and got him a job as a tram cleaner when he was twelve.

It wasn't really what Hans wanted to do but he did like feeling that he was growing up, and seeing his weekly wage packet.

After ten years at the company, he was promoted to tram conductor.

Now, for the first time in his life, as he sawed, planed and sanded, he felt like he was good at something.

Really good at something.

For his first project he carved a smooth thick chopping-board with Anja's initials in an intricate design.

Anja chopped all her vegetables on it from then on.

Over the remainder of the term, he carved smooth wooden fruit, then made a wooden bowl to house them in.

He soaked the wood in essential oils and the bowl perfumed their flat.

When he finished the first course, he enrolled on a second.

He hoped by his third course to move on to small pieces of furniture.

He toyed with the idea of becoming an apprentice carpenter, but he was worried about going back to such low pay when he was just moving up into a better wage, due to his years of service with the Vienna Transport Company.

Anja told him she would support him in whatever he did.

It helped, he knew, that her family had a business to fall back on.

Now, at Newtown Farm, Hans had already put his woodwork skills to use, making some essential repairs to fencing and some gates.

In Fintan Walshe's workshed he'd seen stacks of woodcarving tools and after his first week there, when he felt he had earned the man's trust a little, he asked if he might borrow a plane and a chisel.

He saved any offcuts of wood he found and passed the time in the evening by the fire in his cottage, working on them.

It brought him great peace.

Mrs. de Freyne paid them a small wage for their work as well as their food and board.

Hans thought that if he could carve some things to sell, he could add to his meagre income.

In his dreams, the ones where his mind wandered, he imagined himself with a workshop like Fintan Walshe's, full of tools and all the time in the world to carve out pieces of furniture.

The Hettinger boys would head off to college and they would be educated and they would get good jobs.

They presumed Hans would remain a farm hand because he had little in the way of education and his manner was soft and quiet.

They didn't expect much of him.

But Hans had been given a second chance.

He had made it to Ireland when so many thousands of others had not.

Anja had not been able to come here.

He felt that he owed it to her to make something of himself.

He wanted to make her proud.

Always, he wanted to make her proud.

G2 INTELLIGENCE REPORT

STATUS: INFORMATION
LOCATION: NUNNERYLAND, TERMONFECKIN, CO. LOUTH

Peadar Tracy is a school friend of Mícheál McKee. He has come to Garda attention on a few occasions, notably for leering in the windows of Mrs. Carmody's House in March 1939. He is also suspected of theft – including potatoes from Lynch's farm, a number of wooden poles from Coughlan's yard at Newtownstalaban, and he is suspected of harvesting trees without permission at Blackhall Wood.

In general, he is of a cheeky and belligerent disposition.

Father, Sammy Tracy, was accidentally killed by IRA explosives in 1926.

He lives with his mother, the widower Maggie Tracy. Of low income.

Gisela

CHAPTER ELEVEN

Mrs. de Freyne raised her teacup to her lips and sipped.

The saucer rattled each time she put her cup back onto it.

Gisela noted how she drank from a different set of china than was used at breakfast.

More ornate.

The drawing room was drowned in light, and it was quite comfortable on the soft sofas. A small fire flickered in the grate, even though tomorrow would be the first day of July.

"Nola is ... difficult," said Mrs. de Freyne.

Gisela glanced up at the chandelier that hung over their heads, the light glinting and casting tiny rainbow flecks around the room. A small rectangular rainbow sat on Mrs. de Freyne's face. It moved up and down as she spoke.

"She is an intelligent girl. She's certainly not stupid. But she's flighty. She likes to get her own way. I'm hoping you can help me with that."

Gisela realised that in all the time she had been preparing to come to Ireland, she had given little thought as to what would actually happen when she got here.

What did *companion* mean anyway?

Was she to be a friend or a chaperone?

"I would like you – if you can, as much as possible – to keep her out of trouble."

"Trouble?"

"Keep an eye on her. Go with her. She is forever wandering and I don't, truth be told, know where."

"I will try, Mrs. de Freyne."

"Of course, it is not an easy task. I'm aware of that." She laughed gently. Nervously. "But if you could try ... it is another set of eyes. I do worry about her. She has a very free spirit."

She leaned in closer to Gisela.

"A *very* free spirit."

Gisela's heart sank.

How was she to tail a seventeen-year-old girl?

One glance out the window, across the trees, orchards, fields, barns, showed there were any number of places to hide.

Any number of places to get up to trouble.

"I will try, but please do not think bad of me if ..."

"Goodness, no! Of course not. It is an impossible task! I am only asking you to try. We all do our best with Nola. All of us."

Mrs. de Freyne gestured in a circle, meaning the whole household.

Gisela put down her teacup and cleared her throat.

"There was something I wanted to ask," she said, leaning in a little to her host. "It's about my parents."

"Yes, dear?"

"It was something Eva said at breakfast. To see if we could get them here. I know it's a lot to ask and I've only just arrived myself, but if there was a way?"

Mrs. de Freyne sighed, sadly.

"It is so difficult. I do understand, I do. But it is very unlikely, Gisela. Everything has changed in the last six months. The legations have closed down. It's become almost impossible."

"Can you try?"

Mrs. de Freyne looked at Gisela and Gisela could see the pity in her eyes.

"Yes, I can try, of course I can try. I will speak with my contacts in the Council of Refugees."

"Thank you."

"Now, why don't you go and find that daughter of mine and see what trouble she's getting herself into?"

Who was this seventeen-year-old girl that everyone fretted over, wondered Gisela.

And what sort of trouble did they mean?

* * *

"This way," said Nola, leading Gisela over the lawn and towards a small woodland with a narrow path.

They passed by orchards and fields where corn grew.

The farm, Gisela could see, was busy.

Nola had shown her the animal enclosures and pens, the cottages where the Hettingers and Hans Schmitt were staying, and Fintan Walshe's house and workshop which was located in a row of buildings in the farm courtyard.

"You, like me, are a lady and get to be in the house," she said, smiling.

Gisela did not feel like a lady but she supposed it was nice to be staying in Newtown House itself.

The cottages were simpler, built for working folk.

Gisela was in a more privileged position.

"What did Mummy want to speak to you about earlier?" asked Nola.

"Oh, just to see that I was doing all right," said Gisela.

She sensed that Nola knew there was more to the conversation but Nola did not push any further.

The narrow pathway gave rise to long spiny grass which led across a field to the beach.

Gisela could smell the salt in the air.

They were so close, she realised, so close to the coast it was at their fingertips.

At the top the sand dunes they stood for a moment and looked out to dark, blue sea.

Gisela closed her eyes and breathed deep.

Across that sea was England.

Beyond England was France and, further beyond, Holland.

If she reached Holland, she could take a train right across the land to Vienna.

She imagined going back the way she came, arriving home to her parents, feeling them take her in their arms.

"Look! A dead seagull!" said Nola.

They made their way down the dune, their feet scrambling, and Nola poked the dead bird with a stick.

The tide was in and it lapped right up to the dunes, leaving only a slither of rocky path along the shore.

The bird was white and grey, its spiny feathers pulled out.

"Probably by a rat," said Nola. "Do you know I saw a rat running along here once and it was the size of a fully grown cat!"

The image made Gisela shudder.

"Let's see if we can find the culprit!" said Nola.

Her companion's glee made Gisela feel uncomfortable.

The girl was as giddy as a child.

She felt the gap in their maturity, a wide gulf between them.

She feared they had nothing in common.

Nothing at all.

On they walked, Nola in search of her cat-rat, as far as the mouth of the river, where the Boyne estuary met the sea.

A large ship turned from the wide sea and sailed up the narrow river to the port, where it would arrive, Gisela expected, where she'd seen the cattle standing on the dock yesterday.

"Wouldn't you love to run away with a sailor?" Nola said.

Gisela shrugged. "Not really," she said.

"But imagine," Nola said, "you could see the world. And some of them are very handsome."

Gisela breathed in the deep sea smell – vinegar and seaweed.

She would have to find something to do here in Ireland, she thought, something apart from keeping Nola company.

How long could she stand having to mind a girl who offered very little in terms of conversation, in terms of intellectual understanding?

As they made their way back to the dunes behind Newtown House, Gisela noticed how the tide had turned and was on its way back out.

The beach appeared, brown and dark.

Nola shielded her eyes from the sun then suddenly began to run, pulling off her plimsolls and flinging them into the air.

Legs flailing, she lifted her dress as she ran, right up over her head.

It fluttered in the breeze behind her and landed gently on the wet sand.

Gisela put her hand to her mouth, shocked.

Nola was in her underwear!

Splashing now, Nola reached the sea and ran right into it.

She turned around to face Gisela and peeled her slip up over her head, throwing it too, like the dress, into a ball to land on the sodden sand.

The silk grew dark as it absorbed the salt water.

"*Come in!*" yelled Nola.

Gisela walked towards the sea, anxious now that Nola was practically naked and in full view of anyone who might walk along the strand.

Diving, Nola disappeared under a wave.

"*Come on!*" she called to Gisela again after she emerged, her hair and face drenched.

Gisela shook her head.

"*No!*" she shouted. "*No!*"

Nola dived under again and swam for a distance before turning back again.

She could have been a mermaid, thought Gisela.

How natural she was in the water!

After another few lengths, Nola stood up and walked out of the sea.

Gisela was embarrassed by the dark patch in Nola's underwear, the water having turned the material quite see-through.

She looked away as she realised Nola's nipples were showing through her brassiere, perfectly erect.

"Glorious!" said Nola. "You'd love it – you should have come in."

Gisela felt like a bit of a spoilsport.

But she would never be brave enough to go swimming without her bathing suit and towel.

What if somebody saw her?

Nola bent down to collect her clothes as they walked back up the beach.

She pulled the slip back over her head, oblivious to the discomfort of the wet sand and damp material against her skin.

Looking upwards, she elbowed Gisela.

"Look," she said and nodded her head.

Standing on top of the dune was a man in a hat, holding a walking stick, two large dogs at his heels.

He stared, unnervingly, at the girls.

"You should put your dress on," said Gisela.

The worst had happened.

Somebody did see.

And a man at that!

"Should I?" said Nola, not breaking her stare back at the man.

The man turned and moved off, whistling to the dogs to come with him.

They bounded after him, long legs bending over the rough terrain of the dune.

"What's the matter, Mr. McKee, have you never seen a fanny before?" Nola roared at the top of her voice.

Gisela was embarrassed. She cringed.

And what did that word mean, she wondered – *fanny*?

"Who was that?" said Gisela, when the man had disappeared from sight. "Do you know him?"

"Everyone knows old Seán McKee," said Nola.

"Will he tell anyone?" Gisela asked.

Nola snorted. "He is a man of secrets. Anyway, what is there to tell?"

She shrugged, pulled her dress over her head and walked on.

"I must write a card," Gisela said on the way back up the narrow path to Newtown. "To send to my parents."

"Oh yes," said Nola. "If you need any envelopes and stamps, Mummy's office is near the stairwell, to the right."

"Thank you," said Gisela.

It was a kindness, she thought.

* * *

After luncheon the two went to Nola's room to relax.

Nola grew restless and bored.

She lay on the bed, her feet up against the wall, her long blonde hair drying in sea-salted waves.

She looked quite beautiful, Gisela thought.

Nola sighed repeatedly.

"It's so boring around here," she said. "I was ever so glad to hear you were coming."

She dipped her head back to look at Gisela.

Gisela smiled.

She hoped she wasn't a disappointment to her.

"Yes, I was very glad to come," she said.

She wasn't, of course.

She wasn't glad at all.

But she was grateful.

"Could you have gone anywhere else?" asked Nola.

"Well, I was offered a job in England, but I said no."

"England!" said Nola, turning to sit up now, interested. "London?"

Gisela shook her head. "It was in Dover."

"Oh," said Nola, looking disappointed. "I'm dying to go to London to live. Granny lives there and we've been over a few times. It's so sophisticated! It's *nothing* like here. As soon as I've come out, I'm going to live with Granny."

That meant, Gisela realised, that they would only have a few months to spend together.

She wondered what would happen to her then?

Mrs. de Freyne would hardly keep her here at Newtown if her daughter was not living here anymore.

"I think here is quite nice," said Gisela.

"Nice and boring, you mean."

Safe, thought Gisela.

Nice and safe.

"The boutiques are so wonderful in London," said Nola. "And once I'm out I can attend all the balls and they really are something. *So* fashionable. I'll need a full wardrobe! As soon as I get there I'll have to order, oh I don't know, a dozen dresses at least!"

Gisela played with the tassels on the rug she was sitting on.

"I think I'll go and write to my parents," she said.

"Tomorrow we can go out in the pony and trap."

"All right," said Gisela.

It would be nice to see her surrounds.

And, she thought, Mrs. de Freyne would be pleased to see them travel out together, Gisela spending time with her companion.

She would be doing as she had been asked.

She would be earning her keep.

She would be openly spying on Nola.

Hans

CHAPTER TWELVE

"Hello."

Hans felt the girls startle in the twilight.

"Hans! What are you doing there, lurking in the dark?" said Nola.

It was not dark, but it was dusk.

Summer time here stretched so late.

"I am having a cigarette."

Hans waved his cigarette and the girls watched the red glow of the dot swish back and forth.

Hans had come out to watch the bats, who liked to hunt along the back laneway entrance to Newtown House, which led from the Strand Road.

It was a lush laneway filled with wildlife, narrower than the busy avenue to the front.

It was where he drove Bessie to access the fields.

It was where he spotted a fox sometimes.

He was sure there was a badger sett in the field beside the lane, but he'd yet to see the shy creatures.

He had not expected to meet Nola and Gisela on the lane so late.

He realised he must have appeared like a ghost to them in the dim evening light.

"We were out walking," said Nola.

"So late?"

"Yes. It's all there is to do around here. Give us a cigarette, Hans?"

Hans took out his cigarette case and offered two rolled cigarettes. Gisela declined.

Nola bent her head to the match and pointed at Gisela. "She won't do anything she's not allowed. Gisela is a very good girl."

Hans laughed but then stopped himself.

Nola was not being kind.

She was not being nice to Gisela, who from what he could make out was a shy, timid young woman, desperately homesick for Vienna.

Nola backed herself up onto the farm gate Hans had been sitting on.

The night settled around them.

A bird called out in the distance.

"What's Vienna like, Hans? I'd say it's terribly exciting, is it?" said Nola. "Nothing ever happens around here."

Hans did not respond. He was not sure what to say.

"I'm going to London as soon as I can. After my coming out ball, I'm gone!" Nola blew a puff of smoke into the air. "You know, and I shouldn't be telling you this, but I will because I think it's very funny. The word in the village, Hans, is that you're a spy!"

Hans, stunned, paused before he spoke.

"I'm sorry?" he said. "What do you mean?"

"Well, they're all very suspicious of you new arrivals, you see, and there are rumours circulating that one of you has to be a spy. They say it's you!"

"That's not funny, Nola," said Gisela.

Hans felt the hairs rise on the back of his neck.

"You're not a Nazi agent, are you, Hans? You're not a spy? You have the look of a spy! Don't answer that. Of course, you wouldn't tell me if you were! I read a book once all about espionage. I think I'd make a rather good spy. I'm good at accents and I'm sure I could pull off a wig. I have that type of face. It's why I want to learn German."

She looked towards Gisela.

"Gisela's going to teach me."

"Am I?" said Gisela.

"Anyway, there's nothing to spy on around here, unless you want to try and catch Fusty Fintan slithering around after Maeve."

"We should probably be getting back," said Gisela.

"Yes," said Hans. "I'll walk with you."

Nola leapt off the gate and landed gracefully.

"These are strong cigs, Hans," she said. "Can I rob one more?"

Hans handed her one and watched her put it into her own silver cigarette case for later.

"I'm not a spy," said Hans, as they walked.

"Well, you would never *say* you were if you were, now, would you?" Nola laughed.

They walked through the dark yard, past tall stone buildings, enclosed for the night.

A cow lowed from the shed.

"Are you coming to the parish dance next week, Hans? Anyone can come."

Hans presumed she meant even someone as old as him.

"I don't know," he said. "Probably not."

He found it hard to imagine being at the dance with all the young people that would be there.

"Will Maeve be going?"

"Oh!" said Nola. "Does Fusty Fintan have some competition?"

Hans laughed. "Why do you call him that?"

"I don't know. I suppose he and I have never seen eye to eye. He's been here for donkey's years and he acts like – you know, like he owns the place."

Hans thought that Fintan Walshe probably took no nonsense from Nola and she held it against him.

He had not realised there was a frisson between Fintan and Maeve.

Maeve had been generous to Hans since he'd arrived. Like Mrs. de Freyne, she had a nice manner about her – kindly.

As they came to the back of the house, Maeve herself bustled out.

"Girls!" she said. "Mrs. de Freyne is on the warpath! Where have you been? Come in immediately. You too, Hans!"

Hans had been about to go to his cottage.

"Father Crowley's here," said Maeve. "He called to see the Austrians and nobody's here. The Hettingers went out to the pictures and nobody could find you lot!"

Inside, Father Crowley stood holding a sherry in the drawing room.

"Ah," he said when Nola, Gisela and Hans came in. "So, they do exist."

"We were just out for a walk," said Nola apologetically.

Mrs. de Freyne grimaced at the trousers Nola was wearing.

The priest's eyes fell to the trousers too.

Nola walked over to the drinks cabinet and took out two tumblers.

"Brandy or sherry, Gisela?"

"Nola!" Mrs. de Freyne said.

"Would you like one, Hans?"

Both Hans and Gisela shook their heads.

"Just a small one, Mummy," said Nola, splashing a large brandy into a glass.

"I didn't see you at Mass on Sunday, Nola," said Father Crowley.

Nola turned to face him and shook her head.

"I wasn't feeling well, Father."

"Is that right?" he said. "I'm sorry to hear you were ill. Nothing serious, I hope?"

"Women's problems, Father, an awful curse."

The priest coughed.

"Nola!" Mrs. de Freyne reprimanded her.

"So, Herr Schmitt," said the priest after a few moments.

Hans seated himself in an armchair, while Gisela chose the sofa.

Hans felt uncomfortable. It was late and he was tired; he found it harder to speak English when he was tired.

He wished he had made it past the back door to his little cottage.

"Mrs. de Freyne tells me you came as part of the farm labouring scheme?"

"Yes," said Hans.

"And how are you finding Newtown? Is it to your taste?"

"Yes," said Hans, thinking he understood. "Very good. I like it here."

"Hans was a tram conductor," said Mrs. de Freyne.

"Oh, wonderful," said the priest. "A big change so."

"Yes," said Hans.

Bigger changes than Father Crowley could ever understand.

"And Fräulein," said Father Crowley, turning his attention to Gisela now, "Mrs. de Freyne tells me you are from Vienna too, but did not come with the others?"

"Yes. The others came through the farming programme. I studied mathematics at university."

"Is that right?"

She nodded.

"And things are very bad there now?"

"Yes."

"You must be mighty relieved to have reached Ireland."

Gisela nodded again.

Hans thought how she looked anything but happy to have reached Ireland.

She looked pale and exhausted.

Her eyes, he realised, were puffy from crying.

"Mrs. de Freyne told me your family converted?"

"We converted to Catholicism when I was six."

"And why was that?"

"We weren't practising Jews."

Hans wondered if the priest had any idea of the political climate they'd come from.

Many people had converted to Christian religions to secure jobs or to hide their pasts.

Especially if they had not been active in their Judaism.

"I have been reading about the plight of the Jews," said Father Crowley. "It really is terribly sad. So much persecution. I always remind anyone who has a bad word to say about the Jews – wasn't our Good Lord a Jew himself?"

"Yes, well," said Mrs. de Freyne. "It's the least we can do. To offer a bit of protection with all that's going on."

"There'll be a war, you think?" said the priest, directing his attention back to Hans.

Hans shrugged.

This was not a conversation he wished to have now.

It was late. He was too tired.

And he felt the priest had no understanding at all.

"That Hitler fellow's an interesting character," said the priest. "Can we believe what he says?"

"Let's change the subject perhaps, Father," said Mrs. de Freyne. "I'm not sure talk of war is a suitable topic so late in the evening! Could I offer you another sherry?"

"It'll be all anyone will be talking about if it happens," said the priest, presenting his glass for another drink. "But yes, you are right, my apologies."

"Well, you've no need to worry about anything here," said Nola brightly. She took a big slurp from her glass of brandy. "This is the safest place in Europe. *Nothing* happens around here!"

"Isn't it interesting?" continued the priest, not quite willing to let the topic drop. "The persecution and pogroms. I talk about it every Sunday. Peace and forgiveness. If we could all just try to understand each other a little more, be accepting of one another, then perhaps we could have peace again. True, everlasting peace."

"Yes, Herr Hitler sounds like he's very understanding all right," said Nola.

"Nola!" Mrs. de Freyne glared again.

"No, she makes an interesting point," said the priest. "It's true, people say he is evil. But I don't believe anyone is evil. They simply make bad choices, or become disillusioned with the world. Erring in their judgment."

"He is a murderer," said Hans. The words growled from his mouth.

Everyone looked at him in surprise.

"You believe that?" said the priest.

"I know it."

Two red spots burned now on Mrs. de Freyne's cheeks.

Nola took another large gulp from her glass.

"That's quite enough of that for tonight," said Mrs. de Freyne.

Hans wondered did she mean the conversation or the drinking.

As the priest reached for his refreshed drink Hans couldn't help but notice the skin on his hands.

White, buttery and soft.

Hands that never did a hard day's work in their life.

Mrs. de Freyne in contrast had rough hands, the fingernails short and worn.

Simple, kind hands.

The priest took a sip from his glass. "Can't beat a drop of sherry."

G2 INTELLIGENCE REPORT

STATUS: INFORMATION
LOCATION: CASTLECOO HILL, TERMONFECKIN, CO. LOUTH

A number of IRA brigade members have been observed attending Seán McKee's house.

We are awaiting confirmation that Seán McKee is Acting IRA Chief of Staff following the recent imprisonment of Patrick Dempsey.

MARRIAGE STATUS: Married to Máire McKee, a known IRA sympathiser. Son Mícheál McKee is of a quiet disposition but believed to be a brigade member.

NOTES: Known to have been involved in gunrunning. Believed to have bomb-making and grenade experience. Considered to be highly dangerous and armed.

ACTION: To pay close attention to movements of Seán McKee. Post to be intercepted.

Gisela

CHAPTER THIRTEEN

Gisela went with Nola to the stable where Pinky the pony, a squat dapple grey, was housed.

Nola led him out by the bridle and asked Gisela to steady him while she fetched Fintan Walshe to assist them with hitching him to the pony trap.

"How are you settling in?" he asked Gisela as he backed the pony between the shafts of the trap.

Gisela nodded and smiled.

"Very well, thank you."

"I hope you got a good rest after your long journey?"

Gisela smiled again. She felt bad that she had been rude to Mr. Walshe on the evening of her arrival. He was a warm, friendly man.

"Where are you taking Pinky?" he asked Nola.

"Oh, I don't know, just around," said Nola.

"Well, don't go too far now, he tires easily these days. And don't bring him back lame."

"I won't," said Nola and the threw her eyes to heaven at Gisela.

Gisela climbed up into the trap and felt it rock beneath her feet.

Nola climbed up, confidently took the reins and they were off, leaving by the back avenue of Newtown House.

Gisela looked back at Fintan, who stood staring as the wheels turned and they disappeared down the lane.

"He seems nice," said Gisela.

Nola sniggered. "Don't you think he looks like a big toe?"

Now Gisela laughed. "No!" she said.

"He hates me taking the pony and trap out. He thinks he owns everything on this farm. But Mother won't hear a bad word against him. He doesn't like me. Just watch him, you'll see what I mean."

Gisela thought that Nola was perhaps oversensitive. What she didn't like was authority.

Nola guided Pinky along a twisty, windy road by the coast.

The sea was a deep dark blue, the sun bouncing shiny crystal light off the water.

"This is lovely," Gisela said.

Nola looked out to the coast. "Yes," she said. "I suppose it is."

After two miles or so, they slowed down to descend a small hill into a village with whitewashed cottages and thatched roofs packed tightly together.

Fishing nets were spread out in the sun to dry, stretched across tiny patchwork gardens.

At some houses, people were sitting outside on stools, repairing them.

Nola guided the trap down a narrow little lane and at the end the sea was revealed beyond a wide, pale sandy shore.

Nola hopped down and tethered the pony to a post.

Gisela stood and looked over the beach.

"Another beach," said Gisela.

"Lots around here," said Nola. "If we go all the way over there, there's a cliff walk up to the head."

Coming from landlocked Vienna, Gisela was enjoying this immediate access to the sea.

It gave her a sense of freedom.

A feeling of being able to breathe.

Out towards the sea, on black jagged rocks, people in white linen shirts and rolled-up trousers were milling about with buckets, bending and scooping.

Nola led Gisela to a sheltered spot where they could sit on the sand and watch.

After a while, Nola lay back and flailed her arms to make a star shape in the sand.

"I don't want to get a tan," she said putting her straw bonnet over her face. "Too many socials coming up!"

Gisela didn't mind if she got a tan.

She always got a tan in the summer.

"It's busy this year because I'm coming out and so I have to attend everyone else's coming out ball too."

"Oh," said Gisela.

Coming out was not such a big deal at home in Vienna.

Gisela had only attended her high school graduation.

"Are you looking forward to Saturday?"

In just two days' time, Nola and Gisela would attend their first ball together.

It was taking place in Dublin and Gisela found it hard to believe they would travel so far just to attend a party.

"I suppose," said Gisela.

She was still feeling tired after her travel this week.

And now that she here and settled, the homesickness was setting in.

She was realising that her situation was probably going to be long-term.

The longer time went on, the longer it would be since she had seen her family.

She missed them terribly.

"Let's sort out our dresses when we get back. I can't wait to see what you brought from Vienna," said Nola.

Gisela couldn't help but feel that Nola was going to be disappointed.

Under the glaring sun, Gisela lay back beside Nola and a quietness came over them.

The waves lapped on the shore, breaking over the large rocks at the edge of the beach.

In the distance people called to each other.

When a shadow fell over them, Nola and Gisela sat up.

They found two young men standing, buckets in one hand, long thick knives in the other.

"Mícheál McKee and Peadar Tracy," said Nola smiling.

The boys didn't smile but sat down beside them, rooting their buckets into the sand.

"This is my friend Gisela, all the way from Vienna," said Nola.

The boys nodded and said hello.

Gisela felt awkward at the intrusion into their space.

"Have you been hunting?" said Nola.

Mícheál tipped his bucket towards them. It was full of shellfish, periwinkles and a few mussels. They sloshed in salt water.

The boys' feet were bare, as were their legs.

Mícheál's legs were the colour of caramel, flecked with dark hairs, while Peadar's were white and covered in beige fuzz.

The boys' presence seemed to invigorate Nola.

"Will you be coming to the Garden Fête? Oh Gisela, I haven't even told you about the fête – it really is fabulous, everyone comes. Everyone from the parish. Mummy has been running it at Newtown for years – it's a lot of work, but a lot of fun. Will you be going, boys?"

Mícheál nodded. "Oh, I'd say so."

Peadar shrugged. "Probably," he said.

"Oh, do come," said Nola. "It's nice to have people our age there. And what about the parish dance Friday week, are you going to that too?"

The question elicited the same response.

"Well, we're lucky this year in that we don't have a prior engagement so we can go," said Nola.

"You can grace us with your presence," said Peadar.

Nola looked at him for a moment and then said, "Yes, we can."

An awkward silence hung while they waited for somebody to speak.

Two seagulls screeched overhead, fighting over a scrap.

Peadar asked Gisela what Vienna was like and told her he'd like to see it someday.

"Well, now is not a good time to visit," said Gisela, quite seriously.

The other three laughed, thinking she was being sarcastic.

Gisela frowned.

"Is your family still there?" asked Mícheál kindly.

Gisela explained about Rudy in Czechoslovakia, about how he used to be a pianist in the orchestra, but now that he'd had to flee Vienna he was working as a grocer's assistant.

"But my mother and father are still there, yes," she said.

"And will they come here too?" asked Peadar.

"I hope so," said Gisela, thinking about her conversation with Mrs. de Freyne.

Not wishing to talk about home any longer, Gisela changed the subject by asking what the boys intended to do with the shellfish.

"Eat them, of course," said Mícheál.

"Lovely in butter," said Peadar.

"I love shellfish," said Nola.

"Why don't you come back to the house now? I'll cook them up. The mother's in town," said Mícheál.

Nola clapped her hands. "Yes!" she said. "Great idea."

They got up and Gisela began to fret as they made their way back to the pony and trap.

Was it a good idea to go off with these two young men?

Mrs. de Freyne would hardly approve.

And how far away was the house?

Nola took the buckets of shellfish and put them onto the floor of the trap.

They mounted, Nola carefully manoeuvred Pinky around and they set off back into the village of Clogherhead.

Mícheál and Peadar followed on their bikes.

The breeze was refreshing as Pinky trotted along, holding his white tail high.

"Won't your mother mind?" asked Gisela as they made their way along a quiet lane.

"Well, you're not going to tell her, are you?"

Gisela shook her head.

She felt she was in a pickle now. Should she choose loyalty in her burgeoning friendship with Nola or truth, by revealing Nola's secrets to the woman who had given her refuge?

It didn't take long to reach Mícheál's home, a whitewashed house, capped with a red corrugated-iron roof, set into a steep hill.

It took a while before the boys joined them in the yard, rolling in and swinging their legs over their bicycles.

Peadar's cheeks were the same colour as the roof of the house.

"There yis are now," said Mícheál.

Gisela noted how the house was larger than the other cottages dotted around the hill.

It was not ornate but it was imposing.

Chickens pecked at the door. Flowerpots held pink geraniums, bright against the whitewash.

Inside, the house smelled of peat.

It was dark and musty.

Mícheál switched on an electric light.

The kitchen was cluttered with pots and pans and all manner of utensils. A pair of wellies sat flopped over under the table.

"Sit down," said Mícheál and he swiped newspapers away, trying to make room for everyone.

Did his mother really leave it all like this and go off to town, thought Gisela? What sort of housekeeper was she?

Mícheál rinsed the shells in fresh water before pouring them into a big black pot hanging on a crook over the fire.

He stoked the fire and put a lid on the pot.

The fire was huge, the chimney open.

A person could easily hide up there, thought Gisela.

Socks and dishcloths hung from a string across the mantelpiece, drying.

"Is your father not around?" asked Nola.

"He's always around somewhere," said Mícheál.

When the water was boiling, he gave the pot a stir.

Nola talked about the parish dance, telling Gisela she could expect set dancing and sandwiches.

"You don't wear a ball dress, just something simple," she explained.

"For simple folk like us," said Peadar.

Nola laughed but Gisela wasn't sure that it was a joke.

Mícheál took two bowls and spooned the shells into them. They were all open now and steaming.

He took a slab of white butter, cut a big chunk into the bowl and reached for the salt cellar on the mantelpiece.

After sprinkling the bowls liberally, he reached back up to the mantelpiece and removed four needles with hooks at the end.

He popped them straight into the bowls and pushed one bowl towards the girls.

Gisela shuddered at the thought of the grime on the mantelpiece where the needles had lain.

Nola scooped out a shellfish from the shell.

"Lovely!" she said.

Not wanting to be rude, Gisela wiped her needle carefully on her skirt and copied Nola.

Despite her hesitancy, the fish tasted delicious.

No one spoke until all that remained in the bowls was a pile of shells and greasy water.

"Would you like a sup of tea?" asked Mícheál.

Nola nodded and Gisela noticed that she stared at Mícheál as he filled the kettle and hung it on the crook where the pot had been boiling.

Suddenly it dawned on her.

Nola had a liking for the boy.

After an awkward silence, Peadar asked Gisela if her parents belonged to any political parties.

She thought it a strange and intrusive question.

"Peadar's a political animal," smiled Mícheál. "He can talk about it morning, noon and night."

Peadar looked nonplussed.

"Goodness, all anyone wants to talk about is politics these days," said Nola.

She had taken out her cigarette case and had selected the rolled one, donated by Hans.

When steam poured from the kettle, Mícheál lifted it with a cloth to make tea in a teapot.

He offered them a slice of currant bread which Nola took readily.

Gisela picked at a large chip in her plate.

"Well, that was lovely," said Nola, stretching herself when they were finished their tea. "We'd better get the pony back in case he's needed."

They all walked out to the yard.

Nola skilfully turned Pinky and the trap towards the gate. They waved to the boys who stood in the yard watching them.

"I think Peadar likes you," said Nola as Pinky picked up pace on the road.

Gisela shook her head. "Me?"

"Yes, you!" said Nola. "I saw him looking at you."

"Did you?" said Gisela.

She hadn't noticed. Not at all.

"The parish dance will be fun," said Nola.

"Yes, I suppose so," said Gisela.

"You'll have wear a nice dress for Peadar," said Nola.

Gisela looked quite horrified, which made Nola laugh out loud.

Near the crossroads into the village, Gisela saw the man who had been on the beach with the two dogs, the man who had seen Nola swimming. He carried the same thick walking stick and stopped to watch as the pony and trap passed.

"*Hullo, Mister McKee!*" Nola called out as they passed. "*Lovely day for a swim, isn't it?*"

Mr. McKee did not respond. His face remained blank and impassive.

"That's Mícheál's father," said Nola, jerking her head backwards. "Not a nice man."

When Gisela looked back she saw that Seán McKee was still standing, staring, his stick solid in the road, as they rolled further and further away.

"How do you mean not nice?" asked Gisela.

Nola shook her head. "Let's just say he's not a man you'd want to cross."

"Jewish emigrants in the countries which they have been permitted to enter have created and are creating grave moral scandals and are a source of corruption of the populations among which they dwell."

**Charles Bewley, Irish Envoy in Berlin,
Report to an Taoiseach, Éamon de Valera, 1939**

Gisela

CHAPTER FOURTEEN

"And what shoes will you be wearing, darling?"

Mrs. de Freyne stood, hands on her hips, in Gisela's room.

Nola stood beside her, barely able to contain her excitement.

It was Friday morning and Mrs de Freyne had come to oversee Gisela's wardrobe ahead of the ball they were attending in Dublin the following night.

Gisela had brought her own dresses from Vienna, but to please Mrs. de Freyne she had hung one of the new dresses she'd got in Switzer's on the wardrobe door as her selection for the ball. It was pale yellow, the same colour she'd seen Nola hold up during the shopping trip.

She assumed it would be a safe bet.

Gisela bent down to the bottom of the wardrobe and came back up with a pair of flat brown shoes.

She did have dancing shoes at home but she hadn't thought to bring them.

"Oh, heavens no! No! We'll have to get you dancing shoes. They won't do."

Gisela felt very unsophisticated.

"Why don't you try some of mine?" asked Nola.

She rushed off to her room and brought back three pairs of satin shoes.

Gisela put her foot into one and felt the enormous space at the toe. They were at least three sizes too big for her.

"You are tiny, aren't you?" said Mrs. de Freyne.

Mrs. de Freyne summoned George and the car and the three of them set off for Drogheda to go shoe-shopping.

Gisela felt quite dreadful at the fuss.

The streets of the town were bustling.

West Street, the main thoroughfare, was filled with wooden shop fronts, some with stretched awnings.

There were wares on the street: household goods, baskets, buckets, sweeping brushes; outside one shop a mannequin displayed fishing waders and fishing rods.

George stopped the motorcar outside a shoe shop called Tyler's.

The assistant knew Mrs. de Freyne and smiled when she came in.

After a quick few words, the assistant brought out a range of shoes, most with heels higher than Gisela was used to.

She felt quite clumpy in them.

"Gorgeous!" Nola said.

Gisela balked when she saw the price handwritten on the box. The shoes were very, very expensive.

Mrs. de Freyne took out her cheque book.

Gisela couldn't help but think what luxuries the price of those shoes would fetch for her parents on the black market.

Many boxes of cigarettes. Chocolate. Pounds of tea.

After shopping, Mrs. de Freyne took Gisela on a short walk up the street to a large red-bricked Georgian building.

"Here you are, Gisela, the Garda station," she said. "You have to report to the Guards – that is, the police – with your passport on Thursdays."

The police needed to make sure that as an immigrant Gisela didn't "abscond" and assimilate, unchecked, into society.

"The others usually take the bus in, but they all have different days to report," Mrs. de Freyne went on. "Perhaps you'd like to take the bus into town yourself too? I don't want you to think we're holding you prisoner, accompanying you everywhere."

"I don't think that," said Gisela.

"Mummy's very good at taking prisoners," Nola said.

Gisela couldn't help but smile.

On the way back to the car they passed by a large ballroom and cinema called The Abbey.

"We can go there during the week if you like," Nola said. "Whatever picture you fancy."

It had been well over a year since Gisela had been to the cinema.

Gisela wondered if the people who walked by her on the street knew how lucky they were to be able to go about their business as they pleased. Without restrictions.

Here there was an atmosphere of cheer, women greeting each other in the streets, jovial.

In Vienna, there was an atmosphere that hung over the streets like a cloud.

A feeling of waiting for something to happen.

As they reached the motorcar, Gisela realised what that feeling was: the emotion she felt each time she stepped outside her home, on an errand, on the hunt for bread.

It was fear.

In Vienna, she had been living in a perpetual state of fear.

Now, in Ireland, that cloud was gone.

It was going to take a bit of getting used to.

Was she really safe and free?

* * *

The next evening, Saturday, the trio bumped their way to Dublin, driven by George, the chauffeur.

Gisela found herself clinging on to the door handle to steady herself.

By the time they got to the large manor house where the ball was taking place, they all felt rather groggy.

Gisela wondered why the party had to be so far away. Weren't there more local debutante balls that Nola could attend?

They were greeted in the hallway by the debutante herself and she shook Gisela's hand graciously and made a little bow.

She was blonde like Nola, but unlike Nola had very dainty features.

Inside, the house swarmed.

A string quartet played in the corner of the ballroom and bodies moved and mingled, hands reaching for drinks offered on trays.

The women were dressed in silk and taffeta, and all the young men wore tuxedos.

Gisela was glad she was wearing her new dancing shoes and up-to-date satin dress from Switzer's now.

Mrs. de Freyne touched her on the arm and said, "Just smile, enjoy yourself."

Gisela supposed she could sense her nervousness.

A few girls approached Nola when they came into the ballroom.

"Nola, who have you brought? Is that a cousin?"

"No," she replied. "This is Gisela, all the way from Austria. Or, you know, Germany or whatever it's called these days!"

They all laughed.

Gisela didn't think the annexation of Austria into Nazi Germany was really a joke, but she shook their hands and smiled graciously.

She didn't want to get off to a bad start.

Gisela held her champagne flute and watched as Nola tipped hers high in the air and drained the contents.

She immediately whipped another flute from a tray passing by her shoulder.

Mrs. de Freyne joined the group and asked how the girls' debutante plans were coming along and what finishing schools they were going to.

"We have Switzerland arranged but you know with all the trouble on the Continent we're not quite sure if I'll get to go," said a tall, lean girl.

"Oh, Gisela knows all about that," said Nola. "The trouble on the Continent."

"Not the time or place, darling," warned Mrs. de Freyne.

"She does know, that's why she's here," said Nola. "She had to flee, didn't you?"

Mrs. de Freyne cleared her throat and quickly changed the subject.

"How is your father doing since he had his bad fall?" she asked of the tall, lean girl.

Nola shrugged and took another large gulp of champagne.

An older man approached and began to speak with Mrs. de Freyne, distracting her from the girls and their conversation.

"How exciting!" said the girl whose father had fallen from a horse and now apparently had a permanent limp. "Tell us all about it, did you really have to flee?"

Nola and her friends encircled Gisela, cutting her off from Mrs. de Freyne, her safety net.

"Well, I ... I suppose yes. It is not safe anymore in Vienna. Where I live."

"Are you a Jew?" asked the shorter girl with brown hair. Her eyebrows met slightly in the middle, stray hairs sprouting softly in the shape of a fan.

"Yes, it's strange," Nola interrupted. "She's a Catholic, goes to Mass and everything. Actually they're all Catholics who are staying with us. But because they used to be Jewish they're still classed as Jews. I mean Mummy used to a Protestant but you'd never think that now. Now she's a full Catholic!"

"How queer," said the shorter girl.

"What's Adolf Hitler like, have you ever met him?" said the tall girl now.

"I think he's rather handsome!" said the shorter girl.

"I've seen him, but I've never met him," said Gisela.

"Really?" said Nola. "You never told me that!"

"Well, of course," said Gisela. "He had a parade, on the streets. We all saw."

"I think he's quite charismatic," said the third girl, the first time they'd heard her speak. "We heard him on the wireless. My father says Europe needs someone like him. Somebody who will get things done. Isn't it true he's created thousands of jobs out of nowhere? And now the economy's booming?"

Gisela thought of the thousands of Jewish teachers, lawyers, dentists and college professors, all removed from their posts. All left with nothing.

She thought of her own father and his job, how he swore things would be all right, on account of their Catholic conversion, on account of all the good work he'd done for the tourist board, for his country.

She thought of the day he came home, stunned and jobless.

"Gisela's not the only Austrian we have living with us," said Nola. "We have the Hettingers, they're a family of four. They have two boys our age, Otto and Max."

"Oh, why didn't you bring *them* to the ball," said the taller girl.

"And we have Hans, who is rather old and a bit odd but nice. He helps with the farm. Gisela is my official companion."

"Lucky you with a companion," said the shorter girl. "All I have is my brother and he's a wretch!"

"Yes, well ..." said Nola looking at Gisela now, smiling. "She's not exactly what I expected. Not as much fun! But she is rather nice, don't you think?"

Gisela felt her blood simmer.

They were discussing her as though she were a dog.

A companionable dog.

"And how come you have so many Austrians living with you?" asked the girl who thought Hitler charming.

"Well, because Mummy likes to rescue things," said Nola. "If it's not a poor old lame horse, it's a group of Austrian evacuees!"

They all laughed.

Two red spots burned on Gisela's cheeks.

She was furious.

"Excuse me," she said, pushing past the group and moving quickly through the ballroom.

She opened a door that brought her outside onto a balcony, with a view of guests mingling below on the front lawn.

She placed her hands on the railing and took a deep breath.

How was she going to pass the evening like this?

Listening to their inane chatter?

They had no idea.

No idea whatsoever.

And Nola?

She would have thought so much more of her.

She thought they were friends.

Scrunching her eyes to try and keep in the tears that threatened, Gisela desperately wished that she could speak with her parents.

She wanted to embrace her father, to smell the scent of his pipe and his woollen shirt.

She wanted to see the kind understanding smile of her mother, to listen to her soothing tones, telling her everything would be all right.

Instead, all she could remember were her mother's tears on the train platform and her father's tomato face.

Pulling her gold cross from under her dress she tugged it around her chin and felt the links dig into her skin.

She wished she could run from that big house, away from those silly girls, out of Ireland and its misunderstanding of everything.

It was a mistake to have come here.

Perhaps she should have taken that chambermaid's job after all.

M15 INTELLIGENCE REPORT TO G2 INTELLIGENCE, DUBLIN
SUBJECT: TOP SECRET INFORMATION

M15 have learned that the arrival of a secret German agent to Ireland is imminent. Agent is expected to land along the coast at Co. Meath or Co. Louth with intent to reach Dublin. Sources indicate the agent, in collusion with the IRA, is to develop network for future German operations.

Suggest all IRA targets are closely observed.

EXPLOITATION: Covert

Hans

CHAPTER FIFTEEN

The next morning there was no movement from Nola's room.

Mrs. de Freyne had pursed her mouth when Nola did not come down for Sunday Mass.

Instead, they set off, the Hettingers, Hans, Gisela and their host, down the long avenue at the front of Newtown House and out onto the road towards the large, Gothic church that sat on top of the hill overlooking the village.

"She is sick, yes?" whispered Otto to Gisela.

"She drank a lot of champagne," Gisela told the group in German. "We had to stop the motorcar on the way home because she was sick. She got sick on her dancing shoes!"

Eva looked quite shocked.

"How did her mother let that happen?" she asked.

"She tried her best," said Gisela. "But Nola kept disappearing."

"She is a wild one," said Eva.

Gisela could only nod.

The group entered the church by a side door and were forced to parade all the way to the top of the aisle to find seats.

The men sat on one side, the women on the other.

Heads bowed in whispers as they passed.

Hans distinctly heard one man mutter, "*There's the Jews now.*"

The words make his skin bristle.

Before Communion, Father Crowley gave a long rambling sermon about the subject of evil, inspired, Hans suspected, by his recent visit to Newtown House.

He ended by saying, "It is a very sad situation to see people driven from their homes, to seek refuge with far-off neighbours such as ourselves. Our religious differences should not drive us apart, but unite us. We all believe in one God. The Almighty watches over us and is always there for us. He never leaves us. We keep our friends from Austria in our prayers as the political situation continues and hope that soon they can return to their own land and their people."

Hans looked at Fritz who was chewing his lip.

When the Mass ended, they were forced to wait for the crowds to disperse so that they could leave their pews.

"Did the priest just say he hopes we can go back where we came from and soon?" said Fritz to Hans in German.

Hans nodded.

The priest spoke in slow, low tones. He had managed to understand him. And that was what he had said.

They all felt low-spirited as they walked back together to Newtown.

"Do you know, it's the strangest thing," said Mrs. de Freyne as they walked out onto the road. "Usually after Mass, I'm swamped by people. They all want to speak to me about something or other. I have a few schemes running, you understand," she added in explanation to Gisela. "But since you lot have arrived, well, I can walk out of Mass free as a bird!"

"We have tainted you," said Fritz.

"Not at all," said Mrs. de Freyne. "It's just awfully strange."

"Perhaps they are afraid of us," said Eva.

"Perhaps they think we smell," said Otto.

His mother clipped him on the shoulder and told him to hush.

* * *

As it was Sunday, the Austrians, Mrs. de Freyne and Fintan Walshe all gathered to have luncheon together in the dining room.

Maeve would then take the rest of the day off and the group would later eat cold meats, sandwiches and salads that she had laid out in the kitchen.

The smell of roast beef must have wafted its way upstairs and awoken the sleeping Nola, because she arrived to the table, looking groggy and puffy-faced.

"Morning!" said Otto brightly.

Nola scowled.

"Good afternoon," said Mrs. de Freyne, her face quite hard to read. "Father Crowley missed you at Mass again this morning."

"Sorry, Mama," said Nola.

Hans' mouth watered at the sight of roast beef, gravy and roast potatoes.

He saw Gisela stare transfixed at her food.

He imagined she was thinking about her family back home and what rations they would have managed to find today.

They were probably missing her ability to walk long miles in search of fresher food.

Nola picked at her plate and put tiny specks of mashed potato into her mouth.

Hans could tell she was feeling wretched and felt quite sorry for her.

"I read the planes are circling over Danzig in Poland," said Fritz.

"Very worrying," said Mrs. de Freyne.

"Did you see they are handing out leaflets in Britain?" said Eva. "What to do if war should come?"

"No, I didn't see that," said Mrs. de Freyne.

"They are sending out 45 million this week!"

"Oh my," said Mrs. de Freyne.

"Herr Hitler is going to Danzig but only by ship," said Fritz. "He refuses to set foot in Danzig until it is Reich territory!"

"That man!" said Eva.

"He'll get it too," said Hans. "The territory."

"No doubt," said Eva. "It is so worrisome."

Mrs. de Freyne cleared her throat.

A silence fell across the table.

Time to change the subject again.

"Nola, would you like to go for a walk after luncheon?" said Gisela, for something to say.

Nola looked at her, quite green.

"All right," she said.

"Yes, the fresh air will do you good," said Mrs. de Freyne.

Maeve served fresh apple tart and cream for dessert.

Nola left hers completely untouched and Maeve picked it up and said she'd leave it in the kitchen for her for later.

Hans watched Maeve smile kindly at Nola.

After they had coffee the Hettingers and Hans retired to the drawing room to play cards and backgammon.

As Hans left, he heard Mrs. de Freyne begin her dressing-down of Nola.

"Your behaviour last night, Nola de Freyne, was absolutely reprehensible. You're a disgrace to our good name. A disgrace to yourself. And a disgrace to your new companion. Do you think Gisela came all the way from Vienna to witness you lose your marbles? On alcohol?"

"Stop, Mummy," Hans heard Nola mutter.

"I will not stop. I will not. Now I expect an apology, to both Gisela and to George. I expect he'll be cleaning the car for a week after what you left behind. Do you think you'll attract a suitor with this carry-on? No one wants to marry a drunkard."

Hans couldn't help but feel quite sorry for Nola.

She was young and excitable.

And this morning she looked truly wretched.

"I'm sorry, Gisela," Hans heard her say.

In the drawing room Hans laid out the cards with Fritz, Otto and Max, while Eva read her book on the sofa.

He watched out the window as Gisela and Nola made their way outside, heading it seemed towards the beach.

At the top of the path, Nola kicked at a tall foxglove, swiping it in half.

Hans stared, fascinated.

Nola threw back her head and let out an enormous ear-piercing scream.

"Did you hear that?" said Max as he lifted his cards, looking around. "It sounded like an animal?"

"Must be coming from the farm," said Hans, as he watched the two girls move off, Nola drop-kicking every tall piece of growth in her path.

She was a bit wild, Hans thought. And she was very spoilt. But he wasn't quite sure if it was her own fault. She had never known anything but privilege. She was too young to understand how the world really worked. How life was not a long party and sins were not always forgiven.

Nola would make her own mistakes and have to live with them.

Just like he had.

Just like he was living with, every single day.

"Your turn," said Max.

Hans looked from the window.

"Sorry," he apologised. "My mind was completely elsewhere."

Gisela

CHAPTER SIXTEEN

Gisela's first week at Newtown passed quickly. Most days she and Nola went for long meandering walks, visiting the beaches. Past Termonfeckin was Baltray. If they turned the other way, they could walk along Ganderstown to Clogherhead. There was a hilly walk around the head from which they could see Port beach. Beyond that was Salterstown and Dunany.

On Thursday she visited the Garda Station, sliding her passport over to the officer on duty who set up her file. She was getting her bearings. Getting to know the town of Drogheda and the landscape all around Newtown with its green fields, persistent salty breeze and rain showers that appeared out of nowhere, drenching them as they walked.

She took to carrying a mackintosh.

Nola roamed free.

They all ate dinner together every evening, talking in hushed tones about what the newspapers had carried that day.

Things were getting worse at home. Herr Hitler's power was growing. Nobody wanted to say out loud what they feared was coming,

War.

On Friday afternoon, almost a week after their first ball together, Nola called Gisela for assistance in her bedroom.

She was frantically searching through the rack of clothes hanging in her wardrobe.

They were attending the parish dance that evening, a social event, Nola had been reassuring Gisela all week that you simply did not get 'too dressed up for'.

"It's imperative that I wear just the right thing," she said.

Gisela laughed.

"What's so funny?" asked Nola, turning around in surprise.

"You are funny," said Gisela. "You make such a fuss of your clothes. What does it matter?"

Nola frowned.

"Don't you see?" she said. "If it was a big social in Dublin, it would be so much easier. There's a dress code for that. And I have a ton of dresses. But for the parish dance, well, it's much more complicated. All the locals will be there. And so I must look stunning. But not overdone. I can't look too ... you know ..."

She waved her hand at her wardrobe.

"Posh," she said.

Choosing a pair of green slack trousers, Nola held them up for Gisela.

"Father Crowley would appreciate these," she said.

"Father Crowley would expect nothing less," said Gisela.

Nola sighed and flopped down on the bed beside her companion.

"I know!" she said, sitting up now, excited. "We should take some gin with us tonight. It'll be fun. And it's a wonderful way to forget."

"Forget what?" asked Gisela.

"Forget everything."

Leaning down, Nola rooted under her bed and pulled out an ornate cardboard box.

Inside was a layer of stockings.

From under the stockings, Nola pulled out two large hip flasks.

"Nola!" said Gisela, shaking her head.

"They were Daddy's," said Nola. "A family heirloom. I'll fill them up later and we can take them with us. Oh, it will be fun!"

"Nola," said Gisela, taking a hip flask from her and looking at the silver engraving, "what happened to your father?"

Nola went quiet.

She looked to the floor and then back to Gisela.

"Well, he died. Two days after I was born. That's it. There's all there is to it."

"I'm so sorry."

Nola shrugged.

"Well, it's not like I knew him to miss him."

"Yes," said Gisela, "But it's still very sad."

"Not really," said Nola. "Probably sadder for Mummy. It's just been me and her, always the two of us."

Gisela had seen a gloriously happy wedding photograph on the mantelpiece in the drawing room.

It featured a younger, slimmer Mrs. de Freyne. The man whose arm she was holding was small in stature and had a great big smile. He had the exact same features as Nola.

"What happened?" asked Gisela. "Was he sick?"

"No," said Nola. "Not really. We were living in Burma. Daddy worked for the army there. And then Mummy had me and Daddy got cholera and it just swept him away and there she was, all alone. With baby little me."

"Oh, my goodness," said Gisela, thinking of kindly, matronly Mrs. de Freyne. "What an ordeal!"

All of a sudden, things made sense to Gisela.

Mrs. de Freyne knew what it was like to be away from home.

To be without family.

To be grieving and feeling loss.

"She wanted to go home to London," said Nola. "But because Daddy was Irish, he wanted me to be brought up in Ireland so she bought Newtown and came to live here. I sometimes think that if Daddy didn't die, we would have stayed in Burma forever. Or else come back to London. I doubt we would be here anyway."

"I'm glad you are though," said Gisela, thinking that if it hadn't gone the way it had, she might still be stuck in Vienna.

"I've never felt that I belong here," said Nola. "I belong in London. I know it."

The two girls fell silent, each thinking about the cities they longed to be in.

"When I do go to London, properly, when it's all set up after my coming out ball, why don't you come with me? The two of us, together?" said Nola.

Gisela shook her head.

"I don't belong there," she said, thinking of Magnus and the crowded underground and the yellow blocks of the Tower of London.

"Life is an adventure," said Nola. "You never know where you'll end up."

"You only think that because you've never been on a real one," said Gisela.

A knock sounded on the bedroom door and Maeve put her head around.

"Gisela, pet," she said, "a letter's come for you."

Gisela jumped up and had her hand out for the letter before Maeve could even blink.

She looked at the handwriting and held the letter to her chest.

The letter was from Rudy.

"Thank you, Maeve," said Gisela.

She told Nola she was going to her room to read it.

"So, the trousers or not?" said Nola, but Gisela had already left the room, her letter clutched tightly to her chest.

* * *

Gisela's heart danced.

This was the first letter she'd had since she'd arrived in Ireland.

She'd had no response to any of the cards she's sent to her parents while travelling nor any response to the three long letters she'd posted since setting up home at Newtown either.

She'd written to Rudy twice.

Now, at last, a response.

Holding the envelope tight against her, she thought about what it might contain.

She wanted to savour the moment and make it last.

When she could take no more, carefully she opened the letter, trying not to tear the paper too much.

There were two pages.

The letter was short.

She felt disappointed there wasn't more.

"*Dear Gisela,*" wrote Rudy. The address was the little store where he worked in the small village on the border of Czechoslovakia and Poland. "*I am glad to hear that you have arrived in Ireland safe and that you have found a nice place to live. The de Freynes sound very nice and what luck to be living with other Viennese! I am afraid I do not write with good news.*"

Gisela's heart sank.

Instead of savouring the letter, her eyes raced through it, taking in the lines.

The words bobbed around, not making sense.

"*Ordered to leave.*"

"*Tried to stay.*"

"*Put on a train.*"

"*Fear the worst.*"

"*No word since.*"

"*Rumours.*"

The bottom felt as though it had fallen from Gisela's stomach.

Nausea swirled.

Rudy had got word that their parents had been ordered to leave the day after Gisela had left.

They were made to gather in the square with a number of other families who up till then had managed to stay in their homes.

They had taken a suitcase each and gone to the meeting point as ordered.

The neighbour who had written to Rudy in Czechoslovakia said they had not come back and their apartment was locked up and quiet.

It was understood they were all put on a train.

No one knew to where.

There were rumours of a new city being built to house Jews, half Jews, quarter Jews.

It must have been there.

No one knew of an address.

Rudy had no way to contact them.

Gisela realised her letters had been delivered to their apartment, and fallen with a quiet thud through their letterbox. There were no hands there to pick them up.

She realised that not even her postcards would have reached them, seeing as they'd been ordered to leave the day after she took her train out.

She would have been with them, had she stayed another day.

Curling into a foetal position, Gisela lay on the bed, Rudy's letter at her heart.

She let the tears come as she thought about where her parents might be now.

What sort of city was being built?

Where was it?

Could she visit?

Why could she not write?

The pillow under her cheek grew wet.

She thought she might vomit and wondered if she would make it to the bathroom on time.

Softly, a knock came to the door.

Unable to answer, Gisela went quiet, hoping whomever it was would go away.

Nola opened the door and peered around.

When she saw Gisela on the bed, she rushed over.

"Oh," she said. "What's wrong? Are you all right? Did you get bad news?"

Gisela could not find the words.

Nola sat on the bed and reached over to rub Gisela's arm.

"Is somebody sick?" Nola asked tentatively.

Gisela shook her head.

"Should I fetch Mummy?" asked Nola.

Gisela shook her head again.

Nola walked around the other side of the bed and climbed onto it.

She lay down beside Gisela and wrapped her arm around her.

Gisela reached down and took Nola's hand.

They lay like that till Gisela's tears stopped and Maeve called up that afternoon tea was ready.

"I'm glad you came here," said Nola, when Gisela got up to powder her face and attend to her puffy eyes. "You're safe now."

"Yes," said Gisela, having finally recovered her voice. "I know I am."

G2 INTELLIGENCE REPORT

Status: URGENT ACTION REQUIRED / ALL STATIONS
ON ALERT

BREAKING: A serious arms theft has occurred at
Phoenix Park Barracks, DUBLIN

ITEMS STOLEN: 16 x Thompson Machine Guns, 12 hand
grenades, 4 x Rifles, 400 bullets

SUSPECTS: Three men, believed to have left the area
in a FORDOR SEDAN

ACTION: Senior IRA targets to be taken in for
questioning. Brigade members to be profiled for
possible storage of stolen weapons in Dublin,
Wicklow, Meath, Louth areas.

NOTE: UTMOST DISCRETION AND CAUTION

Hans

CHAPTER SEVENTEEN

Hans did not want to go to the parish dance.

He felt too old and he had never enjoyed social events, not even in Vienna.

And he knew, as had been their experience at Mass and to some extent in town, whenever they had gone as a group, that they would be watched.

Stared at.

And talked about.

He would have preferred to stay at Newtown.

To have sat with Eva and Fritz and Maeve, over tea and cake, and later, as the night wore on and as was becoming their custom on Friday and Saturday evenings, to indulge in a beer or sherry.

As it was, Maeve was called away on urgent business.

She didn't say what it was, but a messenger called to the door with a note and after that she had disappeared.

Hans knew she was a widow with no children.

He was curious and worried for her.

And disappointed that she would not be sitting in that evening.

Fritz reported that Eva had been struck down with a temperature and the beginnings of what looked like a summer cold.

He would stay in their cottage that evening to look after her.

"Why don't you go along to the parish dance," Mrs. de Freyne had said, when she realised Hans would be sitting in Newtown House, quite alone.

"Will Mr. Walshe be here?" said Hans, thinking he could at least share a beer with the farm foreman.

"He too said he had some business to attend to," said Mrs. de Freyne. "Everyone it seems is busy tonight."

Hans, although he very much liked Mrs. de Freyne, did not relish the thought of practising his broken English, the two of them alone in her drawing room that evening.

At least at a dance there would be music to drown things out.

He would not be expected to converse back and forth, to understand the subject and provide an interesting opinion on it.

He could, if he liked, just watch.

He followed Otto and Max as they walked down the lane.

"*Wait up!*" he called.

He ran to them, his long limbs swaying like ropes as he caught up.

"Hans!" said Max. "I didn't know you danced!"

"I don't," said Hans. "Don't get any ideas."

They laughed.

"Perhaps you will meet a nice Irish girl, yes?" said Hans to the boys.

"Perhaps," said Otto. "Although I doubt they will want to be seen with us."

"Not in front of their Irish boyfriends anyway," said Max.

"Maybe it will be different when we go to college," said Otto.

"Yes," said Max. "Maybe we'll be seen differently when we're not just farmhands."

Otto nudged Max and nodded at Hans.

"Not that there's anything wrong with being a farmhand," said Max.

"Of course not," said Hans.

But he knew what they meant.

Without a formal education and poor language skills, Hans did not have many options here in Ireland.

While the young Hettingers would go to university, expand their language skills and come out the other side with a degree in science, or perhaps even medicine, Hans would still be at Newtown, shovelling manure.

"Maybe *you'll* meet a nice Irishwoman, Hans," said Otto, trying to change the subject.

As soon as he said it, he regretted it.

"I'm sorry," he said. "I didn't mean ..."

"It's all right," said Hans.

The three swatted at the midges that batted around their heads, the young men afraid to say any more, lest they insulted their friend even further.

It was hard to say the right thing.

Everything here had a layer of complication to it.

That was what happened when you left your home country.

Challenge after challenge.

A different culture.

And plenty of faux pas.

* * *

With Hans' new-found love of carpentry and Anja's admittance to the Vienna Philharmonic Orchestra, they were able to enjoy the first few months of their married life.

Everything was better together.

Hans no longer hated coming home. Now he longed for his shift to finish so that he could quickly make his way through the streets, back to their warm apartment and the smell of cooking.

Anja's effect was soothing to his father and for a while he seemed to settle better, now that there was a woman living in the apartment again.

Perhaps it was the scent of her, or her womanly things spread about, scarves and hats, shampoo bottles in the bathroom, stockings drying, that reminded his father of Hans' mother.

Or perhaps it was the smell of cinnamon or garlic and onions as Anja prepared warm, hearty meals for breakfast, luncheon and tea.

Most nights Anja advanced towards Hans in bed, wrapping her legs around him and he felt a thrill as she moved closer to him, pushing her pelvis against his.

He couldn't get enough of her.

Not of her warmth nor her smell nor her taste.

Sometimes he felt as though he might disappear completely into her and it was her reaction that he took pleasure in the most.

As they lay there in satisfied silence, he found it hard to believe sometimes that he had found her.

He had, as time had passed over the years, presumed that he was bound to be alone.

His school friends had married early, only a few years after they'd left school.

Hans had not wanted to marry a girl from his class or someone who he knew would make a perfectly pleasant wife, for the sake of it.

He wanted to be in love.

And now that he was, he knew he had made the right decision to wait.

A few months into their marriage Anja became unwell and found that she had an upset stomach.

At first, she thought it was a bug, but when it did not go away and she began to drop weight, Hans urged her to visit the doctor.

When she came back home, she flopped into the kitchen chair, her face pale and wan.

Hans sat down and clasped her hand.

"Did he say what it was?" asked Hans, worried now at her expression and her pallor. She looked like she had got terrible news. "Did he prescribe any medicine?"

"Yes," said Anja. "He said what it was."

Hans squeezed her hand, willing her to look into his eyes.

She turned to look at him and burst into tears.

"What is it?" Hans said. "What is it, my darling?"

Anja took her hand out of Hans' and held it to her face.

"It's a baby," she muttered into her fingers. "It's a baby."

Hans gasped.

He looked at his weeping wife and suddenly burst into laughter.

A baby!

He jumped up and pulled Anja into a standing position.

"*Yes!*" he roared. "*Yes!* Father, Father! Anja's going to have a baby!"

His father, who was seated on the couch, got up when he saw them standing and came to join them.

The old man cheered as though he'd just won a prize.

"*Yes!*" he roared too.

Anja couldn't help but laugh, the tears still falling from her eyes.

The three of them danced around the kitchen floor in a circle, their arms around each other's necks.

"I'm so happy," said Hans and he kissed the top of Anja's head.

"Who's Anja?" asked Hans' father, looking confused.

Hans and Anja looked at each other and laughed again, at their absurd situation, finding hilarity in the sadness of it all.

"You're going to be a great mother," said Hans.

She shrugged.

"What about the orchestra?" she said, looking worried.

"Oh, that," he said. "We'll work it out. They don't play all year round."

Anja sat down again at the kitchen table.

Hans could see she was not feeling well.

"Let's have some tea," he said and he took the kettle and filled it.

His mother always made him tea whenever he was not feeling well.

As he waited for the kettle to boil on the stove, it struck Hans that perhaps now would not be the best time to go looking for an apprenticeship.

If Anja was expecting a baby, he would have to provide for not only the three of them, but the new baby too.

It would probably be best if he stayed on at the Vienna Transport Company.

It was safe and secure, and of course, reliable.

Hans looked at Anja who was sitting, in shock it seemed, at the table.

"Everything will be all right," said Hans, soothing her.

"Do you think so?" she asked.

"Of course. This is big news. Such happy news!"

She gave the faintest of smiles.

It was as though she knew something he didn't.

Of course, she would be worried.

She was a first-time mother.

She would have to face the pregnancy and birth and Hans could do none of those things for her.

Hans sat back at the table and took Anja's hand.

"I will look after you," he said. "I promise."

Anja smiled now, properly.

"You are a good man, Hans," she said.

"You can call me Baby Papa," he said and at this she burst out laughing and squeezed his hand.

Gisela

CHAPTER EIGHTEEN

The parish hall was smaller than Gisela expected; nothing like the large ballrooms she'd been to in Vienna.

The floors were wooden and worn, cracked in places.

There was a high stage at the top of the room and a terrible smell of must.

A band had set up on the stage – three men, playing a violin, tin whistle and a hand-held round drum.

There were chairs around the walls and most were filled with chattering girls.

Nola had asked Gisela if she'd rather skip the dance, knowing how upset she was by the letter she'd received from home.

Gisela had not told anyone of what Rudy had written.

But, rather than stay in her room alone, she had decided that she would attend the parish dance as planned.

It might be a distraction.

It might take her mind away from the images she kept seeing in her mind.

The cattle trains, the ones that left her terrified to get on the train in London. Her parents' faces on board.

A new city where her parents were forced to work, build houses with their bare hands, dig soil and foundations perhaps?

It was the unknown that was the worst.

The fear of what they might be going through.

A long table at the back of the parish hall was laid with plates of sandwiches, sponge cake and a giant silver vat of hot water for tea.

"I know you're sad but I'm really glad you came," said Nola. "I don't think I could have come on my own."

Gisela could see that Nola would have been feeling alone had she come here without her. The other girls stood around in groups, dressed in plain cotton dresses, some floral, some with hand-sewn frills.

Nola stood out as different, glamorous, and despite her best efforts, posh.

The boys, Gisela noticed, all looked very similar.

Roughly cut hair.

Loose country trousers.

Cheeks red from scrubbing and the walk there, the rest of the skin on the face pale.

The fiddle screeched out of tune in warm-up and everyone jumped and laughed.

Within a minute, the band had burst into a tune, a sound that Gisela had never heard before.

The tin whistle seemed to carry the melody, cutting over the chatter and laughter in the room.

The round drum the man beat was loud and rhythmic, so much so that most people were already tapping their feet.

Some clapped.

"Have you heard music like this before?" Nola asked Gisela.

Gisela shook her head.

It was nothing like the classical music she was used to, the orchestras she had gone to see many times, all Rudy's performances.

"I like it," said Gisela, smiling.

She couldn't help herself.

The music was infectious.

The brave first dancers, two girls, began swinging each other round by the arms. Another two girls joined them.

They were light on their feet, their knees bent, ankles flashing.

"Isn't it fun? Would you like to try?" said Nola.

Gisela shook her head.

The door opened and into the hall walked Otto and Max.

They are accompanied by Hans.

On seeing them, Nola grabbed Gisela by the wrists and whirled her out onto the floor, spinning her around and around.

Gisela gasped and laughed, trying to catch her breath.

"*Stop, Nola!*" she cried.

But Nola had a firm grip of her and she would not let her go.

By the time the tune came to an end, Gisela could barely breathe.

She leaned over and laughed.

"Nola, you are a brat!" she said. "I'm dizzy!"

They found the other Austrians and went to get a cup of watery tea.

The girl pouring tea from the silver vat eyed Nola and Gisela suspiciously.

She didn't say a word as she handed over the mugs.

Max and Otto watched the dancers, fascinated.

"It is so fast," said Otto.

Hans stood head and shoulders above the crowd.

He seemed uncomfortable to be there.

"Are you all right, Hans?" asked Gisela.

He smiled and nodded.

"It is a long time since I attended a dance," he said.

Gisela wondered about him, about his background.

Although he was always friendly and civil to her, in the two weeks since she'd been here she'd learned very little of him at all.

The Hettingers were the opposite.

Eva loved to talk of home, of her extended family there, of what it might be like when they returned.

She'd told Gisela all about their life in Vienna, while Gisela had done the same, discussing her father's job and how she had toured all over the country with him as a child, of the struggles she'd faced before she'd left, of her worries about leaving her parents behind.

She had been right to worry.

Look at what had happened now.

Gisela realised that part of her upset today had been the understanding that she couldn't tell the other Austrians about the news she had just received.

To do so would leave them worrying about their own family.

To do so would bring home, to Ireland, what they had left behind.

Instead, Gisela would write to Rudy and see if there was any possible way that they could find out where their parents had gone.

Somebody had to know something.

Somebody had to have a contact somewhere.

"Let's go outside and have a cigarette," said Nola.

The five trooped outside and, as they held the door of the dance hall open for each other, Gisela felt eyes boring into their backs.

They were being watched.

The whole dance hall was staring.

Gisela reached up and touched her plaited hair.

She had wound it round her head in a traditional style.

She realised now, looking around her at women wearing their hair down, long and curly or cut up short in waves, that no one else had a hairstyle like hers.

No one else had a dress like hers either, heavily embroidered and worn over a white, frilly blouse.

Nola had tried to convince her to change into something else, but Gisela had refused.

It reminded her of home.

Now, she felt uncomfortable and she wished she had changed.

Outside, they stood with their backs against a thick hedge and watched people coming and going.

Many were still arriving to the dance, racing in on black bikes and flinging them up against the hedge.

Gisela watched two young men approach the group.

As they got near, she realised it was Mícheál and Peadar.

Peadar's cheeks were rosy.

His eyes were bright blue.

Gisela felt a blush in her cheeks.

Nola had said he liked her.

Did he?

What would he think of her now, in her traditional dress?

On spotting the boys, Nola stood up straighter and stretched herself.

Gisela thought she looked like a swan: beautiful and elegant.

"Miss de Freyne," said Mícheál. "How very nice to see you here."

He spoke in a funny voice, imitating Nola's accent.

They all laughed.

Above them, midges swirled in black clouds, biting.

Nola introduced the newcomers to Otto, Max and Hans.

"That's Mícheál," she said. "Irish for Michael. And that's Peadar. Irish for Peter."

The Austrians laughed.

The Irish didn't.

"And where are you from?" asked Peadar.

"Vienna, like Gisela," said Otto.

Peadar turned to look up at Hans.

"Must be an awful place altogether," said Peadar. "If you all had to leave."

"Yes," said Max. "It was not safe."

"Nowhere's safe," said Peadar.

"Here is safe. Safe and boring!" interjected Nola.

"Perhaps we will get a sandwich?" said Hans.

He seemed uncomfortable in the boys' presence.

Gisela thought he probably would have been better to stay at home.

"Yes, let's," said Otto.

The three Austrian men went back into the dance hall.

Nola turned to Peadar.

"Nowhere's safe?"

Peadar took a drag of his cigarette.

"I just mean things aren't always as safe as they seem."

"And what do you mean by that?" asked Nola.

"I mean ... nothing. I was just making a comment. No need to bother your head over it, Nola."

Nola seemed annoyed about something that Gisela didn't quite understand.

Nola sighed and then looked around her.

"Boys," she said, "go in and get yourselves a nice cup of tea there and come back out. I have a little surprise."

Mícheál and Peadar looked at each other and laughed.

"What are you up to, Nola?" asked Mícheál.

"Nothing," said Nola, looking quite innocent. "Nothing at all."

The two boys went to do as they were bid.

Staring straight ahead, Nola tossed her tea backwards, showering a blackberry bush in the milky liquid.

"What are you doing?" Gisela said.

"You do the same."

Confused and curious, Gisela threw her tea over the same bush.

Nola opened her bag and flashed one of the the hip flasks she'd shown Gisela earlier.

Gisela put her hand to her mouth in surprise.

"Nola!" she said. "You brought it!"

"Well, of course I did. It's what Daddy would have wanted."

Gisela doubted this very much.

And she thought of Mrs. de Freyne and the trust she had put in her to keep Nola out of trouble.

Nola turned around and rinsed out the cups with a tiny drop of the clear liquid she poured from one of the flasks.

"I didn't bother with the tonic," she said.

When Gisela took her cup back she sniffed the shot Nola had poured for her and felt as though she'd scorched her eyebrows.

"What is it?" she asked.

"Gin."

"Nola," said Gisela. "This is pure alcohol? Is that not dangerous?"

"It'll be fine, I do it all the time," said Nola.

"You do?"

"Of course. It helps you forget. It's wonderful!"

"I don't think I can drink this," said Gisela.

The cup smelled like poison.

"Just sip it slowly," said Nola. "You'll get used to it. Ah, boys!"

Back from the hall were Mícheál and Peadar, holding their fresh cups of tea.

"Dump that!" smiled Nola. "I have something much better."

* * *

To Gisela's surprise, the more she sipped the foul gin, the easier it got to drink it.

The effect was immediate, rushing straight to her head, making her feel quite lightheaded and dizzy.

On top of that feeling was a sense of calm.

Mixed with excitement.

It was most strange.

They returned to the dance floor and, with the rushing music and their new dance partners; Mícheál swung Nola around while Peadar gripped Gisela tight.

Gisela was exhilarated.

She laughed and laughed.

It felt good to let some emotion out.

Every time thoughts of her parents slipped back into her mind, she pushed them back out.

After another dose of gin, Nola brought them behind the dance hall where a low wall was overhung by a canopy of trees.

Gisela noticed that the couples along the wall sat close together, some kissing and cuddling.

It was most surprising to see.

While chatting to Peadar, Gisela turned to find Nola in a deep embrace with Mícheál, kissing passionately.

In surprise, she turned back to Peadar to tell him to look.

Before she could say the words, he lunged at her, planting his mouth on top of hers, his hands firmly on both her shoulders.

Shocked by his wet mouth and the warmth of it, her initial reaction was to push him off, but he had such a grip on her that she was unable to.

Instead, she responded as she thought she should.

All around them are courting couples.

Why not her?

She found herself sitting on the wall, Peadar working her mouth with his tongue, moving his hand to her chin, as though trying to dig deeper.

Gisela couldn't work out if she liked it or not.

Her head was spinning.

From behind, a shout rang out.

A flurry of couples jumped up from the wall.

Peadar stopped, allowing Gisela to breathe and suddenly backed away from her.

"Mícheál!" Peadar called in a low voice.

In the dusk, Gisela could make out Father Crowley, his walking stick held high, moving towards them.

The rest of the couples had already disappeared, hand in hand back around the front of the dance hall.

"*Mícheál!*" called Peadar again.

Nola, completely unaware of the cleric's approach seemed to be half-straddling the young Mícheál McKee.

It was most indecent, thought Gisela, as she stood up and began to move away with Peadar.

"*Miss de Freyne, compose yourself!*"

The priest pushed his cane in between the couple and prised them apart.

Surprised, Nola stood up and glared at the priest.

"*You should be ashamed of yourself,*" he said to Nola.

Mícheál, who had been sitting on the wall, stood up now, looking acutely embarrassed.

Nola wiped her mouth and adjusted her blouse.

"*And what would your mother think of this behaviour?*" said the priest. "*Do you think she'd like to see that, huh? And you, Mr. McKee? You ought to know better.*"

Nola moved off.

Mícheál followed her.

The priest followed them, still admonishing them both.

Peadar walked quickly ahead round to the front of the dance hall.

Red clouds fired the sky.

Nola ran to catch up with Gisela.

"*I think now it might be a good idea if you went home and told your mother what you've been up to!*" Father Crowley called after them.

"*Christ!*" said Nola.

"*And I hope you'll be at Confession on Thursday, repentant of your actions.*"

Nola didn't stop in front of the hall, but kept on walking, down the hill.

She beckoned for Gisela to follow her.

Looking back, she nodded at the red-faced Mícheál and waved for him to follow her too.

Peadar followed at a distance.

When they were part way down the hill, still ahead of the boys, the midges nipping them under the low branches of hawthorn trees, Nola began to giggle.

"That man," she said. "You know, I think he gets off on it, standing there spying before jumping out with his walking stick. *Boo!*"

She jumped and grabbed Gisela's arm, startling her.

They both laughed then.

"I kissed Peadar," whispered Gisela.

"You did!" said Nola.

She had been so engrossed in her own beau, she hadn't even noticed.

"Oh, this is perfect!" she said, clapping her hands.

Being threatened by the priest didn't exactly seem perfect to Gisela, but she had to admit that excitement flooded her veins.

They waited for a few minutes for the two boys to catch up.

They appeared, hands in pockets, trying to look casual.

Nola burst into a peal of laugher.

"C'mon!" she said. "Let's get out of here. I've more gin in my bag! Let's go down and watch the sun set on the beach."

G2 INTELLIGENCE REPORT

SUBJECT: ARREST WARRANT
RE: RECENT ARMS THEFT AT
PHOENIX PARK BARRACKS, DUBLIN

A warrant has been issued for the arrest of Seán McKee, Castlecoo Hill, Termonkfeckin, Co. Louth in relation to the recent serious arms theft at Phoenix Park, Dublin

G2 believe Seán McKee is operating as de facto Chief of Staff and ordered the theft to arm the IRA ahead of potential terrorist activities across England and Northern Ireland.

Approach with caution, may be armed.

Hans

CHAPTER NINETEEN

Hans quite liked the musty dance hall, with its bare floorboards and cracked painted walls.

There was something charming about it.

The hall was filled with chatter, with excited voices, mostly from youngsters like Otto and Max but there were a few older men there like him too.

He would have liked to have gone over and chatted, but he was shy about his command of English.

Really, he needed a text book and to study.

But even at that, he knew, it was in-person conversation he needed.

He would never be comfortable making idle chitchat though.

Even in his native German, that had never sat easy with him.

It had probably been a mistake to come to the dance.

He felt that everyone was looking at him and, with his six-foot six-inch height, he was hard to miss.

He took his cup of tea and stood with Otto and Max to watch the dancing.

Hans felt the rhythm of the music as it started up: fast, fresh, free.

The noise level rose in the room as the atmosphere lifted with the dancing.

Otto and Max laughed as Nola dragged Gisela round and round like a rag doll.

Hans thought it was a bit mean on Gisela, who like him didn't like any sort of attention to be drawn to her.

Out of the other Austrians in the house, Hans identified with Gisela the most, probably because, like him, she kept herself to herself.

Eva Hettinger liked to talk and ask questions and found discussing her problems out loud helpful.

Fritz was an upbeat, educated man who had worked as a scientist in Vienna, which left Hans feeling a little inadequate around him.

Otto and Max were full of youthful confidence and exuberance.

Only Gisela carried a worrisome, inward soul.

He knew she had left her family back home and she didn't like to talk about it.

He knew she was missing Vienna most terribly, but each day she followed Nola about and did her best to fit into this whole new world she'd found herself in.

The world of a grand manor, social events and laughing rich Irish kids who knew nothing about what Gisela had gone through over the past few years.

How different it was to what they'd come from.

How things had changed in such a short time.

* * *

Not long after Hans met Anja she informed him that her father's two tailor shops were being targeted and harassed.

SA officers had appeared with placards around their necks, pacing up and down the street outside.

The placards read: *Germans, defend yourself against the Jewish atrocity propaganda!* and *Buy only at German shops!* and *Germans, do not buy from Jews!*

When Hans went for dinner to their house not long after, Gerhard Schafer, his face pale with worry, said, "The newspapers! All these articles. Herr Einaugler showed me one the other day. It said the Jews are kidnapping Christian children for Passover. To mix their blood with our matzah! Have you ever heard such a thing?!"

Miriam, Anja's mother, had shaken her head.

Anja's brothers looked forlorn.

How could they get the truth out when gentiles wanted to believe such propaganda?

The protests affected their business dramatically.

Nobody wanted to come into their shops after that.

"But we are a German business," said Miriam. "We are an *Austrian* business. How can they say such things?"

Posters continued to appear around the city.

Films were released in the cinema, making fun of the Jews.

And the jibes stuck.

The atmosphere changed.

Things got worse.

Anja worried for her father, whose hair had gone from dark and thick to white and thin in a matter of months.

"He is aging before my eyes," she said.

The Schafers kept the shops open, not sure of what else to do.

After Anja and Hans married, Anja told Hans that she was glad her family had one less mouth to feed.

Hans found that he worried all the time, not only about Gerhard and Miriam, but specifically about Anja who was having a hard time in her early pregnancy.

She constantly felt nauseous and was vomiting often.

She was losing more and more weight.

When Gerhard was forced to take time away from work after a brick came through the window of the shop, shattering the glass, spraying suit jackets and trousers and leaving shards buried bloodily in his hands and face, Hans knew that things were going to change permanently.

They had already changed.

Gerhard was lucky he had not been blinded.

"*Jews out*," read a piece of paper tied around the brick. "*Pigs.*"

"What can we do?" said Anja after Hans had been to visit the family and see Gerhard's wounds for himself.

Hans didn't like to say it, but he thought it.

He couldn't see how things were going to get better.

The protests only incited more hatred.

Herr Hitler was not to be stopped.

Hans couldn't see how Jewish businesses could come through this.

In his heart an ache grew, that sooner or later the Schafers would be forced from the city.

When Kristallnacht arrived in all its shattering glory in November 1938, Anja huddled up to Hans in their apartment.

He refused to let her out onto the street to travel to her parents' house to check on them.

Outside they heard the smashing of glass and shouts from the rioters.

Smoke and flames rose across the city in the dark.

The Schafers' shops did not survive that first night of Kristallnacht.

Most of their stock was looted and the damage to one of the shops, which had been set on fire, was too severe to repair.

Hans had gone with Gerhard and Anja's brothers to survey the aftermath.

The smell of scorched wool, burnt carpet and wood from inside the shop was overpowering.

Hans had to put his scarf around his nose and mouth.

He watched helplessly as Gerhard broke down and cried in front of them all.

"What can we do?" he asked. "Why has this happened to us?"

Hans knew there was only one solution.

"I'm sorry, Gerhard," said Hans, as he kicked at a fallen piece of blackened wood. "I don't see how you come back from this. What if you repair it all and it happens again?"

Later, back in their home in Alsergrund, Hans gently suggested that perhaps they should get away for a while till things calmed down and they could look at coming back in the future.

Anja would be safe with him, he said, being married to a gentile.

When Hans came home to Anja and told him what he'd said to her parents, she was angry.

"Why would you say such a thing?" she said. "You want them to go away?"

"No," said Hans, holding up his hands. "Of course I don't. But I don't think it's safe for them here anymore. You've seen what's happened. What are they going to do – borrow money to repair the shops and have it happen again? Your father was already nearly blinded! I think they need to take a break until it's all over. I think they need to go somewhere safe."

Anja's anger turned to tears.

She took to her bed and stopped speaking to Hans.

It was the first time they had ever fallen out and Hans felt absolutely wretched.

He wanted to protect his beautiful wife, not upset her.

He offered her soup and tea, and purchased flowers from a flower seller on Stephensplatz.

He went to a store and bought a baby's smock and blanket, in the hope that it would cheer her up and show her that they had a future to look forward to, even if things had been hard lately.

The sight of the baby's things only seemed to upset Anja more.

She could not face the thought of her family leaving the city without her.

She knew Hans would never leave his father and why should he, seeing as he was not being targeted?

She could not go anywhere in her condition.

Vienna became a dark, hateful place.

* * *

"Hans, come dance with us!" cried Nola.

Hans was pulled from his thoughts by the sight of Nola jigging up and down.

The band had played a few numbers and the music had settled in his ears and despite himself his foot was tapping along, without him even knowing it.

"No, thank you," said Hans.

"Oh Hans, you're so boring!" said Nola.

Hans couldn't help but laugh.

Nola had a wild glint in her eye.

Otto, always braver than Max, made an approach to two girls who were standing nearby with their mugs of tea in their hands.

Hans watched them giggle and turn away.

Otto came back, looking dejected.

"Wouldn't speak to me," said Otto. "Do I smell?"

"Like an Austrian," said Max.

Otto grimaced.

"They are embarrassed in front of their friends," Hans said diplomatically. "On their own I am sure they would have spoken to you."

Still, wounded, Otto did not approach anyone else to try and speak to them.

Instead, the strange trio refreshed their cups, ate some sandwiches and chatted among themselves.

Growing tired, Hans decided that he would be better off calling it an early night.

He had tried.

He had come along, he had stayed for a while, he had enjoyed the music and now he was happy to go back to his little cottage.

"I think, boys, that's enough for me," said Hans.

"Oh, don't go," said Max. "Then there'll only be two of us."

Nola and Gisela had disappeared outside and come back in to dance with two young Irishmen.

As they whirled, Hans thought Gisela looked much happier to be dancing with a young man than dragged around the floor by an over-excited Nola.

It made him happy to see some colour in her cheeks and a smile on her face.

He felt a bit guilty leaving the perturbed Otto and Max to their own devices, but with his poor English and older presence he thought they might have better luck chatting to some locals without him.

He went outside and saw that the sun was beginning to set.

The sky was lit up red and gold.

There was a hum in the air, of insects and swooping birds, of the chatter of the dance goers.

Hans knew there was a pub if he walked the other way home.

He had never been to it but Fintan Walshe had spoken of Patton's and told him he'd take him there one evening.

Perhaps he was there this evening?

Hans took his time strolling through the village.

He felt calmer as he walked further away from the dance hall.

The last time he'd danced properly with anyone had been with Anja, at their wedding.

He realised now that seeing all the elated faces, the chatter, listening to the music, it was reminding him of that.

He could not stay.

He could not remember.

As he rounded the corner in the village which led down a hill past the post office and to the pub, two black police cars drove by at speed.

He waited and watched as another made its way, heaving up the hill.

Three police cars?

Where were they going?

It was an unusual sight.

Something must be badly wrong, somewhere.

He watched as they zoomed off into the distance towards another hill.

He had walked up that hill a few times and knew that there were only a few cottages and farmsteads up there.

He hoped there hadn't been an accident.

He walked on, when the noise of the motorcars had faded and the evening country peace was restored.

As he approached the pub, he debated internally what he should do.

How would be received when he walked in?

Would anyone speak to him at all?

Should he just walk on home and save himself the bother?

But something made him want to go in.

The call of a warm whiskey.

More than that, a man at peace with himself on a Saturday night.

It felt like the right thing to do.

He had the freedom, didn't he?

Making the decision in a split second, he crossed the road and opened the pub door.

He had to duck to go inside.

Every head in the place turned.

It was quiet, with just a few drinkers at the bar.

With as much confidence as he could muster Hans walked up to the bar and waited for the barman to acknowledge him.

"What can I do you for?" asked the grey-haired man behind the counter.

"A whiskey, please, anything Irish."

The barman turned round and Hans looked either side of him to find that every single man in the bar had stopped drinking and was staring at him.

He sat down on a high stool and nodded to each side of him, acknowledging those around him.

Immediately, they looked away and returned to their drinks.

"You're new in these parts," said the barman.

"Yes," said Hans. "Here only a short while. You will have to forgive me – my English is not that good."

"Arra," said the barman, "it's devil's tongue anyway."

Hans had absolutely no idea what the barman meant but felt that it was not an unkind thing he had said.

"Are you staying around here?" said the barman.

"Yes," said Hans, taking a sip of his whiskey and enjoying the smooth sail of it down his throat. "Up at Newtown House."

"Ah," said the barman. "Heard that all right. Working with Fintan Walshe?"

"Yes, that's right," said Hans, nodding. "Yes, I work with Fintan."

He was glad of the connection made.

"He'll be in later," said the barman.

A warmth went through Hans, with the landing of the whiskey to his stomach and also the knowledge that he could stay now and wait for Fintan.

He would not be alone; he would have somebody to speak with.

The barman was polite and asked Hans a little of his background but he didn't pry too much and Hans was happy to talk about the dance where he had just been.

They joked about leaving it to the young people.

As Hans was finishing his second whiskey and about to order a third, the door of the pub was flung open and a man in a flat cap dashed inside.

"*You won't believe it!*" the man announced to the bar.

Everyone stopped talking and turned around.

The young man was panting.

"*Seán McKee!*" said the man. "*The house has just been raided. They've taken him in.*"

The news rippled through the pub in small waves.

A few men stood up, joined the young man and left.

Hans looked around him helplessly.

The news had sent the other men into hushed huddles.

This was some sort of dramatic news.

Seeing his confusion, the barman leaned in to explain.

"A local man, he's been arrested," he said. "Taken in by the police."

"Ah," said Hans.

An arrest.

He understood now.

That must have been why he'd seen the police cars earlier.

"I saw the police motorcars," said Hans. "Before I came in. Three of them."

"Three of them?" said the barman and he whistled.

Hans looked quizzically at the barman.

Seeing his face, the barman bent down and said in a low voice, "Tell me Hans from Vienna, have you ever heard of the IRA?"

Gisela

CHAPTER TWENTY

There were lots of people on the Strand Road as Gisela, Nola, Mícheál and Peadar made their way down towards the beach.

Farmyard carts rolled incessantly by.

Cyclists on black bicycles rushed past, leaving a blast of soap in their wake.

"We better bring these cups back or there'll be an SOS out," said Mícheál as Nola kept them topped up with gin.

Despite the alcohol swirling in her stomach, which brought with it its own sense of bravery, Gisela had a terrible fear that they would be seen by Maeve or Fintan Walshe, or worse Mrs. de Freyne herself.

What if she drove by in her motorcar and saw Gisela and her charges strolling away from the dance hall with two young men?

How would it look?

Terrible.

Thrilling.

A bitter fire crept through her stomach.

The gin made her feel high.

Peadar fell into step with Gisela as Nola and Mícheál led the way.

"And where do you work?" asked Gisela.

She wasn't sure if Peadar was a farmer too, like Mícheál.

Peadar told her he worked the odd day in a bicycle shop in town, but that work was scarce.

Mostly he looked after the cottage and his mother, he said.

"Can fix a puncture in three minutes flat," said Mícheál, looking back towards them.

"Never mind punctures," cried Nola. "Can you shoe a horse?"

Gisela wondered if she was quite drunk.

Peadar was interested in Vienna and asked her questions about the city.

"I have a second cousin who knows the *charge d'affaires* in Belgium," he said. "I'd love to travel, you know, go and work in a foreign country. I wanted to stay in school. But I had to leave when my ma got sick, to mind her like. I applied for the Civil Service exams three times, but haven't ever been called. Ma says to keep trying. But I don't know. I think they have me on a blacklist."

Gisela wondered why Peadar, with his red cheeks and freckles, would be on a blacklist.

She felt quite sorry for him.

If he'd left school young, the Civil Service was unlikely to call him forward for exams.

Similarly, neither would any embassy or foreign affairs office take him on either.

His dream was not logical.

As they got to the pathway to the beach, the sun had begun to dip on the horizon.

It hung, fiery, onto the edge of the earth.

They found a place to sit on the sand, having walked through a shallow tributary stream that cut off one end of the beach from the other, shoes and socks in hand.

It felt private.

There wasn't a soul on the strand.

Nola and Mícheál held hands, digging their heels into the sand.

Despite their kiss earlier, Peadar sat apart from Gisela and stared ahead.

He was as shy as she was, thought Gisela.

She was unsure what he was thinking.

Did he like her?

Could he like her?

Did she like him?

Nola leaned into Mícheál, laughing.

Gisela wished she had her confidence and her ease of spirit.

All of this came easy to Nola: the carousing, the rule breaking, the laughter, holding onto Mícheál as if he was her husband for the past twenty years.

Gisela shifted in the sand, turning her legs away.

They were now down to the last of their gin.

Split four ways, it had dwindled fast.

Gisela's head felt funny, her insides woozy.

"You're settling in well anyway, Gisela," said Peadar.

He had an intensity to his eyes, thought Gisela.

It was a bit unnerving.

"Yes, I'm settling in okay," she said.

Was she though?

She still cried most nights, thinking about her parents and Rudy.

And after today's letter she'd felt as though her whole world had come tumbling down.

"It's nice to have a few new faces around the village," said Peadar.

"Yes," said Gisela.

"You're lucky to get here, you know. Very few are getting in, from what I'm hearing."

"Yes," said Gisela. Of course she knew. She had spent six months sorting her travel arrangements for Ireland. Her father had a path worn to the various embassies going back and forth with her paperwork.

"You can understand why," said Peadar. "They can't just open the borders, let whoever wants to flow in, you know."

Gisela looked down at the sand and scraped at a shell shaped like a tiny unicorn's horn.

"I think Herr Hitler has a lot of interesting things to say," said Peadar. "I can understand where he's coming from, you know, wanting to reunite Germany. It's the same here in Ireland, with the North."

Gisela looked out to sea.

She did not want to discuss politics.

Not now.

"See that boat of Jews that they wouldn't let dock in Cuba? You can understand that too. If they let all those refugees in, then there'd be ships flooding across the Atlantic. I mean it's sad for the refugees. But I can see it from the other side too."

The story of the boat carrying nearly a thousand Jewish refugees had been in the papers.

The passengers, most of them children, who had all been approved for visas before they left from Hamburg were refused entry when they got to Cuba. The boat sailed to Florida, then Canada before turning back for Europe.

What would happen to them now?

The same thing that happened to her parents?

Swept away on a train?

Gislea felt a fury forming where the gin swirled.

"Once you divide up a country, you'll always have trouble," said Peadar. "I'm not surprised the Germans are looking for reunification. The deal they got after the war was terrible."

The alcohol had loosened Peadar's mouth.

Up till now, Gisela had thought him gentle.

"I could have been on that boat," said Gisela.

"I thought you weren't a Jew?" said Peadar.

"I'm converted. But I still could have been on the boat. Anyone with Jewish blood is at risk."

"Ah, it's different with you," Peadar said.

"How is it?" said Gisela. "I am a refugee. Exactly like them."

"Ah, I didn't mean to upset you, Gisela."

"What are you rabbiting on about?" said Mícheál, calling over. "Politics again? Wouldn't Peadar make a fine politician, Gisela, don't ya think? Always up on his soapbox about something!"

Gisela got up and walked off.

She could not bear to look at Peadar after his diatribe.

She'd thought Mícheál and Peadar were lining up to be friends with her and Nola.

How could she ever be friends with someone who had that kind of thinking?

And she had kissed him!

Walking further up the beach, her arms folded, Gisela felt the gin buzz in her head.

This evening was supposed to be a night to forget things.

Instead, it had burned another big hole in her heart.

She would never be accepted no matter where she went. There would always be those who didn't understand and those who didn't want a foreigner like her in their country.

Without thinking, Gisela walked into the water and felt the cold seep to her knees.

She wanted it to cleanse her.

To wash Peadar's words away.

To wash Rudy's letter away.

To wash her own self away.

She wanted to be baptised as somebody new.

Somebody with no Jewish blood.

Behind her, Gisela could hear Nola talking down to Peadar.

"*What did you say to her?*" her voice carried on the wind.

Looking behind, Gisela watched as Nola got up and walked towards her, her arms folded, following the pockmarks Gisela had made in the sand.

"Are you all right?" she said, when she got to the water.

Gisela stood, looking out at the horizon.

"I'm fine," she said.

The tide was going out.

Each wave dipped a little further back, casting a dark shadow on the sand, leaving a grey foam in parts.

Nola dipped her foot in the water and showered Gisela in cold sea spray.

"*Nola!*" roared Gisela in annoyance.

Nola giggled and did it again.

Gisela bent down, plunged her arms into the water and tossed a huge wave of cold water into Nola's face.

"*Gisela!*" shouted Nola now.

She was soaked, her hair dripping. She was utterly unimpressed.

She backed out of the water and walked back over to the boys.

Mícheál and Peadar laughed out loud as she plonked herself in the sand and glared back at Gisela.

"Go for a swim, did ya?" said Mícheál.

Gisela turned back and stared out to sea, feeling the cold water swirl around her shins and knees.

She felt overwhelmingly annoyed.

Angry to her core.

The gin had done something to her.

Awakened feelings she'd pushed deep, deep down.

Today's letter was like a cannonball to the stomach.

Maybe she should try to go home?

Follow after her parents, find out somehow where they'd been taken.

It would be better to be with them wherever they were, than here, alone.

She should never have gone to the dance in the first place.

What was she thinking?

She splashed out of the sea and began walking up the beach to go home.

"*Where you going?*" shouted Mícheál.

She ignored him.

She could be back at Newtown in half an hour.

Curled into her peat-smelling bed.

Alone with her thoughts and prayers for her parents.

She would write a letter back to Rudy, tell him that they must, *must* find a way to contact her parents.

She would talk to Mrs. de Freyne perhaps, again.

Surely she knew a charity or a politician, or somebody who could find out where the new cities were being built in the east for those being sent away?

She would not let herself think about the darkest thoughts that gurgled, waiting, somewhere deep inside.

That the cities were a ruse.

That their parents, like others, had been sent to a camp.

"*Come back, Gisela!*" roared Mícheál, but his voice faded as she walked on.

Let them, thought Gisela.

Let them have their fun with Nola and enjoy the last of their gin.

She had tried.

She had tried to be a good chaperone, but it was an impossible job.

With her head down, Gisela barely noticed the drone that echoed on the wind in the distance.

As she looked at the sand and heard her feet *crunch, crunch, crunch*, on the piled shells thrown up by the tide, it took her a moment to recognise that something had changed.

When she did look up, she saw something silver in the sky.

Squinting as the object seemed to dive and turn, she gasped.

An aeroplane!

How unusual!

An aeroplane, here?

Gisela looked back to see if the others had spotted it.

Nola was wringing out her hair, sulking.

"*Look!*" cried Gisela.

She ran back towards them.

"*Look!*"

They all turned to where Gisela was pointing and watched motionless as the little silver bird approached, growing bigger and bigger as it came near.

The front part of the plane was coloured yellow.

It zoomed right over their heads and they strained their necks backwards as it passed over.

"*Woah!*" shouted Nola.

They all watched as the plane made its way up the beach and neared the mouth of the river.

"*Mein Gott!*" said Gisela loudly as something emerged from the plane.

It fell and billowed into a white parachute.

A man!

A man with a parachute!

He floated majestically towards the ground, slowly, as the white billowing material caught the wind.

The plane carried on further before making a turn back towards the sea and disappearing into the distance.

Peadar's mouth was open.

"*Holy Jesus!*" said Mícheál.

They all looked at each other before breaking into a run, four pairs of feet digging into the sand as they raced towards the dunes where the parachute looked to have landed.

They sprinted until they were forced to stop to catch their breaths.

"I didn't think it was so far," panted Nola.

The hilly dunes stretched on and on up to the mouth of the river.

From back at their spot on the beach, it hadn't seemed such a distance.

It was hard to make their way through the dunes at speed. They were pitted with ankle-breaking holes and rough scratchy grass.

After Nola fell, twice, they stopped for a moment to survey the land.

Beyond the dunes was a flatter area leading down to the river bank at the mouth of the sea.

"*There!*" cried Nola.

They all looked to where she was pointing and there, sure enough, was a glimmer of white.

They all ran quickly towards it and as they approached the glimmer turned into a large doughy mass.

The parachute lay, spread out like a big, thick pancake.

Mícheál reached it first.

He lifted the edges, searching for the man.

Gisela felt her head thump from the gin as she too reached the parachute.

Why had she drunk so much?

Why had she been so silly?

"Where is he?" said Peadar.

They all ran their hands around the edges of the material, lifting it to see if the man could be under it, hidden.

The wind sent ripples across its surface.

It was much rougher to the touch than Gisela expected.

Thick string curled near to where Mícheál was standing.

He picked it up and followed it to a set of straps.

He held them up.

Empty.

"*Hello!*" Nola called out. "*Hello!*"

The only sound to be heard was the flap of the parachute in the wind.

"Do you think he's armed?" said Peadar.

"There's an army base in Gormanstown," said Mícheál. "That's not far from here."

"Maybe he flew from America," said Nola.

The boys snorted.

"America?" said Mícheál. "In that piddling plane?"

"What do you think, Gisela?" Peadar asked.

"I don't know," she said.

She did not want to tell them what she really thought.

That across the skies in Vienna she had seen similar planes.

Silver and malevolent.

The sun had slipped away now and it was hard to make anything out in the distance.

A fog was moving in from the sea, up the river.

They walked away from the parachute and made their way to the banks of the river where there was a rocky drop below.

The tide was out, exposing seaweed and fishing debris – scattered nets, a broken lobster pot.

"He can't have come this far," said Peadar.

They walked along the bank, which sloped down onto the shore.

"I hope he's not lying horribly injured somewhere," said Nola.

"He didn't seem to come down hard," said Mícheál.

"Look!" said Gisela. "What's that?"

Her voice was a whisper.

They all strained and squinted their eyes in the dusk.

Against the bank, tucked in against a grassy overhang was a man.

He sat, his bottom on gravelly stones, his legs at an angle.

"Oh my God," said Nola.

"Maybe we should leave him?" said Gisela. "He could be dangerous."

But they all moved forward and crouched down.

"*Hello there!*" Nola shrilled.

She sprang up like an African deer and moved towards the man, dashing down the bank towards him.

"*For God's sake!*" said Mícheál.

"*Are you all right?*" Nola yelled. "*Yoohoo!*"

Mícheál and Peadar jumped up and followed her.

Gisela lagged behind.

The man was looking up.

Stones dislodged as Nola stumbled down towards him.

Gisela smelled the tidal water now, raw.

The man was in uniform: grey wool, black lapels.

"Where are you from?" Nola asked, loudly, clearly, as though speaking to a child.

The man attempted to sit up and pointed to his leg.

Gisela reached the group and stared in the twilight at the man's uniform.

"Do you know where you are?" said Nola.

"What is name of this place?" asked the man. He smiled, disarmingly. His accent was heavy. German.

"Well, this is Baltray," said Nola. "Bal – Tray. Where are you trying to get to?"

The man pointed at his leg and groaned.

"I've hurt my leg," he said.

He began rooting in his pocket and took out a piece of paper.

Peader nudged Mícheál.

"That leg looks broken to me," he whispered.

Gisela stepped forward.

She studied the uniform closely and then, taking them all by surprise, said, "*Was machst du hier?*"

Her voice was gravelly.

Taken aback, the solider turned to look at Gisela and smiled.

"*Ah,*" he said. "*Deutsch.*"

"*Nach wem suchst du?*" said Gisela.

"*Ein Freund,*" said the solider.

"*Nein,*" she said.

He smiled again.

"Are you Austrian?" asked Nola, looking between them.

"He's German," said Gisela. "A German solider."

"Who are you looking for?" said Peadar. "Have you a name of someone?"

The man beckoned for Peadar to come over and carefully showed him the piece of paper.

Peadar took a step back.

He nudged Mícheál.

"Your da," he said. "Your da's name is on this paper. And your address."

Mícheál stared at Peadar then at the solider.

"Right," said Peadar, turning to the girls. "You leave this to us now, girls. We'll take over here."

"What?" said Nola.

"Run along home."

"We will not!" said Nola, incredulously.

"It's best if you do," said Mícheál.

He turned his back on her and folded his arms.

Nola protested.

"*No way, we found him too!*"

The soldier took a cigarette out of a silver case and lit it.

He pulled on it deeply, trying to ease his pain.

"You should call the police," said Gisela firmly.

"We won't be doing that," said Peadar.

He grabbed Nola by the arm and pushed her along.

"Go on home. I won't say it again."

Nola stumbled and rubbed her arm where Peadar had gripped her.

"*Peadar!*" she said again in protest.

"Come on," said Gisela to Nola. "We are not wanted here."

"What are you going to do with him?" asked Nola. "How are you going to move him if his leg is broken?"

"That's none of your concern," said Peadar.

Gisela turned and began to climb the river bank up onto the dune.

Reluctantly, Nola followed her.

"*And girls!*" cried Peadar as they walked away. "*Not a word to anyone about this. If I hear you've been talking...*"

He pointed his finger at them, then tapped his head.

A threat.

Of what?

Gisela was not sure.

As they walked back up the dunes in the dark, so difficult to see now that the sun had gone completely, Nola and Gisela were forced to hold onto each other, for fear of falling.

"Why are they helping him?" said Gisela. "Do they not know he is a Nazi soldier?"

"He's here to meet Seán McKee," said Nola knowingly.

Gisela looked at Nola in the dark in puzzlement.

"Have you ever heard of the IRA?" said Nola.

Gisela shrugged again.

"The Irish Republican Army? If that German solider wants to meet him then it's something to do with that. Something army-related."

"Germany and Ireland? Together?" asked Gisela.

"*Yup*," said Nola.

"*My God!*"

Was nowhere safe?

Hans

CHAPTER TWENTY-ONE

Hans was glad he stayed in Patton's pub.

Fintan Walshe arrived in, took off his cap and clapped Hans on the back when he saw him.

"Ah, look what the cat dragged in!"

Hans didn't understand the phrase but knew it was said in jest.

Now, he would not be alone at the bar.

Now he had, what some might call, a friend.

Fintan was red-cheeked and said he'd been out walking.

"Did you hear about the commotion?" he said.

Hans nodded.

"Sorry state of affairs," said Fintan.

Hans had seen many people arrested in Vienna, always Jews, always he knew for a minor offence, if any offence at all.

He suspected here in Ireland it was not like that.

The man must have done something wrong.

"What will happen to the man they arrested? Do you know him?"

"Ah, sure everyone knows Seán McKee," said Fintan. "Everyone."

Hans waited for Fintan to say more.

He didn't.

"So do you like our little pub here?" said Fintan, looking around as the barman approached.

Hans smiled.

"They have not thrown me out yet."

"You wouldn't do that, would you, Mac?" said Fintan to the barman.

"Not to a friend of yours," said Mac the barman.

Fintan ordered a pint of stout and looked around him again.

"Ah, you'll be alright here," said Fintan.

Would he, though, wondered Hans.

He hadn't felt very welcome when he walked into the bar.

He knew by the eyes that glared that he was looked upon suspiciously.

Maybe it was just that Fintan himself felt so comfortable here that he couldn't feel what Hans felt.

"You're doing well on the farm anyway," said Fintan, taking a big slurp of his pint when it arrived.

Hans nodded.

"You'll be taking over from me soon!"

"I am learning a lot. I like it here, very much," said Hans.

"Ah 'tis a nice holding she has there, Lady de Freyne. I'd do anything to help improve that farm for that woman. You know, she's the closest thing we have to a saint around here."

Hans raised his eyebrows quizzically.

"Always doing good. See those cottages just outside the boundary gates – she built them for families who needed them. She gave a sports field to the parish too. And she took you lot in, didn't she?"

Hans smiled, as was expected of him.

"As for the daughter …" Fintan leaned in closer to Hans and narrowed his eyebrows. "Nothing like the mother. Nothing. Wayward. Must take after the father. Never knew the father, you see, so no discipline."

"What happened to Mr. de Freyne?" asked Hans.

"Ah, sad story. He died out in Burma. They were living out there – he had a job with the army you see. And sure, Nola was born and two days later Mr. de Freyne was dead from cholera. And poor Mrs. de Freyne had to take the child home all by herself. But she grew up then without him, the father – and I think that's why she's half wild."

Hans thought about Nola.

She was forward and confident, yes, but was she wild?

He thought perhaps Fintan was being a little unfair.

Nola was fun.

She might even be good for Gisela, he thought, taking her out of her shell a little.

"That must have been very difficult for Mrs. de Freyne," said Hans.

"Ah sure," said Fintan, "we all have our crosses to bear."

Hans was at the bottom of his whiskey.

Fintan leaned in again.

"Now, she wouldn't have much time for Seán McKee. Oh no. No, no. Sworn enemies. You see, Lady de Freyne is English. And well, Mr. McKee would see her now as the ruling class and he wouldn't like that."

Hans looked a bit confused.

"It was a long time ago, years ago now, after she first arrived. He had a bit of a campaign against her. He didn't want her here at all. He felt that the house and farm should have gone to an Irish farmer, certainly not an English woman with no farming blood in her. And a widow at that!"

Fintan laughed and took another slurp of his pint.

Mac the barman came over to offer Hans another whiskey and Hans nodded.

He was glad he had left the dance and come to the pub instead.

He was starting to enjoy himself, although he should probably slow down, he mused.

"Isn't that right, Mac?" said Fintan. "Lady de Freyne and Seán McKee wouldn't exactly see eye to eye."

"Ah," said Mac, flicking his head upwards, "sure, that fella. He has a few enemies all right."

"He tried to stop people working for her," said Fintan. "Made out that whoever went to work for her was a traitor. Well, I'm no traitor, and I went to work for her and Maeve McGorry too and she's as nationalist as they come."

Hans nodded, not really fully understanding.

"And when she started doing good then, Lady de Freyne, when people saw what she could bring to the parish, because she's a big employer, you see, and she was planting trees and building cottages and then she started her Garden Fêtes and the whole parish could go and, well, he didn't like that at all. And at the first Garden Fête – you remember this, Mac – during the dancing that evening, Lady de Freyne's car went up in flames. And rumour was that Seán McKee did it."

"Ah, Fintan," said the barman, "you can't be saying things you can't prove."

"Well, everyone knows," said Fintan. "The dogs on the street."

"Fintan doesn't like Seán McKee," said the barman diplomatically to Hans.

"Not many people do," said Fintan, lowering his voice. "I've always said it; I think he's dangerous. But I can't be talking out loud – that's between you, me and ourselves."

"Not very dangerous now that he's locked up," said the barman.

"Aye," said Fintan. "Do you think they have him in Drogheda or took him to Dublin?"

The barman shrugged.

"I'm not the man to know that," he said and he nodded towards a large burly man who had just walked into the pub.

Hans turned and saw the man in his navy policeman uniform.

Immediately he recognised him as the man who had taken his passport when he signed on for his alien status in the police station.

"Ah, Sergeant McKiernan," said Fintan.

The policeman nodded and sat down at the bar.

He ordered a stout, the same kind that Fintan was drinking.

"Evening, fellas," he said, nodding to Hans and Fintan.

Suddenly, Hans felt uncomfortable.

As if he was doing something inappropriate.

"Busy night," said Fintan.

"You could say that," said Sergeant McKiernan.

"All quiet now?" said Fintan.

"Aye, all quiet now," said Sergeant McKiernan. "Detectives taken him up to Dublin. Straight to Mountjoy."

"Must be serious."

"Mountjoy," said Fintan to Hans. "The prison in Dublin."

The three sat in an awkward silence.

"I went to the dance in the hall," said Hans, as though he were confessing his sins.

"Oh?" said Sergeant McKiernan.

"Too many young people so I came here."

At this, the two men laughed.

"Sure, you're in the right place then," said Sergeant McKiernan.

Hans drained his whiskey and, with the arrival of the policeman, found his thirst had gone off him.

"I will be getting back now," he said.

"Ah, so early?" said Fintan.

Hans nodded.

"I won't be staying long myself," said Fintan.

Hans nodded goodbye to both men and left them at the bar.

As he walked through the pub, men in huddles stopped talking and stared at him.

There it was again.

The uncomfortable feeling.

The feeling of being watched.

The feeling of being other.

As he left the pub, turning over the bridge to head for Newtown House, Hans knew that this evening had been a big step forward.

It had been nice to sit in the bar and talk to Fintan and the barman.

It had been nice to be apart from the other Austrians, making his own way in the village.

Yes, he was other.

But one day, one day in the future, he might belong.

Gisela

CHAPTER TWENTY-TWO

All night Gisela dreamed of her parents, locked into the carriage of a train, unable to escape, unable to breathe.

She awoke at one point and was full sure she saw her mother standing at the end of her bed.

Her mother simply stared at her, not saying a word, not even smiling or being her kind self.

It was most unsettling.

The thing was it didn't even feel like a dream.

It felt like her mother was really there.

When the morning came round, Gisela was tired but could sleep no more.

Her head ached.

Was it a hangover?

It was certainly the worst she'd felt in a long time, as though she had the makings of a flu.

At the breakfast table she was surprised to find Nola was already up and in a cheerful mood.

She didn't look tired at all.

She looked alive.

Gisela watched her butter her toast, putting big dollops of it onto the bread and crushing it with her knife.

Gisela's stomach was queasy.

"Where do you think they brought him?" Nola whispered.

Gisela shook her head.

How would she know where they would bring a parachuting Nazi soldier?

She didn't know this land, its hiding places.

"I'd say they'd a terrible job moving him anywhere. I don't think he could walk. You know, they might need you. To translate." She raised her eyebrows as she munched.

Gisela snorted.

There was no way she would translate for that man.

Mrs. de Freyne opened the dining-room door and joined them at the breakfast table.

"Ladies," she said, "you're looking very fresh this morning. Did you have a good night?"

"Yes, we had lots of fun, Mummy. Didn't we, Gisela?" said Nola.

Gisela nodded and spooned muesli into her mouth.

She certainly didn't feel fresh this morning.

Her muesli tasted like sandpaper.

It caught in her throat and she choked and coughed and had to lunge for the orange juice Maeve had poured.

"Rather different from the ballrooms in Vienna, I expect?" said Mrs. de Freyne kindly to Gisela.

She nodded, her eyes red and streaming.

"We did a bit of set dancing," said Nola. "Gisela was actually rather good."

"Well, there you go now," says Mrs. de Freyne. "A natural."

After breakfast, Gisela would tell Nola what she had decided.

That they must report the parachutist to the police.

The solider was there illegally.

He needed to be reported.

Maeve came into the dining room carrying a rack of boiled eggs and fresh toast.

"Did you hear the news?" she said as she put the food into the centre of the table.

Nola and Gisela waited.

So, the new was out.

The parachutist had been discovered; Gisela wouldn't need to report the soldier's arrival at all.

"Seán McKee was arrested last night," said Maeve. "Taken away by three squad cars!"

"Arrested?" said Mrs. de Freyne. "Whatever for?"

"The Guards raided the house when the dance was on. Looking for arms – you know, that big theft up in Phoenix Park? I heard Mrs. McKee is in an awful state with the fright of it all. He put up a bit of a fight. They pulled the whole place apart."

She picked up two empty plates and held them in front of her.

"I'd say Mícheál got some shock when he went home. He was at the dance, I heard. But when they went down to the parish hall to get him after it all happening, he was nowhere to be found."

Nola squirmed and looked at Gisela.

"Never a dull moment around here," said Mrs. de Freyne.

"Anyway, it'll probably be in the paper," said Maeve as she left the dining room.

Gisela watched Mrs. de Freyne chewing her toast.

Her brow was furrowed.

Thinking.

Snapping out of her daydream, Mrs. de Freye smiled at her.

"Now, what are you two ladies planning for today?"

"Nothing, Mummy," said Nola. "Maybe a walk?"

Her voice sounded like that of a little girl's.

Innocent.

"Well, there's a bit of work to do ahead of next week's fête. It'll be all hands on deck. Mrs. Carmody will be here on Monday for a meeting. So make sure you're available for that."

"We will," said Nola.

They got up to leave the table.

Outside the dining room, Nola spoke in hushed, excited tones.

"Do you think they arrested Seán McKee because of the solider?"

Gisela blinked and shook her head.

How would she know?

"I can't believe it," said Nola. "We have to find out what happened. We should call to Peadar, find out what's going on."

"I'd prefer not to be involved," said Gisela quietly.

"Gisela," whispered Nola, "this is so exciting. Can't you see? He must be a spy! And the Guards arresting Old McKee. It's like a … a novel!"

Gisela folded her arms.

"Oh, I know, I know. He's a German soldier and all that. I understand. But it's still exciting. Now whatever you do, don't tell the others. It's a secret. Our secret, okay?"

Gisela grimaced.

She wouldn't be bothering the Hettingers or Hans with this news.

They had enough to be worrying about.

They had travelled right across Europe to escape the Nazi party and its politics.

She wasn't about to shatter that peace again.

* * *

Reluctantly Gisela accompanied Nola up the road after breakfast in search of Peadar and Mícheál.

The air was warm and pungent.

It was going to a fine July day.

"You know Mummy and Seán McKee are old sworn enemies," said Nola, as they walked past the church and into the bend in the road before the river. "He's never accepted her here, because she's English. And he's jealous of the holding we have. And the house."

Nola had, with great aplomb last night, explained to Gisela in detail all about the IRA, who she said were a secret army who wanted to rejoin the twenty-six counties of southern Ireland with the six counties of Northern Ireland, which had been separated in 1921, when Ireland for the first time became a Free State and out from under the rule of Great Britain.

Nola spoke to Gisela as if she would have no idea what all that would be like, considering she was a foreigner.

It didn't seem to register with Nola that Gisela had seen her own home country of Austria annexed only last year. That she too knew what the politics of partition looked like.

Even though the IRA had gone underground, Nola explained, there were families who were staunchly loyal to the cause.

Maeve was a supporter.

Mícheál's family were very involved.

His father, Seán McKee, was high up in the organisation but everything was a rumour and no one knew for sure what his role was, only that he was an important man.

Gisela remembered how he'd stood on the beach watching them that time and the expression on his face when they'd passed in the pony and trap.

"There's been these bombs all through England and they say it's the IRA. That's how they operate. They try to bomb the British Government into giving back Northern Ireland. If that solider wanted to see Seán McKee then it's definitely a secret mission!"

Gisela thought of the planes circling over Danzig.

If the IRA were looking for army supplies from Germany, then they were probably barking up the right tree. She thought of the massive guns she'd seen on her trip across the continent and the tiny useless sandbags in their wake.

Peader's cottage was situated on a small piece of scrubland on a narrow lane leading off the crossroads in the village.

Nola rapped on the door.

It rattled as though it might fall in.

It was almost completely bare of paint, stripped off flake by flake by the wind and rain.

It took an age but eventually the door opened and a tiny grey-haired woman peeped out.

The hand that clutched the door was gnarled and dirty.

"He's not here," she said gruffly and tried to close the door.

"It's me, Mrs. Tracy," said Nola. "Nola de Freyne, from Newtown House."

"Newtown?"

Mrs. Tracy opened the door a bit wider and stared at Nola.

Gisela thought the woman must be quite blind. She was not old, but she looked neglected, as if she were not able to look after herself.

"And how is your mother?" she croaked. Her voice was weak, caught up in her throat.

"She's doing well. Getting ready for the Garden Fête next week."

"Ah yes," said Mrs. Tracy. "She'll be busy all right. Tell her I said thank you for the coffee she sent up a few weeks ago. Much appreciated. I still have a bit left."

"Do you know where Peadar might be at all, Mrs. Tracy?" said Nola.

"I'd say he's up at McKees'. There was a bit of trouble I heard last night."

"Oh?" said Nola, playing dumb.

"I wouldn't know much about that now. You'd have to ask Peadar. That's his business. I don't be paying much heed to all that now."

"Much heed to what, Mrs. Tracy?" said Nola.

"All that politics business. Always running around with those army men. I told him no good would come of it. It didn't do his father any good and it won't do him any good."

She was getting wound up.

Gisela thought that Nola should stop asking questions of the woman, because it didn't seem right.

"I didn't know he was into politics," said Nola, innocently.

"Well, you can call it politics. Republicanism. I understand the fight. I do. But I don't see why they have to be violent. I've no time for it so I haven't."

"No," said Nola, shaking her head.

"Would you like to come in for a cup of tea?" said Mrs. Tracy.

She pulled the door back and inside Gisela could see a bare mud floor and a table propped up on a tin bucket.

A tiny fire glowed in the grate.

A smell like sour milk hit her.

"Ah no, we were just looking for Peadar," said Nola. "Sure, we'll head off, see can we find him. Thank you, Mrs. Tracy."

"Suit yourself," said Mrs. Tracy and she closed the door with a click.

Nola looked at Gisela.

Gisela stared back.

"Will we brave it, do you think?" said Nola.

"Brave what?"

"The McKees, to see what's going on?"

"I'd really prefer not to," said Gisela.

What if the solider was about?

What if that was where they had put him?

"Ah c'mon," said Nola. "How exciting is this?"

* * *

There was a lot of traffic on the road up to the McKees' house: men on black bicycles, women hurrying, shawls pulled tight across their heads.

The last time Gisela had visited the McKees' house, the day of the periwinkle feast, the road had been much quieter.

"Christ, it's like a funeral!" said Nola as they neared the house.

A crowd of men and women stood outside in the yard.

"Excuse me!" said Nola loudly, as she pushed a pathway through.

Gisela felt eyes shift to them as they made their way to the open door and into the kitchen of the house.

Nola might have been fearless but Gisela certainly didn't feel comfortable.

Inside, it did feel like somebody had died.

The atmosphere was sombre and hushed.

Men and women sat at the table and in the armchairs at the great open fire.

Others stood with their backs against cupboards and the sink.

Voices murmured.

Gisela felt her eyes adjust to the light.

On the table were plates of brown-bread sandwiches, jam, butter and scones.

There was a smell of brewing, stewed tea, the same as at the village dance.

More eyes turned to them.

A woman at the end of the table was having her arm rubbed by another woman.

That must have been Mrs. McKee, thought Gisela.

Nola had already made her way through the kitchen, round the table and was standing at the back of the room in front of a sideboard.

Mícheál stood, tall, white-faced, against the dresser.

Gisela followed on tip-toe, excusing herself as she almost fell over the feet of an elderly, grumpy-looking woman.

"Are you all right?" Nola asked Mícheál in a low voice.

Mícheál, who had his arms folded, gave the tiniest flick of his head.

"We came to see about ..." said Nola, her voice trailing off.

Mícheál flicked his head again, pushed away from the dresser and walked out into a back hall.

The two girls followed him.

The back hall was bright, lit by the open back door.

They advanced out into the daylight again.

Behind the house was another yard with small outhouses.

A grassy field stretched beyond the house rising into a hill, where cows munched busily on the summer grass.

A large grey barn stood domineering in the background.

From the road, the farm didn't look as large as it really was.

A group of men stood in the yard in a tight, closed-off circle.

Gisela recognised Peadar, his back to them, small and slight among the older, heavier set men.

"*Peadar!*" called Mícheál.

Peadar turned to look.

His expression did not change, but he left the group and joined them.

They all walked towards the big green field.

Gisela was baffled by what was going on.

Were all these people here just because Seán McKee had been arrested?

Or was it something to do with the parachutist?

When they were a good distance from the house, Peadar and Mícheál stopped and turned.

"What do ye girls want?" said Peadar, matter-of-factly.

Gisela side-stepped a large, crusty cow pat that she had almost plunged into.

"We wanted to know if everything was all right," said Nola.

"Clearly, it isn't," said Peadar.

He had a horrible edge to his voice, thought Gisela. It was unsettling.

"Did they find him?" asked Nola.

"Find who?" said Peadar.

"Well, who do you think? The parachutist!"

Peadar looked off into the distance then back to Nola.

After a pause he said, "You'd be better off running on home now, girls. Leave all this to us."

"Do you think we're complete idiots?" said Nola.

Gisela watched her pull her shoulders up to make herself taller.

She was at a disadvantage standing downwards on the hill.

Peadar stepped forward.

"I think that none of this is your business and you should keep your posh tits out of this."

Nola didn't move. "I think this is every bit of our business seeing as we were there when he came down. I wonder what the Guards would think if we told them what we know?"

A flash of something crossed Peadar's face.

Gisela feared he might lash out and throttle Nola.

Mícheál stepped forward and tipped Peadar on the arm.

"They just want to know, Peadar," he said.

Peadar unclenched his fists.

"It's like this, girls," said Mícheál. "There's stuff going on here way beyond your level, right? Serious stuff. Political stuff. You know my da was arrested. It's serious. We can't talk to you about the solider. We just can't. We know you were there. But you can't tell anyone what you saw. All right? You just can't."

"Was the soldier arrested too?" asked Nola, still staring Peadar dead in the eye.

"No, he wasn't," says Mícheál. "But that's all I'm going to say about it, right? Now you need to go off home. You shouldn't be here. This whole place is under surveillance. We are all under surveillance."

"Are *we* under surveillance?" asked Gisela.

She hoped this wouldn't affect her alien status.

The last thing she needed was to have her visa revoked.

"That's why we want you to fuck off," said Peadar. "For your own good."

Nola and Peadar stared for another age before she said, "You think you know it all, Peadar Tracy."

With that, she turned and stalked off and Gisela was forced to run to follow her.

"Stuff Peadar Tracy. I can't stand him," said Nola. "Did you see the way he looked at us? Like we were dirt on his shoe?"

Nola led her to a side gate in the field which they climbed over, thereby avoiding the funeral-like crowd in the front yard.

"They must have him hidden somewhere," said Nola. "But I wonder where?"

G2 INTELLIGENCE REPORT

STATUS: INFORMATION
LOCATION: MOUNTJOY PRISON, DUBLIN

Seán McKee refuses to co-operate.

He denies any knowledge of Phoenix Park arms theft and refuses to give the names of IRA counterparts.

To appear at Smithfield District Court on Monday.

Prisoner has accepted meals and beverages and requested a solicitor.

Mr. Ignatius Tully, a solicitor well known to represent members of the IRA met with Mr. McKee this afternoon.

A number of requests for visitation have been made from the family of Mr. McKee, particularly his son Mícheál.

All have been denied.

Hans

CHAPTER TWENTY-THREE

With the parish dance on Friday and the Garden Fête happening the following weekend, Mrs. de Freyne had not accepted any social invitations for her or Nola on Saturday night.

Instead, she invited everyone to the house for some drinks and a cold supper.

Hans found he was quite looking forward to an evening of relaxation with the Hettingers, Gisela and Nola – and Maeve who would only have light duties to attend to.

He hoped Fintan Walshe would attend too.

Maeve had prepared a buffet of sandwiches, cocktail sausages, tarts and bread.

Nola, aided by Gisela, made a great fuss of carrying it all from the kitchen and setting it up in the dining room. She was flustered and blew a piece of hair up past her forehead, repeatedly.

By the time the food was laid out, Hans watched as Nola poured herself a large glass of wine. They sat around the dining-room table to eat.

"Oh, do have a drink," said Nola to Gisela, who was pouring herself a glass of apple juice. "Please don't leave me to be the only nonny drinking."

Gisela shook her head and refused the glass of wine.

Hans noticed how much it bothered Nola.

Hans poured a large bottle of beer into a glass and raised it to Nola. She held up her glass and smiled back.

She really was quite a beauty, thought Hans. A dangerous beauty. He sensed trouble for her ahead.

Fintan's words repeated in his mind. That she was *wild*.

They moved into the drawing room where a small fire had been lit, despite the summer weather, and it added to the warm glow of the room.

Candles flickered in candelabras and the gas lights had been turned low.

Fintan Walshe arrived into the room in his jacket and cap, accompanied by Father Crowley.

They nodded to everyone as a flurry of greetings rang out.

After a while, Mrs. de Freyne asked if anyone would play a song on the piano.

Eva Hettinger urged Hans forward.

"*Hans, Hans, you!*" she said.

Feeling a flush burning through his cheeks, Hans stood up and walked over to the piano.

He sat down and pulled his trouser legs up.

His knees knocked against the underside of the piano and he had to sit at an angle to fit under it.

A hush fell on the room.

Trying to think of a song, Hans let his fingers find the keys.

And there it was.

A fun number he knew Anja loved.

He was not an accomplished player – he was nothing like Anja who had the grace and skill of a concert pianist, even though her main instrument was the oboe.

At first his voice was low and faltering.

"Ah!" Eva clapped as she heard the opening of the song.

"*Ist dein kleines Herz für mich noch frei, Baby,*" sang Hans.

Gisela leaned over to Nola.

"You might know it in English as 'I Can't Give You Anything but Love, Baby'," she whispered.

As Hans played he grew in confidence and added power to his voice.

He closed his eyes and there was Anja, as though she were right beside him, smiling and singing along.

Oh, how powerful music was!

He felt tears threaten and had to squeeze his eyes tight and concentrate on the keys and the next line of the song.

When he finished, there was a moment of quiet pause before a burst of applause rang out.

"*Bravo!*" cried Mrs. de Freyne.

Hans opened his eyes and saw that Mrs. de Freyne and Eva Hettinger's eyes were glistening.

Were they tears?

Or the smoky room?

"Oh, do give us another, Hans!" said Mrs. de Freyne.

This time Hans broke into an upbeat march, a German folk song, to which all the Austrians sang along.

Nola made a dreadful bleating attempt at the German lyrics, which made everyone laugh.

As Hans rose to walk away from the piano, he got a standing ovation.

He smiled, bashful.

Fritz Hettinger sang next and, although he was not as good a baritone as Hans was, he paused and winked comically and made the song fun.

"Go on, Gisela, just one tune," said Nola, when Fritz was finished playing.

Hans watched as Nola forcefully pushed her companion towards the piano.

Gisela looked back at the sea of smiling, encouraging faces.

She closed her eyes for a moment and cleared her throat.

"Hand me that wine," she said, opening her eyes dramatically and gesturing for a glass.

"*I've trained her well!*" Nola yelled.

Everyone laughed.

Gisela closed her eyes and, like Hans, her fingers found the keys, softly, naturally.

Debussy.

She played the piece beautifully and it drew tears from her audience.

"You heartbreaker," said Nola, her voice a croak, amid the applause.

"I used to play it at home," said Gisela, her voice quiet. "Rudy accompanied me on the violin. It was funny, you see, because he is the pianist."

"You play beautifully," said Mrs. de Freyne.

After a pause, Father Crowley asked if anyone knew any Irish tunes.

A babble echoed around the room.

Fintan stood up from his seat, one hand by his side, the other planted firmly on his heart.

He closed his eyes and began a mournful ballad.

Hans didn't understand the words.

He wondered if his grasp of English was slipping away with each sip of beer.

"He's singing in Gaelic," Nola whispered, sensing Hans' confusion.

Ah.

So, no wonder he couldn't understand.

Fintan Walshe seemed to disappear into another place when he sang.

The concentration on his face was intense and mournful.

When he finished he got a big round of applause.

Hans looked across to Maeve and saw that she was frowning, as if she'd been upset by the song.

Nola filled her glass with wine again.

Hans saw Mrs. de Freyne watching her from across the room.

When Nola went outside with Eva, to escape the fug of the room which had grown rather hot, Fintan sat down beside Gisela.

Hans overheard him questioning her about Vienna, about her family, about her brother.

"And what are your plans, long term?" asked Father Crowley who had moved into a seat beside Hans.

"I'm sorry?" said Hans.

"Your plans, for the future," said Father Crowley. "Are you looking for a wife?" The priest smiled, then laughed.

A stab like pain bounced through Hans and he shook his head.

"Ah," said Father Crowley, "a man who likes to keep himself to himself, I understand."

"And will you go back to Germany?" Hans overheard Fintan asking Gisela.

Gisela's face registered something that Hans couldn't quite make out.

She suddenly stood up and rushed from the room.

She had looked as though she were about to cry.

"Well, I will stay here and see what happens for me," said Hans.

"Yes," said the priest. "Yes. You might meet a nice young Irishwoman. But the city offers much more opportunity for a fellow like yourself, perhaps?"

Was it rid of him he wanted, thought Hans? He had come to be a farm worker. What good was a farm worker in the city?

Hans watched as Fintan made his way over to Maeve now, making a joke as he sat down beside her.

Maeve turned her head away, looking uncomfortable.

Hans was fascinated.

What sort of the relationship did the two have?

Did they have a past?

Did they have feelings for each other?

"I quite like the country," said Hans to Father Crowley.

"Yes, but does the country like you?" said the priest.

Han looked at him.

What a strange thing to say!

"I hope so," he said to the priest, who wore a smirk on his face. "I would like to think yes."

The priest nodded and laughed.

They both turned to look at Nola who had come back in now and was climbing onto a chair while holding a full wine glass and asking the room to hush, because she had something she wanted to say.

"*Nola*," said Mrs. de Freyne, loudly. "*Please get down.*"

"*A toast!*" said Nola.

Hans heard the hiss in her voice.

She was quite drunk, it seemed – the wine had gone to her head.

Nola looked around.

"Where's Gisela?" she said.

"*Nola ...*" growled her mother.

"*For our Austrian friends!*" Nola shouted and she held her glass high.

Hans watched droplets fly from the glass onto the wool rug below.

"*Who have come such a long way to see us and live with us and we are so glad they did!*"

"Thank you, Nola," said Mrs. de Freyne, gesturing to her to get down.

"*To Austria!*" said Nola, holding her glass up again.

"*Here, here!*" shouted Fritz Hettinger.

"*Or Germany, whichever you want!*" Nola shouted and giggled.

As Hans held up his glass, he looked around the room and saw everyone reach for their own drink to raise it in toast.

The only person who didn't raise their glass was Fintan.

Instead, he stared deeply, directly at Maeve, who didn't seem to notice the special attention at all.

"*To us!*" said Eva Hettinger.

"*To you!*" said Mrs. de Freyne.

Gisela

CHAPTER TWENTY-FOUR

On Sunday morning, Nola failed to leave her bed, as she had failed the week before, and the week before that, for 11 o'clock Mass.

Mrs. de Freyne was furious.

Gisela saw it in her face as they all stood, the Hettingers and Hans, in the hall to leave.

"Has she really not got up?" she said.

They watched as Mrs. de Freyne dragged herself up the stairs slowly, with her bothersome hip, and rapped out of sight on a door upstairs.

They listened to the sound of a door opening and closing.

The group looked at each as shouting came from upstairs, followed by quiet then more shouting.

Mrs. de Freyne came back down alone, two red spots burning on her cheeks.

It was the first time Gisela has seen her lose her cool fully.

Eva whispered to Gisela as they walked down the avenue that Nola had got quite drunk last night.

"You left early?" said Eva.

"Yes," said Gisela.

She did not want to tell her why.

She did not want to tell her that Fintan Walshe's questions about her parents, about Rudy had upset her so much that she had to go to bed, to be alone, to think about them in the sanctuary of her room.

"Was she bad?" Gisela asked Eva.

"Very," said Eva. "She danced Mr. Walshe around the room."

"Oh," said Gisela.

"There was no music."

"Oh."

Eva leaned in to whisper in an even lower voice, despite the fact they were speaking in German.

"Then she called Mrs. de Freyne a boring old fart and asked if she was adopted?"

"She did not," said Gisela, shocked.

Max hid his laughter as they crossed sombrely onto the wet road, having overheard their conversation.

Eva looked at him and admonished him.

"Stop it, Max."

"I thought it was funny," he said with a smile.

"Well, it's not funny this morning," said Eva.

Mrs. de Freyne had marched to the front of the pack and was storming ahead angrily.

"Maeve convinced Mrs. de Freyne to go to bed and said that she would look after Nola," said Eva. "She is very angry this morning, right?"

"Yes," said Gisela. "She is."

At Mass they segregated themselves and felt the usual staring eyes as they made their way into the pews.

Gisela felt like shouting out, *We are Catholics just like you! Do we not believe in the same God? Why do you stare so?*

Father Crowley did not draw special attention to them this week and Gisela was glad.

Still, she was glad to get out of the church and back up the road to Newtown.

* * *

Back at the house, Gisela went up to Nola's room to check that she was all right.

The air was heavy and stank of stale alcohol.

Nola was buried beneath a mound of blankets, barely visible at all.

"Leave me alone," Nola said into her pillow.

"Can I get you anything?" asked Gisela.

"A new head," said Nola. "I want to tear this one off."

"I have some aspirin," said Gisela.

"You do?"

Nola moved in the bed.

"Oh yes, please, I need that. And some water. And could you be a dear and drop me up a cup of tea? And maybe a little biscuit? I can't stomach anything else."

"All right," said Gisela.

"Gisela," said Nola, before she left. "I can't stop thinking about him."

"About who?" said Gisela, stopping.

"Who?" said Nola. "Who else? Do you know any other spies that dropped from the sky in front of you recently?"

Gisela walked back and sat on Nola's soft bed, feeling her weight sink into it.

"Yes, he's been on my mind too. I've been thinking that maybe he was sent to watch us. You know, from home, keep an eye on us? They do that, you know. They spy on Jews and people they don't like for whatever reason."

"Oh, I never really thought of that," said Nola. "Yes, he could be, couldn't he?"

"I'm thinking that I should tell the others. To be on alert."

"*Oh no, don't do that!*" said Nola, sitting up now properly. "No, we must keep this between ourselves. I don't want anyone else to know."

"But what if he's come to do them harm? Or take them away or ... or something? I must warn them!"

Nola went quiet.

"We could try to talk to Mícheál again maybe. Without Peadar. He's more reasonable. He probably won't tell us much but he might tell us if you were under any threat. Or the others."

"Do you think we are? Under threat?"

"No, not really. He wanted to see Seán McKee. That tells us enough. But I'm dying to know where they put him. He has to be hiding somewhere! I wonder is he even in the village or did they move him somewhere far away?"

Gisela shrugged.

She hoped he had been taken far away from them.

"We have to keep this to ourselves though. Don't tell anyone at all. If Peadar found out we spoke, well ... I just don't want to get on the wrong side of him. Or the McKees."

"I thought you weren't afraid of Peadar."

"I'm not. But still, I don't want to make him angry."

Gisela left the room to go and fetch Nola's list of requirements.

As she made her way to the kitchen, passing by the open door of Mrs. de Freyne's office, a voice called out, *"Who's there?"*

Gisela put her head inside the door to see Mrs. de Freyne at her desk, writing.

The office was pleasant and airy.

The mahogany shelves were filled with folders of documents and dense-looking text books.

"Ah Gisela, do come in," said Mrs. de Freyne, smiling.

She closed the notebook she was writing in.

Gisela took a seat and smiled at her sponsor.

Suddenly the thought struck Gisela.

Did Mrs. de Freyne know anything about Friday night?

Had she heard that they had been drinking?

About the solider?

No, she was smiling. She looked pleasant.

"And how are you doing, Gisela?"

"I'm fine, thank you," said Gisela, waiting to see where the questions might lead.

"Good. Good. You seem to be doing rather well. Although you left for bed early last night – was everything okay?"

"Yes. Just tired, Mrs. de Freyne."

"And how about my daughter? Are you finding it easy to ... to be her friend?"

Gisela thought about the drinking bouts and the kissing at the parish dance and the Nazi solider that had parachuted down right into their circle. A circle of potential criminals – of terrorists. Nola seemed to create chaos everywhere she went.

"Yes, I think so. We are getting on quite well."

"Well, she certainly seems happier since you came to live here, so for that I am grateful."

Gisela smiled.

The thought struck her then that now was the time.

Now, she could confess to Mrs. de Freyne about the solider.

She could tell her in confidence and have it so that Nola would never know the information came from her.

It would be a weight off her mind. And surely the police could find out where the solider was hiding? Arrest him and take away?

"I wanted to let you know that I had a letter from the Society of Friends," said Mrs. de Freyne. "About trying to get your parents visas to Ireland. It's not good news, I'm afraid. They have ceased all rescue operations in Vienna and beyond, and they cannot get anybody else out. The legation has shut down and visas are now impossible. Should your parents wish to escape, well, they'd have to be smuggled out of the country."

"Oh," said Gisela.

"I'm sorry it's such bad news. The Society is very good and reliable. They said we were lucky to get you here."

"It's probably too late, I am thinking," said Gisela.

"How do you mean?" said Mrs. de Freyne, folding her hands under her chin.

"I had a letter from my brother on Friday. My parents were taken from the city the day after I left. They were put on a train to no one knows where."

"Oh, my goodness, Gisela!"

Suddenly the tears arrived and Gisela found herself clasping her hands to her face.

"I'm sorry," she said, sniffling. "I haven't told anyone yet. I haven't said it out loud. But it's true. I fear ... I fear the worst."

"Oh, now, dear," said Mrs. de Freyne, getting up and taking a handkerchief from her sleeve to give to Gisela. "Oh, you mustn't fret. Let me see if I can make further enquiries on the ground."

"I just want to know where they've been taken," said Gisela. "So I can write to them. They won't have got any of my letters or cards since I left."

"Oh, that is very troublesome," said Mrs. de Freyne. "You poor thing, carrying all that around by yourself. You know I am always here, if you ever want to talk. And Eva is a good ear. And Maeve."

"I didn't want to trouble anybody."

"It is not a problem. We are all here, together. All trying to get through this dreadful situation, together."

"Thank you, Mrs. de Freyne," said Gisela, dabbing her eyes with the hankie.

She felt relieved having unloaded her burden.

That she had finally said out loud the words she had only read.

The news of the solider could wait. She didn't feel ready to tell Mrs. de Freyne now.

"As for that daughter of mine," said Mrs. de Freyne. "She wouldn't know hardship if it hit her in the face. She's dreadfully spoiled, I'm afraid."

Gisela smiled, weakly.

Well, yes, that much was true.

"I thought you being here and all you are going through might tame her down, but I fear she is only getting worse. You are lucky you went to bed early last night and missed her carry-on."

"She is young, Mrs. de Freyne," said Gisela, even though she was only a few years older herself.

Gisela had never acted like Nola though. She would never have dreamt of it.

"Well, we're going to have serious words today. I've had quite enough now. Things really have to change."

Gisela stood up and thanked Mrs. de Freyne for her efforts.

What she really wanted to say was *thank you for your kindness.*

Back in Nola's room, bearing pharmaceuticals, nourishment and tea, Gisela told Nola what her mother said.

"She said she's going to speak to you later. That things have to change."

"Oh God," said Nola, sitting up in bed and throwing her head back to swallow the aspirin. "Not the lecture again. Why can't she just leave me be? I mean, was she ever young herself? What harm am I doing?"

Gisela thought that Nola was doing a great deal of harm.

To her reputation.

To her family name and all her mother's hard work.

But as Nola sipped and blew on her tea, Gisela didn't have the heart to make her companion feel worse.

She also didn't have the heart to tell her that she had come very close to telling their secret.

"Can I get you anything else?" she asked when Nola had drunk her tea.

"No, darling, thank you – you're a complete pet," said Nola, flopping back down onto the pillow and pulling the blankets over her head.

* * *

After luncheon, the argument between Nola and her mother began.

Everyone was excused from the dining room and Mrs. de Freyne asked Nola to stay behind.

219

The Hettingers, Gisela and Hans sat uncomfortably in the drawing room, trying not to listen to the shouting coming from across the hall.

There were sobs from Nola.

A door slammed, opened and closed and slammed again.

"Oh dear," said Eva Hettinger.

"Should I check on her?" asked Gisela, as they heard Nola fleeing up the stairs.

"Ah, probably best to leave her alone for a bit," said Fritz Hettinger.

They played cards and chess.

Hans went back to his cottage to work on his wood carvings.

Later, as it approached time for afternoon tea, Nola opened the door gently and stepped into the room.

Her eyes were red-rimmed.

"Gisela, do you fancy the pictures this evening?" she said, her voice bright.

Gisela stared at her.

"Um ..."

It had been so long since Gisela had the luxury of attending a film.

But she was quite tired.

Friday had been too much excitement. Saturday too.

A film would require much attention as she translated everything in her head.

"I'll go," said Otto.

"Me too," said Max.

Nola frowned. "I didn't mean –"

"All right," said Gisela.

Nola sighed.

"All right, but we'll all have to squeeze into the car. Let me look at the newspaper – they usually have a show on just after 5 o'clock."

With that she closed the door with a bang.

The Hettinger boys and Gisela looked at each other.

"I'm not sure she wanted you all to go," said Eva Hettinger.

"Too late now!" said Max.

* * *

George, the chauffeur, looked a little ticked off as Nola, Gisela, Max and Otto piled into the Fraschini at the steps of Newton.

Gisela knew that he'd been expecting a restful afternoon.

He lived in a small cottage down the road from Newtown House and was only called when needed.

Unusually, Nola was quiet as they drove.

She carried a fat handbag, which she balanced on her knee.

Max sat in the front beside George.

"What's the film?" he shouted over the roar of the engine.

"Oh," said Nola, frowning. "*The Saint* something. There was one out last year and it was good."

George dropped the four right to the door of the Abbey Cinema and Dance Hall and told them he'd be back at seven o'clock to pick them up again.

They went inside to get their tickets.

Gisela felt a rush of excitement as they moved along in the queue.

How normal it all was!

How divinely familiar!

And yet it was a simple freedom that had been removed from them with such ease by the German Government.

No entertainment.

No dancing.

"I haven't been to the cinema in two years," said Gisela to Nola.

"Two years?" Nola said, looking aghast. "Don't you like the pictures?"

"Of course I do," said Gisela.

Nola looked at her blankly and Gisela realised that Nola still did not understand what it had been like for them all at home.

She hadn't a clue.

Not a clue.

Nola looked at her watch and tapped her foot.

"Are you all right?" Gisela asked.

"Fine," she said.

She didn't seem fine.

Something was off with her, Gisela felt.

She was far too agitated.

They went into the cinema and found their seats in a row near the back.

Nola waited in the aisle till they were all seated then sat in her seat, near the door.

It was quite a thrill when the lights dipped and the loud music came on.

Gisela realised how much she had missed this experience.

As the film began to roll, Nola whispered that she needed to go to the toilet.

She lifted her large handbag.

"I'll come with you," said Gisela, realising that she should have gone before they left for the journey into Drogheda.

"No," said Nola firmly, pushing her back with her hand. "Stay here, I won't be long."

Gisela sat back down, surprised.

Nola had shoved her.

What on earth?

Gisela realised that she really did have to go to the toilet.

Nola could not tell her what to do!

Gisela whispered to Max that she would be back and then made her way in the dark up the steps.

When Gisela got to the foyer, she saw Nola disappearing out the front door, the large handbag slung over her shoulder.

She ran outside.

"*Nola!*" she shouted.

Nola was weaving her way down the street at speed.

"*Nola!*" she cried out again.

Turning around, Nola saw Gisela and suddenly broke into a run.

What was the girl doing?

Gisela thundered down the steps and chased after her.

Had she arranged a date?

Was she seeing a boy?

Mícheál perhaps?

"Nola, wait!"

Nola's head-start allowed her to disappear down a side street.

By the time Gisela reached it, she had gone.

It was such odd behaviour.

Gisela couldn't understand what she was doing.

She ran down the street and when she turned the corner at the bottom, she spotted Nola far ahead.

Gisela chased after her.

She was out of breath by the time she reached where Nola was.

The bus station.

She saw her climb onto a stationary bus, its fumes pumping and swirling round the back door.

To Gisela's horror, the bus began to move out of the station, just as she got there.

To stop it, she ran right into its path and waved her arms.

The bus came to a halt with a jolt.

Gisela climbed on as the conductor angrily admonished her.

"What are you doing?" he said. "Are you trying to get killed?"

"Please," said Gisela, "can you wait? One moment? I need to speak with my friend before she leaves? Please?"

The conductor looked into Gisela's desperate eyes.

"Thirty seconds," he said and he called to the driver up ahead to wait.

Gisela turned to look at the passengers.

And there she was, halfway down the bus, still arranging her bag in her seat.

"*Go away,*" Nola said when she saw her approach. "*Leave me alone!*"

"Nola," said Gisela, "where are you going? Please get off – where are you running to?"

"That's none of your business."

There weren't many other passengers on the bus but they fell silent, listening to the commotion between the two young women.

"Please don't go," said Gisela. "Don't leave me here."

Gisela looked behind and saw the conductor's angry arched eyebrows held high in frustration.

She tried again.

"If you won't get off, then I'm going with you."

And she meant it.

She sat down in the seat opposite.

"*All right!*" said Nola. "*For goodness sake!*"

Scowling, she got out of her seat and walked up the bus aisle.

Gisela followed her.

"Can I get a refund?" Nola asked the conductor.

"No refunds," he said.

"Fine!" she snapped.

She went down the steps and Gisela thanked the conductor for waiting.

He nodded at her.

They bus powered away in a cloud of diesel fumes.

"Why did you do that?" asked Nola.

She looked like a wilted flower.

"Nola, what are you doing?" said Gisela. "What is wrong with you?"

Nola's eyes were filled with tears.

They fell over the brim of her lashes and tumbled down her face.

"Where were you planning on going?" asked Gisela, gently.

"London," said Nola quietly.

"London!"

"Over to Granny. She'd take me in. Away from this godforsaken place. And Mummy."

"Things can't be that bad, Nola," said Gisela. "You'll make up with her. There's no need to leave."

"She said she was going to cancel my coming out ball. That my behaviour is too terrible. That I can't be trusted. And there's no point making my debut anyway."

"Oh," said Gisela. She knew how much the event meant to Nola. "I'm sorry. But wouldn't it better to try and make up with her, rather than running away?"

Nola sulked. Then sighed.

"Were you really going to leave me behind, just like that?" said Gisela, hurt.

Nola looked at Gisela and sniffed.

"I never really thought about you."

"No."

"I'm sorry."

"It's all right. You just need to ... to think. You can't run away just because of a simple row."

"It wasn't a simple row."

"Well, it was, really, if you think about it."

Together, they walked back in muted silence to the cinema.

"Don't tell the boys," said Nola.

"Of course I won't."

When they were back in their seats, Max leaned towards Gisela.

"Where were you?" he asked.

"Women's problems," said Gisela.

Max swallowed and turned away immediately.

Gisela looked at Nola who smiled.

It was hard to concentrate on the film after what had happened.

Gisela worried about what would have happened had she not caught Nola.

She had got to her with only seconds to spare.

There's no doubt she would have made it to Dublin.

Then to the ferry port.

By tonight, she'd be halfway across to England.

And what sort of chaperone would Gisela be then?

Letting her charge escape to another country?

The girl was a total liability.

When George picked them up, it was a very subdued Nola who climbed back into the motorcar.

Max nudged Gisela on the way home when he noticed Nola's tears.

Gisela shook her head in a warning not to ask.

How could you explain a girl like Nola?

To an uncomplicated boy like Max?

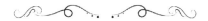

"There seems to be no abatement in the number of aliens upon whom Irish citizenship are being conferred ... We have had too many foreign settlers in the past and the boats which are bringing in aliens to our ports are taking Irish emigrants away to seek in other countries the livelihood they cannot secure in their native land ... Already we have far too many aliens – for a scrap of paper will not make them Irishmen in the eyes of the people."

Editorial, *Irish Independent*, Mon 24 July 1939

Hans

CHAPTER TWENTY-FIVE

On Monday morning Mrs. Carmody, a portly, tall and loud-voiced woman, arrived at Newtown House.

She brought with her an entourage of women in various shapes and sizes.

"Oh God!" said Nola from the breakfast table, as she watched the women make their way up the avenue.

The women were each armed with a basket.

Like a shield.

"Run," said Nola, getting up out of her seat and making for the door.

"Sit," said Mrs. de Freyne.

Nola sat back down and scowled.

"Mrs. Carmody is head of the Irish Countrywomen's Association and is in charge of the Garden Fête," Mrs. de Freyne explained to the Austrians. "She's a very capable woman and she'll expect help from all of you throughout the week. There is much work to be done and we are delighted this year to have so many extra pairs of willing hands."

"She's a total battle axe," said Nola, looking at Mrs. Carmody through the window.

"Nola!" reprimanded her mother. "That's enough of that now. Remember what we talked about yesterday."

Hans looked at Nola.

Her shoulders slumped.

She looked beaten.

The row yesterday with her mother had certainly affected her.

He couldn't help but feel sorry for her.

They waited as Maeve let the entourage into the hall and brought them into the drawing room.

Everyone put their napkins down and went to join them.

"Ah, plenty of helpers this year, I see," said Mrs. Carmody looking at the Hettingers, Hans and Gisela.

"Yes," said Mrs. de Freyne and she introduced them to each other.

Fintan Walshe joined the meeting and Mrs. de Freyne nodded at him in greeting.

"Whatever you need of the group, just ask, they're here to help," she said.

"I have a bad back so I can't do any heavy lifting," said Fritz.

"Right," said Mrs. Carmody and she frowned.

Hans saw Fintan Walshe roll his eyes.

Mrs. Carmody went through a long list of tasks that needed to be completed by the weekend.

Newtown House would be turned into a veritable circus by the sounds of it.

In the dancing hall concerts would be taking place on the half hour.

Ushers would be needed to get the crowds in and out and a stage hand would be needed to attend to the needs of the musicians.

Outside, a variety of tents would house the competitions and show stands.

The needlework tent would display the products of the hard labour of the association and lessons would be available for those who wanted them.

The culinary tent would display the best of cakes, bread and jam from the committee, with the judges announcing the winners at a prize-giving on Saturday evening.

The tennis competitions would run all day at the courts at the back of Newtown.

A golf competition would take place on a freshly prepared green.

Two painters would give both watercolour and oil-painting demonstrations, while a treasure hunt for the children would take place at two-hour intervals.

Hans thought it all sounded wonderful.

"You will be vital in ushering people about on the day," said Mrs. Carmody, looking at Gisela and Nola. "Is her English good?"

She asked the question of Mrs. de Freyne.

"I am fluent," answered Gisela.

"Wonderful," said Mrs. Carmody. "Now, the tents will be going up on Thursday. We've asked competition entrants to drop in their items from Wednesday on. I think we should open the side door like we did last year and let them come and go, otherwise it'll be like a train station."

Mrs. de Freyne smiled.

How generous, thought Hans.

How kind of her to open up her house like that.

Mrs. Carmody said they would be expecting hundreds of visitors to the fête.

Despite his aversion to social gatherings, he found himself quite excited by the sound of it all.

He was itching to get stuck into the work that was needed on the grounds and in the house.

"Whatever you need, Mrs. Carmody, just shout," said Fintan.

Mrs. Carmody nodded her head and wrote something down on her clipboard.

"Thank you very much, Mr. Walshe."

After the meeting ended, the committee, the Austrians and staff followed Mrs. Carmody out for a walking tour of the grounds.

Mr. Walshe had already started the event's hired-in gardeners on the rose beds and weeding around the avenue.

He dipped his hat at them as they passed.

"What a fine job he is doing!" said Mrs. Carmody of Mr. Walshe.

"Yes," said Mrs. de Freyne, "I'd be quite lost without him."

Hans smiled at the compliment to his foreman.

He looked forward to working on the grounds over the coming week.

It was going to be busy, but it would take his mind off things.

The busier he was, the happier he was, Hans had realised.

It was better that he less time to think.

The memories could be too overwhelming.

It was better not to let them take hold at all.

* * *

As Anja moved into the second part of her pregnancy, when she was almost five months in, she began to feel better.

The sickness which affected her so badly abated enough for her to be able to eat again and she regained some of her strength.

Hans was relieved.

He had begun to worry constantly, not just for Anja and her delicate condition, but for his father who Anja was tasked with caring for, when she was barely well enough to care for herself. He worried for her family who found themselves at home wondering what they could do next.

Anja's brothers had taken up some odd jobs doing deliveries and assisting in a Jewish baker's from time to time as well as some small tailoring jobs from the house, but they were waiting in limbo.

They knew they were caught in a desperate situation and their future was uncertain.

Hans had gone to work each day with a knot in his stomach, similar to when his mother had been ill and he'd had to leave her at home with his incapable father.

He finished up with his wood-making course, as it simply wasn't fair to leave Anja in the evenings, especially with the cold, coiled atmosphere of the Viennese streets.

Throughout her sickness she had only missed one rehearsal, as the orchestra happened to be on their yearly break.

Now that they were back up and running, she vowed that she would miss no more as she had worked so hard to gain her position in the first place.

She was a pioneer as the first woman player to be allowed into their ranks.

Discussing what to do about her situation, Anja decided with Hans that she would not reveal her pregnancy till it was impossible to hide.

Hans thought it was a risky strategy and felt that she was setting herself up for disappointment.

He felt, dreadfully, that when the conductor did find out about her situation, she would be removed from her position immediately.

He suggested Anja might feign illness, even get something written up by a doctor to say she needed long-term bed rest for six months, thereby hiding her pregnancy altogether.

But Anja did not want to lie.

Neither did she want to hear of missing rehearsals.

When Hans was not working, he walked Anja to the tram stop and was there for her when she came back carrying her oboe, looking pale and tired but smiling from ear to ear at how well the rehearsals had gone.

The music uplifted her and ignited something in her that nothing else could come near. It was as though music formed part of her soul and, when she was kept from it, that part melted away.

She was in a much better mood when she got to play with the orchestra and Hans knew it would be cruel to take that away from her, to tell her she must stop.

On occasion Hans' shifts meant that he was not able to walk her to the tram stop as he liked and as their neighbour Frau Leitner was already being called upon to mind his father, he had to let her walk to and from the stops alone.

In the strangled atmosphere of the Viennese streets, it was another worry that pressed down on him.

One evening, after a long, boring and quiet shift Hans got back to the apartment and found to his surprise that Frau Leitner was still there.

"Is Anja not back yet?" he asked, taking off his gloves and hat.

"No," said Frau Leitner. "She is not, and I have to keep going back to my apartment to sort out squabbles. My children can't be left alone for so long. She is over an hour late!"

A wave of anxiety rose in Hans.

Something must be wrong.

Anja knew that Frau Leitner was doing them a good turn and would not unnecessarily delay her.

"I am very sorry," said Hans. "Thank you for staying. We really appreciate it."

Frau Leitner folded her arms.

"You will have to do something," she said and she pointed to Hans' father who was swaying back and forth in his chair, listening to an unheard tune in his head. "He tried to hit me earlier. He thought I was his old school teacher."

This made Hans want to smirk.

His father had always grumbled in his lucidity about how much he had hated his old school teacher who had beaten him with a cane. Not surprisingly he associated Frau Leitner and her gruff manner with the school teacher.

"I know," he said as he showed Frau Leitner to the door, "I know."

Now was not the time for a lecture on his father's care.

Now, he needed to find out where Anja was.

Wrapping his father up in his coat, he ushered him out of the apartment and held tightly onto his arm.

"Papa, we are going to find Anja – you must stay beside me, all right?"

His father nodded, and feeling the cut of the wind on his face, began touching his cheeks.

They had stopped bringing him out for walks a long time ago as he tended to dart away suddenly, but tonight Hans had little choice.

He had considered at one point fashioning a type of tether for his father, something he could tie onto his wrist, but he found the whole situation so humiliating and bizarre that he could not bring himself to do it.

Often his father sat at the window and cried.

He hoped tonight the novelty of being outside would keep him amused enough to stay with him.

They walked quickly to the tram stop nearest to their house and waited and watched the trams pulling up.

He watched for any sign of her, checked the faces of the late-evening workers getting off the trams that pulled in, one after the other.

When he realised she was not on any of them, he helped his father onto a tram going the opposite direction. They sat at a seat where his father could stare out the window at his own foggy reflection. It seemed to bemuse him. Hans's leg jittered up and down, uncontrollably. He was anxious, a horrible wave of worry working its way through his intestines. He had a feeling that something had gone wrong, that something bad had happened.

At the stop where he knew Anja alighted for the rehearsal hall, they got off. He had to prise his father from his seat, pinching his arm, forcing him to cry out.

He felt eyes on them as they dismounted.

When the tram pulled away, Hans looked around.

The stop was quiet.

He walked towards the hall, which Anja had proudly brought him to one day, showing him exactly which seat was hers.

As they approached a narrow, badly lit side street, Hans noticed a small crowd had gathered.

His stomach fell into his boots.

Something had happened.

Something had happened to Anja.

The onlookers stood in brown and grey coats, murmuring to each other, in hushed mournful tones.

Hans pushed through them, excusing himself till he could see what they were looking at.

With his clear view over everyone else's shoulders he saw a woman lying on the ground, a coat thrown over her, a pillow made from another coat under her head.

Anja.

There she was lying on the street, a dark-coloured pool of blood ebbing from under the pillow coat.

"*Anja!*" he cried. "*That's my wife! My wife!*"

The crowd parted and he rushed through, squatting down to try to speak to her.

She was unconscious and did not respond.

It was dark and hard to see the colour of her skin, the light coming only from a lamp near the tram stop.

He touched her beautiful head, saw that her cheeks, her eyes were swollen.

Her lips were burst open, black blood pouring from her nose and, from the looks of it, from the back of her head.

"*My Anja!*" he cried, the shock of her crumpled body winding him.

He cradled her in his arms, taking her up from the cold ground on which she lay.

Somebody appeared with a towel and tried to stem the bleeding from the back of her head.

The towel was soon stained black in the orange lamplight.

"Anja," he whispered over and over, "can you hear me, Anja?"

But Anja could not hear him.

Or if she could, she could not tell him so.

An ambulance finally arrived and she was lifted and arranged onto a stretcher.

The ambulance man let him sit in the front with him as they drove at speed to hospital.

"Do you know what happened?" asked the ambulance man.

Hans, in shock, shook his head.

"Is she a Jewess?"

Han nodded.

"The third we've taken from the streets this week. There's a gang," he said. "Young. They're attacking women, old men, the vulnerable."

Nausea rose through Hans and he worried he might vomit all over the front of the ambulance.

"Easy prey," said the ambulance man.

"Cowards," said Hans quietly, disgusted.

Hans watched as Anja was taken away to be examined in hospital.

He was asked to wait in a waiting room and it was well over an hour before a doctor came to speak to him.

Anja was very badly beaten, the doctor told him.

She had lacerations to her scalp, a fractured cheekbone and her arm and fingers had been broken too.

The shock of what the doctor was telling him was almost too much for Hans to bear.

He wanted to scream in horror, to yell and shout that it could not be true.

How could this be happening?

"She has swelling to the brain," said the doctor. "We have her sedated and are treating her, but she is very swollen and we will have to see how she gets through the night."

The doctor went quiet.

"Herr Schmitt," he said, "is your wife pregnant?"

Hans nodded. "She is nearly six months." He held his throat, waiting. Waiting for what the doctor might say.

The doctor frowned.

"She is bleeding," he said. "I'm sorry. We will do all we can, but it is not a good sign."

The doctor asked a nurse to sit with Hans, while Anja was treated.

Hans let the emotion come out then, the tears and snot bursting forth like an explosion.

That night the doctor said the baby's heartbeat was strong.

In the morning, he came to tell Hans the news.

The baby's heartbeat was gone.

But Anja's beat on.

Gisela

CHAPTER TWENTY-SIX

"Gisela! Gisela!"

The voice was a hiss.

Whispered in the dark.

Gisela opened her eyes to see Nola's face right up against hers.

"Gisela, wake up, please."

Gisela sat up and tried to adjust her eyes in the dark.

In her dream she had been back in Vienna, walking down the street towards Stephansplatz.

She was with Rudy and they had spotted Wolfgang sitting outside a café at a bistro table, waiting for them.

What was Wolfgang doing in Vienna, Gisela had wondered.

In fact, what were they all doing in Vienna, together?

But it was a dream.

Here she was, in the dark, in Newtown House.

Without them.

"What's wrong?" said Gisela, her voice groggy.

"You must get up and come with me. Please. Not a sound."

In the twilight, as her eyes adjusted, Gisela watched Nola put her fingers to her lips.

She swung her legs out of bed.

"What's going on?"

"Just get dressed and come with me. I'll tell you when we're outside."

Outside?

Gisela found a dress and pulled it on over her nightdress. She slipped her feet into her plimsolls.

She followed Nola down the corridor on tip-toe, then down the stairs, shafts of moonlight shining from the window box above.

Nola brought her through the kitchen and out the back, unbolting the door with a gentleness that Gisela never knew she possessed.

Out in the courtyard, the moon was bright.

Nola led her round to the outhouses and sheds, where Bessie the tractor lived, where feed and hay was stored, where angry-looking machinery sat looming in the dark.

"Okay," said Nola. "You need to listen to me and stay calm. The spy is here. They've hidden him in one of the sheds. He's sick though and he's gibbering and they want you to speak to him in German."

She paused.

Her face was pale in the moonlight.

"What?" said Gisela, her face registering shock.

Nola touched her on the arm.

"I know it's a lot to ask but I wouldn't ask if ... they ... they're desperate. Please, Gisela."

"Who's they?"

"Mícheál. And Peadar."

"I don't want to see him," said Gisela firmly. "*No. No.*"

"He's very unwell. They just want you to try and calm him down."

Gisela shook her head.

"Gisela, we're all going to get into trouble if he's found, right? Can you just help us? You don't have to go near him. Just listen to him and talk to him a bit."

They stood in the dark, staring at each other.

"Can you just do this for me? I haven't asked you for anything, Gisela.

Not one thing!" said Nola, her voice angry now.

Her anger raised the same response in Gisela.

Why did she care if the man was sick?

He had arrived here in Nazi uniform.

She owed nothing to him.

Nothing at all.

"Why should I help?" said Gisela. "Don't you understand yet, Nola? Why I am here? Why we are all here? It's because of men like him! Him and the rest of his army! My parents were sent away! After I left? Put on a train to God only knows where. I don't even know if they're alive. Put on a train, by men like him!"

"*Shhhhh!* Keep your voice down. All right. I understand. I know you're angry. I know he's your enemy. I do understand, Gisela."

"You don't. You really don't."

"Okay," said Nola, trying to calm Gisela down now. "I'm sorry, okay?"

Gisela turned, walked a few steps then stopped.

She stared into the dark of the yard.

"I don't want to be here, you know," she said, turning around. "I never wanted to come here. I wanted to stay at home. Where I was happy. Where I could go to university. Where I could see my parents every day. What if I never see them again?"

Tears filled her eyes now.

Nola took a step closer to her.

"I'm sorry," she said, reaching out for her arm. "I'm sorry if –"

A door somewhere opened.

Nola grabbed Gisela's arm and yanked her down, low to the ground.

"Be quiet," she whispered.

They waited until it was quiet again, staying statue-still, holding their breaths.

Carefully Nola stood up and opened the sliding metal door of one of the sheds and stepped inside, beckoning for Gisela to come with her.

Reluctantly, Gisela followed.

Inside the shed, Gisela could see a ladder leading up into an opening in the roof – a rectangle of yellow light.

"They're afraid he's going to ... he's really not well. Could you just take a look? I promise, I'll never ask anything of you again."

Gisela let out her breath.

"Fine," she said. "Fine. But I'm not making any promises. This goes against every ..."

"I know. Thank you. Thank you, Gisela," said Nola.

She squeezed her arm and turned around and climbed up the ladder.

Gisela followed carefully into the rectangle of light, feeling the rungs of the ladder press hard into the soles of her shoes.

When she poked her head up through the loft, she was met with the smell of pungent body odour. It was mixed somewhat with the overpowering smell of disinfectant.

Peadar and Mícheál swivelled their heads.

"Gisela," said Mícheál.

He seemed glad to see her.

The parachutist was lying on top of a sleeping bag with a white cloth on his forehead.

He shook and rattled with fever.

His jacket was removed as was the boot on his right foot.

Gisela could see that the trouser leg was dark with blood.

His shirt was wringing wet.

She stood a distance away from him and asked if he could hear her.

"*Kannst du mich hören?*"

"What is his name?" she asked the boys when he did not answer.

"Bruno," said Peadar.

She spoke to him again in a louder voice.

"*Bruno, kannst du mich hören?*"

The soldier's eyes, vacant, darted in her direction.

"Can you come closer?" said Mícheál.

In as loud a voice as she could muster, Gisela asked Bruno if he knew where he was.

The smell was quite overwhelming.

Gisela repeated her question again.

The solider, shaking, turned his head in a gesture that seemed to indicate he didn't know.

Gisela told him he was in Ireland.

She moved closer, seeing now that the man could do her no harm.

He was, as Nola had said, very sick.

She tried to ask him how he was feeling, but he broke into gibberish.

He talked of his mother, of a tree, of a wishing well, how he had to carry the water for his mother. He must get back to the tree, he said. It was washing day.

Gisela looked at the others.

She could see the concern in their faces.

"You need to get his fever down. He's –" *Halluzinierend.* She wasn't sure of the English word.

Nola crouched down and pulled back the flap of the soldier's trouser leg.

It had been torn and ripped to make it easier to open.

Gisela could see why now the boot had been removed.

The soldier's ankle was swollen like a balloon.

A bandage and splint had been applied to the shin, but the blood had seeped through.

"The bone came through the skin," said Mícheál. "It's a mess. We tried using disinfectant on it but –"

"He has an infection," said Gisela. "It's causing the fever. He really needs to see a doctor. Or go to hospital."

"No," said Peadar. "Not possible."

"How can we treat him?" asked Nola. "What do we do?"

Gisela realised they were all now looking to her for advice.

She was, she realised, the oldest.

And they expected her to know how to fix this for them.

"It's not going to get better," said Gisela. "Not without medicine. It will turn to poison. In his leg. It will spread."

"Amputation?" said Peadar and he made a cutting gesture towards the soldier's bad leg.

"*Peadar!*" Nola hissed. "*You're not chopping off his leg!*"

"Well, maybe that's what has to be done," said Peadar seriously.

"What medicine should we give?" asked Nola.

"Sulfa," said Gisela. "If you could get that for him it would help, I think."

"Mr. Morarity he might give it to us," said Mícheál, referring to the village doctor.

"*Arra*, he might," said Peadar, "but he'd be all questions. Maybe one of you girls could get it? In town?"

Nola nodded.

"We'll try in the morning," she said.

"Will you just say a few words to him," said Mícheál to Gisela. "Tell him he'll be all right?"

Would he be all right, though, Gisela wondered.

He was in a very bad state right now.

She moved nearer again.

What could she say to this man?

"Take it easy," she told him in German. "Just rest. You'll be all right."

It was all she could muster.

She repeated the words.

Like a mantra.

Peadar and Mícheál looked relieved when she stood back up.

"Thank you, Gisela," said Peadar. "We appreciate it."

Gisela looked at the soldier's stained trousers and sopping shirt.

"Sponge him down and try to get some water into him. He needs clean, dry clothes."

"Did you nurse before?" asked Nola.

Gisela thought of her parents, of the times when they contracted fevers and she cared for them, dripping warm soup into their mouths from a spoon.

"No," she said.

"She just knows things," said Mícheál.

Yes. She knew things.

Things they knew absolutely nothing about.

Nola climbed down the ladder first and Gisela followed her, careful with her footing in the darkness of the shed.

Outside, they checked the coast was clear, before walking quietly back to the house.

"They're so glad you came out," said Nola. "They were really panicking, you know."

"Did you know he was there?" asked Gisela. "That they were keeping him there?"

"No," said Nola. "Mícheál threw stones at my window tonight and woke me up."

"How did he know which was your bedroom?" asked Gisela.

"Never you mind," said Nola.

* * *

The next morning Gisela and Nola ate a quiet breakfast of eggs and toast in the dining room, before leaving to get the bus into town.

They were lucky that it was Gisela's day to sign on at the Garda Station.

It gave them an excuse to travel in together.

As the bus rattled along, both of the girls were lost in their own thoughts.

Gisela thought about the dream she'd had when she'd gone back to bed the night before.

She'd dreamt of her father, that he was bent down on a kerb, surrounded by soldiers, his Tyrolean hat at an angle, the black toothbrush scrubbing, scrubbing.

When one of the soldiers mocking him turned around it was the face of the solider in the shed.

He was laughing.

She wondered what her parents would think of her situation.

Would they tell her to help a man in such obvious pain?

Or would they tell to stay away because he could be dangerous?

To her and the other Austrians?

"Why did they put him there?" asked Gisela as the bus rounded a bend on the Baltray Road. "Why on our farm?"

Nola looked around to make sure nobody was listening.

"It's all a bit of a mess," she murmured. "It's because ..." she lowered her voice further, "because you-know-who was arrested and they had to scramble to find somewhere to put him. All the safe houses are being watched because of the arms theft. So, he ended up in our shed."

"And you didn't know he was there?"

"No, I swear, I didn't know."

Gisela looked out the window.

"There's a back entrance," said Nola. "To that shed. It's a hayshed, you see, so they've a ladder right up to the roof at the back. You can get in from the other side with no one seeing you."

Clever.

"How did he get up there with his broken leg?" asked Gisela.

"I don't know," said Nola. "Maybe he parachuted in."

Gisela looked at Nola who burst out laughing.

"I'm sorry. I know it's not funny. I'm sorry."

"Where is the parachute?"

"Mícheál told me they buried it."

When they got off the bus they walked quickly to the Garda Station.

Gisela was relieved that the station was quiet today and it didn't take long to have her paperwork signed. It was the same policeman who had signed her paperwork the previous week.

He had thick fat hands and wide shoulders.

He didn't look like he could run fast after any criminal.

The thought crossed Gisela's mind in the same way as it had when she was with Mrs. de Freyne in her office last Sunday.

She could tell the policeman what she knew.

She could lean forward and whisper to him.

I have information about a German spy. Can I speak with you? In private?

What would happen if she did?

The spy would be arrested, she supposed.

Given proper medical treatment, no doubt.

But Nola and Mrs. de Freyne would be implicated too.

Peadar and Mícheál.

And of course, she was caught up in all this too.

What did they do with spies anyway?

They put them to death, didn't they? For activities against the state?

Imagine if the soldier's execution was on her hands?

As she thought about the consequences of telling, the policeman handed her back her passport, wordlessly.

He nodded at her in dismissal.

Too late.

She turned and looked at Nola, who was seated beside a man in a woollen hat.

She grimaced and indicated to Gisela to hurry up.

Outside, Nola waved her hand in front of her nose.

"Oh my God, I was sitting beside the smelliest man in Ireland, did you see him?"

Gisela shook her head, her mind a whirl.

"You must have smelt him," said Nola, looking disgusted.

The girls walked on, past the cinema and ballroom, past the church with its black railings and steep steps.

"Let's go to Cooney's Pharmacy, down near the bridge," said Nola. "He's half blind, Mr. Cooney. I'm sure he'll give us what we need."

Inside the pharmacy, a bell rattled.

Gisela noticed the Victorian tiling on the floor.

Mr. Cooney looked up and peered at them through thick, black-framed glasses.

"Good morning, ladies," he said.

"Good morning, Mr. Cooney," said Nola. "Could I trouble you for some sulfa and some bandages, please? My mother has a terrible leg ulcer."

"And who would your mother be?" asked Mr. Cooney.

"Mrs. Carmody, from Termonfeckin."

Gisela shot a look at Nola.

"Ah, Mrs. Carmody," said the pharmacist. "Has an ulcer, has she?"

"Oh, it's very bad," said Nola.

"I thought her daughter was away in England – Margaret, is it?"

"That's me," said Nola.

The pharmacist turned around and began searching his various drawers.

"And how is your mother keeping? Is she still involved in the Countrywomen's Association?" asked the pharmacist.

Gisela and Nola watched him hold bottles right up in front of his face and use a large, thick magnifying glass to read them.

"She is, she is," said Nola. "Keeping busy. The Garden Fête is on this weekend."

"Ah, that's right. Does she need the ointment for her haemorrhoids?"

Nola stifled a giggle. "No, Mr. Cooney, she has plenty of the ointment left."

"Tell her now she's to rest that leg with the ulcer. And if it doesn't get any better, she should attend the doctor. Can be hard to get rid of if you don't look after it."

"She wanted something for the pain too, Mr. Cooney. What with the fête this weekend."

"That's all right," said Mr. Cooney and he turned around on his treasure hunt again.

"Now be careful with these," he said, rattling a bottle of thick white tablets. "No more than three a day. They're powerful."

Outside, Nola burst out laughing.

Gisela smiled too.

"I cannot believe you," she said. "Maybe you should think about becoming an actress."

"When I get to London," said Nola, "I'm going to try. Really!"

They walked to the bus station to take the next bus home.

They were anxious to get to the parachutist, worried at how ill he'd been the night before. Both of them were keen to see what state he was in this morning.

"Peadar told me last night that Mícheál was going up to Dublin today to try and see his father in prison," said Nola. "He said if they wouldn't let him in he was going to stay over and try again tomorrow."

"Can his father give an order, to take Bruno to hospital?"

"I hope so. We really need him gone for the fête. Mrs. Carmody will be poking around everywhere."

"It would be a lot of trouble to move him, with the state he is in," said Gisela.

Nola nodded and stared out the window.

"Still," she said, turning to look at Gisela, "it's all terribly exciting, isn't it?"

Gisela sighed. She'd had quite enough excitement to last a lifetime.

Hans

CHAPTER TWENTY-SEVEN

"Mr. Schmitt, could you help me with something?" said Fintan Walshe as Hans made his way across the yard.

"Of course," said Hans and he walked with the farm foreman towards his workshop.

Inside the room smelled of oil and wood shavings.

Hans breathed it in, deep.

He loved that smell.

Fintan was mending a table and needed Hans to hold the thick wooden leg in place, while he got it into the right position.

Together they manoeuvered the wood, while Fintan searched in a small toolbox for the right nut to secure the leg.

"Will be a busy week," said Fintan.

"Yes," said Hans. "I am looking forward to the garden party."

"Aye," said Fintan. "I was like that before I knew all the work that went into it!"

Hans laughed.

"Might be an odd one, with all that's going on," said Fintan.

"What do you mean?" asked Hans.

"Well, all this arrest business and people being on edge. Did you know that the police are watching everyone? All the comings and goings in the village?"

"They are?"

"Oh yes. The police are on high alert. That big arms theft in Dublin, a load of guns stolen, they're sure by the IRA. Seán McKee has plenty of friends in the parish. They might not want to be seen at the fête at all. I'm just saying, might be a funny atmosphere."

Hans nodded.

Together they turned the table over and stood it up.

"Thanks for that," said Fintan. "You're handy with the woodwork anyway."

"Yes, I love to work with wood," said Hans. "I would like someday to perhaps be a carpenter. Make some furniture, you know?"

"Would you now, begad?" said Fintan. "Well, you have the feel for it, that's for sure."

"I am making Maeve a wooden bowl," said Hans. "And carving some fruit. You put oils on it and it smells nice."

"Are you now?"

It was project Hans had turned to in the past week.

He relished returning to his carvings in his spare time, feeling them smooth beneath his hands, a comfort.

He had started off making a bowl for Eva Hettinger as a gesture for all her kindness to him during their travels.

And when he was making that, he thought it would be nice to make something for Maeve too.

She also had been kind to him.

More than that, he wanted to give her a gift.

He wanted to see her face light up when he gave it to her.

He would need to make something for Mrs. de Freyne too, he supposed.

She had given him the greatest gift of all.

But he'd like to carve something big for her.

A table perhaps or, as once had been his goal, a cabinet of some kind.

Perhaps Fintan Walshe could help him?

"Is it a fancy you have for her?" said Fintan.

"I'm sorry?" said Hans.

A fancy. What did he mean?

"Do you have a liking for Mrs. McGorry?"

"Yes, she is a very nice lady."

"You know what I mean, Herr Schmitt," said Fintan. "I mean a liking. As a gentleman might like a woman."

"Oh," said Hans.

He shook his head and laughed.

"I don't think she would have a liking for me."

"That's not the question I asked."

Hans went silent.

Fintan didn't seem to be asking him in jest.

"No," said Hans, thinking of Anja. "Of course not."

"All right," said Fintan. "Only asking. I like to watch out for her, you know. She's a lovely woman, Mrs McGorry."

His words stung.

Maeve did not need to be protected from him.

Fintan turned around, unlocked a drawer in his desk and pulled out three brown envelopes.

"I have to go out now to check the green for the golf and the courts for the tennis," he said. "This week is going to be running from Billy to Jack. Would you do me a favour and take these down to the post office? They need to go today."

Hans nodded and took the envelopes.

Fintan then held out some coins and dropped them into his palm.

"Just get the stamps and put them in the postbox yourself. Mrs Pentony the postwoman is terrible nosy altogether. And don't be long. There are signs I need to have put up, seeing as you love your woodwork."

Hans left the workshop and walked through the yard and around Newtown House.

He set off down the avenue, passing the gardeners who were hard at work and Mrs. Carmody who was standing with an audience of rotund women.

She certainly liked being in charge, Hans thought, with a smile.

Near the bottom of the avenue, he met Gisela and Nola walking.

Nola was carrying a paper parcel.

"Hello," he said and stopped to talk.

"Can't stop, Hans," said Nola. "We're in a hurry!"

She walked straight on by.

Gisela stopped then threw her eyes to heaven at Hans.

He smiled.

Nola leading the way as usual.

He remembered that Gisela's signing-on day was today.

His had been yesterday. Fintan had to excuse him from the fête preparations to go into town.

Glancing at the letters that Fintan had given him to post, he saw that they were addressed to a hotel in Dublin.

Mr. Henry Mullins, read the name.

Perhaps he was a relative of Fintan's, he thought.

A cousin?

Hans walked down into the village, past the church and over the narrow humpback bridge.

The water was low and babbled over three levels of rocks, before tumbling into a tighter, deeper flow.

Hans took a minute to stop and stare.

He found the sound of the rushing water calming.

A woman pushing a pram passed him by.

He nodded and said hello, but the woman put her head down as she passed.

Perhaps she did not hear him?

Hans felt his legs sting as he pushed up the steep hill to the post office, which also served as a small shop.

Two men, leaning against the wall outside, were smoking thin cigarettes.

He tipped his hat to them and they nodded.

Inside, Hans had to wait for his eyes to adjust to the dark cave of the shop.

When they did, he saw a bosomy shopkeeper standing behind the counter.

The shelves were lined with packets of tea, sugar, tinned food.

"Good afternoon," said Hans.

The woman nodded, silently.

Hans could smell meat, ham, hear the flies buzzing around it.

"Three stamps, please," said Hans.

"Where for?" the shopkeeper asked.

"I'm sorry?"

"Where are you posting your letters to?" asked the woman, speaking slowly and pointedly, as if she were conversing with a child.

Hans looked down at the address.

"Dublin."

The woman opened her book of stamps and tore out three.

"I thought you might be sending back to Germany, that's all."

Hans shook his head.

A woman in a dark coat came into the shop.

It still smarted to have to his home country called *Germany*. It didn't feel right.

He wanted to correct the shopkeeper. *Austria.*

"Are you one of those fascists, or are you on the other side?" asked the woman in the dark coat.

Hans was taken aback.

"I am not a fascist," he said gently.

"And will she be bringing any more of you in?" asked the woman. "Will there be more coming? There's a fair crowd of you up there now."

She looked Hans up and down as she stood beside him.

"Mrs. de Freyne likes to help the suffering," said the shopkeeper.

"Plenty suffering around here too," said the woman in the dark coat.

An awkward moment hung in the air.

Hans didn't know what to say.

"And what's it like where you're from?" asked the shopkeeper.

"Ireland is much safer," he said.

"I bet it is," said the woman beside him.

"Can I get you anything else? Would you like to try some ham?" asked the shopkeeper.

"No, thank you."

Hans nodded goodbye to the two women and felt their eyes bore into him as he left the shop.

Outside he put the stamps on the letters and posted them in the large, green postbox, all under the watchful eyes of the smoking men.

As he walked away, he felt their eyes on him too.

He expected the women were having a good natter about him in the shop behind him.

It was an uncomfortable feeling, being watched and talked about, finding yourself under surveillance because of who you were and where you came from.

He set off down the road and hurried back towards Newtown.

At least there he could get on with his work.

At least there he wasn't being watched.

"Sir, it is a shame to see thousands of our boys and girls having to seek a living in other lands while foreigners can live and thrive in this country."

Name and Address with the Editor
Irish Independent, **Aug 31, 1939**

Gisela

CHAPTER TWENTY-EIGHT

"We need to be careful," said Nola as they approached the yard. "We can't be seen going in there. Let's go round the back."

Making sure there was nobody around to see them, the two girls climbed up the ladder laid against the whitewash of the back of the hayshed and opened the hatch door high up in the wall.

The shed was stuffy and warm in the mid-morning sun.

They climbed into the loft and made their way over to the bundle in the corner, anxious to see what state the soldier was in.

He lay shivering under a blanket, his face wan like candlewax.

On a crate beside the soldier's head was a tin can of water, candles, a candleholder and a plate with stale bread and ham.

The food hadn't been touched.

Nola took out the small tin the chemist had given her and opened it.

The powder was white.

"Ready?" she said.

Gisela took the nail scissors she'd packed in her bag that morning and cut through the damp bandages on the soldier's leg.

The splint fell away.

They both recoiled at the smell.

"Oh my God!" said Nola, retching.

Her retching made Gisela retch too. She held her arm up to her nose to block the smell.

In the fetid heat, they were both forced to walk away from the corner for a moment to catch their breaths.

"I don't think I'd make a nurse," said Nola, gagging.

Back at the leg, Gisela examined the soldier's wound and removed the small bottle of iodine she'd also added to her bag that morning.

"It needs to be set or else the leg will need to come off. It can't heal like this."

Nola pursed her lips.

"Let's clean him up anyway, best we can," she said.

Gisela pressed the cotton wool and iodine to the wound.

This awakened the solider.

He tried to sit up and cried out.

Nola gently pushed him back down and soothed him.

"*Shhhhh*," she said. "Bruno. There, there."

The soldier's shin had come through the skin.

The bone was shiny, white.

The leg was swollen and red, the wound filled with yellow pus.

Gisela doubted her iodine would repair anything.

"He needs to go to the hospital," she said. "Can't they take him to a different one. Far away?"

"They say it's not possible," said Nola. "He would be arrested, no matter where they went."

"But they want to keep him alive, don't they?" she said.

Nola nodded.

Gisela took the sulfa powder and gently dappled it all over the wound.

Nola helped her wrap the new bandage carefully around the splint and secure it.

They pulled his trouser leg down and covered him again with the blanket.

Nola took the tin can of water and poured some of it into the soldier's mouth.

He spluttered.

"You must drink," Gisela told him in German.

For a moment, clarity came to his eyes.

"We have painkillers. Please, take them with the water."

Nola took two fat pills and offered them to the solider.

When he didn't move, Gisela asked him gently to open his mouth.

When he did, Nola popped one in and poured some more water between his lips.

He spluttered again and choked but the pill seemed to go down.

With painkillers taken and the antibiotics on his skin, they had done their best.

They watched the solider shiver and shake.

"Now we must leave him," said Gisela.

Nola nodded.

They were glad to get out into the fresh air outside the shed.

They climbed down the ladder and made their way back to the house, just in time to meet Mrs. Carmody and her entourage making their way out from the dancing hall.

"Ah, there you are!" said Mrs. Carmody, shrilly. "There's an SOS out for you girls! Where have you been?"

"I had some business to attend to in Drogheda," said Gisela.

"Did you now?" said Mrs. Carmody. "More important than getting this house and gardens ready for the biggest party of the year?"

"Well, yes," said Gisela, thinking of her requirement to attend the police station weekly.

Mrs. Carmody glared at her, sensing insolence.

"Well!" she said. "You're here now. I want you to set to work in the hall there. Grab a cloth and some hot water and get to work on the chairs – we need them all wiped down. No dusty bottoms, thank you!"

She laughed, as did her entourage, faintly, behind her.

"When you're finished with that, we've a stack of trestle tables outside. We need them carried in here and cleaned as well."

"God, that's all we need today," said Nola as she and Gisela made their way into the hall.

The chairs had been arranged in rows.

Easels with paintings sat at the front of the hall.

On a table were stacks of pots of jam and empty cake stands.

There seemed to be wicker baskets everywhere.

Gisela offered to go to the kitchen to fetch the hot water for the chairs.

Nola plonked herself down to wait and blew a piece of hair up towards her forehead.

In the kitchen, Gisela found Maeve standing with Mr. Walshe near the back door.

They stopped mid-conversation when they saw her come in.

"Do you need something?" asked Maeve.

She was quite abrupt in her manner, thought Gisela.

Not her usual warm self.

Gisela waited while Maeve filled a basin with hot water.

Mr. Walshe walked off from the back door without saying a word.

Gisela looked at Maeve, trying to read her face.

She seemed distracted.

Deep in thought about something.

"Is everything all right?" she asked.

"Yes," Maeve answered. "Why wouldn't it be?"

She gave Gisela a weak smile.

Back in the dancing hall, Nola and Gisela got to work.

Nola sighed as she sloshed the cloth back and forth.

Gisela was cleaning at double her speed.

"This is so boring," Nola said. "Why does Mummy take on these things? All this work. God. Every year!"

She sat down on a wet chair and sighed again.

"I can't stop thinking about him," she said.

"Me too."

"I really hope he gets better."

"What will they do with him if he does?"

"I don't know," Nola said. "I mean what do spies actually do? He could have picked a more interesting place. Dublin at least."

"What'll they do if he doesn't get better?"

"Don't say that. Please."

Gisela wiped down two more chairs and rinsed her cloth in the basin, the water turning slate-grey.

"I saw Maeve and Mr. Walshe whispering in the kitchen," she said.

"You did?"

"Just now."

"He's in love with her."

"What?"

"Oh yes. Didn't you know?"

"No."

"Oh, my goodness, he follows her around like a puppy dog. She has no time for him. I'm not surprised. *Ugh*, can you imagine? Fusty Fintan!"

"Nola!" Gisela couldn't help but laugh.

"I think he's jealous of Hans."

"Why would he be jealous?"

"Haven't you noticed? Maeve fancies Hans! It's so obvious!"

Gisela shook her head.

It wasn't something she was looking out for.

Not with worrying about her parents and dealing with the Nazi spy half dead in their shed.

No, that little relationship observation had certainly passed her by.

"Come on, Nola," she said. "Go and get some fresh water for us so we can finish the job."

"Really, Gisela," said Nola as she sighed and leaned back in her chair. "What's the rush? If we finish this job, we'll just get another. Let's just take our time."

Gisela sighed too and found a dry chair to sit on.

Maybe Nola was right.

Maybe she needed to relax.

* * *

They went to bed early, feigning tiredness after the work Mrs. Carmody had them doing all afternoon.

Mrs. de Freyne smiled and said it was wonderful to see Nola so dutifully occupied.

They hoped by going to bed early everyone else would follow and they could sneak out to check on Bruno early.

When finally the house had gone quiet, when all the lights were out and they were both sure that everyone had gone to sleep, Nola and Gisela tip-toed out to the hayloft again.

The moon was high in the sky once more, although it was a damp night and clouds moved across its shadowy white face.

Mrs. Carmody had spent most of the day proclaiming a great desire for "good weather, please god," for the Garden Fête.

She had planted a large red statue of a Child of Prague on the lawn in front of Newtown and had even laid a few flowers before it.

Nola explained to Gisela that this ritual was sure to bring good weather.

Carefully they opened the hatch into the loft.

There was no candlelight.

Bruno seemed to be sleeping.

Nola climbed in first and went to the upturned crate.

She struck a match to light the candle.

Something moved in the hay in the opposite corner to Bruno.

A mouse?

In the illumination, Bruno stirred slightly.

So, he was alive.

His shivering had calmed down by the looks of it, although he was still wan and pale.

Nola touched him on the shoulder.

"Hello," she said. "Bruno, can you hear me?"

Startled, he opened his eyes.

"You are all right," said Gisela in German. "Do you know where you are? You're in Ireland."

He looked at Gisela, his dark eyes darting now in the dim light.

He pulled himself into a half-seated position, groaning with the pain in his leg.

"How long have I been here?" he mumbled in German.

"I don't know," answered Gisela. "A few days."

He pointed at his crotch and told Gisela in German that he needed to urinate.

In the corner Gisela spied a bucket, which must have been brought there for such a purpose.

She went and fetched it for him.

"Nola," she said, "look away."

"I will not," said Nola.

Struggling, the solider undid the button on his trousers and untucked himself from his underwear.

Gisela tipped the bucket towards him.

Looking away, to give him some privacy, Gisela saw that Nola was peering in good and hard.

"Nola!" she said.

Nola widened her eyes.

The soldier didn't seem to notice Nola's examination.

He groaned as the bucket was deposited with foul-smelling urine.

Gisela wondered whether he might have an infection in his bladder too.

"You need to drink more water," said Gisela. "You are dehydrated."

Gisela gave the bucket to Nola and asked her to get rid of its contents.

"*Ugh*," said Nola taking the bucket and holding it as far away from herself as possible.

"My leg is broken," said the soldier.

"We know," said Gisela. "We put sulfa on it today. And gave you a painkiller. You should take more."

She took another one from the bottle and gave it to him with the water.

She asked him to drink as much as he could.

The medicine had begun to work, thought Gisela.

This was the first time they'd seen him properly lucid.

"I landed badly," he said. "It's unfortunate."

"Are you hungry?" asked Gisela.

He shook his head.

"You should eat," she said.

He told her he felt nauseous.

"It's the fever," she said. "Tomorrow, we'll bring you proper food. Please, drink as much water as you can."

Peering past her, the soldier began searching the loft with his eyes.

He patted the sleeping bag.

"What are you looking for?" asked Gisela.

"My radio," he said. "My bag."

Nola, who had tipped the urine out the back of the loft with a splash, put the bucket down and joined in the search.

She spied a shape in the corner of the loft and went to it with the candle. She lifted it up.

A large canvas kit bag, like a long fat pillow, had been half covered in straw.

Nola dragged it over.

The soldier lifted the flap of the bag and pulled out a shirt and trousers.

Next, he pulled out a rectangle leather case.

He opened it and inside was a square radio, fastened to the inside of the lining.

Grimacing in pain, he began to assemble an antenna.

"Ah!" he said after he switched it on and nothing happened. "*Verdammt!*"

"Broken?" said Gisela.

He nodded.

He fiddled with the radio dials and then, seemingly exhausted, fell back onto his pillow.

He lifted his head again.

"Those boys ..." he said. "Who brought me here."

"Peadar," said Gisela. "And Mícheál."

"When will they be back?"

Gisela asked Nola what she thought.

"They'll probably visit you later," Nola said. "They can only come when it's dark. Their houses are being watched so it's difficult for them to get out. But I think Mícheál is in Dublin, with his father. Tell him," she said, turning to Gisela. "Tell him Mícheál is trying to get word from his father about what to do with him."

Gisela translated.

"What are they being watched for?" he asked in English.

Nola looked at Gisela.

"There was a robbery. They've arrested Mícheál's father, Seán McKee."

"Ah yes," said the soldier. "Mr. McKee. I never even got to meet him." The soldier stared for a moment.

"I need to get a radio. I must send a message."

"When the boys come you can ask them about that," said Nola.

As Gisela stood up to leave, the soldier reached out and grabbed her hand.

"Where are you from?" he said. "Your accent?"

"Vienna," said Gisela, looking surprised.

"Ah," he said and he fell back onto his pillow again with the effort of it all. "The City of Dreams."

His eyes began to close.

Gisela saw that the painkiller was powerful.

"We'll come back in the morning," said Nola. "And bring you breakfast. I expect Peadar will come to check on you later."

But the solider was already asleep.

Nola blew out the candle and they made their way out the back of the loft and down the ladder.

"I think he's getting better," said Nola.

"He's going to die if he doesn't get to hospital," said Gisela.

"You think so?" said Nola, shocked. "What should we do?"

"Well," said Gisela. "He's not our responsibility. Perhaps Mr. McKee will give his permission to get him to hospital. So they can save his life."

"That fella," said Nola. "I wouldn't want to be relying on him. We'll go and talk to Peadar about it tomorrow. It's getting too close to the Garden Fête now."

G2 INTELLIGENCE REPORT

STATUS: NOTICE OF ARREST
LOCATION: DROGHEDA GARDA STATION, CO. LOUTH

Peadar Tracy of Termonfeckin village has been arrested on suspicion of TRESPASS at Newtown House, Termonfeckin.

Mr. Tracy has a history of loitering and theft and was found in the garden of Newtown House last night carrying a bag with foodstuffs, indicating he intended to camp out within the yard and surrounds to await various thieving opportunities.

Gardaí are aware that due to this weekend's Garden Fête there are a number of valuable items in situ.

He will appear before Drogheda district court this Friday.

Hans

CHAPTER TWENTY-NINE

When Miriam and Gerhard Schafer saw their only daughter lying unconscious in her hospital bed, they cried like children.

Nobody could comfort them.

Anja was unrecognizable, swollen into a monster.

Beaten to a pulp.

They had lost their first grandchild, before she had even breathed.

Hans stood, silent, watching them, his eyes vacant of tears.

He had not cried since the night he'd found her on the street.

Instead, he swallowed his anger and his grief back.

He felt it, like a lump, travelling back down into this body, where he knew it lay deep, festering.

At home, Hans' father knew that something was wrong but could never understand what.

His dementia, which had stabilised when Anja had moved in, got worse.

Hans was torn between trying to care for his father at home and his wife in hospital.

He had to take a leave of absence from work.

The Vienna Transport Company gave him two weeks without pay.

He couldn't think beyond that.

The grief the Schafers showed on the outside matched Hans' feelings on the inside, yet he could not bear to watch them wail, sob and cry over their daughter.

It was too much.

Usually, he went for a walk when they arrived to her bare hospital room.

When he came back, he hoped they'd have calmed down.

For five days Anja went in and out of consciousness.

Eventually the swelling subsided enough for her to wake up and it was with great joy that they held her good hand and looked into her eyes as she blinked at them blankly and touched her head and bandages.

"You're all right!" her mother exclaimed. "Anja, my love, we are here, we are here, can you hear me, you are all right!"

Two days later she gave birth to a still, perfectly formed baby.

A girl.

Hans held her in his arms, wrapped in a white blanket.

When they gave her to Anja, she did not seem to know what was going on.

Their joy at Anja's waking soon turned to despair.

Anja had woken up but it was not the same Anja who had come back to them.

Something had happened in the beating.

Something knocked out of place forever.

Her parents ignored it at first.

They said she was doing ever so well and exclaimed whenever she did something for herself like get out of bed, or drink from her teacup.

Hans recognised the problems instantly.

It reminded him of his father.

She was there, but she was not there.

She had changed.

She couldn't remember.

He knew that sometimes she did not know who he was.

She did not ask about the baby.

It was as though she'd never even known there was a baby.

The Schafers insisted that with enough care and attention, everything would come back.

The doctors thought differently.

Her brain had been damaged, they said.

She could recover some memories perhaps, but her state, the childlike state they found her in, was likely to be her long-term outcome.

There were therapies they could try.

But the damage, overall, was too great.

When Anja was recovered enough to leave the hospital, her parents wanted to take her home with them to Alsergrund but Hans refused.

She was his wife.

He wanted her home.

And he would take care of her.

He extended his leave from work without pay.

His boss, who he'd known since he was a boy out of school took pity on him but said the time off was the last they could give.

If he could not return to full-time work, they would have to hire a new conductor.

"We are not a charity," he'd said solemnly.

Hans had nodded his head.

He did not want charity.

He just wanted more time.

Frau Leitner did her best.

She came around each day to help Hans with the cooking and cleaning but when his father hit her, giving her a black eye, Hans knew that he could not ask anymore of her.

With the reality of the situation at home, that Anja could not cook or clean and with his frail and sometimes violent father, Hans relented and brought Anja to the large town house where her parents and siblings still lived so that he could return to work.

"Only for a short time," he said. "Until I can organise my father."

Hans had to go to work.

Anja needed to be supported.

Gerhard's white hair fell out completely, revealing a smooth round head.

He took charge of Anja, brushing her hair, singing to her, holding her hand and telling her stories from when she was small girl, about how they'd go boating in the lakes and for walks in the forest.

It was hard to correlate the smartly dressed tailor and business owner with the ravaged teary nurse who now looked as frail as Anja did herself.

Miriam fretted.

Their money was drying up.

Their sons could only do so much.

Time was running out, they knew.

If they wanted to leave, they'd have to do it soon.

Otherwise, there would be no visas left.

In early 1939 the Schafers made a decision.

With their business destroyed and their only daughter's life having been changed irrevocably, they would face up to what had been staring them in the face for a long time.

The intimidation, the rules, the segregation and the hate.

They would have to leave Vienna.

Their good friends, the Engels, were rounded up one morning at 5am and taken away.

The Schafers were prominent in the community. They knew that they would be next.

Miriam, through Jewish friends, organised a passage to Palestine for the family.

She begged Hans to come with them, to bring Anja in the new wheelchair they'd bought for when she needed to travel any distance.

But Hans could not leave his father.

And he did not want to be separated from Anja either.

They belonged together, he told them, in no uncertain terms.

In time, he promised, perhaps they would follow them out.

On the day the Schafers left, Hans wheeled Anja to the train station in her wheelchair.

He knew she didn't really understand what was happening.

Gerhard found it difficult to let go of his daughter.

He cried deep tears, held onto Anja's neck until Miriam screamed that the train was going.

Hans felt sick to his stomach.

He waved them off, waved to them for Anja.

The city was emptying out.

Each day on his tram he saw Jewish families, carrying as many belongings as they could.

They were all on the move, wearing the same, pale, frightened expression.

The children, those who were travelling without their parents, broke his heart, with their placards around their necks, *Vilheim, Marta, Gunther.*

And then he was back to his old conundrum: how could he work and care for his elderly father and his wife?

Hans asked about the neighbourhood and found an older woman who agreed to come and care for Anja and his father while Hans went to work.

It would leave them with very little money, but he would have peace of mind at least.

On the morning the carer was due to arrive, Hans went to rouse his father to give him his morning tea and bread.

He found his father lying at an angle in the bed, cool to the touch, his mouth awkwardly open.

At some point the life had slipped from him in the night.

His father was gone.

In the space of a few months, Hans had lost the beloved wife he had known, all of her extended family and now his father.

Their dreams of a family had evaporated.

The life he had imagined for himself as a future carpenter, while Anja raised their small children seemed laughable now.

He thought about taking her to Palestine.

He thought that maybe it would be the best thing for her, to be back with her family who so dearly missed her.

Perhaps he should have let her go with them in the first place?

Perhaps he had been selfish all along?

Round and round his thoughts went, going over and over how he could have done things differently.

Frau Leitner told him he had to stop blaming himself.

She said terrible things were happening in the city and none of them were Hans' fault.

But Hans could not.

Because he did blame himself.

He blamed himself for getting Anja pregnant in the first place.

He blamed himself for not being there to walk her to her rehearsals.

He blamed himself for leaving her, all by herself, beaten on the pavement.

And he blamed himself for not letting her go with her family to Palestine.

All of it was his fault, he felt.

No matter what Frau Leitner said.

* * *

"Ah, there you are," said Maeve.

She was carrying a basket over her arm.

She took a sandwich wrapped in paper from it.

Hans looked up from where he was painting strips of wood to be hammered into place for the Garden Fête.

All across the lawns at Newtown were various stalls and paraphernalia.

Two lorries had arrived that morning to drop off stretch tents and extra chairs.

Mrs. Carmody was in a flurry of activity, waving her clipboard about and pointing.

Her shrill tones carried on the wind.

Hans was glad to see Maeve.

She brought with her a sense of calm, of kindness.

In the short time that he'd been in Newtown, they had found themselves falling into conversation, at the dining table, on Saturday nights over a glass of sherry.

Nola and Gisela rushed by, heading towards the house.

"Are you running from Mrs. Carmody?" asked Maeve, joking.

Nola threw her eyes to heaven as she scuttled past.

"I'm running from Mr. Walshe," said Hans.

"Aren't we all?" said Maeve.

Hans looked at Maeve's face and waited for her smile.

It did not come.

A pair of goldfinches alighted on the lawn.

They pulled at the white seeds of fluffy dandelion heads.

Maeve sat down beside Hans with an "*Oomph!*"

She handed him a small bottle of milk.

"I'm supposed to be doing the lunch rounds," she said, "but I'm sure I can have a little rest for a minute."

There was that smile again.

A twinkle in her eye.

Hans, trying to fill the void, found himself saying words he never expected to say.

"It is nice to spend time together, Maeve."

Maeve smiled again, deeper this time.

"Yes," she said, "I suppose it is."

"We should do this more often."

"I thought you'd never ask."

They looked at each other.

"If I did ask you to go for a walk one evening, you will go?" Hans said tentatively.

Maeve was quiet.

Then she nodded.

"Yes, I would, Hans. I would."

"You would?"

"Yes. I don't see the harm."

"As more than a friend?"

"Well, we'd have to wait and see, wouldn't we?"

She looked up into his blue eyes and he looked into her dark features, trying to read her face.

She was older than Anja, much nearer to his age but, yes, he could be comfortable with her, he realised.

"Do you think Mr. Walshe would mind?" he asked.

Maeve frowned.

"Why would he mind?" she said.

"Well ... just he ... he ... I don't know. I just wondered."

"What I do is none of his business."

"Yes," said Hans.

He berated himself for asking.

He had annoyed Maeve, he could see.

She got up and dusted down her apron.

He wanted to apologise.

She went to turn around to walk away and Hans stopped her.

"Maeve ..."

"Yes, Hans?" she said.

"I –"

"You what?"

"Nothing. I'm sorry."

He could think of nothing to say.

He could not put into words his feelings and sorrow at upsetting her.

"You're all right, Hans," said Maeve as she walked away, the lunch basket over her arm.

Hans returned to his painting, inwardly cursing himself and his language skills and his inability, always, to say what he really thought, what he really felt.

Anja had always seen beyond it, understood him, deep down.

Maeve, he knew, did too, only they were new to each other and unsure.

That was why it would be nice to step out.

So that he could come to know her better, and her, him.

Gisela

CHAPTER THIRTY

Curious to see what condition Bruno was in following his night of painkillers and sulfa powder, Gisela and Nola were surprised to find him propped up on his sleeping bag, the contents of his canvas bag scattered all around him.

On his lap was a small hardbacked novel and some papers.

The radio was set up.

It seemed he had been trying to get it to work again.

"Good morning," said Nola brightly.

"Ah," he said. "The girls."

Gisela produced the bread and boiled eggs she'd snuck from the breakfast table.

Nola had a lump of hard cheese.

"How is the leg?" asked Nola, pointing at his bandages.

"Bad," he said. "Feels bad."

Gisela set to work, cutting off the wet wrappings and preparing the sulfa powder.

When she uncovered the wound, the powerful smell almost made her fall backwards and she had to steady herself.

She felt as though she might retch and had to turn away.

The solider lay back on the sleeping bag.

Gisela noticed a thin film of sweat on his face, down his neck and across his chest.

His fever was back, she realised.

He did not look very well at all.

Examining the wound, Gisela cleared her throat and caught Nola's attention.

Where the bone had broken the skin, a dark black colour had appeared.

Instead of cleaning the wound as she had done yesterday, Gisela simply poured the sulfa powder onto it and wrapped up the leg tightly.

The solider groaned, deeply.

Nola took the bottle of painkillers and shook them.

She showed it to Gisela.

"You must have been taking a lot of these?" Nola said.

The soldier spoke in German.

"He said he had to," said Gisela. "For the pain."

Nola spoke loudly and clearly to the soldier in English.

"You need to go to hospital."

The soldier nodded.

"You must be seen to."

He nodded again.

Gisela asked him something in German and he shook his head.

"Peadar didn't come here last night," said Gisela to Nola.

Nola frowned.

Before they left, Gisela and Nola helped the solider with the bucket again.

He found it hard to urinate, as though he were all blocked up.

"It's going to be busy around here today," said Nola, projecting her voice. "We have a big party coming up. Lots of people. But we will come back this evening. Please don't make any noise."

Gisela translated what she had said.

The changing of the dressing seemed to have triggered a new pain in the soldier.

He pushed away the papers and radio and moaned.

He muttered in German.

"He doesn't want us to leave," said Gisela, translating.

"But we must," said Nola. "Mrs. Carmody will be looking for us."

Gisela found herself feeling quite sorry for the solider as they climbed their way out of the hayloft. He was in a pitiful state.

Outside, they hurried away from the shed, ducking in behind a tree near to the walled garden.

"What do you think?" said Nola.

"I think he has gangrene," said Gisela.

"Is that bad?"

"Very bad. It will spread. It probably has spread. I think he was only able to talk to us because of all those painkillers inside him."

"What will we do?" asked Nola.

"Can we speak to Peadar? Or Mícheál?"

"We'll have to do something. I can't understand how they can abandon him like that. Although Mícheál must still be in Dublin."

From behind, Mrs. Carmody called.

"Girls! Where have you been hiding? Please come here at once!"

Looking at each other, the girls threw their eyes to heaven in solidarity and made their way over to Mrs. Carmody to receive their latest instructions.

"Now, I've run out of ribbon for the cake-stand table and I need one of you to call to Mrs. Hodgins in Baltray. She's donating her spools – since the arthritis took over her poor hands, she can't sew a thing. Gisela, you take a bike over. If I let Nola go, I might not see her till next week."

Nola scowled.

Gisela nodded.

She borrowed a black bike leaning against a shed in the yard and freewheeled down the avenue, leaving the chaos that was Newtown behind.

She waved to Otto and Max who had joined a group of gardeners weeding at the entrance gates to the house.

The large limestone pillars looked magnificent against the closed, black gates.

Tomorrow they would be flung wide open for the many visitors who were due to descend on the estate.

Gisela enjoyed the pull of the air on her skin and hair as she cycled along the winding road to Baltray.

She had walked the road a few times with Nola and felt confident about where she was going.

It was funny how she was getting used to this place now, so different from home.

It took just a few minutes to reach Mrs. Hodgins' small whitewashed cottage overlooking the marsh.

Gisela felt the sun on her face as she rapped on the door and waited for an answer.

She smelt the tidal water, sour in the heat.

Reedy grass grew in the garden around a broken footpath.

A bushy red geranium sat in a cracked earthenware pot.

Mrs. Hodgins, a stooped woman, who looked like she should have retired from any laborious work at least a decade ago, opened the door and peered curiously at Gisela.

"I have come for ribbon," said Gisela. "Mrs. Carmody sent me."

"Ah, come in," said the old woman.

Inside the cottage, a low fire glowed in pile of ash in the grate.

A pot hung over it on a crook.

Gisela saw a flat-looking bread on the table and a large pot of potatoes.

The cottage was warm but not stifling, its thick walls and small windows offering protection in the summer heat.

"Just a minute now," said the woman and she shuffled over to a dresser laid out with china, newspapers and crafting materials.

Rooting in a bulging drawer she pulled out three spools of ribbon, two red and one blue.

"If she needs any more than that, she'll have to go into town, I'm afraid. Or Mrs. Healy might have a spare few bits, she's only over the road there."

She handed the spools to Gisela.

Gisela nodded and said thank you.

The woman was right up close to her.

Gisela smelled peppermint on her breath.

As Gisela turned to leave, the woman gripped her by the arm.

"Are you one of those Austrians?" she asked, studying her face.

Gisela nodded again.

"Ah, you are. Isn't she very good now, that Mrs. de Freyne? Taking yis in. Manys a wouldn't, that's for sure. Don't mind any talk you hear in the village. Yis are most welcome."

She released her arm and smiled.

Gisela felt something warm spread in her stomach.

They were *most welcome.*

It was an unexpected kindness from this stranger.

And it was the first time she'd been told she was welcome by anyone outside of Newtown House.

Gisela pedalled the bike back up the hill, passing cows in fields, a few sheep scattered among them.

Back in the grounds of the house she hunted out Mrs. Carmody who took the ribbon and immediately passed it over to another woman to go and dress the stand.

Nola, carrying three stacked chairs, spotted Gisela, dropped them and raced over.

"*Major news,*" she hissed. "*Major!*"

The girls turned away.

"Peadar's been arrested!"

"*What?*" said Gisela.

Had they been found out?

Had they discovered the spy?

"Here, last night. For trespassing!"

"Oh, my god!" said Gisela.

She went quiet for a moment.

"Can we talk to Mícheál then, about what to do?"

"He's not back yet, Maeve told me!"

"So, we have no one to speak to. We're running out of time, Nola."

"I know."

"*Girls!*" called Mrs. Carmody.

"Oh, piss off, Mrs. Carmody," said Nola.

"Excuse me?" said Mrs. Carmody.

Nola turned and smiled sweetly at the committee leader and pointed at the flowerbed in front of them. "I was just saying to Gisela that the petunias are lovely."

* * *

The rest of the day passed in a flurry of activity.

Gisela and Nola were sent in all different directions, fetching, carrying, holding, hanging and generally being on hand to assist with whatever Mrs. Carmody demanded of them.

Mrs. de Freyne seemed to revel in the work and floated about overseeing all the activity.

"It's all coming together marvellously," she said at the dinner table that evening.

Gisela saw Hans smile up at Maeve as she put some extra vegetables on his plate.

She liked to see Hans smile.

"Tomorrow we will spring open those gates," said Mrs. de Freyne. "I tell you, those faces, especially of the children – when you see them, it'll all be worth it."

Exhausted, everyone retired to bed early.

When the house had settled and the moon rose in the sky, Nola gently opened Gisela's door and sidled into her room.

Gisela was in a deep sleep and Nola had to rouse her.

Gisela turned away.

She felt too tired to get up.

"Please, Gisela, we need to check on him. I don't want to go out on my own."

Reluctantly, Gisela pulled herself from her bed.

In the kitchen, Nola put bread and leftovers from supper into her bag, which also contained their kit for tending to the soldier's wound.

Gisela did not relish the thought of playing nurse again.

How had this happened, she wondered, as they went outside in the dark.

How had she ended up sneaking about at night looking after a Nazi solider?

A yellow light in Mr. Walshe's window glowed.

Further back, where the other cottages were, Gisela saw that Hans' light was still on too.

Not everyone must have been as tired as they were, she thought.

They hid against the wall to make sure there was no movement in the yard.

Slowly, they made their way round to the back of the hayshed and climbed up the ladder.

Nola went ahead of Gisela.

She spoke in a low voice to the solider to alert him to their presence.

"Hello, Bruno! Sorry we couldn't get back to you any earlier. Are you awake?"

As Gisela righted herself, standing up in the low loft, she saw Nola peer down at the solider.

Nola moved closed and touched the soldier's arm.

"Hello," she said. "Bruno? Can you hear me?"

Nola looked back at Gisela.

Gisela moved closer.

Bruno was lying perfectly still.

There was no rise to his chest and, as Nola struck a match to light the candle beside the sleeping bag, Gisela crouched down and put her ear to his mouth.

"Nola," she said in a quiet voice. "Nola, he is not breathing."

Gisela put out her hand and touched the soldier's forehead.

She yanked her hand back in fright.

"He's cold!" said Gisela.

"Is he … ?" said Nola.

"Yes," said Gisela nodding, her voice faint. "Bruno's dead. He's dead."

Hans

CHAPTER THIRTY-ONE

Maeve's interest in Hans made him swell with pride.

Till now he had felt like such an outsider, somebody other who would always be apart.

Now, somehow, he felt as if he had been accepted.

He had been accepted, by Maeve at least.

On Friday evening, back in his cottage, he sat up late, sanding his carvings with a piece of fine sandpaper.

He was tired, but he felt elated.

He wanted to finish his gift for Maeve.

She had said she would step out with him.

Here again, was a chance at love.

The oil lamp flickered on the table.

Dusting the soft wood shavings off his knee, Hans stood up and shook out his trousers.

His back ached and his eyes were tired.

He set the carving aside.

It was almost finished but he didn't have the stamina to keep going.

It would be better to rest than to make an error now when it was nearly done.

As he moved across the kitchen towards the narrow stairs for bed, a sharp knock came to the door.

The rap made him jump.

He turned around.

Who could want him at this hour?

Mr. Walshe, perhaps?

Something had happened on the farm?

He carried the oil lamp to the door and opened it.

He was shocked to have Nola and Gisela rush past him and into the cottage.

Nola slammed the door shut behind her and stayed leaning against it.

"Something's happened," said Gisela in German. "We need your help."

"What?" said Hans, surprised by their sudden intrusion. "Are you all right?"

"You're not going to believe this," said Gisela.

Hans looked from Nola's white face to Gisela's.

"I swear I'm not making this up," said Gisela.

"It's not my fault," said Nola. "Please, we don't want to get into any trouble."

* * *

Being married to a young Jewish woman and watching her family try to cope with the duress they found themselves fighting under the Nazi Party regime, Hans had come to know the campaigns of intimidation they raged.

The loss of the Schafers' business had been devastating.

The SA officers who had marched outside in protest, the brick through the window, the pogroms, Kristallnacht had intimidated and shocked.

There was a campaign, however, that had mostly passed Hans by until he realised as he pushed Anja in her chair along the street one day that it was directly aimed at them.

It was against those who could not contribute to the state.

He stopped Anja's chair at a poster that had been plastered to a lamppost.

It pictured a working man carrying a disabled man on one shoulder and a mentally ill man on the other.

50,000 Reichmarks is what one person with a hereditary disease will cost the state in their lifetime, read the caption. *Fellow citizens, that is your money too.*

He touched Anja on the shoulder and she put her hand up to grip his.

Always she liked to be stroked, a reassurance that he was there.

After seeing the poster, Hans noticed them more and more.

They were plastered to posts, in some shop windows and even, he noticed, in some apartment windows in their building.

He began to lose trust in where he lived.

He'd heard whispers about Anja being a Jewess, something that had never mattered before, but ever since Kristallnacht everything had changed.

Frau Leitner told him that some of the neighbours weren't happy.

"This is not a Jewish neighbourhood," she said, holding her palms out. "You should be careful. Somebody could report her. They're taking people away, you know. You could come home from work and she would be gone."

Frau Leitner snapped her fingers.

Just like that. Gone.

The sound reverberated off Hans' insides.

Frau Leitner was right.

Anja as a Jewess was not welcome.

Anja as a disabled Jewess was even more a target.

He had been denying it to himself, too consumed with his father, with the Schafer's departure, with coping with Anja's illness and recovery and trying to work.

Until then, he'd clung to a glimmer of hope that she would get better.

That her state was temporary and that given enough time and love and care she might hopefully return to the old Anja.

He had found it hard to believe that the attack could leave her so permanently changed.

If she was no longer disabled, she would be safe with him, wouldn't she?

One evening Hans came home from work and Anja's carer said a man from the municipal council had called.

She did not know who he was or what he wanted, but he had asked questions about Anja and taken notes.

He had watched her in her chair and stayed while she ate a bowl of soup.

The visit was enough for Hans to make his decision.

He too would leave Vienna.

Anja was in great danger.

There was no time to try and organise Palestine.

It could take weeks to bribe their way out.

So many people had moved in the weeks after Kristallnacht that getting out now was almost impossible.

Hans cursed the fact that he had not allowed Anja to move with her family when they had gone at the very start of 1939.

He wished he'd realised how desperate the situation was earlier.

He wished he hadn't been so naive as to think things would get better.

He skipped work and visited legations around the city to see who might support a Catholic man and his Jewish wife with emigration.

He told no one about the state of her health.

She was a good worker, just like he was, he promised.

One evening, as Frau Leitner washed up the dishes after putting her large brood to bed, she got a knock on the door.

It was Hans.

He handed her the key to his apartment.

"Tomorrow," he told her, "we will be gone. Tell no one. You can have whatever you like. Take anything you need. You can stay in the apartment if you want. Until the landlord realises we are gone."

Frau Leitner had nodded solemnly, as if she had expected such a visit all along.

She squeezed his arm and wished him good luck.

They both knew it would be the last they ever saw of each other.

The next morning, Hans took a small bag of belongings for himself and Anja and pushed her in her chair to the train station.

They took a train far out of the city until they reached farmland.

Hans had great difficulty trying to get Anja's chair down onto the platform.

No one came to help.

Through a charity run by some Christian Churches and the Society of Friends, Hans had managed to get himself onto a farming scheme at Kagran, outside the city.

There he would retrain as an agricultural worker and work with the charity to get a placement away from Germany.

They were securing passage to Bolivia and Peru in South America, to Rhodesia in Africa and to Canada and the United States.

Hans felt lucky to have got on the scheme, which was made up of nearly 200 Jews.

The accommodation provided was basic, little more than wooden huts for the families who had managed to secure a place.

Light appeared all around the bottom of the cabins, where insects and vermin could creep in.

They ate in a cafeteria hooded by a large plastic roof.

Although the emigrations were funded by monies raised by the charity, the farm work was overseen by Gestapo soldiers in uniform, some of them armed, as the scheme itself was organised by the German Government.

Anja was assigned the most basic of tasks in the kitchen, while Hans dug ditches and worked in the fields.

He worried about her constantly and explained to the staff that she was still recovering from her injuries.

They took pity on her and allowed her to take breaks back to her cabin to rest.

She was confused by her new surroundings.

She wanted Hans to stay with her all the time.

One morning Hans got up to go and fetch some drinking water for Anja.

She had suffered a bad night with disturbed dreams and pain.

Outside, he met a family who had just arrived with their belongings and bags on their back. They'd been assigned the hut next door.

They looked tired and washed out, gaunt and pale-faced.

"Hello," said Hans and he watched how stooped the man of the family seemed to be.

"Hello," said the man and he smiled in greeting and held out his hand.

"Fritz Hettinger," he said.

Hans pumped the man's hand and smiled.

"Hans Schmitt."

"This is my wife Eva and my sons, Max and Otto."

The two tall boys, standing back, waved.

Eva smiled.

"Pleased to meet you," said Hans.

He was a glad a woman had arrived next door.

He hoped she would be friendly towards Anja.

She needed all the support she could get.

Gisela

CHAPTER THIRTY-TWO

"Rise and shine, sleepy-head!"

Maeve stood over Gisela's bed, smiling.

"My, my, you are tired this morning. Miss Nola is the same next door. Were you up talking all night or something?"

Gisela lay still.

Did Maeve know something?

She put a jug of warm water on Gisela's washstand.

"Breakfast is early this morning so you'd better get a move on."

At the breakfast table Mrs. de Freyne was wearing a beautifully cut jacket and her hair was coiffed. She was beaming with excitement.

"There you are," she said when Gisela and Nola arrived. "Look at what a bit of hard work has done to you! You look worn out!"

The girls sat down.

Gisela looked at Hans who raised a small glass of orange juice to his mouth.

He nodded in acknowledgment before looking away.

After their breakfast was served – sausages, bacon and eggs on account of the special occasion – Mrs. de Freyne rapped her spoon on her teacup.

She cleared her throat and looked around at the Hettingers, at Gisela and at Hans.

"Today is a very special day for Newtown," she said. "It's a day for us to shine. I am so glad you get to experience this day with us, getting to meet all of our lovely villagers and seeing them enjoy what we enjoy here every day. Here's to our wonderful 1939 Garden Fête!"

She held up her teacup.

Everyone else held up their teacup or glass.

"*Here, here!*" said Fritz Hettinger.

A ripple of applause broke out and Gisela and Nola caught each other's eye.

It was a lovely speech.

But Gisela felt nauseous and her chest felt tight.

What was going to happen today?

When would he be found?

Gisela and Nola left the breakfast table to go to the dancing hall for a final meeting with Mrs. Carmody and the committee.

Mrs. Carmody, like Mrs. de Freyne, had donned a suit for the occasion, although hers was badly fitting and coarse.

Her hair was swept up and pinned back.

"She looks like a trussed-up turkey," said Nola to Gisela.

Gisela couldn't help but smile.

Mrs. Carmody also gave a little speech but it wasn't quite as warm as Mrs. de Freyne's. Instead, she warned that she would be keeping a close eye on everything to ensure things ran smoothly.

"Thank God she'll have gone back to roost from next week on," said Nola.

Gisela wondered what next week would bring.

The nauseous worry in her stomach swirled.

She felt that something was going to happen, something bad, something terrible.

She didn't know what. Only that they were going to get in trouble somehow.

She could feel it.

An army of volunteers had appeared for the day and were moving around the grounds, getting ready for the gates to open.

The stallholders were busy setting up their shops.

Gisela watched a man set up a roulette table.

He was dour and moody but she expected that later, as he called for bets, he would have a smile on his face.

At eleven, Newtown House gates were thrown open wide and Gisela and Nola made their way out to the avenue to watch.

They stood beside Fintan Walshe who had his arms folded as he watched the visitors arrive.

"You know this place was closed up for two hundred years," said Fintan to Gisela. "Nobody ever came in except the staff and, even at that, the staff weren't local. And then Mrs. de Freyne came along and she opened it all up and that's why so many people come here, you see. They want to look. They want to feel what it's like, to live in a big house like this."

Gisela looked at Mr. Walshe.

He looked tired, with purple folds of skin under his eyes.

It seemed the fête preparations had taken their toll on him too.

Gisela was staggered by the volume of people that came flowing through the gate.

Families with small children rushed in.

Groups of young boys abandoned their bicycles all along the stone wall at the perimeter of the property.

Motorcars pulled up and unfurled many squished-up people.

The tea tent was soon full.

Guests took their seats for the first concert of the day.

The painting demonstration was packed.

A large Rolls Royce moved at a snail's pace up the avenue, through the crowds.

Motorcars were not permitted past the gates.

As the car passed, Gisela saw that inside was Mrs. Mulvany whom she'd met on the very first day of her arrival and Nola's cousins, Kate and Margaret.

"The Mulvanys won't go round the back," said Mr. Walshe, smirking.

"We'd better go and say hello," said Nola.

Reluctantly Gisela followed Nola.

At the front door of Newtown, the Mulvanys put a delicate foot each out of the car and stepped out.

"Ah, Nola," said Mrs. Mulvany, "another raucous occasion. I'm sure you're in your element."

Nola smiled.

Gisela noticed that Nola's hair was quite tousled and that she was dressed in her favoured trousers, while the Mulvany girls had smooth pearls in their ears and wore A-line dresses with wide bands around the middle, which they'd matched with low heels.

"It's like a zoo," said Kate.

"Is your mother about?" asked Mrs. Mulvany.

"If you can find her. I think she's manning the tea tent," said Nola.

The group made their way around to the lawns.

There, as expected, they found Mrs. de Freyne, red-faced in the tea tent.

"Really, Laila," said Mrs. Mulvany, kissing her sister-in-law on the cheeks, "I don't know why you bring this upon yourself."

Mrs. de Freyne laughed.

"Let's go and watch the tennis," said Nola to her cousins.

The tournament was in full swing when they arrived and found a place on the grass.

Gisela watched Nola's cousins stare at the more handsome player who had dark features and bulbous, hard calves.

"That's Father Crowley's brother," said Nola.

"Really?" said Gisela.

Sure enough, they spied Father Crowley standing on the side-lines, looking on.

"He's much better-looking than Father Crowley," said Margaret.

"That wouldn't be hard," said Nola with a laugh.

"I don't know," said Kate. "I don't think Father Crowley is that bad.

He has something about him."

"Too short," said Nola.

"Your father was short," said Margaret.

Nola scowled.

"Well, he was, like all the de Freynes."

"Have you put any plans in place for your coming out ball yet?" asked Kate.

"Not really," said Nola. She looked down and pulled up a tuft of short grass. "Things have been a bit tense."

"How do you mean?" asked Margaret.

"Well, Mummy and I haven't been getting along. She said I was on my last warning. If I do one more thing wrong, she's going to cancel my coming out ball. So, I can't get in any trouble whatsoever." Nola glanced at Gisela.

"That'll be difficult for you," mocked Kate.

"I'm trying to behave," said Nola, still holding Gisela's eyes.

A large cheer rang out from the crowd as the handsome tennis player scored a winning point.

Father Crowley made a little leap of joy.

"Are you keeping her out of trouble?" asked Margaret, turning her attention to Gisela now.

Gisela shrugged and smiled.

"Yes. She's a very good influence," said Nola.

Gisela felt the warmth of the compliment.

"Oh well, I suppose that's something," said Margaret.

After the tennis match, which Father Crowley's brother won outright, they went to look at the golf and then made their way back to the tea tent for some cake and lemonade.

As the four girls sat at a table with their drinks, the sound of a siren wailed in the distance.

They all looked around.

"Oh goodness," said Kate, "somebody's in trouble."

"Gisela, let's go and see what's going on," said Nola.

She and Gisela stood up.

"You stay here," said Nola firmly to her cousins.

Gisela and Nola moved quickly around to the front of the house, where they spied a black Garda motorcar, siren wailing, pushing its way up the avenue.

"Oh my God," said Nola. "Do you think ..."

Gisela was silent.

Mrs. de Freyne appeared, drawn by the noise.

The Garda car reached the top of the avenue and pulled in beside the Mulvanys' Rolls Royce.

"Mrs. de Freyne," said Sergeant McKiernan, getting out of the car and pulling a navy-blue Garda hat onto his head.

Two younger Guards followed.

"Is there a problem, Sergeant McKiernan?" asked Mrs. de Freyne.

"We're looking to speak to a Mr. Hans Schmitt. Is he here?"

"Yes, he is," said Mrs. de Freyne.

She led Sergeant McKiernan away, followed by the two other Guards.

Gisela and Nola looked at each other.

"Let's go upstairs," said Nola. "We can see everything from up there."

They raced up the stairs, taking two at a time, and ran to the back guest bedroom which overlooked the yard, the cottages and the lawns where the fête was set up.

"There," said Gisela and she pointed to Mrs. de Freyne and the three Guards who were making the way towards the bandstand.

Hans stood with his back to them, listening to the music.

They watched as Sergeant McKiernan tipped him on the shoulder.

"They know," said Nola. "They know."

"Oh my God," said Gisela.

She had felt that something was going to happen today.

She knew it.

And now, here it was.

The girls watched as the Guards, Mrs. de Freyne and Hans made their way through the crowds.

Mrs. Carmody ran from the painting tents to follow them.

People stood apart to let them through.

They were drawing attention.

"I think they're going to the yard," said Nola.

They lost sight of them for a moment before they appeared again, crossing the courtyard.

The group walked towards the cottages where the Hettingers and Hans lived.

Gisela and Nola, watched, silent.

The Guards disappeared into Hans' cottage, while Sergeant McKiernan stood outside with Hans, Mrs. de Freyne and Mrs. Carmody.

Within a few moments they reappeared again.

"What have they got?" said Nola, straining to see.

From across the yard, Fintan Walshe made his way to join the small group.

"What if they want to speak to us?" said Nola, turning to Gisela. "We need to know what we're both saying."

Gisela stared.

What was it they took out of the cottage?

As Fintan Walshe and Mrs. Carmody stood back, the Guards walked Hans forward.

"He's in handcuffs!" said Nola.

Mrs. de Freyne and Mrs. Carmody looked shocked.

As the Guards got nearer, the girls could clearly see what had been removed from Hans' home; it was a heavy bulky grey kitbag.

The girls looked to each other in startling realisation.

It was Bruno's bag.

They'd found the parachutists' belongings in Hans' cottage.

"Oh my God," said Nola.

Hans walked through the courtyard, tall, loping, his arms pinned back, arrested.

G2 INTELLIGENCE REPORT

STATUS: NOTICE OF ARREST
SUBJECT: HERR HANS SCHMITT
DETAINED: DROGHEDA GARDA STATION, CO. LOUTH

Mr. Hans Schmitt of Newtown Termonfeckin has been arrested on the suspicion of MURDER in relation to the discovery of a body, believed to be German Solider BRUNO MAYER on Strand Road, Termonfeckin.

Bruno Mayer's army issue bag was discovered in Hans Schmitt's residence at cottage at Newtown House.

Enquiries are under way as to what role Mr. Schmitt played in the arrival of the secret agent to Ireland.

We await further information from M15 and autopsy report.

Please see appendix for COVERT FILE on witness testimony in relation to this incident.

Hans

CHAPTER THIRTY-THREE

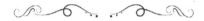

To Hans' surprise, the work on the farm outside Vienna, while intensive and tough on the body, brought him a sense of satisfaction.

He enjoyed being out in the open, feeling the fresh air sweep into his lungs and the warm sweat turn cool on his skin.

The soldiers took pleasure in putting the city types to work, watching rotund men, who had spent their lives at a desk, struggling to lug half-cut trees and fence posts and push heavy wheelbarrows of stone.

Hans grew in strength, and although he was still tree-tall and thin, his long arms became defined and his legs lean and tight.

Fritz Hettinger struggled with the work.

He'd been born with a slight twist to his spine which had started causing trouble when he'd finished growing.

If he spent too long hunched over in the lab it bothered him and Eva had learned to massage his stony muscles with an ointment that drew heat.

Within a week of the hard labour at the training camp, he was finding it hard to walk.

The soldiers mocked him.

Hans often saw tears in his eyes from the pain.

Otto and Max tried to work with their father as often as possible to assist him with the heavy tasks.

Hans too, stepped in when he could.

The hope was that they would find a placement sooner rather than later, so that wherever Fritz went he could try to find more suitable work than the heavy digging and dragging on the training farm.

Eva Hettinger, much to Hans' relief took Anja under her wing and took her around the camp like a daughter.

They had to keep a close eye on her because, although she was not able to travel long distances, she could still wander off and many dangers lurked.

Beyond the flat lands of the farm was a steep hill, behind which was a deep ravine. Eva, like Anja, helped in the kitchen cooking for the farm trainees.

Anja sat with her most days, doing small tasks that Eva assigned her.

They tried to keep Anja out of everyone's way, particularly the soldiers and the orderlies who ran the camp.

They knew they'd have little time for someone like Anja, who although she looked quite well from the outside, was simply not able to complete tasks like others.

She frightened easily.

She hated loud noises.

She didn't like the smells of cooking in the kitchen.

Outside the farm, where the pine trees rose high along the hill, she pointed and wanted to be brought there to sit or sometimes walk.

After the work for the day was completed, the Hettingers and Hans took turns to take her out to the bottom of the hill, knowing how the birdsong calmed her, watching her stroke the cracked honey-coloured bark of the trees and smile.

They watched as families disappeared in the mornings, packing up their meagre belongings and taking the train out.

Most were going to South America.

Only a few other families trickled in.

They were lucky to get on this scheme, they knew.

Soon, they were told, it would finish up.

Hans met with the Society of Friends each time they visited the camp, but with Anja's impairment they were finding it hard to place her.

After six weeks of the training camp, an Irishman who was a volunteer at the camp told him he thought he had a solution.

"Ireland is very rural," he said. "I think they will take in workers. If I can find a host family, we might have a solution."

Sure enough, the man, by the name of Hugh, returned with good news in just a week.

"I've found a family. They will take you and Anja and the Hettingers."

They were all overjoyed.

Finally, their backbreaking time at the camp would come to an end.

They would travel together.

And what's more, they would remain in Europe – something they all wanted.

On the morning before their departure, Anja woke up vomiting.

Hans tended to her and felt her warm forehead.

He rushed to get her water, to lay a cloth against her head and to scrub down the cabin before starting work.

Eva said she would keep an eye on her but that she had to get to the kitchen to prepare for the workers' lunch.

Hans hoped they wouldn't be put to work too far away in the fields that day.

When he left the cabin, Anja was tucked under her blanket, sleeping.

Before lunch break, he looked up to find Eva Hettinger running across the field towards him.

Her arms and legs flailed as she ran.

He stood up to meet her, a wave of fear rushing through him.

"*Hans!*" she cried. "*Hans, Anja's gone. I went to check her on, but she's gone!*"

Hans ran.

Fritz, Max and Otto chased after him, back to the cabin where only Anja's blanket lay.

They split up and went into the forest, cupping their mouths and calling her name.

"She can't have gone far," said Hans.

He knew that her gait was weak and her balance poor.

Their biggest fear was that that she would fall.

When they came to the ravine leading down to a small swollen stream, Hans' worry rose through his throat.

"*Anja!*" they called. "*Anja!*"

Stumbling down the steep incline, Hans reached the bottom of the stream and waded in.

There was no sign of her.

They spread out, Eva staying on the top of the slope to get a good view.

They walked for an age, seeing nothing, calling her name, finding not a sign, their hope turning to despair.

And then, a shout from Fritz, who had stopped near a tree, frantic.

"*Hans! Hans!*"

When Hans reached him, he saw what Fritz had found: his beautiful Anja, underwater, her body wrapped around a tree.

Fritz scooped her up.

Hans pulled her towards him.

Her face was swollen, white, gone.

When Eva and Otto and Max reached them, they put their hands to their mouths in shock.

Nobody had expected this.

Everyone blamed themselves.

In a slow procession the group made their way back to the camp, Hans carrying Anja, a limp ragdoll in his arms.

Word filtered through the camp about what had happened.

The Hettingers fretted about what to do.

They were all booked to leave the following day – any delay could see their safe passage taken away permanently.

That night, by Anja's bedside where she was laid out, wild flowers tucked into her long dark hair by Eva, Hans told them that they must go ahead.

"Hans," said Fritz, "you must come too."

"No," said Hans, shaking his head. "I can't leave her."

They left him with her all night, where he slept, his arms around her, clutching her cold body, dry-eyed and dry-throated.

In the early hours of the morning Fritz came to the cabin again.

"Will you help me bury her?" asked Hans.

"Of course," said Fritz.

Under a tall pine tree, at the bottom of the hill where Anja loved to roam, Hans, with the help of Otto and Max, dug a grave.

Eva came before they gently laid Anja to rest.

At the end of their prayer, as the sun rose in the sky, an eagle called from overhead.

Fritz squeezed Hans' arm.

"I am so sorry," he said.

Hans nodded.

Eva wrapped her arm around Hans' waist.

"I will come with you to Ireland," said Hans, staring at Anja's grave. "I have nothing left here now."

He had left his job.

Anja's family were beyond his reach, his parents dead.

At least, in Ireland, it would be a new start.

At least he would be with the Hettingers.

Fritz told him he was doing the right thing.

They packed their meagre belongings and called to the office where the Irishman Hugh was there to give them their tickets and paperwork for their journey ahead.

He touched Hans on the arm and said he'd heard what had happened to his wife.

Hans nodded in thanks.

"The camp closes on Friday," he told them. "You are lucky you are getting out."

Yet, in his shock and raw white grief, Hans did not feel lucky at all.

They took a train to Prague where they stayed for a night and then on to Dresden, majestic against the skyline. Eva cried silent, desolate tears over Anja, over leaving, over everything.

By the time they reached Hamburg, Hans felt as if he'd been on a train forever.

With no J on his passport, his passage was uncomplicated.

The Hettingers had to wait in long queues to have their paperwork processed as they did carry the stamp.

He kept Anja's passport with his, taking it out to look at it throughout the rocking journey, touching her picture, her face, the black, ominous J.

Eva vomited non-stop on the sea journey to England.

Fritz worried that there was something seriously wrong with her, but a ship steward assured them it was a simply a bad case of sea sickness.

"She is unfortunate," said the steward.

They were relieved when they got to Ireland to learn that they were being housed on the southern coast and they would not have to travel far.

In Waterford, Hans pumped his grief into his labour.

He ploughed his thoughts of Anja into sowing and planting and tilling the soil.

The farmer at Ardmore allowed him small pieces of wood, and crucially his tools so that he could pick back up the craft he'd had to drop once the care needs for his father and Anja took over.

He began to carve again.

When they were moved to Enniskerry he had to leave the tools behind.

When they moved to Termonfeckin, he discovered Fintan Walshe's large, well-stocked tool shed.

When his anxious thoughts over Anja became too much, he picked up his carvings.

He sanded his regrets and loathing for himself into the wood, over and over, round and round, smoother and smoother.

The gifts he would make for Eva and Maeve and Mrs. de Freyne were a project to keep his mind off things.

The woodwork stopped him tipping over the edge when he felt like he might not be able to come back.

He could not cry but he could carve.

It was how he got by.

It was how he survived.

* * *

In the small cramped cell of Drogheda Barracks, Hans' fingers itched.

He longed to have a chisel in his hand.

He longed to have a round hollow bowl to smooth.

The questions they had bombarded him with rang out in his head.

When did the spy arrive?

How long were you hiding him?

Do you know the secret codes?

What else have you hidden?

How long was this planned?

How did he die?

Why did you kill him?

A detective had arrived from Dublin. He sat stony-faced beside Sergeant McKiernan.

Hans had said nothing at first.

He remained silent as was his natural demeanour.

But, he worried, his silence would lead to a worse outcome.

He felt that he should say something.

He should try to explain that he had only helped move the soldier's body, but how to do that without implicating Gisela and Nola?

He thought about simply saying he had found the soldier's bag and put it in under his bed.

But that was a lie. And he did not want to lie.

He asked to speak to Mrs. de Freyne.

He wanted to ask for her advice.

He wondered if he needed legal representation.

She might pay for that, he thought.

Eventually he spoke.

"I did not kill him," he said. "I only moved him."

"Where did you find him? Who asked you to move him?"

He could not tell on Gisela and Nola.

He could not.

"We don't believe you, Herr Schmitt," said the detective.

More and more questions, over and over they asked.

Hans grew exhausted.

His language skills deteriorated, he found it hard to understand what they were saying at times.

"What happened to your wife?" said the detective. "How did she die?"

The mention of Anja saw a flare of anger shoot through Hans.

How dare they bring her into this!

What did she have to do with any of these circumstances?

"Got you going there, Mr. Schmitt, have we? Is that what happened with Bruno Mayer? Did you get angry with him too? He was a member of the Nazi party, wasn't he?"

"I told you, I only moved him, I did not kill him."

"We've heard rumours that *you* are a spy, Mr. Schmitt. Were you working for the Reich? You knew Mr. Mayer was coming to Ireland, did you not? Did you arrange it? Did you organise to meet him here?"

Hans shook his head.

Of course not.

Where was this all coming from?

"You do realise that no matter what happens you're finished here?" said Sergeant McKiernan. "We don't want aliens coming into this country, working against us."

Hans realised that the Guard was right.

No matter what happened, his visa would be rescinded now because he'd been involved in a crime.

If Gisela was implicated, hers would be rescinded too.

He could not see her sent back to Germany.

It would be a death sentence.

Not for him, but for her.

After hours of questioning, Hans was put back in his cell.

He lay there on the thin stripy mattress, his arms by his side, wondering what to do next.

He thought of Anja and her family.

What would they think of him now?

A criminal?

But he had done the right thing, he felt.

Hadn't he?

* * *

After Gisela had firmly told Hans that there was a dead Nazi parachutist in the hayshed, he had to take a minute to close his mouth.

It kept dropping open.

He knew by the girl's faces that they were not lying.

He knew it was not a practical joke.

They were scared, Nola's eyes wide and white.

Gisela would not lie, he knew.

"We can't leave him there," Nola had said. "Please can you help us move him, anywhere? Anywhere off the property?"

Under the moonlight, Hans had followed the girls all the way round to the back of the hayshed where they indicated for him to follow them up a ladder.

In the loft a candle burned on an upturned crate.

Beside the crate lay the man.

He was perfectly still.

Perfectly dead.

"Where did he come from?" asked Hans. "How did he get here?"

"It's better if you don't know," said Nola.

Hans cocked his head.

"He was here to meet with the IRA," said Gisela. "You know who they are?"

Hans nodded.

Seán McKee.

The guns theft.

Trouble.

"But then there was an arms theft and arrests and they had to hide him and he ended up here."

"*We just want him gone!*" said Nola, jittering now with nerves, almost shrieking. "*The fête is tomorrow. We can't have a dead body on the property!*"

"Calm down," said Hans.

He surveyed the scene.

"We can move him. But are you sure you just shouldn't call the police? Tell them you found him?"

"No," said Nola. "No police. Not with the IRA involved. Let's just get him out of here and then no one will ever know he was here."

"All right," said Hans. "All right."

He looked around him.

"Stay here," he said.

Outside he found a wheelbarrow and brought it in through the front door of the shed, leaving it at the foot of the hayloft ladder.

When he got back into the loft, he got the girls to hold the soldier's feet, while he lifted the shoulders.

Using all his might, he managed to lift the torso and swing it around in a semicircle.

When they moved the body, a terrible odour emerged.

"Oh God!" Nola said.

Hans grunted and managed to pull the body right over to the hole in the loft.

"Right," he said. "We're going to push him through."

He dragged the solider forward until the body dipped forward into the empty space.

Liquid seeped across the loft floor.

"I think I'm going to be sick," said Nola.

"*Ssshhh!*" said Gisela.

Suddenly, the body toppled down through the hole and landed, like a sack of potatoes.

They all looked at each other.

Hans climbed down first and pushed the body away from the ladder.

Gisela climbed down next, carrying the sleeping bag which was soiled and smelled terrible.

Nola came down with the soldier's bag.

Together, with effort, they got the solider into the wheelbarrow.

Gisela covered him with the sleeping bag.

Nola opened the shed door and looked out.

The night was still.

Quietly they set off into the yard, rounding the corner to move past the other sheds, the farm machinery, making their way to the top of the lane that would lead them to the Strand Road.

The trees along the path were black.

An owl hooted in the distance, spooking Gisela.

"You go home," Hans said. "Go back inside, I will look after this."

"Are you sure, Hans?" said Nola.

She looked glad to be allowed leave, away from the smell of the soiled soldier.

Hans nodded under the moonlight.

Gisela looked torn, torn as to whether to accompany him or not.

"Go," he said.

Partway down the lane the girls stopped and watched as Hans walked off into the dark.

He felt their presence turn and go back towards the house.

He passed the gate where he'd had a cigarette with Nola.

How long ago that seemed.

How much had already changed.

It was better to do this alone.

They had less chance of getting caught.

The wheel of the barrow bumped in and out of dry potholes.

He walked fast, anxious to complete the job.

At the bottom of the lane, Hans crossed the Strand Road, wheeling the wheelbarrow up a slight incline into a large empty field.

He pushed the barrow as far as he could across it.

Near the perimeter ditch he tipped the barrow up, letting the soldier's body fall out awkwardly onto the dewy grass.

He pulled the soldier around, face up and tried to move his arms and hands across each other, as though he were laid out in a coffin.

He wanted the man to have some sort of dignity.

The soldier's arms were solid and stiff.

He could not move them.

He laid the wet sleeping bag over him, like a blanket.

Back out on the road, he watched for a minute before crossing to make his way back up the lane to Newtown.

Along the lane, he thought he heard a noise behind him and he stopped to listen.

Nothing.

He moved on again, quickening his pace.

Near the top of the lane, he heard a noise for certain this time, like a shoe scuffing a stone.

He broke into a trot and raced the barrow into the yard.

At the hayshed, he ran the barrow inside and waited, listening again.

In the dim light he noticed the soldier's kit bag lying at the bottom of the ladder.

Damn it, they had forgotten to take it with all the heaving and effort of getting the body into the barrow in the first place.

He didn't want to risk going down the lane carrying the bag back to the body.

It felt like there was somebody out there, somebody watching.

Lifting it onto this shoulder, he opened the door and looked out.

Skulking as best he could, he closed the door behind him and carried the bag on his shoulder back to his cottage where he put it under his bed, the only available hiding place in his sparsely furnished home.

Who had been following him outside?

Somebody that might have known about the solider?

Or somebody else?

Fintan

CHAPTER THIRTY-FOUR

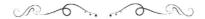

Fintan Walshe sat in the kitchen of his cottage and thumbed the crumbs on his plate.

Brown crumbly soda bread.

Made by the fair hands of Maeve McGorry.

She'd always been a good baker.

Even as a young girl.

When Maeve was young, she used to help her mother in the kitchen of their small cottage on the Strand Road and then drop loaves and scones around to his mother, who had been sickly all her life and rarely, if ever, baked herself.

The Washes lived right next door to Maeve and her family.

But the two families couldn't have been more different.

His mother never baked.

She rarely cooked either.

She always seemed to suffer from something that stopped her getting up and looking after her children.

When she was pregnant with his siblings, she was sick.

After she had them, she was unwell.

She got a neuralgic problem in her face, causing such pain that she took to the bed for months.

When this resolved itself, she fell into a black depression.

Their mother's complaints sent their father to the drink.

And so, it left young Fintan to mind his two brothers and sister, having to make do with a mother who wouldn't cook and a father who wasn't there to.

Maeve's regular appearance with a batch of warm scones had warmed his heart as well as his stomach.

He had always loved her.

Always.

When he grew older and of age, he wanted to ask her to step out with him, but he was shy of himself, of his manner.

His skin was bad, all boils and bumps, which he tried to scald off with hot water and sulfate paste but that just made his face raw.

His teeth weren't good and he was small and undernourished in his stature.

What's more, he knew Maeve was the type of girl who liked a different kind of fella.

Someone louder, more confident, who could tell jokes and hold the attention of a room.

The day he saw Maeve walking down the road arm in arm with Malachy McGorry he knew that it was too late for him.

Malachy was tall and wide-shouldered; he had a great big smile of good teeth when he laughed.

Malachy had a charisma that attracted both men and women.

He was highly thought of.

Popular.

Fun.

Fintan Walshe couldn't compete.

He could never get a woman like Maeve, he realised.

It sent him into a black mood, a mood he realised that was just like his mother's.

She had passed her melancholy on to him.

And it was a very hard thing to shake.

One by one he watched as his siblings took jobs that led them away from home.

His sister emigrated to England, to Manchester where she took up factory work. She married an Englishman and never crossed the Irish Sea again.

Johnny, the brother closest to him in age, took off to America.

Anthony, the youngest, followed him.

After their father passed, struck down in the road by an instant fatal heart attack, it left just Fintan and his mother, a miserable duo eking out an existence in the dark rundown cottage on the Strand Road.

Over time, what little respect Mrs. Walshe had for her eldest son diminished and she shouted and cursed and took out her frustrations on him.

It was Maeve who came to his rescue.

She got him a few days' work up at Newtown House as a grounds keeper, when a young English widow swept into the parish called Mrs. de Freyne.

Lady de Freyne, Fintan liked to call her, because to him that's what she was.

A lady.

Like Maeve.

When the farm foreman retired, Fintan found himself in a position to take over.

He gained status, a good wage and a spacious cottage and workshop on the grounds of Newtown House itself.

He was proud of all that he'd earned.

And he knew it was all thanks to Mrs. Maeve McGorry.

Fintan wasn't a big drinker, but he liked to call into Patton's bar each evening.

It was a break from his mother.

A chance for a bit of warmth and chat.

His mother hated that he worked away all day and went out in the evening too.

She didn't want to be left alone.

Fintan went to the pub anyway.

He'd had enough of minding her all his life.

He'd had enough of looking after everyone but himself.

It was during these nightly visits that he came to know Sergeant McKiernan, a burly man who drank there, originally from County Clare.

Fintan liked Sergeant McKiernan.

He was full of laughing stories and he always stood Fintan a drink.

He made Fintan feel as though he had something to offer.

Fintan found himself telling the Guard small bits of stories and information that he thought might be of interest to him.

"Is that right?" Sergeant McKiernan would nod.

"Aye," Fintan would say and he'd lean in closer and tell him a bit more.

Fintan had a good ear for things.

He could sit and talk to someone and tune in and out of the various conversations going on all around him.

He was also an observant fellow.

He noticed things.

Fintan knew that Maeve was a nationalist, as her husband Malachy McGorry had been.

Often, without her knowing it, Fintan followed Maeve home.

He liked to look in her windows late at night in the dark.

He noticed that she had regular visitors, but they weren't lovers, as he had suspected at first.

No, it was worse than that: they were brigade members of the IRA.

Fintan despised the IRA.

Over the years he had come to see them as a troublesome, quarrelsome organisation, out to do more harm than good.

He disagreed with their bombing campaigns in England.

His sister lived there.

In his eyes, they were a group of organised bullies.

If he could do something to stop that, he would.

He wanted to let Sergeant McKiernan into some of this information as he knew it would be of interest to him.

But he had to be careful though.

He didn't exactly want Maeve to get in trouble but, still, he didn't want her to get away with the work she was doing.

He knew that being seen speaking to Sergeant McKiernan so often could get him into trouble.

Nobody wanted to be labelled a snitch.

And so, they came to an arrangement.

Fintan only passed the time with Sergeant McKiernan at Patton's, the same as any fellow might.

Instead, he began writing things down.

Sergeant McKiernan gave him a special address to post the notes to, a hotel in Dublin and the code name Henry Mullins.

Every three months a payment was sent back to Fintan.

He became an official informer.

Working at Newtown gave Fintan access to people and information.

There were so many suppliers coming and going.

So many involved in the running of the estate.

He attended meetings, became involved in community projects.

Wherever you looked, really, Fintan was there.

Fintan gave Sergeant McKiernan detailed information on Seán McKee, on the movements of his wife Máire, of Mícheál McKee, the son, of his friend, that *amadán*, Peadar Tracy, who Fintan had never liked either.

He'd seen Peadar spying in the windows of Mrs. Carmody.

He caught him trespassing in the lead-up to the fête, bag in hand, sandwiches and all, ready to camp out and steal from Newtown House.

And all the good that Mrs. de Freyne was doing.

He'd enjoyed phoning that one in, he had.

When the Austrians arrived, Fintan was beside himself.

Mrs. de Freyne had brought a whole group of unknown aliens into the sanctuary of Newtown.

They all needed to be examined and studied.

He took each of them aside as soon as he could and spoke to them, gleaning information about their background and plans for their time in Ireland.

It was easy to get to Fritz, Max and Otto.

There was always a job on the farm that he needed help with and he could speak to each of them alone, gain their trust, have them laughing and telling him things that he used in his notes posted to Henry Mullins, Dublin.

Hans was a different sort of fellow.

Quiet.

Secretive.

He felt he had something to hide.

He watched him closely and came to understand after a very short time that Hans had a liking for Maeve.

What was worse, she had a liking for him.

It sickened him, that did.

An alien coming into the country, trying to take up with a good Irishwoman like that.

He would not sit by and watch the two of them form a bond, just like she had with Malachy McGorry all those years ago.

This time, he would not lose her.

Fintan took Maeve aside in the kitchen of Newtown House and told her his plans.

They should marry, he said. It was time.

They were both suited and they could continue their life together, happily, at Newtown House.

Mrs. de Freyne would approve.

They would have a life of domestic happiness, knowing that neither would die alone.

Meave had laughed at first and dismissed him, not believing that he was serious and when Fintan became angry, she grew quiet and told him she wanted to be left alone.

"You'd want to watch yourself, Maeve McGorry," he'd said. "There's things about you I'm sure you wouldn't want anybody to know."

"And what's that supposed to mean?" she'd said.

"You act holier than thou, all smiles and scones and tending to everyone's needs here. But I'm sure if the truth were to come out, Mrs. de Freyne wouldn't be long letting you go. I don't think she'd keep you on, if she knew the truth about you and your activities."

Meave had stood, open-mouthed.

Gisela had appeared in the kitchen then looking for hot water.

Fintan had walked away, knowing he had rattled Maeve, worried he had given the game away on himself too.

As part of his informing activities, Fintan had over the years taken to night watches, walking about the village, hiding in ditches, dressed fully in black, observing who was coming and going and what they were up to.

He kept an eye on the McKees' house at Castlecoo Hill, the Tracys' house in the centre of the village and the cottages all along Strand Road.

He watched everyone and noticed everything.

The night he saw a tall, spindly man pushing a wheelbarrow across the Strand Road, his heckles had raised.

Here, he knew, was a man up to no good.

He'd spotted him coming out of Hanrattys' field and as he got closer and saw him going up the back lane to Newtown, he realised he knew who it was.

It was Hans Schmitt.

Out at this hour!

Quietly he tracked him, picking up his pace and, in his effort to keep up, he'd nearly fallen over a stone.

He'd had to wait for Hans to move off as he had stopped to listen.

When he rounded the yard, he saw Hans disappear round the corner to his cottage, a large bag on his back.

He waited to make sure that Hans had gone inside before turning back down the lane and retracing his steps into Hanratty's field.

In the field, he'd stepped in a wet squelchy cowpat and couldn't help but curse out loud.

"*God in the bejaysus!*" he yelped.

And then he saw it, a bundle lying in the moonlight, over by the perimeter ditch, crumpled into a heap.

What was it?

What had Hans dumped there?

When he got close, he saw that the mound was covered in some sort of padded blanket.

He'd pulled the blanket back and the surprise gulped in his throat.

A body!

A man's body!

Dead!

He rushed back to Newtown, galloping up the lane, and let himself into the house to use the telephone as quietly as he could.

"Send someone quick," he told the barracks at Drogheda. "There's a body in Hanratty's field."

Fintan didn't know who the person was lying in that wet, dewy corner.

He didn't look at it long enough to work out if it was a local or even to observe that the man was in uniform.

When it came to it, Fintan was, it turned out, scared of things like that.

He went to his cottage and climbed into bed after he made the call.

He couldn't be seen to know anything about what had happened.

Early the next morning, the morning of the fête, he had quietly called the Barracks again and arranged a rendezvous with Sergeant McKiernan.

When they met on the back roads of Almondstown, at a secret quiet spot they liked beside a Mass rock, Sergeant McKiernan broke the news that the dead man looked to be a Nazi agent.

They'd found papers in his pocket.

His name was Bruno Mayer.

Sergeant McKiernan told Fintan that G2 had taken over, the intelligence unit of Irish Army, and that even M15 were involved.

"This is big," said Sergeant McKiernan.

How could Fintan have missed such a thing going on, under his very nose at Newtown?

After their meeting, Fintan went back home, his feet heavy, his head pounding.

All this time a real German spy had been there, on his watch, and he'd known nothing about it.

Some informant he was.

He felt it creeping on, the black depression, as the fête kicked off all around him.

He felt the tiredness sweep in, the gut-wrenching disappointment, the feeling, knowing that he had let himself down, let the Guards down, let Lady de Freyne down.

He stuck close by Hans, waiting for the inevitable arrival of the black police motorcar up the avenue.

He watched as he was taken away in handcuffs.

And now, he sat, over the soda bread Maeve had made and thought again about how he must have been the laughing stock of the Garda Barracks and the G2 unit itself.

How could he have missed a thing like that?

How could he stay on as an informer now?

There were the feelings again.

He was a failure.

Fintan Walshe was a failure.

He'd always known it.

And now, here was the proof.

G2 INTELLIGENCE REPORT
STATUS: INFORMATION

Mícheál McKee visited his father Seán McKee in Mountjoy Prison last night.

We believe they were speaking in code, yet to be deciphered.

G2 INTELLIGENCE REPORT
STATUS: INFORMATION

Peadar Tracy has been released on bail, with a file sent forward to the DPP for prosecution on the charge of TRESSPASSING at Newtown House, Termonfeckin, Co. Louth. Bail stood by Mrs Máire McKee.

G2 INTELLIGENCE REPORT
STATUS: INFORMATION

Hans Schmitt is refusing to co-operate.

He will appear before a special sitting of Drogheda District Court.

G2 has put in a transfer request to Dublin, based on the severity of the charge and the sensitivities involved.

Gisela

CHAPTER THIRTY-FIVE

The shock of Hans' arrest sent ripples through the staff and residents of Newtown.

Nobody could believe that quiet, affable Hans could be in any sort of trouble.

When news filtered through the fête, not just of Hans' arrest but that a body had been found in Hanratty's field that morning, an audible bubble of gossip went from mouth to mouth, behind cupped hand and cupped hand, until everyone, even the children, were aware of what was going on.

We always knew they'd bring trouble.

She should never have taken them in.

She's a good woman but she's too soft.

Mrs. Carmody was horrified that all her planning was on the verge of being horribly, irrevocably remembered for all the wrong reasons.

She clapped her hands and told people not to be whispering and to get on with things and enjoy the day.

"The sun is out, ladies – are you entering the golf? Have you tried your hand at the roulette table yet?"

That evening, after Mrs. de Freyne had finished her prize-giving and the hundreds of revellers began making their way back through

Newtown's front gates she telephoned Drogheda Garda Station for information on Hans.

She was told that he would be staying for questioning and that they'd like to speak to her too.

She agreed to attend the station by appointment the next morning.

"What about legal representation?" she asked on the phone. "Does he need it? I will call Mr. Weldon."

When Mrs. de Freyne made the call to her solicitor his wife told her that he was away for the evening and not expected back until the next day.

"Could you ask him to call me as soon as he gets back?" asked Mrs. de Freyne. "It's very important."

Nola's cousins demanded to know what was going on.

They eyed Gisela suspiciously, the thought all across their faces that the Austrians, including Gisela, really were up to no good and now here was the proof.

It had put a dampener on the whole event.

"Do you think we'll be arrested next?" whispered Gisela to Nola, as they helped stack some chairs.

They both felt exhausted.

"I don't know," said Nola, close to tears.

They waited into the late evening for the arrival of a Garda motorcar, but none came for them.

After a light supper there was no mood for an after party, as there usually would have been on the night of the Garden Fête.

The residents of Newtown House sat and spoke in subdued tones, trying to work out what possibly could have happened.

"You two didn't know anything about this, did you?" asked Mrs. de Freyne, eyeing Nola and Gisela.

"No, Mummy, of course not," said Nola.

She made a convincing liar.

"I don't understand," said Fritz.

The rumours spread at the fête were that Hans was a German spy all along.

"We know him," said Fritz. "We know he would not do something like that."

"Aye," said a sombre Fintan Walshe. "That's what made him a good spy. Very convincing."

Maeve was white-faced and silent.

She excused herself early and made for home.

"I'll walk you," said Fintan.

"I'm fine on my own, thank you very much," she said.

The door slammed when she left.

It added to the tense mood.

Soon after, everyone made their way to bed.

In the corridor, Gisela and Nola whispered.

"What'll we do?" said Nola.

Gisela shook her head.

"I don't know."

"I think we should go and talk to Peadar and Mícheál tomorrow," said Nola. "Peadar was let out. Maeve told me. And Mícheál's back from Dublin now."

"They didn't come here today," said Gisela.

"They didn't dare."

"What can they do now?"

"I don't know, but maybe if they came forward or something? Explained it was all to do with them?"

Gisela nodded.

It would help all right. But would they confess?

In bed, Gisela's fears ran like wildfire through her head.

What if Hans had already told the police what he knew.

If the police thought he'd actually something to do with Bruno's death, then he'd have to save his own skin and tell how he'd come across the body in the first place.

Wouldn't he?

They hadn't told Hans about Peadar and Mícheál – he couldn't even point them in that direction.

The only way he could direct them was to her and Nola.

Tossing and turning in her bed, the cold realisation of the situation dawned clearly in Gisela's mind.

If she was implicated in this, if Hans did tell the truth, then there was no doubt but that her visa to Ireland would be revoked.

She would be sent back to Germany.

Hans too.

That's if he wasn't tried for murder.

Did they put people to death in Ireland for murder, she wondered.

She wasn't sure.

She would have to ask.

Poor Hans.

It was all their fault he was in this mess.

* * *

The next morning it was a subdued and silent bunch that made their way to Sunday Mass.

They missed Hans' presence terribly.

They knew all eyes were on them in the church.

Afterwards, there was a rush towards Mrs de Freyne of well wishers to comment on yesterday's fête. Gisela watched as the crowd surged forward and an elderly head-scarved woman politely and firmly enquired about the 'tall Austrian fellow' and his link to the body in Hanratty's field.

"They're saying they found a spy. A real Nazi spy?"

With the crush of bodies around her, Gisela felt as though she would suffocate.

She pushed her way out of the crowd, as did Mrs. de Freyne who thankfully had George waiting for her at the gates of the church.

"I must dash," said Mrs. de Freyne, politely waving to the crowd like a royal. "Thank you, speak to you again!"

They watched her go off for her appointment at the Garda Station.

Little did the crowd know, thought Gisela, where she was going.

Quickly the girls and the Hettingers pushed their way through the baying Mass-goers and walked hurriedly back to Newtown.

At the gates, Nola whispered to Gisela.

"Let's call to the boys now that Mummy's not here," she said.

Gisela nodded.

"Eva," shrilled Nola, "Gisela and I are just going for a quick walk. We'll be back for luncheon."

Eva nodded and carried on up the avenue.

It still bore the signs of the fête – trampled grass and worn verges.

"Who first?" said Gisela.

"Let's try Peadar," said Nola.

A glorious morning was building, with insects buzzing in bushes and songbirds flitting from branch to branch as they passed.

Mrs. Tracy answered, dressed in her Sunday best.

She still had a small black hat on her head from Mass.

"He's already gone up to McKees'," she said. "He's not here."

"That's all right," said Nola. "Thank you, Mrs. Tracy."

"He was in trouble, you know. Caught trespassing. Trespassing! Did you ever hear the like?"

The woman peered out, trying to read the girls' faces.

She stepped out with a lunge onto the doorstep.

Gisela got a strong waft of sour milk and must.

"*You,*" she said. "You're the young de Freyne."

Nola nodded, stepping back.

"Will you ask your mother to see to it that they don't hold anything against Peadar? She knows he wouldn't do anything. She knows he's a good boy!"

"All right, Mrs. Tracy," said Nola, nodding. "I'll tell her."

She was backing away, anxious to leave.

"They're saying he could go to jail! There's a snitch up there in that house, a snitch. Watching everything."

Nola looked to Gisela.

"What would I do if they put him in jail, *huh*? No firewood for the past three days since the Guards took him in!"

"I'll tell my mother, Mrs. Tracy," said Nola.

"You know I was giving out saying he shouldn't be running around with republicans, but it was the republicans who helped him when he needed it the most!"

Nola half waved, turned and walked away quickly.

Gisela followed.

"The poor woman," said Gisela, when she'd caught up with her.

She looked behind to see Mrs. Tracy standing, hunched over, holding onto the door jamb for support.

"Poor woman having a son like Peadar," muttered Nola.

They walked in silence up to the McKees' house, neither wanting to make their way into the farmyard, both lost in their thoughts of Hans, trapped in a prison cell.

Chickens scattered as Gisela and Nola rapped on the door.

A minute later Mícheál answered.

A dark look crossed his face.

"We need to talk to you and Peadar too. Outside," said Nola.

Gisela was surprised at Nola's forcefulness.

And proud.

With a flick of his head, Mícheál indicated for the girls to go round the back.

They made their way round to the field where they had stood the day after the parachutist had landed. Today there were no crowds of supporters or funeral atmosphere for Seán McKee, just the same few cows munching and grinding their jaws.

After a few minutes, both Peadar and Mícheál came out and walked towards them.

They all moved as a group towards the brow of the hill where they could talk in private.

"An eventful week," said Peadar quietly.

"*Eventful?*" said Nola, her voice angry. "He died, Peadar. You left a man to die with us."

"We didn't know he was going to die," said Peadar.

"How would you? You never came back for him?" said Nola.

"I did," said Peadar. "I got arrested, or have you forgotten that? Was it your mother that set the Guards on me?"

"What are you talking about?"

The two glared at each other.

"The whole thing is a mess," said Mícheál. "We're sorry you got dragged into it. We never wanted that. We told you to go home the first day as we didn't want you part of it. These things are complicated."

"They're complicated now, all right," said Nola.

"What are we going to do?" said Gisela. "Hans, our friend, he is in prison now. They think he killed him."

"Why do they think that?" said Peadar. "Sure, he didn't, did he?"

"Of course not," said Nola. "But he helped us move him. And he had his bag in his house somehow. I don't know why he brought it back to his cottage. And then because he's Austrian, they think it's all part of a plan or something. Somebody must have seen something and now he's in trouble. And it's not right."

"You need to tell them," said Gisela. "You need to tell the police that you put Bruno in our hayshed and that he died and Hans had to move him. That he had nothing to do with his death."

Peadar looked at Mícheál.

"We won't be talking to the Guards, ladies," said Peadar.

He held his hands out like Jesus at the Last Supper.

"*But you have to!*" said Nola.

Both Mícheál and Peadar shook their heads.

"But you can't leave Hans in there, in prison," said Gisela. "You must!"

"No one's going to admit anything, all right?" said Peadar. "Mícheál's 'aul fella's up there in Mountjoy. He could be looking at twenty years in jail. Do you see him cribbin' and running to the Guards tellin' tales? No. It's not the way we do things. We don't talk to the Guards. I'm sorry for your friend. But he didn't have to involve himself."

"Well, we'll tell on you then," said Nola. "We'll tell the police what we know. About how you two put him there!"

Mícheál stepped forward.

"If you know what's good for you, girls, then you won't do that."

He was calm and clear-eyed.

Gisela had never seen him like that.

Cold.

Menacing.

Like his father.

"And why wouldn't we?" said Nola, making herself taller now and folding her arms.

"Your mother's done well to get away with herself all these years," said Mícheál. "Plenty more English bitches have been run back over the water, tail between their legs. That's a fine house yis have up there. It'd be a pity if anything happened to it."

Nola took a step back, as if she'd been hit in the face.

"*You wouldn't dare!*" she said.

"Wouldn't we?" said Mícheál.

Nola stared deep into Mícheál's eyes.

Then she turned and stalked off, her arms still folded.

Gisela had to run to catch up with her.

"What were they talking about," said Gisela, out of breath.

"*Bastards!*" said Nola. "*Absolute bastards!*"

"I don't understand," said Gisela.

Nola looked at Gisela as they walked across the field, rushing now, their feet scrambling on the incline.

"The IRA burnt out all the English landlords. Years ago. They always left Mummy alone."

"Can't you tell the police they're threatening you?"

"We can. But it won't make the threat go away. There'll always be somebody who would go ahead with it."

"I'm sorry," said Gisela.

Nola nodded.

They were both sorry.

They were both sorry for the mess they were in.

"Let's go and see if Mummy is back yet," said Nola as they climbed over the field gate and out onto the road. "I want to see what they're saying about Hans. And about us."

Hans

CHAPTER THIRTY-SIX

In his cell, Hans thought about many things.

He thought about Newtown House and the wonderful fête he had been part of, the smiling faces and children who queued up for ice cream and games.

He thought about all the hard work that went into the event, how everyone had pulled together, even lazy little Nola who always bolted from hard work when she could.

He thought of how proud Mrs. de Freyne was of what she had built.

Of her generosity in bringing them there and giving them all a second chance.

Of saying yes when everyone else had so readily said no.

He thought of the house and its gardens, of the rich farmland and the trees she'd planted, that would for hundreds of years offer shelter and wood and warmth.

He thought how it all seemed to be enough for her, in her widowhood.

It was enough for her to give. To others. To do good. To be good.

He thought about the Hettingers, who had eased his passage to Ireland, who had provided such comfort over the harrowing few months as he tried to come to terms with the loss of Anja.

They were they only ones who remembered her, the only ones left that knew her, that had memories of her.

He thought of the future Max and Otto would have for themselves. College, an education, marriage no doubt and good jobs.

Last week Mrs. de Freyne had told them she was thinking of investing in a property in Dublin, a small hotel where Austrians could go, people like the Hettingers and Hans, who could meet their fellow countrymen, speak in their language and cook their home food stuffs.

"What do you think of the name, *The Old Vienna Club?*"

Eva had clapped her hands.

"It's wonderful," she'd said.

"Well, I would need a safe pair of hands to run it," said Mrs. de Freyne and she had peered closely at Eva and Fritz.

"Us?" said Fritz.

"Well, that back of yours is no good for farm work," said Mrs. de Freyne. "Much better suited to hosting, I expect?"

Fritz and Eva had looked at each other.

Tears welled in Eva's eyes.

"And if Max and Otto will be attending college in Dublin, well then, better to be near them, I think."

"Oh, Mrs. de Freyne," said Eva. "I cannot tell you what that would mean."

"Newtown was always meant to be temporary," said Mrs. de Freyne. "Except for you perhaps, Hans. I think we might keep you."

Hans had laughed.

"I think Mr. Walshe will keep me," said Hans.

"Indeed," said Mrs. de Freyne. "He does seem to be fond of you."

And then he thought of Mr. Walshe.

Of how he had welcomed him, always so interested in where he'd come from, asking questions about his life there, about his parents, about his wife.

Hans had not wanted to tell him the most intimate parts about himself.

It was only Maeve who managed to scratch that surface.

What would he think of him now, he wondered.

He would, like them all, believe that somehow all along he had not been truthful and not who he said he was.

Only the Hettingers knew.

Only Gisela would know the full truth.

The Guards told him a solicitor would come along that evening, paid for by Mrs. de Freyne. A Mr. Weldon.

But, the detective had also made it clear that the solicitor could not do much for Hans.

He was in too deep now.

No matter what happened his time was up.

They had a witness who had seen him leave the field with the wheelbarrow on the night in question.

The witness had also seen him with the soldier's bag.

They had the bag, with a German radio, maps and codes.

They believed he was involved in an elaborate plan with the German Government, that he had known about the secret agent's arrival, likely he had even planned it, by infiltrating the community in the village and setting up home at Newtown House.

All he needed to do was to admit the truth.

Why did you murder him, Hans? they asked. *What went wrong?*

Back in his cell, Hans had gone over the events in his head.

He didn't regret helping the girls.

They were young.

They had their whole lives ahead of them.

Somebody, somehow, had left them to deal with a terrible, ludicrous situation.

As he lay there, waiting, knowing that sleep would not come, he thought of Maeve.

Lovely Maeve.

In his conversations with her, he had found himself confessing his darkest thoughts.

All his regrets over Anja, the things he could have done differently, the things that would have meant she could have come to Ireland with them as planned.

He told Maeve how he blamed himself for leaving her that morning in the cabin on the farm at Kagran.

How he blamed himself for not being there to accompany her home that fateful night of her attack.

After too many whiskeys one night at the kitchen table in Newtown he told Maeve how he blamed himself for ever even marrying her in the first place.

He felt she would be alive and well in Palestine, had he not.

Maeve had reached across and touched his arm and told him that it was normal to feel guilty thoughts after the loss of a spouse.

She told him that she too had found it hard to go on when she'd lost her husband Malachy.

"Whenever I smiled after he died, I thought 'Look at you smiling – how can you smile and your husband dead and you all alone?' But life goes on, Hans. You are here now. You've been given a whole fresh start. There's a reason for that."

They had a lot in common, the widow and widower.

Maeve had been a great comfort.

Like the Hettingers, he trusted her.

She understood his deep well of grief, hidden behind his quiet aloofness, his stoicism.

She had known the real him.

Sergeant McKiernan told Hans that Mrs. de Freyne had been to the station that morning.

She said she knew nothing about Hans' activities.

"We'll be bringing everyone in for questioning," Sergeant McKiernan told Hans. "All the Austrians. We'll get to the bottom of this."

Hans thought about the Hettingers.

About quiet, thoughtful Eva, about warm, eccentric Fritz.

About the two boys.

And then he thought about Gisela.

Poor Gisela, alone, without her family, lost in a world she did not want to be in.

If he took responsibility, full responsibility, it would free up all the other Austrians, so that they could get on with their futures – futures that now, thanks to Mrs. de Freyne's continued generosity, looked so bright.

If he owned up to the soldier's death, said that everything was to do with him, that he and only he had kept that German solider in that loft, it would allow the rest of them to get on with their lives.

Gisela could not be caught up in this.

Max and Otto could not be implicated.

Only he had nothing left to lose.

There was, of course, the question of God.

What would God think of his actions?

But perhaps this was all part of God's plan anyway?

Perhaps this was the reason he'd come to Ireland.

Maybe this was his sacrifice?

Eternal damnation?

He deserved it, didn't he?

He lay on his pillow and let the thought form.

It has been swirling and stagnating, rinsing through his mind, but now it was becoming clearer.

Those girls could break, he knew.

Gisela was weak, honest and full of heart.

Nola was silly, unreliable and like Gisela might find herself swallowed up by the guilt of what was going to happen to him.

There was only one way to buy their silence, forever.

He asked for a pencil and paper.

He told Sergeant McKiernan he would like to write out his confession.

The Sergeant was surprised that his charge was now willing to co-operate, but it was something he'd seen time and time before; when a guilty man was left alone with his thoughts, he often came to reason.

Hans wrote that he was sorry for what had happened and for sullying the good name of his fellow Austrians.

He said that only he had been a support to the agent that had landed.

I acted alone, nobody else was involved.

He was sorry the agent had died.

He thanked Mrs. de Freyne for her kindness, the Hettingers for their support and wished Gisela and Nola well in their futures.

My time here is done, he wrote. *I am sorry it has ended in this way.*

He lay the paper down on his bed.

And then, he got to work.

INTELLIGENCE G2 REPORT

STATUS: URGENT INFORMATION

Herr Hans Schmitt was found hanging in his cell at 7.35pm this evening.

His sponsor Mrs. de Freyne has been informed.

No immediate next-of-kin.

Confession note left and contained within.

The matter has been referred to Garda Headquarters, Dublin.

Also Autopsy Report had been received: BRUNO MAYER cause of death has been confirmed as SEPSIS.

Gisela

CHAPTER THIRTY-SEVEN

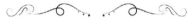

October 1939

As they climbed aboard the train at Amiens Street Station, Dublin, Gisela couldn't help but admire the Hettingers.

Eva was dressed in a new coat in a dark bottle-green.

Fritz had oiled his hair back – his cologne carried in the air.

Max and Otto stood tall, a confidence that their first few weeks at University College Dublin had given them.

Max was studying physics.

Otto was doing a pre-course for medicine.

He would make a good doctor, Gisela thought.

He had a calm, thoughtful manner about him.

The sights and smells of the big echoey train station had become familiar to Gisela over these past few weeks.

It was from Amiens Street Station that she'd been catching the train lately to travel out to Clontarf, where she went to meet Brian.

Brian was a plumber.

Brian was what she could now openly call her boyfriend.

The big echoey station, with its high arched roof and the smell of metal on tracks of dark, oil-slicked stones, reminded her of him.

Of their evenings spent walking.

Of taking tea with his parents.

Of stopping by the Schrödingers' house, where she was invited, as a guest, having made Herr Schrödinger's acquaintance at the Old Vienna Club.

There was quite a community now of friends.

They were of different backgrounds and they had come to Ireland in various ways, but they all had one thing in common.

They were all Austrian.

And they were all exiled from home.

She had met Brian one evening at the Schrödingers' house.

He'd been called in to deal with a problem with a leakage in the back yard and, because he only lived a few doors up, he had made it his business to leave the task until his last job of the day.

He happened to call at the same time Herr Schrödinger was hosting some friends.

It happened that Gisela was one of those friends and had taken a liking to Brian and he to her.

Gisela took her gold chain and wrapped it around her chin as they waited for the train to move off.

She was looking forward to the trip and yet an anxiety wrapped itself around her centre too.

She hadn't been back to Newtown in three months – not since she'd moved to the Vienna Club with the Hettingers.

She was looking forward to seeing Nola.

She was looking forward to seeing Mrs. de Freyne.

But there was one person who'd be missing, one person who should have been there.

Slowly the train powered its way through Dublin.

Past Croke Park the skyline changed from terraced houses to detached houses before they reached Howth and Malahide.

She loved to see the sea open up and the coast appear.

She loved it too at Clontarf where Brian lived.

She could see herself settling there eventually.

If they ever made it that far.

She was shy and quiet with him, which he said he admired.

He was a quiet man too.

The group chattered about the weekend ahead and the special occasion planned.

They wondered how Mrs. de Freyne had been coping with organising Nola's coming out ball, mostly by herself.

"I'm expecting live tigers," said Otto.

"Jugglers," said Max.

"And she'll definitely be wearing fur," Otto replied.

Gisela smiled.

She didn't think so.

She knew, from her letters to Nola, that their summer had changed her.

Yes, it would be a big party.

But she expected to see a more mature, less frivolous Nola now.

Would she?

Gisela opened her hatbox, which contained her make-up for tonight and a small wrapped box, containing Nola's coming-out gift – she had been saving for it for weeks.

She didn't earn much waitressing and hosting at the Old Vienna Club, but with her meals and accommodation covered, she was able to put some money aside for such a gift.

She had chosen a charm bracelet, the heaviest she could afford.

The Old Vienna Club, was, as Mrs. de Freyne had imagined, a triumph.

It was busy with Austrians who had made their way to Ireland, some coming over from England, although with the outbreak of war since September, they knew they could not expect many more arrivals.

Travel to Europe was no more.

They were the lucky ones who had got out.

At the club, they were safe to speak and debate for hours in German.

They cooked the home food they were used to and played music in the evenings.

Eva and Fritz organised a series of lectures and classes, socials and dances.

Being back in the city helped Gisela with her terrible homesickness.

She woke up each day to the sound of traffic on the street, to people around, to the park nearby.

She could walk to the shops, visit the markets and feel the swell of people all around.

Her room at the hotel was fresh, new.

She ate breakfast in company, in the evenings she helped the Hettingers cook and serve meals for their guests.

When Gisela had moved to Dublin, much to Nola's sadness, but with the blessing of Mrs. de Freyne who understood that Gisela was wilting in the countryside, she had taken up a book-keeping course.

It wasn't the maths she was used to in university, but she liked it and it suited her logical brain.

Over four months into her stay in Ireland, she felt she had found a good place to be in.

She enjoyed living at the hotel.

She saw her fellow countrymen and women.

And she had Brian.

Brian was perhaps the most unexpected meeting of all.

Finding someone and falling in love with him – well, it had never even crossed her mind over the past year as she fought to find a way out of Austria.

It was funny, she thought, how things happened.

How things, people, found you.

Mrs. de Freyne had found her.

And now she had found Brian.

As the train passed Balbriggan, Laytown and eventually pulled into Drogheda station, slow and steady, sending diesel fumes into the air, she thought about how far she'd come.

She was a different Gisela to the young woman who had arrived just a few months ago.

She was changed.

All of them, she expected, were changed.

George had come to meet them in the Fraschini, the same nonchalant look on his face as always.

They were lucky to have the car sent for them – soon fuel rationing would see cars put off the road.

They all piled into the motorcar, arms and legs touching, their cases tied to the boot and roof.

"You must be very busy this weekend," said Fritz to George.

"Not a moment's rest," he said.

George did not like to be inconvenienced too much.

Gisela smiled as they drove through the town, out past the river under the viaduct bridge.

It was all familiar.

But it did not feel like home.

At Newtown the avenue was showing its autumn colours, something she had not experienced before.

The golds, reds and browns reminded her of the lush alpine forests outside Vienna.

When would she see *those* trees again?

The gardens had been freshly raked.

Lanterns had been placed all along the driveway, ready to be ignited later.

At the steps of Newtown they got out of the car and walked up to the door.

Before they could ring the bell it was flung back by Nola who had curlers in her hair and was dressed in a robe.

She looked quite beautiful, Gisela thought.

If, as always, a little inappropriate.

"*Gisela!*"

She flung her arms around Gisela, gripping her tightly.

Dramatically.

Uncomfortably.

Inside in the drawing room, Mrs. de Freyne appeared, and touched all of their hands, squeezing their arms.

"How are you? So good to see you," she said, beaming.

They all nodded.

They all smiled.

It was good to be back.

It was so lovely to return to Newtown.

But there was a glaring absence.

One empty chair.

A space that could now never be filled.

Gisela blinked and tried to push the reminders out of her mind.

She had known this would happen.

She knew being here would bring it all back.

* * *

Newtown House was filled to the brim with noise, commotion and event organisation.

It reminded Gisela of the Garden Fête, although there would be smaller numbers in attendance tonight and the guests would certainly be dressed in finer clothes.

Mrs. Carmody had been seconded back in to help manage the staff who had been hired in to cater and serve the event.

Her hairstyle was again a bouffant.

Maeve was both glad of the help and rattled by the shrill tones of Mrs. Carmody as she strutted about the place.

As Mrs. Carmody's voice carried all the way down to the kitchen, Maeve gripped a tea towel and twisted it into a knot in her hands.

"That woman," she muttered.

Flowers decked out every table and surface the eye could see.

Candles sat ready in polished candelabras.

The plates were stacked ready to be dished out, the linens starched and folded.

"It's as though the Queen herself is coming for tea," Maeve moaned as she tried to find room on her counter to make the Austrians a quick sandwich after their arrival.

The band was setting up in the dance hall, the odd *'parp'* travelling along the corridor to the kitchen from the brass instruments.

Gisela went to listen.

From the back of the room, she watched the musicians set up.

Her eyes fell on the piano player.

He looked like Rudy, small, like her, dark.

He played Brahms and Gisela, struck by a desperate moment of longing to see her brother, felt tears at the back of her eyes.

They wrote every week.

He had yet to give her any news.

Nobody, nobody had heard anything from her parents.

Her hope, she realised, had all but run out.

Tearing herself from the dance hall, and not wanting to get upset on what was supposed to be a celebratory occasion, Gisela made her way upstairs to find Nola.

It was easy to identify Nola's room by the cloud of smoke seeping out from under her bedroom door.

"Come in!" she called, when Gisela knocked.

Gisela entered.

"Ah, there you are," said Nola.

She had a thin cigarette in her hand.

She had been painting her nails.

Gisela gave her the small package she'd brought, her gift.

"Oh, you shouldn't have," said Nola.

"I wanted it to be bigger, but I have to save for my course," said Gisela.

"When I'm working, you can expect bigger gifts!"

"Nonsense," said Nola, "I'm delighted, thank you."

She unwrapped it while trying to smudge her nails and exclaimed at the bracelet, examining the three charms.

"A heart, from me. A house, because we shared this one," said Gisela, waving her hands around to indicate Newtown. "And an aeroplane. So we never forget. What happened here."

Tears welled in Nola's eyes. She was silent and then reached for the tumbler on her dressing table.

She saw Gisela looking.

"Don't worry," she said. "I'll pace myself. I won't make a fool of you. Or Mummy."

Gisela smirked and cocked her head.

"I hope not, Nola."

She sat down on the bed.

"How are you doing?" said Nola, turning around now. "I mean really doing. With everything?"

"I'm all right," said Gisela. "I get sad. But I am busy also, so I get on with things."

"Are you happier in Dublin than here?"

Gisela was silent for a moment.

"Well, it's a city. I'm used to city life."

"So yes, then."

"I suppose, yes."

Nola sighed.

"I can't wait for my city life to begin."

Next week, Nola would be travelling to London, to move in officially with Granny.

"You could come visit," said Nola.

"I don't think my visa would allow."

"Oh, would it not?"

Still, each week, Gisela had to sign on at a Garda station.

Now, her assigned station was in the heart of Dublin city centre.

"How is Brian?" asked Nola.

"He's fine," said Gisela, smiling.

"Look at you!" said Nola. "Will you marry him?"

"I don't know. It's too soon to know. Perhaps."

"Well, I hope I'll be bridesmaid!"

Gisela smiled again.

Yes, she thought. Yes, Nola could be bridesmaid.

"What about ... what about ... everything?" said Nola, lowering her voice. "How do you feel about ..."

She raised her eyebrows and Gisela understood.

She didn't need to say his name.

Hans.

How did Gisela feel about the death of Hans, now that some time had passed?

"I feel so sad," said Gisela. "All the time."

"Me too."

"I feel it's our fault. It is our fault."

Nola nodded, tears pricking her eyes.

"I hate not being able to talk about it," said Nola. "I miss you, you know. So very much."

Gisela stood up and went to embrace Nola.

Nola held her head against Gisela's chest.

"I think he missed his wife very much," she said, tearfully. "That he couldn't really see a future for himself here. Not after what happened. I feel we took all that away from him. Just by asking him to help."

"I know," said Gisela. "I know."

Together, they locked in their embrace, letting their tears flow, feeling the tension run through their bodies.

"Sometimes I wish I could just float away, from all of this, from here," said Nola.

"Yes," said Gisela. "Sometimes I wish I could just float away home, up into the sky, all the way back to Vienna."

Nola pulled away and checked her wristwatch.

"What time is it? Yes, we've time. The hairdresser won't be here for another forty-five minutes. Come on!"

She jumped up.

"Where?" said Gisela. "Where?"

But Nola was gone out the door.

Surprised, Gisela followed her out into the corridor.

Nola was ahead, quite a sight in her rollers and robe, racing down the stairs.

She took the side door out onto the lawn, past a marquee that had been set up, under string lights that would be lit soon for the evening.

Gisela had to run to catch up.

"Where are you going?!"

"Come on!" said Nola.

Picking up her pace, Nola ran towards the path behind Newtown, the one that led, narrow and gravelly, across the field to the dunes and the beach.

Gisela smelled the familiar scent of salt, of spiny grasses.

Nola slowed as she reached the dunes, forced to walk by the rough terrain.

She stood at the edge of the dune when she reached it, looking out to the horizon, to the sea.

A clump of sand loosened and scattered before them.

Gisela, panted, out of breath.

This is where it all started, where the parachutist landed, where their nightmare began.

How could he ever have known what lay ahead?

How could Hans have known what they would involve him in?

Nola reached her arms out like Jesus on the cross.

Gisela did the same.

Together, they threw their heads back, opening their mouths to howl at the wind.

It was freeing, exhilarating.

"You said you wanted to float," said Nola.

She ran down the dune, shoes scrambling, and raced towards the sea.

This time she did not take off her clothes.

This time, Gisela followed her.

When they reached the water, Nola waited for Gisela and they joined hands.

The shock of the water was like a knife to the skin.

It pulled the blood from their chests, their stomachs as they ran into it, deep.

They laughed with the thrill of it, screamed with the madness of it all.

Gisela felt delirious.

The waves washed over them and Nola dived under, swimming, taking Gisela with her too.

The shock of the water on Gisela's head was overpowering.

When they came back up, they allowed themselves to float, sent back in to shore by the waves, their bodies tingling, responding to the cold.

"We're going to be okay," said Nola.

"Are we?" said Gisela."

"Yes," said Nola. "We are."

"We couldn't save Hans."

"No, we couldn't. But he saved us."

"Yes," said Gisela. "He did."

They stayed hand in hand as they walked out of the water, leaving the power of the waves behind, feeling the water pour from their clothes, shivering uncontrollably now as the cold air hit them.

They moved quickly up the path, towards Newtown House, where the lights were starting to come on in the dusk.

"If your mother sees you, she'll be terribly angry," said Gisela, looking at the water dripping from Nola and her now soggy hair-rollers.

"What's new?" shrugged Nola and Gisela laughed.

They walked by Hans' empty cottage on the way back and bowed their heads as they passed.

The Hettingers' cottage was lit up and would be back in use this evening.

"Oh, I almost forgot," said Nola. "I have something in my room for you."

In the courtyard they walked by Fintan Walshe's cottage which lay dark and uninhabited now that the new farm foreman lived off site.

"Do you miss him – Mr. Walshe?" asked Gisela as they passed.

"No, I do not," said Nola. "And Maeve doesn't either. Fusty 'ol Fintan, eh? Who would have thought?"

They made it back to the house, unseen by Mrs. de Freyne, slipping up the stairs towards Nola's room to change and bathe quickly.

"What in the unmerciful?" said Mrs. Carmody, who was coming out of Nola's room, having just been inside looking for her. "Girls! What *have* you been doing?"

"Floating," said Nola. "We were floating."

Gisela looked at Nola, squeezed out her damp braid and smiled.

"Please get yourselves cleaned up. The guests will be here soon," said Mrs. Carmody. "And Gisela, Mrs. de Freyne asked me to check if you'd like to perhaps play some piano tonight."

Gisela nodded.

"Yes," she said. "I'd love to."

She'd been practising at the Old Vienna Club.

"Something in honour of Hans?" said Nola.

Gisela nodded.

Yes.

"*Ist dein kleines Herz für mich noch frei, Baby?*"

"Oh yes!" said Nola.

Mrs. Carmody rushed away telling the girls to hurry.

In her room, Nola opened the bottom drawer of her dressing table.

"This is for you."

Into Gisela's hand Nola dropped a small, wooden apple, smooth and carved.

"There's one for you and one for me, one for Mummy, one for Maeve and one for Eva. We found them in Hans' cottage after ... well, afterwards. There was a bowl but Mummy took that. If you put oil on them they scent the air."

Gisela rubbed the wooden apple in her hands, feeling the grain of the wood.

She imagined Hans' long fingers and rough palms, working the wood over and over.

"Thank you, I will treasure it," said Gisela and she held it right to her heart. "I will treasure it forever, Nola, thank you."

Youth gets ten-month gaol sentence for trespassing at Newtown House

A YOUNG MAN has been sentenced to ten months in gaol for trespassing at Newtown House, Termonfeckin, in July earlier this year. Peadar Tracy of Nunnery Land, Termonfeckin was found by Sergeant Joe McKiernan in possession of a bag and was thought to be lying in wait to commit robbery. Sergeant McKiernan told Drogheda District Court that this was not the first time Mr. Tracy had come to the attention of the Gardaí and that Mr. Tracy was belligerent and kept "bad company". Justice Michael McNamara imposed a sentence of ten months, warning Mr. Tracy to "clean up his act". Mr. Tracy was removed to Mountjoy Gaol, Dublin, to serve his sentence.

Drogheda Democrat,
Wednesday 15 November, 1939

IRA trial scheduled to take place next year

THE TRIAL of a number of men accused of IRA membership will take place next year to allow for evidence gathering, according to our court reporter. The trial had been expected to take place in the autumn of this year, however prosecution lawyers for the State filed a request this week to seek more time to allow Gardaí to gather further evidence and witness testimonies. There have been accusations of ongoing threats of violence and intimidation of witnesses in the case, SC Barry Gillespie told Dublin Central Criminal Court on Monday last. One of the accused, Seán McKee of Termonfeckin, Co Louth, has been incarcerated since July of this year on the charge. His son Mícheál McKee was arrested in August, after arms were found in the family home, believed to be connected to the Phoenix Park arms robbery in July. Justice Pat Maloney granted the request and adjourned the case until 23 February next year.

The Irish Reporter,
Tuesday 12 December, 1939

G2 INTELLIGENCE REPORT
STATUS: TOP SECRET INFORMATION

Detectives have discovered the remaining arms missing from the Phoenix Park robbery at the home of MR. FINTAN WALSHE, Newtown House, Termonfeckin.

We believe he was acting as a DOUBLE AGENT.

Advise immediate detention based on COVERT OPERATIONS and SENSITIVITIES involved.

EPILOGUE

Maeve McGorry sat in the kitchen of Newtown House, a single sheet of notepaper on the scrubbed-clean table in front of her. She had taken it from Mrs. de Freyne's office, something that she was allowed to do whenever she needed.

She didn't write many letters though. Not usually.

Over the past few weeks however, she had felt the urge to write. A build-up of desire to say something.

Dear Fintan, she wrote. That was the easy part. *I hope you are well.*

She didn't wish him to be ill, she supposed. But she did want him to suffer. In some way. For what he had done. For what had happened, in the end.

I hope these scones reach you in one piece. Mr. Finnegan the milkman assured me it would be no problem to take them up as he does a drop to Mountjoy Gaol most days anyway. He's a nice man.

Unlike *you*, is what she really wanted to say.

All is well here in Newtown. Well, there have been big changes of course. Gisela and the Hettingers have moved up to Dublin, they run the Old Vienna Club now, a small hotel on Upper Pembroke Street for Austrians. It is all going very well, I hear. Nola has moved to London and Mrs de Freyne will spend Christmas in Belgravia this year. She misses her terribly

353

of course. Though, it is peaceful now at Newtown, for sure.

Maeve tapped her lip with the lid of the pen. Yes, she would tell him about the new foreman. She knew it would pain him terribly, although what else did he expect? Just because he was gone, Newtown House and Farm could not fall apart.

The new farm foreman is doing wonders. An agency hire. He's very experienced and used to dealing with large holdings so Mrs de Freyne is very, very pleased with him.

That would rub it in a bit.

I am sure you miss the house here terribly and I suppose it's unfortunate how it all worked out for you in the end. I have to say we were all shocked to hear the news. We never would have taken you for an IRA man, Fintan, not ever.

She smiled as she wrote those words. She couldn't help herself.

It was, after all, her idea in the end.

When their sources verified that Fintan Walshe was indeed a Garda informant and believed to have been for many years, providing covert information on everyone at Newtown House as well as IRA brigade members, it was clear that something would have to be done.

Some members wanted him taken out completely – a silenced bullet to the head – taken from his cottage at Newtown in the dead of night.

But she had come up with a different idea.

Wouldn't he suffer more if he was pinned for being the very person he hated? For being an IRA man?

She had brought up the idea at a meeting. She attended regularly, some held in her own cottage next door to old Mrs. Walshe's, although they had stopped meeting there in the past few months, as they had expected there was an informant operating somewhere.

Fintan Walshe had never been considered. Nobody thought he had the guile. He was too snivelling, too weak. But people could surprise you. And Fintan Walshe had surprised everyone.

"We could plant some arms on him," Maeve had said on the night they discussed what should be done with him. "Nothing much, we don't want to give away what we have, but a few guns and maybe a grenade or two."

She knew it would be easy to do that. She could easily place a package in his cottage at Newtown when he was out in the fields or off driving Bessie somewhere.

She could tip the Guards off anonymously. The guns would be easily identifiable from the Phoenix Park arms theft.

The idea was liked.

It would put Fintan Walshe away and finger him as an IRA man, which they knew was a revenge in itself. It would also take some of the heat off the search party and the pressure brigade members were under ever since the arms robbery. It was too late for Seán McKee, who the Guards were never going to let go. A new leader would be elected in due course.

The secret German agent had been above Maeve's involvement in the brigade.

If she was to be honest, she was a little hurt that she had been left out of the plan. She felt she could have assisted, especially when it had turned out the way it had.

But, the leadership had kept it very tight. A need-to-know basis. It was unfortunate the way it had all worked out, with the timing.

And of course, for Hans.

Poor Hans.

Meave thought of him now, remembered him sitting at the table, taking his cup of tea, smiling at her.

They could have been a good match. She might have stepped out with him. There was a softness to his soul that she liked and it had been so long since her husband Malachy.

But it could never be now.

He had made the ultimate sacrifice.

Still, the fight went on. Still, Ireland was not free. Still, she would continue her work with the IRA.

Things would go on at Newtown as always.

She was settled there. She had Mrs. de Freyne to look after and all the comings and goings of running such a big house and holding. She was happy to be busy. And it was a bonus that Fintan Walshe was no longer in her life, no longer hanging around, his moony eyes following her.

It'll be a different Christmas for you now, Fintan, but I'll say a prayer for you. I will ask that God forgive you for the error of your ways. I will look in on your mother. She says she misses you and she has been hit hard by what happened.

It's a pity what happened to you, but I suppose none of it can be helped now.

All the best and Happy Christmas,
Mrs McGorry
Newtown House
20th December 1939

AUTHOR'S NOTE

I came to write this story, not because I particularly wanted to write a World War II story, but because I was led there by a very unique and memorable woman called Vida Lentaigne.

Vida (née Haslam) was born in 1894, the daughter of a Liberal MP and industrialist Lewis Haslam, and grew up in Belgravia, London, as a very wealthy and privileged young woman. She married an Irishman, Joseph (John) Lentaigne, who worked as a solicitor attached to the British Imperial Civil Service and they moved to Burma where she spent two blissful years of early married life. Two days after her first daughter, Jojo (Josephine) was born, Joseph died from the effects of cholera. Vida returned, as a young widow, not to her home country of England, but to Ireland, to carry out two express wishes her husband had made on his death bed: that their daughter be raised a Catholic and Irish.

With the guidance of Joseph's extended Irish family, Vida purchased a large property and holding at Termonfeckin, County Louth, called Newtown House, in the late 1920s and began a two-decade crusade to establish a farm that would give local employment as well as improving the lives of local residents. She was appalled by the rural poverty she saw all around her in 1930s Ireland and was determined to help improve in some way the lives of rural people.

She built houses, provided employment, donated sports fields and planted thousands of trees. She was elected to Louth County Council in

1934, quite an achievement for a recently arrived Englishwoman. She was a member of the Society of United Irishwomen, which later became the Irish Countrywomen's Association and offered Newtown House as summer school for the organisation in 1933. In 1954, the house was purchased by the association and renamed 'An Grianán'. To this day it remains the headquarters of the association and is a meeting centre for women who travel from all over the country to experience the grounds of this beautiful, coastal property.

As a convert to Catholicism, Vida took her religion very seriously and this led her to co-found and chair the Catholic Council for Refugees. This was how she came to take in a small group of converted Jewish refugees forced to flee persecution in Vienna in 1939.

I discovered the story behind these refugees while searching through the local parish history books during lockdown 2020 and was struck by their plight. Little did I know when I began writing that the issue of war refugees and what role other countries play in helping those displaced would again be top of the news agenda when the war broke out in Ukraine in early 2022.

Vida is, of course, my Laila de Freyne in *The Emerald Spy*. Her daughter Jojo is my Nola. I was privileged enough to track down and interview family members and parishioners who helped me discover what life was like at Newtown House in 1939 and although I have fictionalised much of the story, I hope the sentiment of these characters remains the same. They are based on real people and I wanted to bring them back.

'Gisela' is also based on a true person and I was extremely lucky to interview her real-life daughter at length about her mother's experience of coming to Ireland as a refugee in 1939. She read her mother's diaries from the time to me and so it was from this that I gained much of the detail of the story.

For reasons of privacy I have changed some details, but the story of Gisela, her parents and her brother is true. The truth is that Gisela's parents perished in the Polish concentration camp of Treblinka, 1942, although it wasn't until a few years later that Gisela would discover the full truth.

They were deported from Vienna to a ghetto in Poland and from there found their way to a small Polish village. They remained there for some months in hiding until they were eventually rounded up and taken away to be executed.

It was one of the most poignant moments I've ever experienced in an interview, to talk to a grandchild whose grandparents had died in the Holocaust and I hope I have done Gisela's story some justice.

The story of the Nazi agent is also based on truth, although in reality my characters at Newtown House never did have a run-in with a parachutist that I know of. It's believed that eight Abwehr/Security Service agents landed in Ireland during World War II. You can read more about this fascinating time in Mark M. Hull's book *Irish Secrets – German Espionage in Wartime Ireland*, from which I gleaned a lot of my knowledge about how exactly these agents landed and what they did when they got here. I was fascinated by the story of Hermann Görtz, who landed at Ballivor in County Meath, walked to Dublin and went undetected for about nine months. I thought Meath was close enough to Louth and so my story of *The Emerald Spy* was born.

The IRA too sent their own personnel to Germany throughout the 1930s to establish solid links with the Nazi Government – it was felt that both had a natural enemy in England.

If you are interested in reading more about the Germans and Austrians who fled to Ireland at this time, I can highly recommend Gisela Holfter and Horst Dickel's *An Irish Sanctuary*. Dermot Keogh's *Jews in 20th Century Ireland* also provides an intriguing account of this time period.

There were times when I didn't think this book would ever see the light of day. It took quite a while to establish the story line, plot and characters but, as it was, Mrs de Freyne, her daughter Nola and quiet, stoic Gisela, just would not go away. I am glad that now they exist here and forever more, between these pages.

Nicola Cassidy
August 2022

ACKNOWLEDGEMENTS

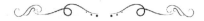

Thank you to all the characters' family members who gave me their time in the research of this book, particularly to Gisela's daughter who wished to remain anonymous but gave me so much of her heart and insight into what it was truly like for her mother to be a World War II refugee to Ireland. Thank you to Victor O'Reilly who gave me a fascinating insight into his grandmother Vida and mother Jojo and to Victor's son Bruff O'Reilly for helping to arrange our call.

Thank you to Mark M. Hull who was very kind and supportive in my mission to write this book. His research into German agents in Ireland is a truly fascinating account of the time. The book is currently out of print but Wendy Logue in Irish Academic Press kindly tracked down a copy in the US and imported it for me. It would be wonderful to see it back in print.

Thank you to Lilliput Press and publisher Antony Farrell for allowing me to use the opening quote from Hubert Butler's *Children of Drancy* which gave me an insight into the Kagran farm scheme the refugees took part in. The character Hugh at the Kagran camp is a nod to Hubert who did great work in helping secure passage out of Germany for many refugees.

Thank you to Gerry Mullins, Pat Wallace and David O'Donoghue for their knowledge and company on all matters World War II related, and advice on visiting Berlin. This book was originally intended to be something different and I still have another story waiting to be told.

Thank you to Jim Cooke of Rathfarnham who provided me with information and an essay on the Old Vienna Club. A sincere thanks to Declan Quaile of the Termonfeckin History Society who spoke with me at length and sent me on some brilliant information on Vida herself. If it wasn't for Christine Everitt of Termonfeckin who kindly lent me her own journals from the Termonfeckin History Society, I don't think this story would now exist, so I am very grateful. I suppose I should give them back now.

Thank you to Gerry Rubin in the UK for sending me on some surprise newspaper cuttings on espionage in Ireland when I purchased a book from him – academic historians are brilliant for the archival clippings!

Turtle Bunbury, Irish author and historian kindly corresponded with me when I discovered a family member of his as a flower girl in the wedding photo of Vida Lentaigne. It turns out a branch of his family (no relation to the flower girl) used to live at Newtown House throughout the 1800s, so it was a unique and fascinating link.

Turtle put me in touch with Anne Hyland, another family member of the Lentaignes who gave me such fascinating insight and information on the family. I am very grateful for the correspondence.

Thank you to Poolbeg Press and publisher Paula Campbell who waited patiently for the many, varied drafts of this book. Thank you to editor Gaye Shortland for her firm guidance in whipping the text into shape. My sincere thanks to editor Sally Vince, who helped me through a very large quagmire I found myself in as I tried to complete multiple drafts of the text. She has a wonderful bookshop called Banner Books in Ennistymon, County Clare – go visit it!

Thank you to Irene in Academy Books in Drogheda for her unending support. Thank you to my writing buddies Sheila Forsey and Andrea Mara who understand the difficulties of being a working writer and Mam, and to Sam McGrane who is always on hand to cheerlead.

Finally, a very big thank-you to my parents, family and friends who love to tell everyone all about my books. My five-year-old currently claims she wants to be a writer when she grows up but I'm very surprised by this as she knows at first hand the neglect she faces as I disappear into my writing cave, only coming out to fire food at her and her sister. My husband Ronan, a creative himself, is probably my biggest support and I am very grateful that his faith in me never wavers, even though, from my point of view, it often, really, should.